SLAVE BOY

SLAVE BOY

Book One of The Democ'Chu Series

NATH BRYE

Dawn Publishing

Published by Dawn Publishing
www.dawnbates.com
The moral right of the author has been asserted.

For quantity sales or media enquiries, please contact the publisher at the website address above.

Cataloguing-in-Publication entry is available from the British Library.

ISBN:
978-1-913973-07-0 (paperback)
978-1-913973-08-7 (ebook)

Book cover Illustration – Ben Sampey (aka Sampey)
Book cover design – Jerry Lampson

To my son Sam, and my daughter Maddison.
You both inspire me to becoming the person I was meant to be. I strive every day to being a better person, a better human being that one day you can be proud of.
I love you both and hope you enjoy the story.

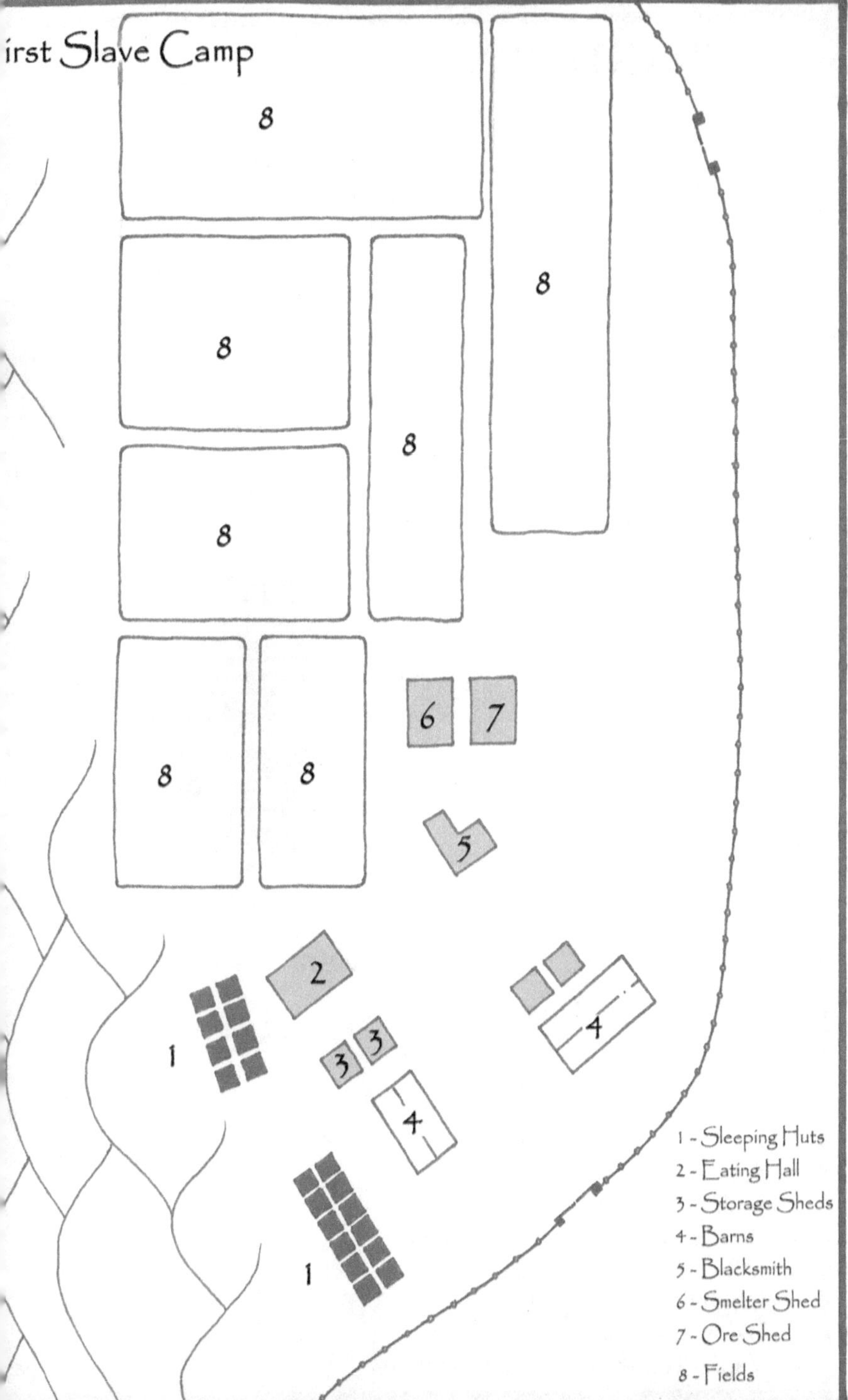
irst Slave Camp
8
8
8
8
8
8
8
8
8
6
7
5
2
1
3
3
4
4
1
1 - Sleeping Huts
2 - Eating Hall
3 - Storage Sheds
4 - Barns
5 - Blacksmith
6 - Smelter Shed
7 - Ore Shed
8 - Fields

OUTLANDER Nation

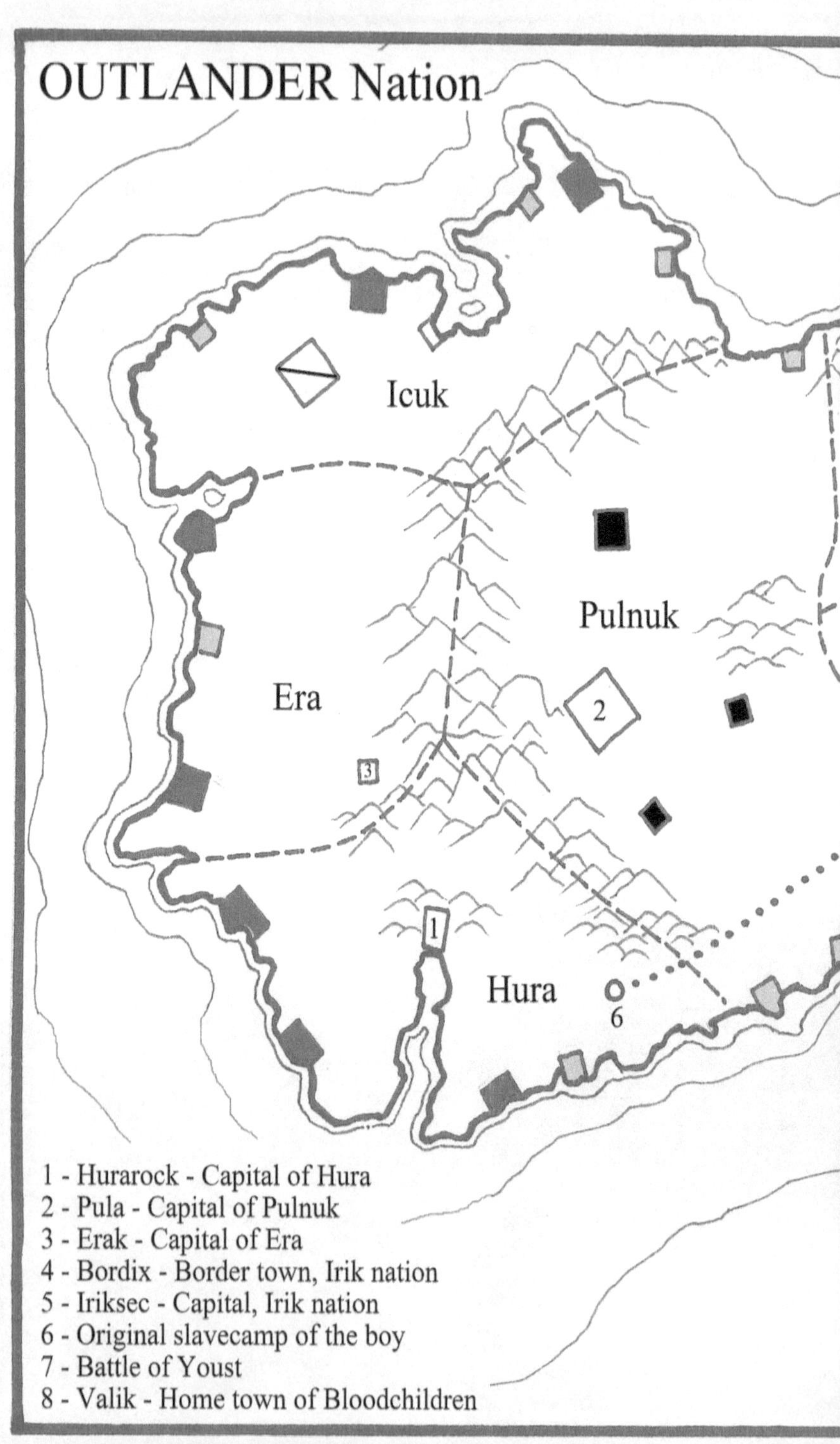

1 - Hurarock - Capital of Hura
2 - Pula - Capital of Pulnuk
3 - Erak - Capital of Era
4 - Bordix - Border town, Irik nation
5 - Iriksec - Capital, Irik nation
6 - Original slavecamp of the boy
7 - Battle of Youst
8 - Valik - Home town of Bloodchildren

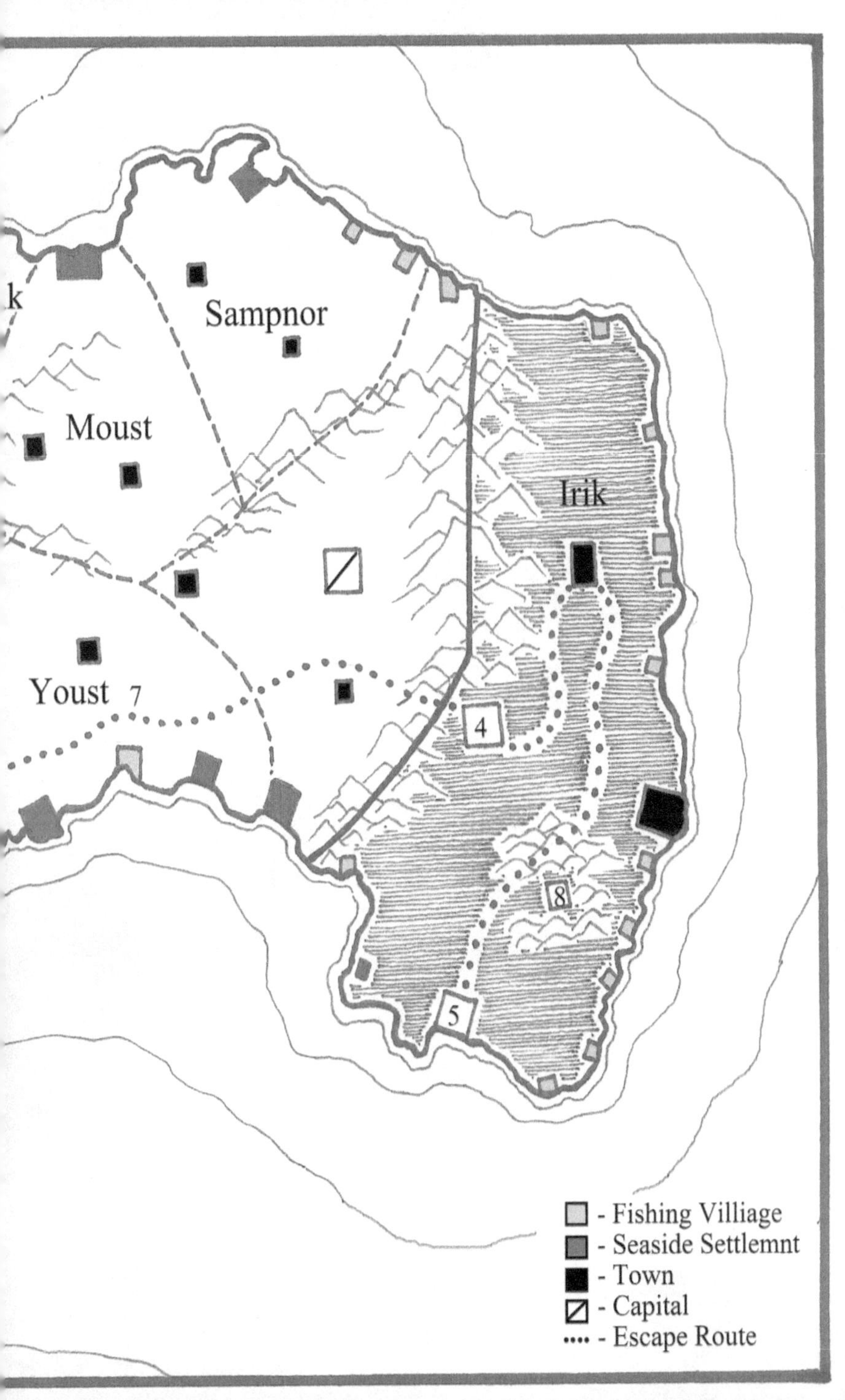

k
Sampnor
Moust
Irik
Youst 7
4
8
5
- Fishing Villiage
- Seaside Settlemnt
- Town
- Capital
- Escape Route

A young boy woke startled and confused. He peaked out of the blankets covering him as he lay warm and secure in his bed of straw. It was still dark inside the hut that he shared with his mother and father. The only light came from the dying embers of the fire. He looked over at his parents' bed, but they were nowhere to be seen. He could hear shouting and the occasional scream coming from outside. He screamed for his mother but heard nothing. He started to sob as fear started to take hold; then screamed for his father but once again nothing. Every instinct told the boy to hide under the blankets, but he couldn't. He slowly climbed out of his bed, still sobbing and made his way to the door of the hut. Moving aside the curtain nailed to the frame of the hut, he peered out. Everywhere, there was fire. He could see strange men walking in the distance, silhouetted by the neighbouring huts that were on fire.

He heard a muffled scream from the right. He saw two men holding his mother down, one of them had his hand clamped over her mouth. He ran outside screaming for his mother. A third man swung around to face the small boy, just five summers old. He stepped towards the boy and lifted him up. He said something in words that the boy didn't understand. The two men holding his mother down laughed a cruel laugh. The boy was kicking and screaming as the strange man held him, then walked towards his mother. His mother stared at him, tears streaming down her face. The man put the child down on the ground and backhanded him. The boy flew two metres before hitting the ground in a heap. The mother screamed and renewed her struggle, trying to bite the hand over her mouth, trying to pull her legs from the man holding them; she couldn't.

The man who had struck her son was now standing over her, loosening his trousers. He bent down and kneeled in front of her. In that moment, she saw movement that confused her. Two small hands holding a piece of firewood smacked the kneeling man in the face.

When the small boy fell over, she saw a small piece of sharp wood had snapped off from the piece of firewood and was now buried in the man's eye. He screamed, toppling backwards. The boy turned to run but one of the men holding his mother down was faster and punched the child full in the face, sending him flying once more.

The child got a quick look of surprise on his mother's face before the world went black and he sunk into darkness. The mother crying as she saw her only child lying like a sack of potatoes on the ground, lifeless with blood pouring from his nose and mouth.

The boy slowly came back to consciousness. At first, it was bright, and he could make nothing out. All he heard was the crying of other children. He couldn't move, no matter how hard he struggled. He blinked many times to adjust his eyes to the light. When he could finally see details, he realised that he was sitting on his bum, legs out in front of him. His legs had been tied with rope. His hands sat in his lap and had also been tied. He felt head pain where the punch had hit him, felt tired and disorientated. He tried to speak but nothing came out.

He realised that he had cloth tightly bound around his head, gagging him so he couldn't speak. He looked around and saw about fifteen other children similarly tied and gagged. One or two were young but most were older than his five summers. One large lad looked close to ten summers. They were in the back of a wagon and he could feel the wheels bumping slowly along the stony road. He looked around and noticed nothing familiar. He started crying again. He was hurt, he was terrified and even though gagged, he tried to scream for his mother. Other children looked at him and joined in the screaming.

A rough-looking man jumped in the back of the wagon, yelling and waving an axe at the children. Most went silent, with only some sobbing. The small boy blacked out again.

When he came to again, they were all gathered around a fire – tied together so they couldn't run. He had wet himself and could feel the wetness through his little trousers. He silently sobbed. The ten summers boy he had seen yesterday was looking at him. He shook his head slowly and the little boy closed his eyes. When he opened them again, the youth was looking away. He remained still, looking down at his little feet.

The same angry man from the wagon strolled past and laughed at a joke that one of his fellows had said. The boy couldn't understand what they were saying and confusion swept over him. His stomach rumbled from lack of food. They had given him water in the morning and in the afternoon, slipping the water nozzle past his mouth gag; but no food. Only water.

The angry man came back and stared down at the little boy, looking menacing and saying something to his comrades; his comrades laughed. The boy stared at the man, not knowing what he had done wrong. With an angry curse, the man backhanded him, bringing darkness once again.

After four nights, the wagons arrived at a small port. The boy could smell salt in the air for the last day. He had never seen the ocean before. At some stage over the last two days, more wagons had joined the convoy. Now, there were up to nine wagons, all filled with tied and bound children. The boy hadn't cried on this day. No more tears came and even though he was still scared, a strange feeling of numbness had come over him.

He and the other children had been only fed once on their journey. On the second night, the gags had been removed and the children had been passed a bowl of porridge. One child chose this time to scream at the top of her lungs, as soon as the gag had been taken off. One of the angry men had grabbed her and pulled her up, looking at the other children, he had opened her throat with a knife and let the body drop. Some of the children started sobbing quietly, others went into shock, but the boy felt dread, and even though he wanted scream for his mother, he didn't. He dropped the bowl of porridge on the ground but didn't notice. The older lad was watching him again and nodded his head towards the food he had dropped. The older lad using eye movement and nods to try and give the small boy reassurance. It was this day that the boy had run out of tears. He was emotionally spent and had no more tears left to give.

As the wagons reached the port, all the children were carried and loaded into the ship. Deep in the hold, they were tied to the wooden hull of the ship. The older lad that had tried to calm the boy in the wagon journey was also tied to the hull, directly across from the boy. They stared at each other, seeking reassurance in the other. Most of the children stayed silent for fear of further punishment. Except one small girl that had cried and sobbed non-stop from the time that she was bundled into the wagon. Only now, she did it quietly and the boy could only tell she was crying as her little body shook.

As the final child was loaded and tied in, two candles were lit in lamps and hung from the roof. The door to the hold was then slammed shut. No more sunlight, just two candles flickering in the lamp holders. The small boy rested his head on the child beside him and drifted off to sleep. Sleep was his escape from this nightmare, and the boy had come to rely on it. The gentle rocking of the ship as it made its way out to sea had him drifting off to sleep quickly. Praying with all his heart that when he woke up, it would all just be a bad dream. Praying that when he woke up, his mother would be there to hold him; his father there to play hide and seek with, his life back to normal, in the small hut he called home.

The boy woke to another cold morning. He raised himself from his bed of straw and threw on his tunic. He wrapped the scraps of cloth to each foot and bound them with strips of rope. Slaves were not allowed boots. They had to make do with wrapping and binding their feet every morning to keep out the cold of winter. By the end of the day, the cloth was wet all the way through, his feet were damp and cold. He rose from his two blankets of straw and left the hut that he shared with three other boys. They had also wrapped their feet and had moved outside. It was spring, and the morning was chilly, with a light frost on the ground.

"Move it, slave," said one of the other boys as they all

moved off towards the fields. Slave – a name, a title, a life! The boy never knew any other name and couldn't remember any other way of life. None of the slaves were allowed names, this was a part of their lives. Some of them had nicknames for each other but never used them in front of the masters. The boy clearly remembered two of the masters overhearing a slave refer to another slave by a nickname. Both slaves were beaten hard. Both slaves left unconscious where they had fallen, bruises and blood all over their faces. There were long bruises where the masters had used their batons. The baton, a wooden stick as thick as a man's wrist and as long as a man's forearm. Each master carried one on their hips, used for tapping cattle and sheep to get them to move and, of course, very handy for disciplining slaves. The boy had felt the rod more than once.

After a short walk, the four boys arrived at the fields, each of them trying to rub warmth into their hands by rubbing them together vigorously. The light of the new day was just starting to stretch across the sky when the master arrived to let them into the tool shed. Once opened, the master would disappear to breakfast. No such luxury for the slaves. They got their first food for the day around mid- morning. The boys grabbed the wooden shovels and started to work. With spring here and the snow melting, it was time to prepare the fields for the sowing of crops. The slaves digging over the field in preparation for planting. The boy looked up and around the field, where roughly forty other slaves of various ages worked. This earned him a whack from one of the boys that he shared quarters with.

"Back to work, slave boy!" said the oldest of the four boys.

He rubbed his arm where the shovel had hit and went back to work. The whack was not to get him to work, more for the cruelty of it. The masters encouraged the cruelty, it added to their amusement. And what did the masters care if the slaves beat each other? He received another whack this time to his other arm, a lot harder than the first hit. Another of the boys hit him for the fun of it. This was the way of it for the boy, wake, work, be beaten, work some more, then sleep. His daily routine over the last five summers since he had arrived at this camp. He had been the victim of the three boys since the day he had arrived in this camp. He had received many beatings from them, which only earned laughter from the masters. He tried to fight back on occasion but being younger by a few seasons and outnumbered, he stood no chance.

Working away at the hard ground, he felt his sweat start to run down his back. The good part about the physical work was the slaves didn't stay cold for long. It was more difficult in the middle of winter as the cold would freeze the sweat as soon as it began. During winter they would be in one of the larger buildings doing boring tasks like rope making, the snow too deep for working outside. The only outside work that they did during winter was collecting wood for the fires and carrying it from the woodshed to the main hall. This was not because the masters cared for the slaves, but more because they didn't want to lose a worker that they would have to replace. They were treated worse than the animals in the camps. At least, the animals got two meals a day. The slaves didn't. They got a watery porridge mid-morning that couldn't be called a meal, and in the evening they got a bowl of stew that was made up of vegetables, water and not much else. There was no flavour and it barely left a slave full. The boy had one memory of a harvest three seasons earlier that had stayed in his memory. The slaves had been awarded with half a small loaf of bread to go with their evening stew. He smiled at the memory, the wet bread being a welcome change to their normal diet of vegetables that the boy had no idea what they were.

He dug all morning, working as hard as the other slaves, even though they were older and stronger. He laughed internally when one of the older boys struck his own foot with his shovel. The other boys saw the amusement on his face and dropped tools, taking it in turns to punch the boy as he cowered on the ground. A master saw them and ran over to break it up but when he saw who was being tormented, he laughed. He told the others to go back to work and walked away. The boy picked himself up and moved to another patch of ground and continued to work until the bell was rung for the mid-morning meal. Upon hearing the bell, all slaves would drop their tools and move back to the main hall where food was served.

The boy was last in line and angry. He'd have been further up the line had the three other boys not foot tripped him. By the time he had got back up, he was behind all the other slaves. Once he'd arrived at the serving lady with his bowl, he watched as she slopped two scoops of thin, flavourless porridge into his bowl. He didn't care what it looked like or how it tasted, it was food and it was hot. He moved off to sit alone as he always did and eat his morning meal. As he walked away, one of the other boys' foot tripped him, and he went down in heap on the ground, his porridge spilling to the ground. He looked up and saw the three boys laughing. He didn't care if he took another beating. He stood up and charged, throwing a punch at the oldest one who led the two others. The punch connected to the youth's jaw and dropped him. Before the other two could react, the boy had picked up the youth's food bowl and started raining down blows on his face; the strong wooden bowl quickly breaking the skin around his right eye and mouth. The other two boys finally grabbed him by the arms and pulled him off, throwing him to the ground. They spent some time kicking him until the masters told them to stop. The masters had been watching and when they picked the boy up off the ground, they punched him back down again. If the boy was capable of tears, he would have cried but the boy had no more tears to cry.

The boy picked himself up after the masters had gone and walked to a water barrel to clean himself up and then drink deeply. He would be returning to the fields shortly on an empty stomach. It was not the first time that he had missed a meal and he doubted it would be the last. For the remainder of the day, he worked alone, away from the youths. He knew he would get another beating from them and accepted it like everything else – he had no choice. This was his life.

The boy had made no friends in his five summers in the slave camp. There were over sixty slaves in this camp and around twenty masters. He sometimes got a smile or a kind word from the cook, an old woman with stringy, grey hair and weathered face. This was the only positive interaction that he had with anyone. Apart from the three youths that he shared a sleeping shed with; all of the other slaves ignored him.

As the light started to fade on another day, the other slaves all stopped their digging and headed to the tool shed to put away their tools. The boy waited until all the slaves had moved off before putting away his shovel. He followed behind as all the other slaves made their way to the food hall.

The food hall consisted of wooden poles supporting a wooden roof. The walls had been built with mud from the ground to the height of the roof. It was a poor building, but warmer to sit in with the fires going and the press of slave bodies in it. The boy walked in and made his way to the end of the hall where the eating bowls sat upon a large table, the cook serving from a large black, cauldron like pot. The boy was hungry and tired. After not having the mid-morning bowl of porridge, it had left him feeling weaker than usual. His stubbornness fighting through the hunger pains, he'd continued to work throughout the day. He saw the other three boys as he walked toward the cook; they pointed at him and laughed. The eldest shouted. "You are too late, slave. The food is all gone."

The boy's heart sank. It had happened before, but he still walked towards the cook.

She saw him coming and smiled. "I saved you a bowl!"

His eyes brightened and he thanked her. As he took the bowl, she slipped a fist-sized piece of bread loaf into his hands. He didn't look at it but slipped it straight into his tunic. He smiled at her and walked off the way he had come. It was cold outside but still he preferred this night to eat alone. He sat under a tree, the new growth of spring grass cushioning his bottom. He pulled out the piece of bread and dipped it in to the broth. He savoured the feeling as the wet bread went into his mouth. He must find a way quietly to do something nice for the cook. She was the only one that paid him any attention, and this was the third time, she had saved him some food when the others had eaten it all. He finished his meal quickly and took a drink from the water skin hanging at his side. He only relaxed for a short time before getting up and walking over to the supply shed. Here, he rinsed out his bowl and left it on the ground next to the supply shed door for the cook to find.

He ran all the way to his sleeping shed before the others finished their meal. Rushing inside, he grabbed his two blankets and returned outside. There was no way that he was sleeping in there tonight. Not with the three others looking for vengeance, which they would most certainly take whilst he slept. He made his way to the large barn and the hay loft, as he had done a few times before. Once he reached the door, he pulled it open enough for him to slip through before closing it behind him. He reached the hay and climbed to the highest point. The top hale bay was almost at the roof and there was just enough room for him to slip his body into the gap. He managed to wrap the blankets over himself and for the first time that day, he relaxed as he started to warm up. He would as he had done a few times before, sleep here away from the others, emerging in the morning and running off to join the slaves once more in their daily work. As he drifted off, he tried to remember what his parents looked like but as always, their faces had faded from his memory. He drifted off to sleep warm and secure, ready to face the continuing battle of being a slave.

Chapter One

The boy woke automatically before the sun started to rise. His summers as a slave setting his body clock to wake at the same time every day, no matter what time he got to sleep. He didn't move for a few minutes, just relaxing in the warmth of the hay and his blankets. It's a shame that he couldn't sleep here more often but knew if his three tormentors found his hiding place, he would have no more place to hide from them. Not to mention the beating he would get if the masters found out.

He slowly rose and got out between the hay and the roof, pulling his blankets with him. Climbing down, he hurried to leave the barn and get back to his sleeping quarters to return his blankets. He ran across the ground that was cold under foot and arrived at the sleeping shed. He went in and went to drop his blankets on top of his straw bed, but there was no straw bed! He knew straight away, the other three had taken his straw for themselves. He felt a small spike of anger and left the shed as they roused themselves. He ran to the supply shed and opened the door. He folded his blankets quickly and shoved them beside a sack of vegetables and closed the door behind him.

All of the other slaves were awake and starting their day as he headed to the tool shed. The master had already opened it, so he grabbed a shovel and headed to the far side of the field to stay away from the others – his tormentors and his bullies. He was still angry as he started digging out the ground, the anger helping him to ignore the cold spring morning as he began to work up a sweat.

Before long, the sun started to rise, and other slaves had joined him in the fields. The ground was only a couple of days from being prepared for planting, a task the boy looked forward to. Their next task of planting the seed was less physical, and gentler on the body. He looked over and saw the other three boys watching him. They were one hundred paces away, working in a different part of the field from him, but still they watched him. He knew they would eventually catch up to him and he couldn't hide for ever. Throughout the morning, he dug at the cold earth, turning it over and over, preparing it. He had almost forgotten about his troubles and was heavily lost in the work that he was doing when he heard the bell ring for the mid-morning meal. He stopped and took a swig of water from his water skin. He then dropped his shovel and headed once again to the food hall. He'd thought about taking his shovel with him as he knew there was going to be trouble. However, he knew he would earn a few whacks from the masters for fighting; if he fought with a shovel, the masters would kill him. His anger was still swirling as he thought of his three tormentors, remembering back to all the times that they'd beaten him, hassled him and caused him problems. Usually his anger was short-lived as angry slaves usually became dead slaves. Today, as he reached the food hall, he couldn't contain his anger.

Outside the food hall were three masters standing with a slave that he had never seen. He wore the tunic and brown trousers of a slave but held himself with a dignity that no slave deserved to have. The slave had short-cropped blonde hair that was just starting to grey. He had a round face with a thick slave beard that was also blonde and peppered with grey. He had massive shoulders and favoured his left leg for standing on with all of his weight. He bowed his head when the masters looked his way as was the custom of all slaves. This had been beaten into them from a young age.

Looking up, the young slave boy saw his three tormentors sitting down and eating their meals outside. They put down their bowls and stood as the boy approached the food hall. Here it comes, he thought to himself.

"Where did you get to last night, slave? We missed your company!" said the oldest and largest.

He had said it loud enough for the masters to hear, informing them that he hadn't been in his sleeping shed. A whipping offence at the very least. The other two laughed as all three approached him. The boy felt his anger floating below the surface, and as it started to bubble over he didn't care if the masters were watching; he was tired of their games, all of them.

"Well, slave? Nothing to say?" said a second of the three.

As the boy approached, he could think of anything to say, so said nothing. The eldest was about to say something else, but the boy didn't give him the chance. Without stopping, he walked up and kicked his foot as hard as he could between the eldest's legs, straight into his groin. The eldest dropped to the ground, screaming in pain. One of the others came flying in with a wild right hand punch, which the boy easily ducked.

On his way up, he punched the second slave's throat as hard as he could. The slave fell back clutching his throat, struggling to breath. As this slave went down, the boy aimed a kick at his head which connected with his jaw, cracking it. A punch landed on his shoulder, a badly timed punch from the third slave. The boy took the punch, then threw one of his own, then another and another. All three connecting with the face of the third slave, knocking him over as he tripped backwards, rendering him unconscious.

The boy looked over and saw the eldest had got back to his feet. Without giving him a chance, he charged and tackled him, landing on top of him. Using his legs to pin the slave's arms, he rained down punches into his face. Punches coming down, over and over again! From somewhere, the boy heard a feral yell, then realised that it was him as he punched the eldest slave.

All of a sudden, his feet were in the air as one of the masters had lifted him off the boy and into the air. The boy, his blood boiling threw back an elbow, connecting with the nose of the master. As the master dropped him, he stood his ground and charged in to tackle the master. The master saw it coming and backhanded him with all of his strength, knocking the boy to the ground. As soon as the boy hit the ground, the second master arrived, his wooden baton coming down on the boy's body, time and time again. Before he slipped into darkness, he got a quick look at the new slave, who was watching and shaking his head.

"Well, father?"

"He is a good candidate for the pit boy," said Chief Hura, leader of this province of the Outlander nation.

"You're going to use him in the pit? You're not going to hang him?" replied the son.

"No. You heard my sister. She wants him to die in as much pain for what he did to her husband in the raid."

"I still can't believe that he was killed by a boy no older than five seasons," said the son.

"Accident. Freak turn of events. Anyway, he may make us some coin before he dies in the pit. He certainly beat the crap out of those three other slaves."

"What are their injuries, father?"

"One with a broken jaw, the other two just bruised and bloody. They will return to work soon enough. Although, I have moved them to the orchard camp."

"Moved them, father?"

"Yes. They will work the season in the orchards, after that who knows!"

"Would the Demon-child have killed them, do you think?"

Chief Hura smiled. The slave boy that they were talking of had earned the name Demon-child in the raid that had taken the Chief's sister's husband by accident. Some of his warriors had said that he was possessed by a demon to be able to kill a warrior in his prime. The Chief knew; however, it was a freak accident. His sister had demanded the boy be tortured, then killed. The Chief had promised the boy would know pain, but in a different way. That is why he had originally placed the boy into the same sleeping shed with the older slaves. He knew they would torment him, and of course, they had.

The Chief had come from his main settlement bringing with him the new slave blacksmith and to inspect the progress. He had arrived just in time to witness the fight. He was quietly impressed and amused at seeing a ten summers boy win over the three older youths, then try to fight one of his own warriors. His son prompted an answer.

"I think the boy is vengeful enough to kill them in their sleep, but who knows. It will certainly be a while before he works again," said the Chief.

"What injuries does he have?"

"We think a cracked skull, a broken wrist and a broken nose," replied the Chief.

"Well father, after the beating he took, it will be a while before he tries to fight us again!"

"I hope so. We need to beat that defiance out of him, if we are to train him for the pit."

"Perhaps get the Smith to watch over him, father. He may hold himself a little too proudly for a slave, but he has never showed defiance and has always worked hard."

The Chief thought about it. "Not a bad idea, son. However, we cannot linger here anymore. I still want to inspect the work at orchards before we return to Hurarock. Tell the Smith that his duties now include teaching the boy humility, and if he fails, tell the Smith that we will return him to working in the mines."

"Your will, father."

As the son moved off to talk with the blacksmith, the Chief looked over the slave camp. It was one of many that he owned. This one focusing primarily on the growing of Kuen that were like the potatoes the southerners grew, but a little sweeter. He breathed in the air before turning and walking back to his horse. Yes, the pits would be the best place for the young slave boy.

The boy woke in his sleeping shed; a fresh pile of straw under him and two new blankets thrown across him. His body screamed in pain as he tried to move. He had a pulsing headache that shot from one side of his head to the other. The day light was shining through the door. He saw his wrist was splintered and he could feel the wrist throbbing. He lay still to prevent further pain. He looked up at the thatched roof before closing his eyes. He must have dozed, because when he woke the light of day was gone. His blanket door had been closed and a small candle was burning on a small wooden chair beside his straw pile bed, he now rested on. Next to the candle was a bowl of stew. He was hungry and thirsty, but as he moved to reach for the bowl, the pain all came rushing back. His wrist pulsing with pain, his head throbbing. He lay back down and fell asleep again.

He woke to the sun was shining through the open doorway. He looked up and moaned aloud.

"So, you are awake, boy?" said a gruff voice.

He slowly turned his head and immediately wished that he hadn't, as the pain in his head started again. He looked over and saw the slave that he had seen with the masters sitting against the wall, small bowl of porridge in one hand and a wooden spoon in the other.

"You have been in and out of consciousness for three days now. The pain paste that they gave you making you sleep."

The boy looked at him, getting a better look at him now that he was closer. His shoulders which looked large from a distance looked massive to the young boy now in the small shed. He had a large chest with strong arms. His hair more silver than blonde now he could see better. His slave beard closely trimmed, also with greyer than blonde.

He managed to croak out a question. "Who are you?"

The man looked at him before smiling. "Don't have a

name; I am a slave after all. I am the new blacksmith at this settlement. The masters call me Smith, so I guess you can call me that."

"What's a blacksmith?" croaked the boy, his throat very dry.

"A blacksmith is someone that works the metal, boy. I make tools but mostly, the bastard-masters will use me to make their weapons."

The boy looked over and beside him was his water skin; he reached for it but slumped back down. The Smith put his bowl down, then moved over and grabbed the water skin. He pulled the stopper and moved it to the boy's lips. The boy took in big gulps of water, feeling the coldness ease his throat. He finally had drunk his fill; the Smith took the water skin away and put back the stopper.

"Thirsty eh, boy?" said the Smith, as he resumed his original sitting position. The Smith rubbed his right knee with a grimace on his face. He saw the boy watching. "Busted my knee up pretty good in a battle with the bastard-masters eleven summers ago now – the same battle that saw me taken as a slave."

The boy nodded before speaking. "How old are you?"

"Thirty-one this summer, boy. You?"

"I'll be eleven this summer. You have been a slave for all these summers?"

"No, I have been a guest of the bastard-masters for eleven summers," the Smith said with a smile on his face.

The boy closed his eyes again. He was hungrier than he had ever been but had learnt not to trust slaves that he didn't know well. A lesson that he had learnt as a new slave five summers ago.

The Smith rose and stood. "The cook will be in soon with some food for you. I'll check in on you later."

"Why?" the boy asked.

"Why what, boy?"

"Why would you check in on me later?"

"The bastard-masters want me to teach you."

"Teach me what?"

"To keep a cool head and do what you are told, boy."

"And you will teach me this?" the boy said, with more feeling than he intended to.

"Yes, boy. That and more."

The Smith left the shed and the boy closed his eyes once again. He slept and woke a few hours later when the cook arrived with a bowl of broth for him. She knelt and fed him, as he hadn't the strength to feed himself. She smiled at him once he was finished. She then pulled a small leather pouch from her cloth belt and opened it; inside was a grey paste. She scooped up some on her finger and went to put in the boy's mouth. He moved his head away.

"Trust me, boy. It will help with the pain," she said in a gentle voice.

If there was anyone in this slave camp that he trusted, it was the cook. He opened his mouth and she smeared it around his gums. It tasted foul and the boy started to gag.

"Do not spit it out, give it time to work."

He did as he was instructed and lay there, resisting the urge to spit it from his mouth. Slowly, he felt himself getting sleepy. He was not sure when he fell asleep but when he woke, it was dark once more.

His days followed this pattern for three quarter moons. Sleeping, being fed by the cook and sleeping again. Some evenings, the Smith would visit and talk of faraway battles that he had been in. He focused on the words and listened intently before falling asleep. When he woke on the morning of the fourth quarter moon, the Smith and the cook were both there standing over him.

"Time to get up, boy. You have been lying in your own filth for long enough. The smell in here could drop a bull."

The boy hadn't noticed before, but as the Smith had said, he could smell the foul odour coming from his blankets. He moved to a sitting position and was surprised when it didn't hurt. He had put no weight on his wrist just in case but was glad that his head had stopped throbbing. With the help of the Smith, he slowly stood. The world spun and it took minutes for it to stop spinning. He looked down at his blankets and the straw and saw the filth there. He was ashamed of himself and the Smith saw the shame.

"Don't worry about that, boy. You have been injured. We will get it cleaned up. But first, outside."

With the Smith's arm around his waist, he made it outside. It was a warm day and the boy knew spring was upon them properly now. He stood in the sun and breathed the fresh air. He found he could stand by himself as the Smith moved away. The Smith picked up a bucket of warm water.

"Strip those rags off, boy; you need to wash before sores start to grow."

The fact that he was standing outside in full view of people didn't stop him. Slaves were not worried about nakedness, as some cultures and people were, and well used to stripping down before their masters. He stripped where he stood and stood naked in the sun. The Smith handed him a soapy rag from the bucket.

"Here boy, wipe down your private areas. The cook will do your back."

The boy took the rag with his uninjured hand and began to clean his private areas. His groin and between his legs got a good clean with the warm soapy water, all the time the cook was washing his back and neck. While this was happening, he noticed to other slaves entering his sleeping shed with buckets of their own. He looked at the Smith.

"They will change the straw and scrub the mess up. It will still smell for a few days. Don't forget to wash under your balls, boy!"

The boy went back to cleaning himself. Once he was clean, he was handed a large rag to dry himself, which he did with the help of the cook. Once his body was dry, the Smith handed him a new tunic. He slipped it on, along with some trousers that had been cut off above the knee. Once cleaned and dressed, he felt better. His head had started to throb a little, but not like it had been a few quarter moons ago.

"Come on then, boy. Time to eat. You must be starving."

The boy nodded and followed the Smith to the food hall. He stopped and called back to the cook. "Thank you!"

She smiled at him before disappearing with his old clothes, to no doubt burn them.

He sat in the food hall sharing the mid-morning meal with the Smith. The Smith said little, just concentrating on his bowl of porridge, although he could be heard muttering "bastard porridge."

This almost brought a smile to the boy's face, almost.

For the next few quarter moons, the Smith was waiting when the boy had woken and come out of his sleeping shed, a place he now slept in alone. The other slaves had indeed cleaned it and placed a large stack of new straw on the ground for him to sleep on, along with two new blankets to replace the soiled ones. Once awake, the Smith had the boy walking the perimeter of the slave camp. His legs at first were a little weak from spending so much time healing on his straw bed, but soon enough he could make it around the camp without having to stop and catch his breath. He spent the entire morning walking the camp, slowly building his fitness up, and stopping when he heard the ringing of the mid-morning meal bell. He would eat alone in the food hall, or sometimes next to the Smith, and then be given other exercises to perform. His wrist had stopped hurting a few days before and after inspecting it, the Smith removed the wooden splint. It felt very weak and the Smith gave him daily exercises to increase its strength.

In the evenings, he would eat with the Smith and once again, would be told of faraway battles. The Smith explained in great detail the ways the battles were lost or won. The boy started to enjoy the evening talks, and his nervousness of the Smith slowly draining away. He still didn't trust the Smith, his slave weariness still telling him to be careful. As he ate, he looked at his body and saw the softness of it. For two full moons, he had been healing from the beating of the masters; the thought bringing anger to him. The Smith must have seen the look on his face. "I hope that anger is not directed at me, boy!" he said.

"No!"

"Who then?"

"Masters."

"Hide it, boy. You can feel all the anger you want, but never let it show."

The boy said nothing, just looked at his food as his appetite left him all of a sudden. He bid the Smith good night, and after returning his bowl to the cook, left for his sleeping shed.

The Smith watched him go and shook his head. "Boy will get himself killed," he said under his breath before returning to his food.

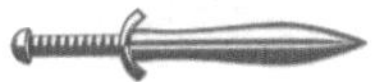

"Well, Smith. How are the Demon-Child's injuries?" said Chief Hura.

The Smith bowed his head and looked at the ground before replying.

"He is healed, master. His wrist is almost at full strength and his mind shows none of the grogginess that he had. His head must have healed by now as well, master"

The Chief nodded. "Start him back to work in the field's tomorrow morning then. He has a full moon in the fields, digging and weeding the crops, before we move him to other duties."

"Yes, master."

"How is his anger, Smith?"

"I have just started instructing him to keep it under control, master."

"Good. As you know well, usually a slave is hung for attacking one of us. We have other plans for that slave and would hate to have to kill him, and you, before those plans can be realised."

"Yes, master"

"Back to work then, Smith. I leave for the summer raids in two days. I hope to see a fit, compliant slave on my return."

"He will be that, master," the Smith said, before leaving and heading to the food hall.

The Chief's son looked to the overseer of the slave camp, a trusted older warrior of his fathers.

"After a full moon of the fieldwork Onik, move him to

carting iron ore from the mines to the smelter shed. He will need to gain his fitness back and start to build muscle on that frame of his."

"I will. Any other instructions?" the overseer replied.

The son looked at his father. "Father?"

"No. He can spend all summer carting ore and we will have a look at him when we return," Chief Hura replied.

"Yes, my Chief," replied the overseer.

"But, allow him to spend time in the evenings with the Smith."

"Yes, my Chief."

With that, the Chief and his son walked to their horses. The overseer watched them leave the camp and returned to his rounds, checking that all the slaves were where they were meant to be before going for a mid-morning meal himself.

The boy had been back in the fields for three days. Weeding and ploughing the ground around the crops was not hard work, just mundane. Once again, the other slaves never talked to him, ignoring him as he went about his work. As always, the boy didn't care and was left alone with his own thoughts, of all that had happened since the beginning of spring and over the last two full moons. The fight with the three slaves, the beating he took after it, the healing and of course, the Smith. Another two full moons and spring would be over, and the first harvest of these fields would take place. A hectic quarter moon with the slaves working harder and faster to get the crops out of the ground before quickly planting the next one. In this way, the Outlanders could harvest two crops out of the same ground within one season before the first snows of autumn fell.

His wrist had hurt a little at first when using a shovel, but the pain was short lived as his strength grew. In fact, by the end of the third full moon after his beating, he was almost back to his normal strength. He was getting back into the routine of the field work when one morning his life changed again. He had woken as normal and left his sleeping shed to find a master waiting for him.

"Change of job for you, slave," said the overseer.

The boy nodded and fell in behind the master. They had walked over to one of the tool sheds that the boy hadn't been in before. Other slaves were already waiting, slaves that the boy recognised but had no idea of their tasks. He saw them for evening meals but in the mornings, they disappeared.

"Follow these slaves and do what they do."

"Yes, master," he said, as the master unlocked the shed door.

As the overseer left, the other slaves went into the shed and returned with wooden wheelbarrows. The boy had seen these but didn't know what the slaves did with them. He grabbed one by the handles and followed the other ten slaves through the camp. He would soon learn exactly what they did.

He had finished his first day and his body was sore, very sore. He had followed the other slaves through the camp and out of a gate behind the slave camp that he didn't know existed. They then started half running along a well-worn track into the hills. After a while they arrived at a small camp with no walls. At the end of the camp, was a large hole in the side of the hill that he learned from one of the others was called a mine. He had no idea what a mine was and didn't have time to ask. The other slaves he was following put their wheelbarrows next to a large mound of rocks, and then started loading them into their barrows. The boy copied their actions and when the barrows were full, they took off back towards the slave camp, pushing their wheelbarrows full of rocks. On arrival, they had dumped their barrows into a pile outside what they called the smelter shed, another word the boy didn't know.

The first journey from the mine back to the slave camp had been uncomfortable, the weight of the wheelbarrow pushing down on his recently healed wrist, his legs straining with the load as he ran to keep up. Of course, the boy had never done this work before, so had to constantly stop for a quick rest. The barrows where heavy and he could not push them for long. The second trip harder, the third trip was truly painful. By the end of the day, he could hardly move his legs and his wrist was weak. He barely managed to finish the last two trips as he no longer had any strength to run or walk or even lift the barrow. He hadn't kept count of how many trips that they had made, just focusing on trying his best to keep up, which of course, he couldn't. He returned his barrow to the shed and made his way to the food hall. He collected his bowl of food and slumped down against a wall, food bowl sitting in his hands. He had no energy to eat.

"Tough day, boy?" said Smith, as he sat beside the boy.

The boy just nodded.

"Eat boy, otherwise tomorrow will be harder. Trust me."

The boy began to eat slowly, looking forward to his straw bed. As he ate, the Smith explained what a mine was and what a smelter was for. His brain taking in the information, even though he was more tired than he could ever remember being. He was not looking forward to the next day, as he finished his meal and listened to the Smith. He wondered how long he would be doing this new work and wondered if it would always be this hard.

Of course, the next day was harder than the first. His body still stiff and sore, groaning as he picked up his wheelbarrow full of iron ore for the first trip of the day. He used an extra piece of cloth that he'd found to bind his wrist, helping to take the weight of the wheelbarrow. He could not keep up with the pace of the others, even though they had slowed to a walk. As he reached the gates of the camp, the other slaves where already returning for another load.

"Keep up, boy!" yelled one of the slaves.

The boy increased his speed as best he could and dumped the iron ore in the pile outside the smelter shed. He turned quickly and with the wheelbarrow empty, tried to increase his speed and catch up. He was just passing through the gate when a foot that he didn't see stuck out and he tripped over it, his face landing straight into the mud.

Two masters stood there laughing loudly as another master that had been hiding beside the gate stood up and pointed at the boy. "Don't be clumsy, slave. Pick that barrow up and catch up. You fall again and I'll beat you, scum!"

The boy picked himself up and ran as fast as he could to try and catch the others. What was worse, is he knew the masters at the mining camp would also punish him for being late. It was all a game to them. As sure as the sun rose in the morning, he was yelled at and received a baton against his legs for returning late. The other slaves had waited for him to return before setting off, a rare gift of kindness. He loaded up and then followed when they took off towards the main camp for their second trip of the day.

As the second trip turned into the third, then the fourth, the other slaves set a slower pace to give their youngest member a chance to keep up. His body was screaming by mid-morning, not being so used to this intense workload. As they stopped to break their fast, he could hardly walk. His legs stiff, his wrist aching, and he was very out of breath. The eldest of the group dropped back to wait for him as they headed to the eating shed.

"Did you fall over?" It was a genuine question, asked without malice.

"Master foot-tripped me," was all the boy said.

The elder slave shook his head. "We will keep to a slower pace this afternoon and once we finish tonight, make sure you stretch before you sleep, otherwise your body will be in just as much pain tomorrow."

Before the boy could ask what 'stretching' meant, the elder slave ran off to catch up with the others.

At the end of the day his body was hurting even more, and he could no longer lift his wrist. He had eaten his meal automatically, ignoring what small amount of flavour there was. Once he had finished, he headed outside to his sleeping shed. He collapsed on his bed of straw, wrapping himself in his blankets. He looked up at the roof of the shed wondering to himself what the hell 'stretching' was.

Chapter Two

The boy sighed as the other lad dropped the barrow of rocks that he was carrying. The boy continued on with his load of rocks passing the boy that he had named Clumsy-boy. Determined to meet today's quota, he powered through the work. He didn't look back at Clumsy-boy, who was known to be lazy and was frequently being beaten by the masters. He was of similar age to the boy but his attitude, his work ethic was summers younger. Reaching the shed, he emptied his barrow of rocks onto the pile outside the smelter shed. He stretched his back, then turned and started returning to the mine. Already, he could see one of the masters laying into Clumsy-boy with his baton. As he drew closer, he saw that the master was the one that some of the slaves had named Monster, due to the fact that he was the ugliest man that any of them had ever seen. Of course, not one of the slaves would ever repeat this nickname in front of any of the masters. That would be a bad beating, if not worthy of a slave being killed. As the boy ran past with his wheelbarrow, he kept his head down, focusing on putting one foot in front of the other and not drawing attention to himself. He heard the whimpers of Clumsy-boy and the laughter of the masters. As he got further away, the noises drifted away and until all he could hear was the wind and the birds. His mind started to wonder.

It had been a full season since he had fought with the three slaves that had tormented him, and then taking a beating from the masters. He had slowly healed with the help of the cook and the Smith. Once he had healed, he was given this new job of carting iron ore from the mines to the main smelter in the slave camp. He now understood all of the words the Smith had taught him, along with the making of weapons from the first point when the iron ore was dug out of the hill, all the way through the process, to where the Smith would heat the iron ingots and bash them into the shape that he wanted. He was learning many things from the Smith in their evenings. The process of making metal, different ways to farm and of course, they talked more of the battles the Smith had fought. The boy enjoying learning what the Smith called tactics.

He reached the mine in the normal amount of time that it took him, started loading up his barrow for the trip back to the slave camp. Back to the smelter shed where the iron ore would be separated into iron ingots ready to be made into whatever the blacksmiths needed to make, and not once, did he move his eyes from what they were doing and look at the masters who watched as he loaded up. He ignored the masters and trotted off, his breath slightly laboured but easy. His fitness had improved in the summer that he had been doing this work. He was just starting to gain height, and with the growth of his teen muscle, the boy was starting to resemble the man that he would become. His dark brown, chin long hair flowing in the air behind him as he ran down the track towards the camp.

There were now fifteen slaves running the iron ore from the mine to the smelter and the amount that they moved each day was impressive. Although the boy often wondered why the masters used slaves and not a large horse and cart? Like the one he had seen dropping off supplies to the slave camp. He asked the Smith.

"Horse and cart costs coins, boy. Slaves do not," the Smith replied.

He lengthened his stride until he was at an easy lope, with the barrow moving smoothly over the well-worn track which wound around and down the hills towards the camp. He thought back to the first days he had carried this barrow on these ore runs. He had struggled and it was painful. His body now however fit, strong and capable.

At the end of the day as the sun was slowly setting, the boy was walking away from the smelter shed, his last load delivered. He and the other youths had gone beyond their quota. The other youths inspired somewhat by the boy and his work ethics, although the boy would never know that. He approached the food hall and upon reaching it, was handed a bowl of vegetable broth and a half loaf of bread handed to him. He smiled at the cook and thanked her. Bread was starting to be included in the evening meal and the boy was thankful. He was not sure why this had happened but didn't take it for granted.

He took the food and walked outside towards his favourite spot some way from the food hall. He sat down on the grass in the falling sun. Taking the water skin from his belt, he drank the last of his water and slowly made his way through the meal. The boy was not unhappy! Yes, he hated the masters with their cruel ways, dreaming boyish dreams of hurting them all when he was a grown man. The Smith had, of course, taught him over the seasons to hide his anger and he had been taught well. Hiding his emotions when they laughed at him, spoke harshly, or threatened him, he looked at the ground like the willing slave and said nothing. He hadn't felt the baton of the masters since his beating a summer gone by, and he intended never to feel it again.

Of course, he was no longer sport for the other slaves. He hadn't seen his three tormentors again as they had been moved to another camp, so he'd been told. The other slaves had heard the story of his fight and chose never to cross his path if they could help it.

At the end of the day, life seemed peaceful. Work hard, get fed and fall into a peaceful slumber. This was the routine of his days and the boy didn't know of any other life. The work that he did now left no time for imagination, a little time for reflection and no time to rebel. His life was more peaceful since he was changed to this type of work. As he scooped the last of the broth out of the bottom of his bowl using the last piece of bread, he heard a bird calling to his mate. He looked up into a tree and watched a bird that he didn't know the name of. It was dirt brown but with a bright red tuff on its chest. He watched the bird flitter through the branches and smiled.

The next day, not long before their mid-morning meal, the boy was once again running effortlessly back to the mine having completed a load. He was in front of two other slaves that had kept up with him and stuck just behind him all day. This happened on some days and it didn't bother the boy unless they started talking, which they sometimes did. As the three of them rounded a bend, they all saw that Clumsy-boy was once again lying on the ground. His wheelbarrow was lying on its side empty, and the slave was not moving. As the three slaves reached Clumsy-boy, they slowed to a walk. The boy had slowed to check on the slave. Upon reaching him, he saw a line down his inside left arm that had pumped blood everywhere and soaked the ground. In his right hand was a sharp rock covered in blood. One of the slaves behind him spoke. "He has taken his own life!"

It was not uncommon in the slave camps for some slaves to want to end their own lives. The boy had heard of it but never seen it. He looked down at the grey face of the slave that he had nicknamed Clumsy-boy. He now felt guilty for all the times that he had lost his patience with him. He breathed deeply before lifting the dead slave's wheelbarrow and putting it atop his own.

He turned to the two others. "Let's continue. We will tell the masters at the mine," he said.

The other two slaves nodded and picked up their wheelbarrows. The boy, carrying the extra weight of another wheelbarrow, moved off with the other two slaves behind him. He shook his head as he ran; he just didn't understand it. His life had been one of cruelty, violence and hard work. Never had he ever thought of taking his own life in this manner. It confused him and he made of point to ask the Smith later that night.

They reached the mine and as the other two slaves started loading up with iron ore, the boy took the second wheelbarrow off and put it next to other spare wheelbarrows. He walked over to the master, the one they called Monster and stood before him, his head and eyes down on the ground.

"Well slave, what is it?"

"A slave is dead master, back down the track."

"Which slave is dead?" he said, with menace.

"The slave you were instructing yesterday, master."

"How did he die?"

"It looks like he cut his wrist with a sharp rock master and has bled out."

"WHAT?" screamed the master.

The boy stood still, waiting to be dismissed. He didn't see the blow coming as the master backhanded him, sending him crashing down to the ground. The blow hadn't hurt too much, more so given the boy a fright. He knew better than to get up, so stayed on the ground with his eyes looking down on the dirt. His anger in check as the Smith had taught him.

"Go back with your barrow and cart the body back to the main camp. Throw it in the garbage pit!"

"Yes, master," said the boy.

He got up and retrieved his barrow. Soon, he was running back towards the body of the dead slave.

"Smith, why did he do it?"

The Smith took a drink of water before answering. The boy had asked the Smith to join him for dinner under the tree where the boy usually sat at alone. "He just couldn't take it any longer"

"Have you ever felt that way, Smith?"

"Never boy! That would be letting the bastard-masters win and I won't do that. There is always hope, no matter how small that hope feels."

The boy continued to eat as he took in the words of the Smith.

"Life as a slave is bloody unpleasant and sometimes downright nasty boy. You know this more than most. We make the best of it in order to keep living, in the hope that one day, we will be free."

"And will we ever be free?" asked the boy.

"No, never boy."

"Then why carry on, working in these conditions with bad food, the constant threat of being beaten?"

"We only get one life, boy! We have to make the most of it! Besides, you seem slightly better off than you were a summer ago when I first saw you!"

The boy nodded. "The work is slightly better; the food has also improved a little and yes I do enjoy having a sleeping shed to myself and not worrying about being beaten during my sleep."

"See! There you go, boy. Small improvements can make all the difference. You never know where small improvements will lead you."

The boy didn't understand what the Smith was speaking of and continued to eat.

"You understand what I am talking about?"

"No, Smith."

"The bastard-masters have a plan for you. This I know! I do not know what it is, but you have to look on the bright side. They have a plan, which means they don't intend to kill you anytime soon."

"Good to know."

The Smith laughed loudly. It was the first time the boy had heard the Smith laugh and it was a pleasant sound. He looked at the Smith and noticed the way his whole body joined in with the laughter.

"Things could be a lot worse boy, you know that."

The boy nodded. He looked out at the hills as the sun slowly disappeared behind them. They had a plan for him! He tried not to worry about it but knew his mind would not let him sleep with that information. It would be a restless night with worrying over what will happen. He felt anger rise again but stuffed it down as the Smith had taught him. He finished his food and took the Smith's empty bowl as he rose.

"Thanks Smith, for explaining, I still don't see how someone could give up like that," he said. His thoughts drifting back to the slave that had ended his life.

"Hopefully, you will never understand that level of surrender, boy."

"What does surrender mean?"

"Giving up, boy!"

"I hope I never understand surrendering either. Thanks, Smith," he said as he walked off to return the bowls.

The Smith watched him walk away, thankful the boy had come to him with these questions. There hadn't been a suicide in this camp for over ten summers. The slaves had been shocked, but still carried on with their tasks. Shocked that it had happened at all, as opposed to who had done it. There were never many friendships in the slave camp. The boy and the Smith were a rare case. The Smith told himself not to get too attached to the boy. Anything could happen and he had lost friends before in the last slave camp that he was in. However, there was something about this boy, something that marked him different to the other slaves. It would be a few more summers before the Smith worked out exactly what it was.

The summer continued with the boy carting iron ore. By the end of his second summer of doing this work, his body was well muscled. His shoulders and arms were firm and toned, his legs long and strong. He could run his wheelbarrows full of iron from the mine to the smelter shed very quickly and the other slaves reacted to this by trying to keep up. The other slaves doing their best to bring more barrows of ore to the smelter in a day than the boy could; they never succeeded.

The Smith continued his lessons in the evening, teaching the boy how to control his anger and many other things. The boy showed that he had a sharp mind and soaked up all the information that he could. He learned about different planting seasons, different ways to water crops, the many different ways to do battle and different tactics to employ in certain situations. He learnt how to read people and their moods. All manner of things he learnt from the Smith, never for one moment in his wildest dreams that he would use any of it.

One of the things the Smith did teach him was the basics of construction; a skill that he actually got to use. When autumn arrived, the Smith had informed the masters that most of the sleeping sheds were ready to collapse and unless fixed, they would fall over with the winter snows. The masters didn't take him seriously, until one of the masters walked over to a sleeping shed. He had shaken it as hard as he could and fell on his backside when it did indeed collapse. The masters then tasked the Smith with building new sleeping quarters before the winter, only four full moons away. He asked for the boy to help him; the boy finally putting into practise what he'd learnt from the Smith. Of course, they were not given hammers and nails to accomplish the task; these being deemed too expensive for constructing slaves' sleeping sheds. The Smith said thin rope, which they had lots of, would do for what he had planned. While half of the slaves gathered the last harvest of the season, the Smith had the other half digging large square holes into the earth. He had chosen a site on the side of a small hill, behind the food hall, which rose until it joined the other hills. The square hole was four paces long by three paces wide. The holes' depth was shoulder height to the Smith when he was standing in the hole. He then instructed the slaves to dig an opening to the far left inside wall leading outside. As the holes were dug into a hill, when the entrances were completed, you could walk straight into the dugout holes without stepping down.

It took over seven days but once fourteen of these holes were dug, one beside the other in a perfect line, the Smith taught the slaves how to make a paste from limestone dust, sand and mud. Once it was the perfect consistency, the slaves spent another seven days coating the walls and floor of the dug outs with the mixture. As the days moved on, the pastes hardened into a white colour and a solid barrier protecting the dug outs from moisture. Roof construction was next, using the recycled wood from a few of the sleeping sheds and sloping roofs were made to cover the holes. The slaves without sleeping sheds, slept in the food hall. The long timbers were laid in place covering the holes from side to side, with only a foot gap in between the timbers, then brush was used to cover the entire roof. This brush was everywhere in the valley and was not used for anything else. The brush was tied down to the timbers. The lime mortar was then coated over top of the brush, sealing the dugouts. The slaves thought they were finished, but the Smith smiled to himself and then told then no. They packed some of the earth that they had taken from the holes onto the lime mortar mixture. Then the sod, with grass still attached that had been carefully taken off, was put back piece by piece.

The finished result was an underground room that could sleep five slaves comfortably. A room that was watertight and as it was in the ground, provided natural insulation from the cold. A wooden door frame was made and placed in the entrances to the new sleeping holes. Smith would not hear of using blankets as doors, so with the help of the other slaves, wove small branches into a tight frame to resemble a door. Then, the doors were coated in the lime mortar. Once dry, rope was used to attach them to the door frames. As autumn was coming to an end, the slaves all slept a lot more comfortably in their new sleeping holes.

As the Smith stood admiring his handiwork, he turned to the boy. "See. Small improvements, boy."

The boy now understood. The old sleeping sheds had been torn down as all the slaves moved into their new accommodation. The boy, of course, no longer had a room to himself, but as he was not plagued by the same problems that he'd had when he last shared a sleeping room, he didn't mind. This winter would not be as cold for the many slaves that lived in the camp and many were very thankful.

"So, they have made new sleeping quarters then?" asked Chief Hura.

"Yes, Chief," replied the Orik, the master who was the overseer of the camp.

"What was wrong with the old ones? Surely, their time could have been spent doing other chores?"

"I thought that as well, Chief, but tested the sleeping sheds myself. One fell over when I gave it a shove; fell on my arse, I did!"

The Chief roared with laughter, as did his son. "The Smith supervised the construction?"

"Yes, Chief."

The son turned to his father. "He is too clever for his own good, that one," said the son.

"Yes, he is, but he makes fine weapons which is why I

brought him off the Chief of Pulnuk. Over the winter, I look forward to seeing what else he will make for us."

"Anything else to report, Onik?" the Chief said, turning his attention back to the overseer.

"No, my Chief. The last harvest was a good one, better than last year, in fact. Also, we have so much iron ore piled up at the smelter, I doubt they will run out this winter."

"So, the slaves worked well for a change then?" asked the son.

"Yes, with no squabbling. It has been a productive summer!" the overseer said proudly.

The Chief looked over the slave settlement and the many slaves going about their duties of securing the camp for winter. "Good to hear and good work, Onik!"

"Thank you, Chief."

The overseer left to check on the slaves as the Chief and his son toured the new sleeping quarters. They carried a candle lantern so they could see. Both were impressed with the new sleeping quarters of the slaves; especially how warm it was inside.

"Slaves should be cold, father!"

The Chief laughed loudly before replying. "Slaves that are content are usually productive slaves, son. Fear is not the only way to push them to work!"

"Is that why you are thinking of the offer made by your favourite pit-rat?"

"Yes. It is an interesting idea."

"We will see, father. I do not like the sound of it myself."

"You're not sick of losing money on the pit fights?"

"I am father, but feeding slaves proper food and training them? It will end in disaster!"

"Maybe." The Chief lay down on the straw pallets used by the slaves. "Interesting. Try it, son!"

With bad humour, the son also laid down beside his father on the straw bed.

"Comfortable, yes?" said the Chief.

"It is father. I think whatever the Smith coated the floor and walls with, is stopping not only water coming in from the dirt, but also keeping away the cold."

They both rose and left the dugout. The son muttering to himself and the Chief smiling. The son annoyed at his father for letting the slaves be too comfortable, the Chief smiling as he anticipated what the Smith would come up with next.

The first winter storm arrived right on schedule during the night. Of course, the slaves were now quite cosy in their new sleeping quarters. They could hear the wind blowing, but the wind, snow and cold, didn't bother them at all. The boy was resting in his straw pallet with both blankets; the warmest that he had ever been. He smiled as he heard the other slaves in the dugout compliment the Smith and comment on how warm they were. The Smith was, of course, right. Small improvements! This small improvement had made the world of difference to the slaves and now they would be warm through the winter; they would be happier. The boy took a little pride in that, that he had been beside the Smith as they went through construction step by step. He was still smiling as he drifted off to sleep. The last thought through his mind was the Smith's voice. "Never underestimate the power of small improvements, boy!"

The boy woke with a start. A master had kicked him whilst he was asleep.

"Time to be up, boy; work to be done."

The boy got out of bed. It was still dark outside and

usually he woke as the sun started to rise. He got a cuff around the side of the head for not moving fast enough that knocked him back down on his pallet. It didn't hurt but caught him off balance. This was a reminder and not punishment. If it had been punishment, it would have hurt. He got straight back up to his feet. The others that he shared the sleeping dugout with were awake and started to rise as well.

"Not you lot!" the master said.

The boy looked at the others as they lay back down, interested in more sleep.

"Move it, boy!" said the master.

He grabbed his water skin and spare shirt and followed closely behind the master that they called Monster into the darkness. His feet crunched through the snow as he followed Monster for a few moments before arriving at the blacksmith shed. He had been past the shed before, but never been inside. Monster walked through the door and into the shed. The boy hesitated, and then followed. The inside was warm, and light blazed from the forge. The whole inside was light, and he could see everything. The well-cared for tools were hanging on the wall to his left, the forge in the right-hand corner and the blacksmith with his apron on appraising the boy with a smile.

"You work here today, help out the Smith," said Monster, before leaving the shed.

The blacksmith stood staring at him with his hands on his hips. The boy smiled at the thought of working with the blacksmith.

"It seems the bastard-masters have decided that I need a helper and I asked for you. You will be working with me for a while as I have weapons to make for the upcoming raids. Your first job is to bring back five barrows of iron from the smelter."

The blacksmith turned and continued to set up his tools, not bothering to see if the boy had understood the instructions. He had, so left the Smithy and half ran to the smelter shed. Grabbing a barrow, he went to the double doors and banged loudly. The doors opened quickly and standing there was another boy slave, one younger than himself.

"Iron," was all the boy said.

The young slave pointed to the corner of the shed where shining pieces of rocks where stacked. He walked to the huge pile and picked up a rock. The rock was the size of large adult hand; heavier than it looked. It had a dull shine to it that reflected the light coming from the furnace that was just being lit. The rock was smooth and in a regular shape. The boy had been taught by the Smith and now knew the basics of how the iron ingots were made but had never held one in his hands before. He shook his head and started hand loading the iron rocks into the barrow. Once full, he ran back to the Smithy, creating a small pile of them on the floor where the blacksmith indicated. It took him a few trips to get all the shiny rocks for the blacksmith. Once he completed this, he took a swig from his water skin outside the door, refilled it from the water barrel and returned to the Smith.

"The rocks are done, Master. What do you need next?" the boy said, with a small smile.

"Do not call me that, boy. It would be a beating for both of us." Replied the Smith with a small smile

"Well, boy. Have you eaten?

"No, Smith."

"Then sit on stool next to the bench. I'll toast some bread for us. A man can't be expected to work a full day with nothing in his gut."

The boy sat on the stool and watched the Smith. He carved a loaf into many slices, then put them on the roof of the forge hood; it didn't look a very clean, but the boy said nothing. The Smith then poured two cups of a white liquid. He put one in front of the boy and the other he took a sip of before putting down beside him.

He reached up to turn the slices of bread and put them back down on the hood of the forge. He went to the shelf next to the door and grabbed a jar. Returning to the boy, he placed the jar down. The boy watched him without saying anything.

"You are not saying much, boy! You okay?"

"I am fine. Just surprised is all. But as you said, small improvements make all the difference sometimes."

The Smith smiled at having his own words said back to him. "Small improvements, indeed."

Taking the sliced bread off the hood, he piled it on a wooden plate and put it down next to the boy. He lifted the jar and prized open the lid. Taking his dagger, he took a generous amount of the contents and spread it on one of the slices of bread. He then handed it to the boy who took it. He prepared one for himself, then sat on the edge of the bench and took a bite. The Smith smiled as he slowly chewed.

The boy looks at the bread, not knowing what the spread was.

"It is honey, boy. Have you never had honey?"

"What's honaay?" he replied, never having heard that word before.

"Honey. It's called hun-ee," he spoke slowly to give the boy the chance to hear the pronunciation. "It's made by bees, try it."

The boy hesitantly took a bite and was surprised at the taste. He closed his eyes enjoying the sweetness on his tongue.

The toasted bread was crunchy but still soft on the inside. The boy also chewed slowly, enjoying the new experience, the new taste of something he had never tried before.

"Good?"

The boy nodded. His piece was quickly consumed, even though he thought he was taking his time.

He looked at the jar and the bread.

"Help yourself, boy. Do not be shy."

The boy took a slice and the Smithy gave him his knife. Copying the action of the Smith, he smeared honey on his bread. Passing back the dagger, he sat there and chewed his second piece of toasted bread with honey. Then a third and fourth piece followed, until all the bread had gone. He went to get his water skin and the Smith pointed at the cup. The boy hesitated before reaching for it. He lifted it and smelt it. It looked like milk but had never tried it before. He took a sip. The taste was strong but not unpleasant; the texture smooth and creamy as it went down his throat.

"Goats' milk. Good way to start the morning. Better than porridge and water, yes?"

"Yes," the boy replied.

"As I said, I am a slave but live slightly better than most slaves in this camp due to my skill with the metal."

Once they'd completed their breakfast, the Smithy cleaned up and told the boy to fetch to more loads of the iron ingots. The boy left the Smithy and once outside, noticed the sun was just coming up. The rest of the camp would soon be waking to start their work. The masters would be waking the other slaves with kicks and punches, bad words and bad attitudes, half smiles and violence. He grabbed his barrow and ran all the way to the smelter shed to stretch his legs.

The Smith banged on the glowing metal over and over again with his hammer. Sparks flew all over the shed. The boy watched with wonder as the long glowing rod started taking on the shape of a sword. All morning, the Smith had talked whilst he worked, the boy fetching things that he needed and listened as the Smith spoke. The Smith, of course, threw questions at the boy to test his recollection of all he had taught the boy over the last full moon. The boy answered quickly and confidently. The Smith was once again reminded of the boy's quiet intelligence. The Smith changed questions quickly.

"So, when and how were you taken boy?" asked the Smith.

The question hit a sore spot in the boy's emotions. A memory the boy had spent his young life trying not to think of. Feelings that he locked away in the deepest part of his being. The boy felt his anger rise and tried his best to quell it. He stared at the Smith without saying anything, a long stare that looked through the Smith. He could feel his muscles tense.

The Smith stopped his hammering and stared at the boy with mild surprise on his face. "No need to get all moody, boy. It was just a bloody question. If you don't want to say anything, I won't ask again."

The boy shook his head.

"Get yourself outside for a few moments. Dunk your head in the barrel of water out there and cool off. The heat is getting to you, boy."

The boy looked at him, his breathing coming in long intakes as he tried to calm himself.

"That was not a request, boy. Go! Now!"

The boy stormed outside. The fresh air was a relief. He walked to the water barrel and dunked his head down into it. He held it there for some time before coming up for air. He ran his fingers through his long brown hair. He sat under a tree and drank his water skin dry. His breathing came back to him as he got himself under control. Memories that he had tried to forget, came back to him. His mother on the ground crying, the men around her laughing. He slowly shook as he tried to push the memories away. He kept his breathing even and closed his eyes. He sat for some time before he heard footsteps.

"You calmed down now, boy?"

He nodded his head.

"Well, one day, when you are ready to talk about it, we can swap stories. You tell me yours and I'll tell you mine sort of deal. But until you are ready, we will speak of it no more."

"Thank you." The words escaped the boy's lips in almost a whisper.

"You're welcome boy. It's time for lunch, so we will sit here and eat our lunch before getting back to work. Run to the food hall and grab two bowls of the mush, that they call food."

The boy nodded and ran off.

Chapter Three

"How is the Demon-child?" the master called Monster asked.

"He works well, master. He is absorbing the information. I think that he finds the work interesting."

"He is not here to find it interesting. He is just here to help you get as many swords and axes completed before summer is here."

"You could leave him with me, master! Let me train the boy as a blacksmith. It would be useful."

"No," the master slurred in anger. "He is here for now to get strong. Then, it's the pit for him."

"You're going to waste him in the pit?"

"Don't question me, slave. You are given leeway on a few things as you make good weapons, but never forget, you are still a slave."

"I shall never forget that, master. Imagine how good your swords and axes would be if the boy started learning now. I won't be here forever."

The master sent a right cross to the Smith's face, then followed up with an uppercut. As the Smith struggled, the master sent a right cross that dropped the Smith to the ground.

"When you're dead Smith, I'll just go back to your homelands and find another." The master stormed off.

The boy had come around the corner with the two bowls of food, just as the master had attacked the Smith. The boy put the food down under the tree. He rushed to the Smith, then fetched another water skin and a cloth, returning as the Smith was picking himself up off the ground. He handed the water skin and cloth to the Smith.

"Thanks, boy. See, not even I am immune to their anger. Bastard-masters!"

The boy sat by the tree as the Smith cleaned himself up. After he'd finished cleaning himself up, he sat down. They ate their lunch together in silence.

Once lunch had finished, they went back to work. The Smith explained that the fastest way to make as many swords and hand axes that the bastard-masters wanted, was to create molds. The metal was not as strong, but he explained that they could make many more in quick succession using this process of moulding. They spent the morning with large, thick planks of wood, as wide as a man and just as tall. The Smith had two such pieces and using charcoal, marked out shapes of short swords and axe heads. With the Smith watching at first, the boy took up chisel and hammer, and started to dig out the marked areas. The boy picked it up very quickly and once he had got used to using the correct amount of pressure on the chisel, the Smith took up another chisel and hammer, and started chiselling as well.

By the end of the day, they had a large slab of wood carved out to resemble the rough shape of ten short swords marked into the large slab. The remaining slab had the carved-out shapes of twenty axe heads. The Smith has started teaching the boy to count so he could use this work to continue his education. The Smith said, "The bastard-masters do not want slaves to be able to read or write or even know their numbers, but a basic grasp of numbers is essential."

They were sweeping up all the wood chips when the Smith turned to the boy. "We are done for this day. I'll see you here a bit earlier tomorrow morning."

The boy nodded. It was still a while before end of the day. He decided to do some iron ore runs before the end of day. He knew if the masters saw him doing nothing, they would either beat him or give him a nasty job, or worse, he would do both. This had happened before! He had finished his work early and the masters found him sitting down doing nothing. They had beaten him, then ordered him to clean out the toilet huts. Emptying the shit pots, then scrubbing them with warm water and cloths. The job had made him vomit over and over again. Since then, he had learnt to always be working. If he finished his work early, he looked for something else to do.

He grabbed a barrow and loped off to the mines. He worked out in his head that he should be able to get two or three loads in before the end of the day. As he ran along, he welcomed the chance to stretch his legs. Although he was happy at the change of work with the Smith, the work was not hard on his body like his normal workload and he felt the need to stretch his legs. As he ran easily over the path leading to the mines, he thought of the Smith. He was stunned how quickly that he had accepted the Smith into his life. The easy friendship growing between them. He realised the Smith was the first slave that he truly trusted.

He sped up to truly stretch his legs. He was sweating lightly as he arrived at the mine for his first load. By the fading light, he had gotten his three loads in. He returned his barrow, then headed to the food hut; finished his meal in silence like he always did. He washed himself up in a water barrel, then headed to bed. He walked into his sleeping dugout, running his hands along the limestone mortared walls, still amazed by what the Smith had built. He got to his pallet of straw and laid down, wrapping his blanket around himself. He fell asleep satisfied and quickly.

The moon had completed its next full cycle, and in that time, the boy had settled into his new routine. He was up early before the sun came up and was at the Smithy. He would help the Smith until a few hours before last light, then he would spend the remainder of the day once more carting iron ore from the mines to the smelter shed, whilst the Smith prepped for the next day before sorting his bed. The Smith continued to teach the boy everything he could think of; happy to pass on his experience and knowledge while they worked. The boy was learning to make weapons quickly and the Smith knew if given a summer or two to teach, the boy would make a fine blacksmith. Of course, that was not an option. The Smith hadn't told the boy of the master's intentions to throw the boy into the pit like a dog, to fight for his life. Unfortunately, there was nothing the Smith could do to keep the boy from this fate.

By the time the moon had completed another cycle, they had established their routine. Whilst the Smith hammered out new weapons that they had taken from the molds, the boy would dress, sharpen and oil the newly created weapons. During this time, they had completed twenty axes and thirty swords. The Outlander preferred axes to swords, but a few liked the sword as a backup weapon.

One of the masters, the one that they called 'Monster' came into inspect the work one morning and although didn't show it, was impressed with the work. Later, Monster returned with the Chief's son, the master the slaves had started referring to "Son-of-Angry-man". He was one of the tougher masters and very unpredictable. He was volatile and would often explode into a rage, killing slaves or anyone else that got in his way.

When Son-of-Angry-man had entered the smithy, he looked around at the boy who was concentrating on an axe that he was sharpening. Son-of-Angry-man had a look of irritation on his face and he started walking towards the boy. He was intercepted by the blacksmith, who was holding a parcel wrapped in a large cloth. He bowed his head and presented the parcel to the master. The master's face dripped with malice about being intercepted until he opened the cloth. In the cloth was a hand axe of shining silver. The blacksmith had melted down an old broken silver mug and added the silver to the last tempering of the axe. It shone in the light from the forge. The Master took it outside admiring it in the light. The hand axe was roughly three and a half feet long; it was well balanced. The blade of the axe was the same width as two hands side by side. It was as sharp as anything the master had ever seen. On the reverse side of the blade was a long spike, designed to pierce armour and as long as two pointer fingers.

The master smiled as he swung it in an attack routine. The Smith watched from the door as the Son-of-Angry-man took joy in the balance of the axe. The boy moved in quickly, had a quick look around the edge of the door, then went back to the bench and continued his work.

"This is your best weapon yet, Smith."

"I thank the master."

"I won't kill you today, then." He spoke as he continued to swing the axe.

Once he had finished, he took his own hand axe out of his belt and replaced it with this new axe. He threw the old axe at a tree, it dug in and held fast, buried up to half its blade.

The Smith continued to keep his stare to the ground. He never knew if the Son-of-Angry-man was joking or not. The master approached him.

"The boy's path is set in stone. No matter how good he works for you, that will not change that. Question one of the masters again and I'll see you dead."

The Smith kept his head down. He knew that he had taken a risk by speaking for the boy. Life was easily ended in this slave settlement. The Smith had perhaps overestimated his worth to these barbarians. "Your will, master."

The master sent a punch that smacked against the Smith's face, dropping him to the ground. The Smith stayed there and didn't move.

"Always my will, Smith. These are my lands, my villages, my slaves."

The Smith wanted to say 'you mean your father's lands and slaves', but he didn't; that would mean death. Although the Smith was not scared of dying, he was not yet ready for death.

The master continued. "The boy will be a pit-rat. That was decided the day that he killed my uncle. The boy should be grateful that we didn't torture him to death!" The master laughed hard and loud. "I hated my uncle. He had less brains than the Demon-child does. Getting himself killed by a child." He laughed again. "My auntie asked for the boy to be punished and demanded that he be thrown into the pit to live out his life there. Who would my father be, if he denied his sister?"

The Smith took all of this information in. He had heard rumours of the boy but had never been sure what was true.

"You have the boy for another half-moon, Smith. Use him well, as I need as many hand axes now as you can manage. Don't worry about swords. As you know, I am not a man to disappoint."

"No master, you are not. The weapons will be ready."

"See that they are"

The masters walked away. The boy came to the door as the Smith was picking himself up of the ground. They returned to the forge where the Smith had a long drink of water. The boy offered him a cloth to wipe the sweat from him.

They continued to work the rest of the day, the boy staring at the Smithy, not returning in the afternoon like normal to cart more iron ore. He finished sharpening the two-handed axe and oiled it. He put it in the rack against the far wall with the finished weapons.

The Smith went back to his forge as the boy approached. "Smith?"

"Yes, boy."

"What's a pit rat?"

The Smith turned and faced the boy. He saw the confusion on his face, the uncertainty.

"He said I was going to be a pit rat. I have never heard the words before. What does it mean?"

The Smith sat down on the stool. He pointed to the shelf where a clay jug was hidden at the back. The boy knew what he wanted and grabbed the jug that was filled with strong spirit. The Smith had acquired a few jugs of the stuff full moons ago, even though slaves were not allowed to drink, he risked more beatings or even death to indulge on the odd occasion. The Smith took the jug, pulled the stopper and took a large sip. He offered it to the boy. The boy shook his head.

He once again offered it to the boy. "Trust me. Relax and take a sip."

The boy took the jug and took a gulp. It burned all the way down and he coughed. The Smith smiled then took the jug back of him. The boy sat on the centre work bench.

"So, what does it mean?"

Outside, the three masters walked away from the Smithy. Son-of-Angry-man rested his hand on his new hand axe and smiled.

"You think the Demon-child will last long in the pit?" the red-headed master called Fire-Head said.

"He will or he won't. He will win a few fights and make us some coins, or he will die painfully. Either way, my father will be happy."

"What do YOU want to do to the boy?"

"Beat him, slowly and until he breathes no more, but my father has forbidden it. I think he is impressed with the story of a child killing a warrior. Although you and I know, it was just sheer luck. Still, my father has said what will happen and we have to follow his orders."

"The child is a demon. It concerns me!"

"What?" said Son-of-Angry-man as he stopped walking and rounded on Fire-Head, standing directly in front of him. "You are scared of him? He just a slave!"

"I didn't say that I was scared of him; I said, "He concerns me". Everyone knows that he is possessed, that's why he's called the Demon-child. You have beaten him, cousin. How many times did he scream out like the other slaves? How many times have you seen him cry when he was a small child?"

"None. He never makes a sound when beaten. He does not have the brains to realise the pain he is in."

"No, he has a brain. The slave is calculating. You saw the beating that he gave the other three slaves last winter. He destroyed them and had no emotion on his face; just a blank stare as he tore into them. Even when you beat him as punishment, he just stared you in the eye and made not a whimper. I saw the hate in his eyes. I wouldn't trust him with a knife. He is possessed by a demon."

Son-of-Angry-man laughed as they continued walking.

"You are too superstitious; he is just a slave. One that fights back; nothing more. Although the Smith has taught him well and the child is more respectful. I think he has finally realised his lot in life."

As they walked back to the barracks, Fire-Head just shook his head. The boy had spirit. Yes, he knew to keep his eyes to the ground and watch what he did in order to stop from being beaten. But still, Fire-Head was always unnerved around the slave. Anyone that killed a full-grown man at five seasons old would unnerve him.

The Smith took a large gulp from the jug. It slightly burned on the way down. He passed the jug back to the boy, who copied the action of the Smith and took a large gulp. He was not prepared for the burning sensation as the fiery liquid went down his throat. He almost gagged and stopped himself.

The Smith chuckled. "Takes a bit to get used to, but it does make you drunk and warms the soul. What more could a lowly slave want, eh?"

"You didn't answer my question!"

"No, I didn't."

The boy looked over at the Smith. The Smith looked back seeing the seriousness in the boy's face. The Smith got to his feet and went over to the door, closing it. He then went over to the oven and closed one of the shutters closing of the air supply. The oven immediately started to die down. Grabbing a second jug like the first, the Smith came over to where the boy was sitting against a wall. The Smith got down and sat next to him on the floor.

"It seems the masters have decided to make you a fighter."

"A fighter?" The boy didn't know the word.

"Yes, a fighter. You will be trained how to fight. Not just fight back which you are more than capable, but how to fight properly. You will spend a few seasons been shown different techniques on how to fight, getting your body stronger and faster. "

The boy was hanging of every word as he took another sip from the jug, although this time took a smaller one. He could already feel his body relaxing and it felt fine.

"Once they have deemed you are ready, they chuck you into the pit with another young fighter."

"And, what is a pit?"

"The pit is a large hole they dig into the ground. As large as the new sleeping dugouts that we made, just deeper. The walls are lined with stones or wood. The two fighters thrown in and then fight until only one is left standing."

The boy looked at the Smith to see if he was lying. "That does not seem too bad, Smith."

"It's not, as its hand to hand fighting, but that is why you are still young. Once the masters deem you are a man, the fights turn deadly."

"Deadly?"

"Yes, deadly. They become death bouts, boy. Both fighters are given weapons and have to fight until one or the other is dead. The Outlanders see it as sport. They make many wagers and win or lose massive amounts of coin on the death bouts. All of the settlements in this land have a stable of fighters that they train. They turn slaves into dogs for their own amusements."

"So, if you lose, you are dead. What happens if you win?"

"If you win boy, you actually lose!"

"If you win you lose? That does not make sense."

The Smith took another large gulp of the spirit. Normally, he would not have been so forthcoming, but he liked the boy, he truly did. He was the smartest slave that he had come across since he had been captured himself ten winters ago. Beneath his blank nasty looks, he cared for others around him; although you had to look hard to see this. The Smith had been around rough men all his life and knew to see into the soul of a person.

"Yes boy, if you win, you return to your work. The next time that there is a pit fight, you are thrown once again to fight for your life. If you keep winning, you will keep getting thrown into the pit, over and over again until one day, you meet someone stronger of faster than you and you finally get killed. It's no life boy. That's why they use slaves."

The boy looked at the ground. This is what the masters had decided he was good for. Life as a slave was hard, but at least in the last four seasons, his life had become steady and predictable. He had food, the other slaves kept away from him, and as long as he worked hard and kept his eyes to the ground, he would not get beaten – usually. Sometimes, the masters would beat him anyway, but he was used to this. Although he didn't like the life of slave, he never knew of any other life.

"So, I have no chance of doing anything else then? They will throw me into this pit to see me fight and die?"

"I'm afraid so, boy. I did question the master Fire-Head, as he is not as violent as the others and can see the value of a hardworking slave unlike the others. But, of course, I took a beating for it. I think you would be more useful here in the Smithy learning the trade. You take instructions well and seem to enjoy the work."

"I do enjoy it. I enjoy learning something new." He looked across the Smithy into space. "What do I do then? Fight and die? My life is over!" he said in a half whisper.

"You have no choice and your only hope is to be the best fighter there is and hopefully win enough fights to earn enough favour from the masters, so that when you are too old for the pit, they give you quiet work."

"How many times has that happened, Smith?" The boy returned to looking at his feet.

"Never. Every person that enters that pit dies. I won't lie boy, it's a death sentence."

The boy took a few more gulps of the spirit, not caring how it burned on its way down. He could feel his body getting drunk. He had never been drunk before and he liked the feeling. The Smith continued to drink his jug. Both of them said nothing further of importance, just small talk whilst they consumed the spirit and drunk themselves to sleep, where they sat.

He woke with a start. He could hear banging and swearing. He opened his eyes to see the Smith slowly making his way around the smithy. Swearing as he struggled to relight the forge. It had gone out last night whilst they had drunk themselves into a stupor. The boy could feel a strong pulsing headache behind his left eye. His head was pounding, and he felt sick. He struggled to rise and once he stood, he instantly regretted it. His stomach started heaving and he ran for the door. Bursting through it, he made it in time to throw up the contents of his stomach on the ground. He was bent over with his body trying to heave up all that was in his stomach. He kept retching until only liquid and bile came out. The blacksmith came out with a skin full of water. The boy took it and drank deeply. As soon as the cool water hit his stomach, he threw it up. The Smith smirked and walked away. The boy heard him mutter.

"You need more practise boy."

The boy walked over and sank down beside the water barrel. He wanted to stand up and drown his head into the barrel, but whilst he sat down his head didn't hurt as much. The Smith returned with another water skin.

"Trust me, boy. Drink as much water as you can. We need to make up for the lost time of yesterday and have lots of work to do. Keep drinking until it stays down, then you had better run and get some more iron ingots for today's work. Once you have a few loads, go and grab us some porridge. By then, I will have this damned oven started again and we can finish off with some heated goats' milk."

The boy only nodded. "Does it always hurt like this? Why are you not throwing up?"

"I've had more practise, boy. If you drink as much spirits as we did last night, it always hurts like this."

"Then why do it?"

"Did it not feel good last night? Did you not enjoy the feeling of all your worries being forgotten about?"

The boy thought back to the previous night and remembered the conversations, the laughing. He had never enjoyed anything in his short life, as much as he enjoyed the bonding and drinking with the Smith last night. "Aye, it was fun. Does it always have to be this bad?"

"That's a decision that every man must make for himself.

You need to learn the magic line where you drink enough to be happy, but not enough to feel like this in the morning."

"Have you learnt this magic line?"

"No, boy. I always end up like this."

"It doesn't make sense, Smith."

The Smith chuckled to himself.

"No, it doesn't. Better get those loads of iron. I'll get this forge started."

The Smith headed back into the shed to fire up the forge, whilst the boy picked himself up. He threw his head into the water barrel and held it there. He then lifted up his head and felt better. He walked over behind the smithy and grabbed his barrow. He started running and instantly regretted it, having to stop and throw up again. He continued by walking briskly with his barrow.

As they ate their lunch, they sat in silence under the boy's favourite tree. The morning had been hard. Normal tasks became more complicated, but they managed to right the smithy and hide all evidence of their drinking session. The boy buried himself in his work of sharpening and oiling the finished axes, whilst the Smith continued to bang his hammer on his anvil, shaping the axe heads. The boy's head had slowly cleared once he had eaten, the warm goats' milk settling his stomach. By lunch time, he felt almost normal. Sometime during the morning, the Smith had stopped and looked at the boy.

"Boy, did I tell you my name last night? My real name?"

"Yes, you did, Corvin!" the boy said with a smile, remembering their drunken conversation.

"Well, do me a favour and forget I told you. You know the rules!"

"Yes."

They had one quarter of the moon left to complete axes for the summer raids. Axes were slightly easier to make than swords as the steel was thinner and didn't need to be tempered as much. The time-consuming part was shaping the heads and sharpening. The boy was confident that they would have it finished in time. They spent the rest of the afternoon hard at work. Instead of running more loads of iron from the smelter shed, the boy continued to sharpen and oil the finished pieces before stacking them in the large wooden crate next to the main door in the smithy.

Three quarters of the moon had passed, and they had reached their target. As the sun rose on this rainy morning, the fifth day of the full moon, the boy stood looking at his work. Next to the door of the smithy, there were five large stacked wooden crates. In each crate, there were ten completed hand axes. All sharpened, oiled and wrapped in cloth. Fifty hand axes in three full moons was as the Smith said, good work. The Smith had confessed that although they were adequate axes and better than any the Outlander could make, they were nothing compared to what he had made in the past. The Outlanders wanted good steel but didn't want them to take too long to complete. Preferring quantity over quality, there was one small surprise for the master, however. The Smith had, on top of the boxes, placed a large object wrapped in cloth. The boy knew it was a much larger one than the hand axes they had been making. He didn't know when the Smith had found time to make it.

"When did you make that?"

"Some nights, I can't sleep. So, I use the time to make something special. It's a gift for Angry-man. It's good to occasionally keep the bastards happy."

The boy laughed as the door to the smithy was flung open. Son-of-Angry-man stood in the doorway.

"Bring out the finished weapons Smith, my father will inspect them." He didn't even ask if the work had been completed; just assuming the Smith had finished on time, as indeed, he had.

The boy had stopped laughing as soon as he had seen the master. As was habit, he dropped his gaze to the ground. As the master turned around and walked outside, the Smith and the boy started manhandling the crates outside. Once they were all lined up outside on the ground, the Smith opened them all for the master to inspect. He would sample one or two from every box before replacing them. The Son-of-Angry-man also tested a few. Once the inspection was complete, Angry-man stepped back.

"Good work, Smith. They are a good enough for my warriors. Not as good as the one you made my son," he said looking over at the hand axe that his son wore on his hip. "But, good enough. Perhaps you can make me one!" Even though the Angry-man's words were polite, the underlying threat could be heard in his tone.

The Smith turned to the boy. "Boy, go fetch the package for the master here."

The boy ran into the shed and grabbed the massive bundle wrapped in cloth. As he carried it outside, he could see the surprise of the master. Upon reaching him, he lowered his eyes and looked at the ground whilst offering the package in two outstretched hands. The master took it and teared the cloth off. The Angry-man, Son-of-Angry-man and Fire-Head were all amazed at what he pulled clear. In his hand he held a large two-handed axe, double headed and five feet long. One side of the axe head was shining silver and round headed, much like seeing a half moon. The other side was an oversized hammer for no doubt bashing instead of cutting. The hammer had been made big to offset the weight of the large axe blade. The shaft was solid oak, smooth yet solid. The shaft had been oiled to stop rot from the sea.

The master actually smiled. Something the Smith had never seen before. He hefted a few times before moving apart from the others and started swinging it in mock battle.

"It is well balanced."

With his eyes on the ground also, the Smith replied. "Yes, master. That is why I made the hammer on the aft side, to balance the weapon."

The master continued to swing it, smiling while he did. "This is amazing work, Smith. You have done well."

Son-of-Angry-man was looking with envy at the large axe. "Perhaps, the Smith can make me one as well, father?"

"No. You have a very fine, new axe. This weapon is made for a chief. You can have this the day that I die."

The Smith could see the anger and jealously in the look the Son-of-Angry-man gave his father. He looked at the Smith with hatred. The Smith continued to look down.

"Well Smith, not only have you made the axes that I demanded, but you have made a masterpiece for me. As your reward…"

"I need no reward, master."

"I'll say what you need, slave. You can either take the rest of the day off with the boy or we can see how sharp this axe is…"

The threat was real. The Smith bowed over, without looking at the master. "Your will, master."

"Get you both gone. Take the day off and my son will come for you both in the early light."

The Smith and the boy disappeared back into the smithy.

Chapter Four

"Day off?"

"Yep boy, does not happen very often but occasionally, the master grants it."

"What is a day off?"

"It means that we do not have to do any work today. We can relax."

"No work?"

"Correct. We will clean up the smithy and get everything ready for whatever the master has planned for us tomorrow."

With that, they cleaned up and prepped the smithy for the following day. The boy did a couple of trips to get more iron ingots. Once the smithy was prepared for the next day, they took a pack of food, then went and sat by the river which was some walk from the settlement. This was the furthest the boy had been out of the settlement and it was a little nerve racking for him. Once they were seated by the river, he started to relax. They slowly ate some of the food they had packed.

"So how long have you been a slave, Smith?"

The Smith smiled. "Remember our agreement? I'll tell you my story if you tell me yours!"

The boy looked at him; he had forgotten. He looked at the slow-moving river, emotions welling up inside him. He had never spoken of his capture to anyone. He had buried the memories deep.

The Smith said nothing as he leaned his head back against the tree that he was sitting against. The boy took a deep breath and slowly started to speak. The words didn't come easy but eventually, he had told the Smith all he remembered, with tears in his eyes. It was the first time that he had felt tears in many summers. He thought that he was all out of tears, recalling the story had made a mockery of that. Memories of his parents, the beatings and the long ship ride bringing pain.

"I'm sorry to say that it's not a unique story, boy. Believe it or not, lots of young slaves have a similar story. However, killing someone at that young age..." the Smith blew air between his lips. "That is something, boy. I see why they call you The Demon-child. I had heard rumours but was not sure whether to believe them."

The boy sat quietly looking at the river. Feeling the emotions roll around in him, emotions that he had left buried for his whole life. They had been released in the telling of his story. He was surprised that he had cried but felt better for it. He breathed slowly whilst he waited for further talk from the Smith.

"Well boy, even though as I said, it's not a unique story, it's still a sad one. "

The Smith looked back to the river and slowly started to speak.

"I was, I can't find the word in the language of the Outlanders, but it is someone that fights other people's battles for coin. A warrior for hire so to speak. I was 17 when I joined these warriors. I was apprenticed to the company blacksmith, so when I was not fighting or carrying out other duties, I was mending or making weapons for my fellow soldiers."

"What's a soldier?"

"Boy, a soldier is a warrior that fights the entire season, over and over again. A warrior that does not have to go home and plant crops or go home and work. They fight constantly and that is what I trained to be from a young age; that and metal work of course. By twenty, I was a sergeant and before you ask, that is someone of better rank and in charge or leading the other soldiers."

The boy shook his head in understanding.

"A minor master?"

"Yes. A sort of minor master. I had twenty men under me. I still worked the metal but when fighting, I was leading my men. I enjoyed the life and I was good at it. I hate to speak highly of myself, but I had good skills in leading other men. I was a sergeant for three further summers until our company was hired to defend a land across the sea from here. The land called DuNoor."

The boy froze. The name seemed familiar to him, but he couldn't put his finger on why.

"We were tasked with defending a certain area of this land from the Outlanders, the same masters we both are slaves to now. Our company staged an ambush one night but to our downfall; it was a trap. We are not sure how or why, but we think the leader of the land betrayed us. There's no way to prove it, of course, but the raiders knew exactly where the company was and avoided us. Raiding time and time again over a six full moon cycle period, always where we least expected it. When we realised what was happening, our captain approached the leader or master of the province and explained that someone was feeding the raider information.

He didn't take the accusation seriously and three moons later while waiting in ambush, we were ambushed ourselves by raiders three times our numbers. Most of the company was slaughtered! Eight of us remained alive out of a hundred soldiers. We were tortured and beaten. One of the raiders must have found some of my blacksmith tools. One of the survivors of my company pointed at me. I was then taken away and never saw any of my men again. We learned all too late, it was the master of the province giving the raiders our position. It turns out that he was taking a cut from the raiders. They gave him money and in exchange, he let them raid his small villages. He also let them use is province as a staging area to raid the neighbouring province. A nasty business!"

He stopped to let the words sink in. The boy was watching him and listening intently. His own grief and emotions forgotten.

"I'm not sure if my men were killed or turned into slaves, but I was chucked on a boat and brought to a camp to work the mines. I tried to escape a few times, of course, but after a few beatings, I learnt not to. The last beating was so severe, I got given this limp. They smashed my knee to bits, and it has never healed properly. That was ten summers ago now and I have been a slave ever since. First working the mines, then making substandard swords and axes for these Bastard Outlanders."

They both sat in silence. The Smith reflecting over his life and the boy trying to understand the words. It was sometime before the boy asked his next question.

"What was the name of the land again?"

"DuNoor, boy. Why?"

Once again, something triggered in his memory. He couldn't quite grasp it.

"Don't know. Seems familiar is all."

"Don't know why it should, boy. It's a two full moon by sea voyage away from this cold place."

"Can you describe it to me?"

"Sure." The Smith searched his memories. "Not quite as cold as here in the winter but it can get cold. It rains a lot more and only snows a little in the winter. In the summer, it is very much warmer than here, and a man would sweat from dawn to dusk, if he was working. A large range of mountains on one border and the sea on the other border. Serfs that work hard all their lives for an early grave. A master that treats the serfs like slaves."

"What's a serf?"

"A serf is like a slave, but you have a slightly better life. You work as hard, but you are fed slightly better, given a warm place to live. Serfs can marry and have families, but the main difference is that serfs can leave the land, if they choose to. In theory, a lord of master has to look after serfs and provide them with the basics of living in exchange for their working his land. Unfortunately, the master of the province in question treated his serfs like slaves. Evil bastard."

"Did they speak the same as us or did they speak other languages, like the cook ladies do?"

"A strange language that I could never pick up. I only managed to learn a few words."

"Can you speak some for me?"

The Smith laughed. "If I was to say good morning to you, I would say 'Greta moringna'. In reply, you would say…"

"Greta moringna mah lerd," said the boy, without thinking.

The Smith stopped and stared at the boy. "How did you know that, boy?"

"Know what, Smith?"

"You just said good morning to you sir in the language they speak in DuNoor. Where did you learn that?"

The boy looked surprised. "I'm not sure. "

"Where would you learn that here? Who in this camp apart from me could teach it to you?"

"What does that mean, Smith?"

"It means, boy, that either the Outlanders have taught it to you, or you came from DuNoor or another province on the nation of Ex'Na and that is where the masters got you from."

The boy didn't know what to think. His short life thus far, he had expected that he would never know where he came from.

"It's only a guess boy, but I can't imagine any other way you would know those words."

"I come from DuNoor, then?"

"Or somewhere close. The whole nation of Ex'Na speaks that language."

The light was starting to fade. They had been sitting here in conversation all afternoon. The boy was relaxed but also confused. He didn't know what to do with this information.

"Better get back. We should get back in time to grab some food."

They stood and made their way back to the camp.

"Can you tell me more about this land called Ex'Na."

"Of course, boy. Although not tonight as I need my sleep! Tomorrow, I can fill you in more whilst we work."

The boy was woken as the door to the smithy was thrown open. He had taken to sleeping on a makeshift pallet in the corner of the smithy over the last few quarters of the moon. The masters hadn't stopped him. Standing in the doorway holding a torch was Son-of-Angry-man. The boy rose up from bed, then stood to attention with his eyes lowered. The Smith came out of his room that was built on to the smithy and also stood to attention. His eyes, although not looking at the ground, where lowered as not to anger the Chief Masters son.

"Smith grab all the tools of your trade and load them into the back of the wagon once it arrives. Demon-boy, grab whatever small smelly possessions you have and then help the Smith load his tools."

The Son-of-Angry-man turned and left not even making sure they were following.

The Smith was wide-eyed and surprised.

"Where do you think we are going, Smith?"

"Not sure boy. I suspected they would take you to one of their training camps but have no idea where they are taking me. Look on the bright side."

"What bright side?" said the boy, with little enthusiasm. The memories of the conversations of yesterday reminding him of his death sentence.

"Wherever you are going, I am going with you."

The boy gave the Smith a half smile and then ran to the sleeping shed to grab his two spare shirts, his spare trousers and his blanket. He loaded his meagre belongings into his blanket, then tied the blanket's ends together to make a rough carry sack. He then ran back to the smithy. As he arrived, a wagon with two oxen was just being pulled up to the front of the smithy.

He tossed his sack into the back and ran into the smithy. The Smith had loaded his possessions into a large leather backpack by the front door. He started putting all his tools into wooden crates that would normally hold finished weapons.

"Give me a hand boxing up these tools boy."

Helping the Smith, they boxed up the tools and then helped the Smith carry the crates to the back of the wagon.

When they had finished, three weapons crates sat on the back of the wagon. The Smith grabbed his leather backpack and chucked that on the back as well. The boy ran in and grabbed the broom and other small items. He saw two hidden jugs of spirits that the Smith drank and hid them in a sack. Running back to the wagon, he placed the items safely. He hid the sack with jugs of spirits carefully under his own blanket sack.

It had not taken them long to get the smithy broken down of the basic tools and store them on the wagon. As the sun was rising, the Son-of-Angry-man came back with masters that the boy had never seen before.

"Both of you, get on the back."

The Smith and the boy jumped and sat beside the crates of tools. The boy using his bed sack under him as a cushion. One of the masters climbed up into the wagon's front seat. Grabbing the reins, he gave them a flick. The other two masters had left and returned riding war horses. Huge beasts, at least sixteen or seventeen hands high. They followed the wagon, watching the Smith and the boy.

As the wagon rolled through the settlement, the boy watched the other slaves come from their sleeping sheds to stare at him. It had all happened quickly, and the boy hadn't had any time to realise what was happening. As the wagon reached the gate of the slave camp, reality came crashing home. His entire life had been spent in this miserable place. However, this was still his home and had been for seven summers. An empty feeling fell in the pit of his stomach. The feeling of uncertainty, the same feeling that he experienced all those summers ago, when first loaded into the slave ship. He looked to the Smith who had fast become the rock in his life over the last five quarter moons. He hadn't realised until now, how he had become to rely on this man. The Smith turned and saw the boy staring at him.

"I was just starting to get settled at that camp. It feels a little strange to be leaving it now," said the Smith, with a half-smile.

The Smith had summed up his feeling and the boy realised that the Smith was feeling the same as himself. He rested his head on his knees as the wagon bumped along. He tried to keep calm as he watched the trees and the world go slowly by. He had plenty of time to think on the death sentence that he had been handed. It scared him but it was more the uncertainty that scared him, as he was too young and inexperienced in life to fully appreciate what fighting in a pit was really like. Although, he would learn, and he would learn it all too well.

The journey had taken a full three days by wagon. They followed a dirt track that had wound its way around ragged hills and tundra, snow covering most of the hills and ground. Both the Smith and the boy had wrapped their blankets round them to keep warm as the weather even though clear, was still cold. The boy could tell the season was turning and spring was almost here.

They had camped on the side of the road the first night, both the Smith and the boy with one of their legs chained to the wagon. They were not fed but then neither of them had expected food. The Smith had foreseen this and had a small pack containing some food, so neither of them would starve. At the start of the journey, the Smith warned the boy on speaking too much, so the conversation had been limited. There was small talk on the odd occasion, but mainly they rode in silence. The boy could see the Smith was struggling with his own thoughts and the boy was no different. He was trying to work his way through the feelings of his new life ahead of him.

On the afternoon of the second day, they had ridden around the base of a hill; before them was a large valley. When the Smith told the boy to take a look, the boy looked with surprise on his face. It was the largest settlement that he had ever seen. On the open side of the valley was a large bay that was sheltered but opened up into the open ocean. The valley floor consisted of many dwellings. More than the boy had seen in his life. The far side of the valley hill was farms, although the boy couldn't see what they grew from this distance. He only saw tiny little figures using tools to till the fields. As they made their way close to the settlement, the boy noticed that on the right side of the valley, the hill was animals grazing. Many of the paddocks had been fenced using stones. In those paddocks, he saw horses running, large cows and the occasional oxen. On the beaches, he saw many raiding ships beached with workers swarming over them. The people were hammering, sanding and oiling the large ships. The spring was almost here, and the boy realised the ships that he saw would soon be out capturing more young boys like himself. He felt anger surge up deep inside of him.

As the wagon headed for the settlement, he noticed there was no walls or fences around it.

He asked the Smith why this was.

"No walls? They don't need them, boy. No slaves to run away and what force would attack this far north?"

The Smith asked the driver of the wagon a question.

One of the masters riding beside the wagon answered. "This place is called Hurarock. It is named after our Chief. It's the biggest settlement in the lands of the Chief with over twenty thousand people living here. Now keep your mouths shut as we ride through the settlement."

They both stayed silent as the wagon entered the settlement. The wagon was on what looked like a main street. The main street was long and straight with buildings and homes either side of it, stretching to the valley side. The road was wide enough to accommodate four wagons being driven side by side. The noise and the smells assaulted the senses of the boy. He could smell a mixture of wood smoke and smoked fish. The sounds were of the lives of twenty-five thousand Outlander barbarians going about their lives. They passed a smithy and the boy could hear the familiar ringing of hammer on steel. He turned to look forward and could see the largest building that he had even seen standing at the end of the road. It took them some time to reach it, but as they arrived at the large building, he could see it was so different to everything around it. Whereas most of the buildings in the settlement were made from wood, with the occasional one being half stone and wood, this one was solid stone. Three storeys high and as wide as ten wagons parked end to end. As they got close, they noticed the road forked and the left and right branch wrapping its way around the large building.

The guard that had spoken before spoke up again. "The home of our Chief Hura."

The boy gazed at the size of the building, noticing the roof that had been tiled using slate. The many windows that went along the left side of the building on the second and third storeys, but none on the ground floor.

As they made their way past the Chiefs home, he noticed children his own age playing. He hadn't seen many children his own age. He had been the youngest at the slave camp apart from two other boys. He certainly had never seen a girl his own age and he gaped at two of them as the wagon passed.

"Don't you stare at us, slave boy!" said one of them, while

the other girl picking up a rock and throwing it at the boy. He was too caught up in his own surprise and the rock hit him square in the face. He yelped and the guards all laughed hard. The girls were also laughing at him. His anger once again started creeping to the surface. Although he had only ever been used to being a slave, always used to beatings and bullying, he had never before felt as low as he did in that moment. He rubbed his right eye where the rock had hit.

"Take it in your stride, boy. You will learn now that these Outlanders are animals. The women as much as the men."

"Silence, Smith," said one of the guards.

The boy looked at him, anger in his eyes. He had never defied the masters before, but the feeling of uncertainty making him careless. The second guard saw the look that he was being given from the boy. He rode his horse up to the wagon and backhanded the boy. The first guard laughed as the boy was knocked unconscious, he struck the wagon as he fell back. He was not out for long and when he came back around, he kept his gaze down.

At the end of the settlement, they approached a large walled enclosure. The wooden walls were as high as two men and stretched across the entire end of the valley. As the gates were opened, the boy and the Smith caught a look of their new home for the foreseeable future. The enclosure was almost as large as the slave camp except the wooden walls ran the entire perimeter of the camp. The camp was perfectly square, and the boy could see the far wall had been dug into the hill, so the enclosure was perfectly flat. The left side of the camp was an odd assortment of buildings. The largest, a three-storey building which looked like the living quarters. The boy thought to himself that it could house at least two hundred people. The building ran parallel to the wooden wall and was almost half the length of the enclosure. Around it where other smaller buildings that looked like storage sheds. To his right on the inside of the wooden wall was another huge building. It was only single storey that he could see but was as tall as the three storeyed living quarters. To the far right and towards the back of the enclosure, he saw a massive field. Rimming the field was a dirt track that had many young men running around the outside of it. A master on horseback following and yelling.

The wagon came to a halt outside a small shed that was only slightly larger than the smithy back at the slave camp. It was double story with the second story boasting a few windows, but the ground floor only having two that he could see.

"Unpack the wagon and put all your tools in this building. There is a forge in there but has not been used in the last two seasons."

The Smith and boy looked closer at the building.

"You are to get the shed set up as another smithy. We have much metal for you to shape, slave. Your living quarters are upstairs, and the Demon-child stays with you for now."

The boys and the Smith hopped down and strode towards the building. The Smith opened the large double door and walked in. Opening the two front floor windows, light flooded in illuminating the inside. The place stunk of staleness and mouse droppings. The huge forge was at the far wall directly in line with the double doors with a massive hood above it. The forge was easily twice the size of the previous one the boy and the Smith had worked in. In front of the forge were two giant anvils. The far-left corner was taken up by shelves made to store blacksmiths tools, although empty. Along the left wall was a workbench that ran the complete length of the wall. In the right far corner was a small smelter with its own tools. This was for the moulding of weapons, a faster and easier way to make steel weapons of war. The Smith had used moulds at the last smithy but had been doing it on a smaller scale than was possible here. The right wall in the middle had another wooden door, whilst the right corner had large crates that would be used for storing iron ingots.

"Your sleeping quarters are through that door. The boy stays here for now as the fighters' barracks are currently full, but that won't last long, the Demon-child is the last to arrive" the guard said with a smile.

The other guard laughed. The third guard who was driving the wagon had disappeared back into the main settlement.

The first guard continued. "You never know, Smith. You may last longer than the last smith."

The Smith looked to the guard; the question left unsaid. The guard looked to him smiling.

"We killed the last Smith for not doing as he was told."

Both guards laughed as they headed away and left the two of them to it.

"Right, boy. Let's get this room aired out. You clean up whilst I set the tools up. Let's get those crates in here first, then you start cleaning. Then, we can look." It always sounded like a request and never an order.

Once the wagon was emptied, the boy spent some time cleaning whilst the Smith wiped the dust out of the shelves in the left corner and then stacked and arranged his tools.

"This place smells better already, boy," the Smith remarked as the boy had picked up the last of the rubbish and mouse droppings. With the double windows open the smithy was well lit. The air was starting to circulate, and the room did indeed start to lose some of its stale smell.

"Let's check out those living quarters, boy," the Smith said as he headed towards the door on the right wall. Opening the door, the boy right behind him, they noticed there was a set of stairs going left, then up. They moved up the stairs that took them to the second story. They arrived at a medium size sitting room. Against the outside wall to the right as you walked in, was a huge fireplace with wood stacked neatly beside it. In front of the fireplace, but not too close were sitting chairs, enough room for two people per chair. To the left of the door was a table with three wooden chairs. The far wall had three doors. They investigated and found three small bedrooms with a single bed in each. Also, in the rooms were storage cupboards to store clothing.

"Bloody luxury, boy," the Smith commented.

The boy looked up and smiled. "Small improvements, Smith."

The Smith laughed. "You ever slept in a real bed, boy?"

"No."

"Well, we better air out those blankets and open up the windows to get the musty smell gone. Also, I'll need to check with the Outlander bastards where I get wood and coal for the forge."

As the boy straightened the living quarters and aired them out, the Smith went for a walk. It did not take long before everything was clean and tidy. He had taken the far-left room for himself, putting his four items of clothing in the cupboard and putting his blanket with the other ones back on the bed. The boy was alone when another boy a few summers younger stepped into the living quarters holding a blanket rolled up with his possessions.

"Sir, the masters told me to come here and see the Smith."

The boy looked him up and down. He couldn't be any older seven summers. "I am not a sir. I'm a slave. What do they call you?" He could see the smaller child relax a little.

"They call me quick-hands!"

"Quick-hands?"

"I used to steal food. The other slaves just call me Quick."

"Have a seat, Quick. The Smith will be back shortly."

"What do they call you?" Quick asked as he sat down on one of the chairs.

The boy thought about. He had never had a name and to be honest, he never bothered with wanting one. Everyone just called him boy. "They call me Boy or sometimes the masters call me Demon-child."

The younger boy shrank back. "It is said that you killed one of the masters when you were younger than me!"

"How did you know that?"

"All the slaves here speak of it. It is said you are to become a pit rat"

The boy shrugged. "Apparently."

At that moment, the Smith arrived carrying a basket of food and an arm full of cloth. "You must be the one they call Quick?"

"Yes, sir."

"I am not a sir. Just call me Smith."

"Yes, Smith."

"This lad is my new apprentice," the Smith said to the boy.

The boy's heart broke, again. Even though he knew his life was for the pit, he had still held out hope that he would be apprenticed. The look of disappointment was on his face when the Smith said, "At least we still get to share quarters here, for a short time anyhow."

The Smith chucked some clothes at the boy. Opening up the folded clothing, he inspected it. Two tunics of cotton, the cleanest and nicest that he had ever touched. They were a grey colour which the boy knew was the chosen colour for slaves. The tunics were sleeveless and had a large whole for the neck. The other two items were short trousers that ended at his knees. He walked through to his room and stored them with his other clothes.

"I see you have chosen your room, boy?" the Smith said with a smile.

"I'll take the one at the far end. Quick, you can take the room in the middle."

"Yes, Smith," the young lad said as he ran off to inspect his new room.

Just then, the Chief arrived in the room.

The boy automatically bowed his head and looked at the floor. The Smith also bowed his head.

"Settled in then, Smith?"

"Yes, master."

"The last smith was killed for questioning his masters. You won't do that will you, Smith?"

"No, master."

"Good. I understand that they have given you an apprentice. Train him well. As for the Demon-child, he can stay with you for now, but will move to the large building when there is space." The master then turned to the boy and spoke directly to him. "Be on the training field at dawn, do not be late."

"No, master. I will not be late."

"Train hard and when the times comes, fight hard. This camp is almost luxury compared to the other camp and if don't want to go back to your flea-filled hut, I suggest you mind yourself."

"Yes, master."

"Meals are served at dawn and dusk in the large building across from here. Eat there or bring your food back here, I care not. Some other food will be set aside for you and Smith for lunches. Never forget, these are luxuries that can be taken away as easily as they are given."

"I thank thee, master. May I ask what metal work I'll be doing here?"

The master stiffened at being asking a question, then relaxed and smiled.

"You always did have large balls, Smith. That's why you have lasted so long in our camps when others have not. You know when to push and when to stay silent; I admire that. Your task here is like any blacksmith. You will do pots and pans whilst also making my weapons for my pit rats. The previous smith produced poor weapons, which is why he was here in this pit camp. One of my men has suggested with better weapons, my pit rats may win more fights. I have decided to humour him and have you here to make better weapons for my pit rats. Make the weapons and remember they need to the same standard as you make for my warriors."

"I will, master"

"Never forget, Smith, this is just an experiment. I do not believe slaves should have good steel even if they are fighting in the pit for me. Over the last three seasons, I have lost many slaves to death bouts. I don't care if a slave dies, but I do care when I go two winters without winning at least a few bouts."

The Smith was now understanding why he was here. He also knew exactly why the boy was here as well. The master no doubt wanted to turn the boy's anger that he has demonstrated a few times in the slave camp, into something useful.

The master said nothing more but left through the door. The boy was trembling slightly, whether nerves or anger he didn't know.

The Smith looked at the boy and saw the anger there. He shook his head. "C'mon you two. Let's go get some dinner."

As Quick left the room first, the Smith put his hand on the boy's shoulder as he walked past. The boy didn't even notice it and with head hung low, left the Smith staring around the living quarters.

"Could be worse," the Smith said to himself as he headed downstairs.

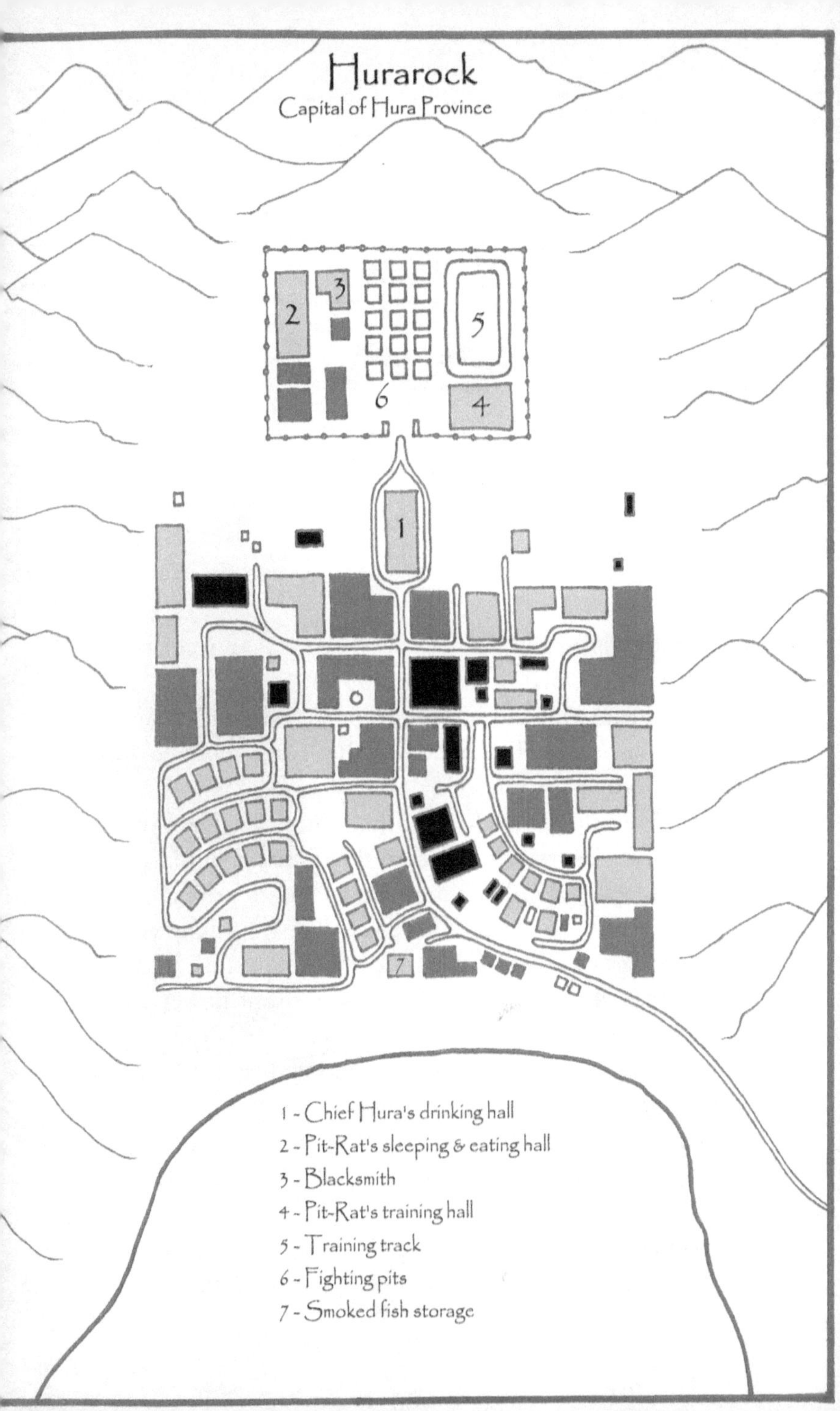

Hurarock
Capital of Hura Province
1
2
3
5
6
4
7
1 - Chief Hura's drinking hall
2 - Pit-Rat's sleeping & eating hall
3 - Blacksmith
4 - Pit-Rat's training hall
5 - Training track
6 - Fighting pits
7 - Smoked fish storage

Chapter Five

The Smith shook the boy awake. "Up boy and get dressed into your tunic. Don't want to be late."

The boy jumped out of bed. He chucked on his new tunic and short trousers. He stopped in the living room to splash water on his face then headed down the stairs.

Once outside, he could see other youths leaving the main building, some he recognised from the dinner room last night. They nodded but said nothing. He followed behind as they made their way to the training field. The sun light was just starting to light the sky. Taking a deep breath, he could smell fresh grass and a light fragrance of a pleasant flower that he didn't know the name of.

More than one hundred youths had gathered on the field. All wearing the same tunic and short trousers. They sat down and waited for something. The boy followed suit and waited. The morning was cold but not as cold as a normal winter's morning. There was no talking and all he could hear was the light wind and the early morning birdsongs that greeted a new day. He looked around at the other youths sitting down. All were slightly older than himself. Most were taller apart from a couple. None seemed remarkable apart form one tall and large slave. The boy's eyes were drawn to him straight away. He stood taller than any other youth, and he could not begin to guess his age. He was larger than all the others, in fact he was huge. But the one thing that made him stand out from all the others was the fact his skin colour was dark brown. He had never seen anyone with that colour skin, he did not even know they existed. In a sea of white faces, he stuck out. The boy was staring at him when the dark-skinned slave looked back at him. He gave a small smile, the boy embarrassed, looked away.

"They are coming," whispered someone in front of him. He looked towards the buildings over his left shoulder and saw two masters walking towards them. They walked fast and it was not long before they were standing in front of the huge group of boys. One master, the boy recognised. He was the grumpy silent guard that had driven his wagon. The other, he didn't recognise.

The grumpy one started to speak. "You pit rats are here to learn to fight!" he said. "You don't know what that means, so I'll explain it. You will be trained in how to fight. By next winter, you will be fitter than you have ever been before. You will be stronger; you will be meaner. We will teach you to kill and finally you will teach US how you die."

The boys were all silent. If they had no clue as to why they were here, they now did.

"This man is not a master. He was a slave like you are. But he won his freedom by being the best fighter that we have ever had."

The words slowly sunk in. The boy grasped at the words, grasping at hope. Perhaps there was a path.

"You will call him Trainer. He can have you whipped; he

can have you killed. Just because he is not a master, does not mean he does not have power over you. Obey him in everything."

With this the master walked off. Once he was gone, the Trainer added his own words.

"You have all been slaves. You will find life here difficult but not unpleasant, as long as you obey. There is food, there is a bed to sleep in and warm clothing. All you need to do in exchange for these things is obey. Train hard to die hard! You may not understand the words but by god, by next winter you will."

He looked over the group in silence, searching all the faces. He continued to stare until the silence became uncomfortable. Finally, he spoke again. "Trust me, you will learn. Now everybody up and follow me."

The boys all jumped to up and followed the Trainer until they were standing on the dirt track that circled the field of grass. The sun was now beginning to creep over the horizon and its light was bathing the land.

"Right. You will run ten circuits. If I see anyone slacking, the whole group will run it again. Now GO."

As he shouted go, the boys all set off. It was not a jog, but it was not a flat-out run either. The Trainer hadn't told them how fast to go, the boys just started running. At first, they were all in a bunch. As they completed their first lap however, some of the fitter lads that could keep the pace started to pull a head, stragglers had started to appear at the back. The slaves that were not very fit not being able to even keep up with the medium pace that was being set. The boy, of course, was fit. The work he had been doing over the last two summers had strengthened his legs and he was in the front pack that started to pull away from the others. As was the slave with dark skin he had seen before.

By the seventh lap, his group of eight had gained a half lap on the others. He was pleased to stretch his legs after the wagon ride. He knew that he could have shot to the front but didn't want to stick out. He stuck with the leaders and matched their pace. He looked over his shoulder as the Trainer was yelling at the lads that had drifted to the rear. Once they started being yelled at, they quickened their pace to not bring displeasure to the Trainer. By the final lap, the boy was breathing heavily but still managed to match the speed of those he followed. As they retuned back to where the Trainer was standing, they sank to ground. It took a short while for the others to catch up. Once everyone had assembled, the Trainer started to speak.

"The five that finished last, stand and face your peers."

The unfit five that hadn't been able to keep up, stood slowly and walked to stand next to the Trainer. They turned to face the other boys that were sitting down. The boy looked at them. They were all older than him, as indeed most of the others on the field were. The five boys standing were panting and trying to catch their breath. Not one of the boys sitting down could see who was approaching and couldn't understand the fear on the faces of the boys standing. It became clear when the original master appeared into their vision. He strode forward. "These were the last five?"

"Yes, master," the Trainer replied.

The master went to the first lad and punched him full in the face. The boy hit the ground and the master bent down and laid into him; raining blows down on him. All the other youths stayed silent. They had learnt through their slavery not to utter a word if punishment was being dealt out, least they call attention on themselves.

One by one the master beat all of the five youths. Punches and blows raining down on all of them. Some of them whimpered, others cried. It was a bad sight to see! Young men that had already been beaten so much that they had lost their spirit. They were all lying on the ground blood covering all of their faces.

"Stand up!" the master yelled.

As quickly as they could, the beaten boys stood. You could see the some of them could barely move. Either pain or fear making it harder for them to get up. Once they were all standing the master spoke again.

"Which one, Trainer?"

The Trainer didn't speak. He pointed to the large blonde lad that was on the end. The master approached him and stood behind him.

"This is a lesson for all of you. Fail, disobey or if you don't work hard enough, this is your reward."

He gripped the youth around the head and is eyes locked on the boys sitting down. He slowly dragged a knife across the youth's throat. Blood began spurting out onto the ground. The youth started to scream, but found the blood clogged up his airways. The boy watched the master with hate in his heart. He felt his heart beating faster and faster. The boy didn't deserve to die for being last. Not on the first day.

The master dropped the body to the ground as it bled out. The blonde youth closed his eyes and never again would they open. The harshest object lesson was not lost on all of the slave boys, the new pit rats.

The master walked off, but not before cleaning his knife on the tunic of the boy that was still standing in shock beside him. As he walked off, the Trainer turned and addressed the seated lads.

"The four of you that are still standing, take his body and throw it in the pit behind me," he pointed to the far right on the corner of the field. "I would advise you four, and the rest of you not to be last again. The rest of you get up and walk another two laps to cool down your muscles."

The boys all stood and started walking around the track. Somewhat shocked even though they had grown as slaves and seen beatings before or heard of killings, they had never seen such a disregard for human life. Others were just accepting, not having enough imagination or intelligence to register what had happened. One of them however, one boy, the one they called Demon-boy was still furious! He had learnt to curb his temper, to not stare down the masters, to say nothing and obey! The Smith had been teaching him slowly over the last season to control his emotions. Right now, all the boy felt was rage. He walked with the other boys stretching his legs. His face was a calm and yet a slight show of anger if one knew what to look for. He started thinking and making his plans.

'Trainer how did the first day go?" asked the master.

Trainer had been called to the building that Chief Hura had called his home. He looked around at the other warriors drinking and eating. "It goes well, master."

'I have told you, you are no longer a slave, Trainer; address me as Chief."

"My apologies, Chief. A lifetime of being a slave, it can be hard to change some habits."

The other Outlanders where smiling at him. They knew of his history. They laughed at him but none of them would challenge him now that he was not a slave and could fight back. He had earned a reputation in the pit as one of the most ferocious fighters. Trainer turned back to the Chief.

"First day went well, Chief. The boys ran well and once

their 'Object Lesson' had been completed, they all trained very hard throughout the day."

The Chief didn't miss the hesitation when he said, 'Object Lesson'.

"You do not think killing one of them was a useful tool, Trainer? It didn't motivate them to train harder?"

"It did master, but I feel…" he breathed slowly. He may no longer be a slave, but he was still not one of them and had to guard his words. "I feel that it was a little harsh on the first day but yes, Chief, it did make them train harder."

"Good. Just remember that this was your idea, to gather a whole lot of the lads and train them for a full season before throwing them in the pit!"

"Yes Chief. I believe it will allow you to win more fights and therefore win more coin."

All the warriors cheered at the words. Gambling was their second favourite thing to do in the outlands. Of course, their favourite thing was fighting!

How many do you think will work out?"

"Hard to say, Chief! Out of the 100 youths you have provided, I would say by next winter, you would have at least twenty to thirty that can win some coin for you. But it's far too early to say"

The Chief thought about it. He replied, "It has certainly cost me enough to set up this training camp of yours. By the way, how is the Demon-child settling in?"

All the warriors in the room stopped chatting amongst themselves and listened. All of them had heard of the child that killed one of them many summers before in a raid. All of them had heard this same child was now training in this camp their Chief had built.

"Don't hold back, Trainer. I will not single him out…. yet."

The warriors all laughed again, hefting their cups in the air and then sculling them back.

Once the commotion had died down, the Trainer spoke. "He is fit, Chief. He was in the lead pack for the first run of the morning for your object lesson. Throughout the rest of the training, he was always in the front pack, whether lifting stones or running. He is fit and strong."

"We can thank my son for that. He gave him the toughest work to do in the slave camp. And his, attitude? Did he step out of line?"

"No Chief. He did all that was required of him, but he did it with an absolute look of hate and anger on his face."

The Chief smiled.

"Good. In the pit, he will learn above anything else that anger is a gift. Return to your camp, I'll call you here again in ten days for the next report. How long before you will pit them against each other?"

The Trainer had already made his mind up on this. "In seven days' time, they will start training against each other. I wanted to focus on fitness first, Chief."

"As you were, Trainer."

The Trainer turned and walked from the large hall. On the walk back to the training camp, he pictured the face of the Demon-boy. He knew he had seen it before. Without knowing why, his memories drifted back to the slave ship that he had once been on. He thought of the little boy that he had been seated across from. The small boy that he had given reassurance to and helped to calm down with just head and eye gestures. The thought then jumped into his head.

"No, it can't be."

The boy made his way up the stairs to his shared living quarters with the Smith and Quick. He moved through the door and sank into the soft double chair. The windows were still open, and he could see the light fading as the sun was slowly going down. He saw there was hot food on the table in the corner. The boy Quick must have fetched his meal for him. He must thank him. His thoughts were going back over his first day of training. Even though he managed to keep up and complete all tasks set for him by the Trainer, his body still ached. He was thankful now for all the hard work of carting iron ore over the last two summers. It had prepared him for today. The iron ore work still didn't prepare him for how spent his body was. He was enjoying the cool breeze that was coming through the open window when the Smith appeared at the door.

"How was the first day, boy?"

"Hard."

"The training or watching some boy's throat being cut in front of you?"

The boy breathed out hard before replying. "Both"

"It's not like you have not seen a slave being murdered before. Not that it's a good thing mind you, but it is not exactly new."

"I don't know, Smith. Yes, I have seen slaves be killed before."

"Murdered boy, not killed, murdered. Never forget that."

"Murdered then. I have seen it before and thought I had become numb. I have never seen the lights of someone eyes fade before me."

"Snap out of it, boy! Yes, it's hard, but you have been a slave for most of your life. Life is hard! And, life is short and can end in an instant. You know this! Do not get distracted or it could be you."

The boy looked at the ground. He hadn't heard the Smith be this hard before. Not having any energy to get up from the soft chair, let alone argue.

"Here boy, eat," he said passing a bowl of stew with a slice of bread across the top of the bowl.

"Thanks."

The Smith sat down in the other chair.

"Dam, I could use a drink. I suppose no matter how grand our accommodation is, we are still slaves."

"Not found any spirit yet?"

"No. Apparently there is none in this training camp. Would be easier to have this conversation with you with a jug that's all."

"What conversation?"

"Listen, boy. The reason I like you so much is you never let life as a slave effect you. You still worked hard and if you got beaten, or watch someone else get beaten or even killed, you carried on with your life. Head down and got the work done. As if you were immune to the life around you. It was an inner strength that not many slaves have."

The boy looked up, not knowing where the conversation was going.

"Since we got in that wagon three days ago, you have been quieter than normal. You are not asking as many questions, you are not smiling that little half smile of yours."

"Perhaps it's knowing I will die in the pit! Perhaps it's knowing that I have no future."

"You never had a future boy. You are slave. That does not mean you should wallow in it. It does not mean you should mope around with the burden of the world on your shoulders. Look around you!"

The boy did.

"At the slave camp you shared sleeping quarters with four

other youths. Youths that beat you until you learned to stick up for yourself. You slept with one blanket on the straw bed of that sleeping dugout. Before that, on a dirt floor! Every mid-morning you got porridge for your first meal and only a small bowl. You never got lunch until you started working with me in the smithy. Dinner was vegetables in both with the occasional slice of bread. Yes, the food was better than a lot of other slaves get but still shit."

The boy looked at the Smith, never seeing him so wound up.

"Now look around the room again."

The boy did.

"You had breakfast this morning that was porridge, yes? It actually has a little sugar in it along with goat's milk. Last night, you slept on a bed in your own room. Your own room! You got some fresh fruit at midday and sitting in your hands going cold is some stew with actual meat in it."

"Sorry," the boy replied, putting the spoon in the stew and started to eat.

"Yes, today a boy died, but it was not you was it? You have good food, you have a warm bed to sleep in and you share an apartment with someone who cares about you, boy."

The boy stopped eating. He swallowed the food that he had been chewing. He dropped his bowl of food on the floor and jumped up; two steps and he embraced the Smith as the Smith rose. They stood there for a few minutes and the Smith kept his powerful arms wrapped around the boy.

"Sorry Smith, I never thought of all that."

"Life as a slave is shit boy, I know that. You know that. If you can't appreciate the small things, then it's over."

They let go of each other when they heard steps coming up the stairs. The boy thinking it was a master, picked up the bowl and used the bread to clean up the stew that had split onto the wooden floor. He had just cleaned up the mess when the door opened up; the Trainer walked in. The Smith and the boy stood there with guilty looks on their faces. The Smith spoke first.

"Master, what can we do for you?"

"I'm not a master and well you know."

Without hesitating, he walked quickly over to the boy and grabbed him. The boy froze as the Trainer put his hand over the boy's mouth.

"Trainer?" The Smith said in alarm.

The Trainer just stood there looking at the boy's eyes and face with his hand covering the bottom of his face. Analysing, trying to remember. The boy stood still as his life depended on it. The Trainer was of thin to medium build, but he was slim muscle from the top of his shoulders to his feet. The boy had seen him lift a boy today and throw him for not complying. All three of them stood there and time seemed to stop for the boy and the Smith. Finally, the Trainer smiled.

"By god, it is you little one!"

He took his hand down from the boy's face and took a step back. "No harm meant, Smith. I needed to be sure."

"Be sure of what?" replied the Smith.

"That, this boy is who I think he is."

If the boy has ever been as confused as he was now in this life, he couldn't remember. The Trainer sat down on the couch and continued to stare at the boy, smiling.

"I was wondering what happened to you. Now I know."

The Smith sat down at the table in the corner. "You know the boy?"

"Not really, we never spoke in words. Did we, boy?"

The boy looked back to the Smith, then back to the Trainer, trying to figure out in his head what the hell was going on. The Trainer spoke again.

"You may not remember but we shared something, you and me. A dark damp hold. A place that only had two oil lamps for light and other frightened children for company."

Realisation hit the boy. He got up and made his way to the Trainer. The Trainer also stood, and they embraced, holding each other for some time. The Smith sat there trying to work out what was going on. As the two broke loose of each other, the Trainer sat back on the soft chair and the boy moved back to the couch.

"How the hell do you two know each other?" the Smith finally said.

"Smith, you remember me telling you of my journey here?"

"Of course, boy. It was only three quarters of the moon ago, when you opened up and told me."

"You remember me telling you of the older lad in the ship hold with me? The one that sat across from me that gave me comfort with his eye gestures?"

"This is him?"

"Yes, Smith. I believe it is."

The boy and the Trainer were both smiling.

"How did you end up being a Trainer?"

"Can we speak in private here?"

"You don't have to worry about me saying anything!" the Smith said.

"Where is Quick?" the boy asked.

"He is fast asleep in his room. His first day as a Smith's apprentice was hard on him. Speak softly and you will be fine."

The Trainer launched into his story but did it softly. The Smith joined the boy on the two-seater chair and they listened.

"After we were taken out of the ship, I was brought

straight here and started training just like you are doing now although the camp was not as set up as it is now. I saw you being loaded up in the wagon with the other smaller children."

He pulled his leather bag up from the floor, the boy hadn't noticed he had been carrying it. From it he pulled two water skins. Taking one he threw it to the Smith and then took the other one, pulled the stopper and took a drink. The Smith followed and also took a drink.

"Man, that is fine. Mighty fine."

He passed it to the boy, who also took a quick drink. It was spirit but smoother than what he had drunk at the slave camp.

"It's their white spirit that they make from potatoes. Good stuff."

"Very!" said the Smith taking the skin from the boy and having another drink.

I remember if it was yesterday, the day that I was brought here. There was not a large camp like there is now for training, just a simple shed that ten of us slept in. There was not even a fence, let alone the building when you arrived. Every day, we were made to run, lift rocks and other activities until we dropped. There was barely enough food in the evening to keep us fed, then collapse on a dirty blanket. After a few quarter moons, they started pitting us against each other. We would strip down to our trousers and then fight whoever the masters put in front of us. At first, we didn't fight hard enough and on the first day, one of the losers was killed like the boy today was.

After that first death, we all fought as if our life depended on it, which it did. For full moons, we fought each other, arriving back at our sleeping shed covered in bruises. Unfortunately, grudges quickly built with the constant fighting. The fights started to kick off again once we got back to our shed. In the end, they had to tie us to posts when we slept.

After the first full moon, they started teaching us how to use axe, swords and knives; wooden replicas at first. They trained us with these and of course, once we started getting the hang of it, they would face us off against each other. It was horrible!

One day, the Chief came to witness our progress. One of the masters picked two of us to fight with weapons for the Chief. I was one of them. The master said that the loser would die and then turned to me to say that if someone does not die in the fight, both fighters would die. So, when the fight started, I went at the other slave, slightly younger than myself and killed him. I beat and bludgeoned him with my wooden sword until blood was pouring out of his face. In the end, with the Chief smiling, I jumped on the slave and rammed him through the throat with my wooden sword. After that, I was a favourite. When the following winter had arrived, only four of the original ten slaves were left. We were all thrown into the pit for our first fights, which were not death bouts but all of us lost. That night in the shed, we were beaten by the masters. The next time in the pit, two of us won, the other two lost. The two that lost were taken away from the sleeping shed that night and never returned. We saw their bodies on the next day during training. They had been hung from a tree by their necks. After that, the final slave and I won all our fights. We did this for many seasons. Train during the summer whilst the Outlanders were raiding. Then in winter, quarter moon after quarter moon, we were thrown into the pit to beat on whoever they threw in front of us. Eventually, when we came of age, they threw us into the pit for our first death bouts. The other slave, Teric his name was, died. He didn't even fight back, he just let the other slave kill him. Even though I won my first death bout that day, I was beaten to almost death that night by the masters for what Teric had done.

I started death bouts on my sixteenth summer. I fought for two summers, winning the Chief much coin. Other slaves who came and went, were trained by the masters. Most died on their first or second death bout. I never became friendly with any of them, knowing how life is short when you are fighting in the pits.

Towards the end of last winter, the Chief visited me in the shed. I was tied to my sleeping post with a blanket around me. He informed me that my next fight at the pit was going to be facing two slaves. A rival chief had offered him a huge wager to take the fight. The Chief asked if I could win it. By this stage, I was numb and just didn't care anymore. I asked him why I would want to win it. I think I was trying to provoke the master to killing me. He was not called Angry-Man for nothing. The Chief laughed at me and then asked if I thought I would just roll over and die like Teric did. I had nothing to lose , so I asked him what he would give me if I won. He just looked at me and asked what I wanted. So, I told him!

"If I win perhaps I want to be raised up to be more than just a slave sleeping in the dirt."

The Chief smiled, then laughed like I have never seen an Outlander laugh before. He then said to me, "You are not special but you have won me much coin." Then, he said, "If you win the next fight, you will no longer be a slave and will be in charge of training the other pit rats."

At my final match, I tore into the other two slaves, not caring for defence but just intent on killing them as quickly as I could. I took many stabbed wounds from them both, but the fight was over very quickly. I will not repeat the details as it still sickens me to look back at what I had become. One died with a throat cut and the other with my dagger in his chest. Before I had finished healing from the stab wounds I took, I was dragged from the sleeping shed and brought in front of the Chief. He exclaimed before all in his great hall, that I was no longer a slave. He said I was now a Trainer of pit rats and my wins would be the talk of his people. I was given a bowl of food and strong drink, then sat down at a table whilst the Chief and his men celebrated their win. The Chief has won many coins on me. During the feast one of the masters that trained me, sat beside me and asked if I was going to do anything different to train the new pit rats. He hated me and was just trying to embarrass me in front of the Outlanders. I told him I would discuss that with the Chief, and not him. He then called out to the Chief that I had some new ideas for training pit rats. The hall went quiet as all eyes turned to me. I stood and told the Chief.

"I do have some ideas, Master."

"Go ahead, 'no-longer-a-slave'."

"Decent pallets to sleep on sir, to rest their weary bodies."

All the warriors in the hall laughed. I still continued.

"Decent food in the morning and the night. A pit rat needs strength in that pit to overcome an enemy and you can't have strength without decent food."

"You survived without decent food," said the master that had trained me.

The warriors of the hall laughed, and the Chief just stared at the 'no-longer-a slave'."

"I didn't. It was snuck to me by one of the other slaves. Food and shelter are not the only things. They need different training, better training."

Finally, the Chief spoke, "If I provided all of this, you could guarantee the pit rats would win all their fights, win more coin for me?"

"No. I could only guarantee that they would win more fights than they have over the last two seasons."

The Chief was slightly drunk, but he was not a fool, but he still thought about it. Winning more fights and coin would be good. His slaves over the last four summers had failed miserably. "How long would you need to achieve this?"

"Two seasons, master. Two seasons with better training, better food and restful sleep and I would say your pit rats would win more often."

"So, he agreed to it and that's how you became a trainer?" said the Smith.

"Yes. I am forbidden to tell any other slave this story in case they get thoughts of no longer being a slave themselves. The work on this camp was completed quickly. In fact, it was only finished a few days before the first of the slaves arrived." The Trainer finished his water skin filled with spirits.

"A remarkable tale, Trainer. Hopefully now you know who this boy is, you can guide him."

The Trainer shook his head.

"Yes and no. I can offer little advice here and there, but I cannot show favouritism. The master that trained me, the same one that killed the boy today, still hates me. If he sees I know the boy, he will kill him."

"We best not tell him then," replied the Smith.

"I must seek my bed," the Trainer said as he rose.

"The advice that I can give you now is give them your best, run faster and work harder than all the other slaves. When the time comes, fight harder than the other slaves."

"The boy already knows that," said the Smith.

"I know but do these things to start with and I'll try to give you other advice where and as I can."

The boy rose and hugged the Trainer again.

"Let this be the last time we hug. Trust me, the master that was my trainer would delight in slaying you, just to see me hurt."

The boy nodded his head.

"In exchange, Trainer, if you ever need advice in training people to fight, ask. I was a sergeant and have some experience in training men for battle. Thanks for the drink also, it was most welcome."

The Smith and the Trainer shook hands.

"I may take you up on that. This business is just a big gamble. I know how to fight but passing on that knowledge…" he let the words fall away.

"Let's just say, I may yet be killed for failing the Chief," he smiled.

With that the Trainer left them and returned to his quarters.

The Smith looked at the boy and saw a load had been lifted. He smiled. "I'm glad someone has lightened the load, boy."

The boy was still a little bemused by the Trainer. He had never thought to see him again and was amazed at his story. His story also gave him hope.

"I better see if I can get some food as this stew has been on the floor."

"Then you best get some rest, sounds like you are going to need it."

Chapter Six

At dawn the next day, the boy was with the other slaves on the field as the sun was coming up. All had remained standing. A voice yelling broke the silence of the morning.

"Just because I am not there yet, does not mean you cannot start. Ten circuits, GO."

The boys took off running. This time, they all stayed together. The boy was near the front. They ran their ten circuits without incident, and all arrived together the end of it.

The day continued much like yesterday. All of the slaves on the ground stretching their legs slowly like they had been shown yesterday. After stretches, it was fifteen more laps but this time at a slightly slower pace then stretching again. This was followed by a breakfast of porridge that as the Smith had said, actually had taste and a little goats' milk on top gave it some creaminess that was pleasant. After breaking their fast, the group was split in two. One group spent time lifting large rocks above their heads and holding them out in front of them for a count of a hundred, then resting for a count of a hundred.

The other group was doing laps around the track as fast as they could, pushing barrows filled with rocks. The boy, of course, excelled at this. The slaves would run a lap, then stop. Another slave would take the barrow and run a lap, whilst the first slave rested. They did fifty laps each in this manner. Once the group on barrow runs had finished, both groups' swapped places. Even though the boy was well used to wheelbarrows filled with rocks, he was not used to running so fast with them. He performed better than the other lads but it was still hard.

The Trainer was supervising the group of slaves lifting rocks, the other master who the boy had knick-named Murderer, supervised the barrow running. He had already backhanded a few of the slaves for not running fast enough. None of the discipline had come near the boy. He took the advice of the Trainer and ran as fast as he could with the rocks. Fortunately, the other slave that he had teamed up with was not as fast as the boy, giving him time to almost catch his breath. Almost.

Towards the end of the day, more stretching was done, followed by some simple ground exercises called chest press that the slaves didn't understand a first, but soon got the hang of it. The boy found these hard. All of his strength was in his legs and lying face first on the dirt, raising himself up with arms alone, whilst he kept his legs straight was difficult. For this, he got a smack around the back of the head by the Trainer but then again, most of the slaves did.

The end of the day came again, and the slaves ran another ten circuits of the track, followed by another ten circuits at a walk.

When done, they all were exhausted. A lot of the slaves could hardly move after the first day, let alone after the second. They all slowly walked back to the food hall to eat.

The tall dark-skinned slave that had also performed well walked beside him.

"Another hard day, eh?"

The boy looked at him but said nothing.

"Had your tongue cut out?"

"No. Just don't want to be seen talking, then get another beating."

The other slave smiled at him. The boy looked around and saw the Trainer was back in the field talking to Murderer.

"How are the legs," asked the boy.

"Sore. Perhaps I'll get the cook to give me a massage when we get back."

The large boy winked at him and he had to hold back a laugh but smiled widely.

"Food time. Maybe chat tomorrow." With that, the slave who the boy would now think of as Funny-boy walked fast towards the cook hut. The boy was wondering whether he was merely hungry or wanted to see the cook. He smiled to himself. The cook lady was the ugliest old crone that he had ever seen. If someone had told him that she had maggots in her hair, he would have believed them.

With his body hurting, he slowly walked with the other slaves towards the food hall. Looking forward to some food before collapsing on his bed to sleep.

The Smith continued to beat the metal in front of him. Apart from the swords and axes that he made for the Outlanders, plus the wooden practise weapons that he would start carving tomorrow for the pit rats, he also had to take care of other more domestic smithy duties for the camp. Currently, he was banging the curve of a sheet of thin metal. The cook had asked for another larger pot and the Smith had started it this morning.

Sweat was dripping off him from the forge and he was concentrating on his work. He didn't hear or see the Trainer enter. When he finally noticed, he put the pot into a large barrel of water with a hiss of steam. Once it had cooled, he placed it on the anvil.

"What can I do for you, Trainer?" said the Smith.

"Advice like you offered last night is what I have come for."

"Anything in particular?"

"No. Apart from making the slaves exercise and then fight, I have no idea on how to teach them."

The Smith looked at him. He had offered last night but didn't think the Trainer would take him up on his offer, certainly not the next day. This showed the Trainer cared and the Smith appreciated that. He led the Trainer out into the fresh air, and they stood in the fading light.

"Firstly, you need to treat them harsher."

"Harsher?"

"Yes. Be mean, yell at them more. Insult them every moment of everyday. Call them names!"

"Why?"

"Spend full moons treating them worse than slaves until they hate you more than the masters."

The Trainer looked at the Smith wide eyed.

"Then once they hate you, and I mean really hate you, start slowly complimenting them when they do well. Trust me. It will take a while but by doing this, you will give them a little pride piece by piece."

"I don't think the masters will be happy with slaves having pride!" said the Trainer.

"Pride or backbone, it's all the same. Do this and they will follow your orders; they will give you their best. Man is a simple creature and most crave a little validation."

"So, treat them meaner, harsher and call them names?"

"Yes, Trainer. It is how we trained soldiers where I come from."

The Trainer didn't look convinced but he was open to try it.

"Also add speed work to their daily training. You are building strength and stamina, but you also need speed. I have seen a form of fighting similar to what these slaves will be doing, although not as brutal as what I have heard of the pits, and the men fighting had amazing speed."

"True, but still unsure how to add this, Smith. Speed training was not taught to me when I was in the pit. I had to learn it for myself and learn it quickly."

"I have a couple of ideas for speed work," said the Smith.

They spent the next twenty minutes deep in conversation; the Trainer hanging on his every word, soaking up all the experience the Smith could share with him. When the Trainer departed, the Smith nodded to himself slowly as he watched the Trainer walk away. He was still young, but because of his life, had more experience than many men. 'Young heart but old head' as the saying went. The Smith decided he liked the Trainer. He showed the same spirit as the boy and even though the Trainer had a darker aspect to him. He hid his emotions away from the world by a scowl that he wore on his face, the Smith saw through this. He was an excellent judge of men and saw the inner strength, the caring for his fellow men and the indomitable spirit that was like a candle in a dark room. It would take more than a few summers in the pit or beatings from the masters to extinguish that flame. The exact same qualities that had drawn the Smith to the boy when he had first met him.

The Smith smiled and returned to the smithy. Picking up the pot using tongs, he stuck it back into the coals of the forge.

The Smith had been surprised to be brought to the training camp and he didn't like being surprised. However, life at the training camp after two days had shown him life could be better here. As long as he could keep the boy alive, of course! As he stoked the coals of the forge, he decided that whilst the Trainer would work the boy's body during the day, the Smith would continue to work his mind in the evenings. Many tactics and strategies, he could teach the boy from his life as a soldier for hire. Some of them would not be useful in the pit, but some of them would. As he drew the pot out of the coals and moved it across to his anvil, he smiled to himself. Passing on his knowledge was something that he never thought would be possible. Now he had two lads to pass this information and lessons on to: the boy and the Trainer. So similar and yet so different as well. It should be an interesting summer, he thought as he started to bang away on the pot.

The boy stood on the training field, blanket around his shoulders. Lost in thought as he welcomed the early morning, staring at the stars as they began to fade and listening to the birdlife as they started to rise. He smiled as he heard footsteps on the snow behind him. He didn't need to turn to see who was joining him. Bulldog-boy and Funny-boy arrived and stood beside him.

The three had made this their morning ritual, all meeting earlier than the other slaves to talk in privacy. Since the three had started talking, a friendship had grown between them and following the Smith's advice, the boy had shared his story with the two of them. It was easier this time, unlike the first time that he had told the Smith. In return, the two youths had also shared their stories with him.

Funny-boy had told of a land, hot and dry. He didn't know where it was, only that he had spent almost a full summer on a large ship to arrive here in this cold and harsh land. He had explained how after many seasons here, he was still not used to the biting cold of the winters. He had told of his memories of brothers and sisters, of living in a large village that was peaceful. He had told of his people's surprise when these Outlanders, skin so white that it was almost transparent, arriving in his land and raiding many villages. His people, an extreme warlike people when they needed to be, had managed to fight off the Outlanders and the bastard-masters were driven off their shores. Not before, of course, they had managed to kill and destroy villages and take a few slaves. Funny-boy was quiet when he mentioned the four others on the ship with him, others that had fought at every opportunity and eventually been killed by the Outlanders until he was the last one. Being the youngest of those taken, he hadn't yet been trained to fight and was inexperienced. He said he had tried to put up a fight, but it was no use. Funny-boy knew that he would never see his homeland again and knew even if he were freed, he would have no idea in which direction to start off in.

Bulldog-boy had attached himself to the other two. The boy was not sure when he had meet Bulldog-boy, he just seemed to drift into his life. His story was similar to that of Demon-child. He had been taken when the Outlanders raided his settlement. He remembered his settlement being large with many people, a settlement surrounded by low hills that held many sheep. When the Outlanders had raided in their hundreds, his people had hidden the vulnerable and the young, before fighting to hold them off. He had been hiding in a food cellar under his home when they found him, dragging him out into the day. When he had opened his eyes, it was to see large piles of corpses. He never saw any of his family in the piles! He was also chucked into a wagon, traveling for many days before being thrown into the dark hull of a ship. The boy and he could have very well been taken in the same raid but there were no way to tell. Bulldog-boy had been named such, as he was short, stocky and unbelievably bad tempered. Just like the hunting dogs with the same name the Bastard-masters kept. It was these two that had given the boy his first slave name. He was now known as Demon-boy to the other slaves.

The three young men complimented each other nicely. Each one of them ready to be there for another when the need was there, ready with a joke or banter to calm things down, ready to stand beside each other when there was the occasional tension amongst the pit-rats.

Funny-boy, of course, the clown of the group, finding humour in almost any situation! Demon-boy had never seen him lose control and become angry, which is a good thing as Funny-boy was the largest and strongest in camp and if he lost control of himself, well Demon-boy didn't even want to think of the implications.

Bulldog-boy also enjoyed a good joke and was very quick with the banter. However, there was also a dark side to him. His hatred for the bastard-masters was the strongest in the training camp, outstepping the hate and anger Demon-boy had for them. When the masters were around, Bulldog-boy kept his head down as the other slaves did, but Demon-boy knew he was fighting his urges, controlling his anger, lest he does something stupid. Many times, Demon-boy looked over at his friend when the masters were present, watching him as he stood still as his veins showed on his neck and forehead as he fought for control. He was also known to talk to himself sometimes, which made the other slaves stay clear of him.

"Morning, Demon-Child," said Funny-boy.

The boy smiled. The slaves had heard by now of his history, although how they knew was beyond him. Although his new nick name was Demon-boy, Funny-boy or Bull-dog-boy would often when alone, refer to him as the Outlanders did. However, it was always said with a huge grin on their faces. None of the other slaves had called him that and the boy was not sure what he would do if they did.

"Horse face," the Demon-boy said in greeting.

Funny-boy's grin turned into a smile as he approached. Some of the slaves had made small friendships, but only showed it when the masters or the Trainer was not around. Even when they shared a meal in the eating house that was underneath the slave rooms, they ate in silence and only occasionally sharing a quick word. Perhaps that is why he enjoyed arriving early, getting the chance to talk to Funny-boy and Bulldog-boy, who had started joining him in arriving early.

"Going to be a wet day," said the Demon-boy.

"Yes. Although I think the Trainer has something else for us," replied Funny-boy.

"What makes you think that?"

"Did you not see all the shovels leaning against the storage shed next to the smithy?"

"No."

"There was a large pile of them. Looked enough for about half the slaves."

"Guess we will find out soon enough."

"Yes. How is the ankle?"

He had twisted his ankle last quarter moon and it had

been strapped heavily since then. Of course, the masters would not think of letting him recover.

"It's fine. I'll take the strapping off tonight."

"Did you hear some of the slaves got sent away after yesterday's work?"

"No. What happened?"

"About ten of the slaves were taken after last night's meal. Three masters came in and dragged them away."

"Do you know who?"

"Yes, it was that lazy sod Purple-eye and some of his mates."

Purple-eye was his name amongst the slaves after Funny-boy knocked him on his arse in the first quarter moon. Purple-eye had made a comment about Funny-boy's mother. He was named as Purple-eye the next day as he was sporting a huge black eye that turned purple and stayed that way for a few days.

"Do you think it was for not training hard enough?" said the Demon-boy.

"Must be, I cannot think of any other reason. Purple-eye and his mates always did just enough to stay with the pack, just enough to not be singled out by the bastard masters."

The boy smiled. The way he said 'Bastard masters' was the exact way that Smith described the masters.

"The Trainer did warn them! Who was the other five?"

"Never spoke to them, only knew them by their faces. They were also the ones lagging behind."

They stopped talking as the rest of the slaves started arriving. The sun was just starting to rise with its small slivers of light starting to clear the mountains west. Once most of the slaves had arrived, they started running. They had learnt that the Trainer expected them to have started by the time he arrived. They had now started running slow laps before they started their harder training. It stretched their legs from the previous day, and they found they would not be as stiff in the evenings. The Trainer had said nothing and let them do it. This was surprising as three days into the training, the Trainer had become nasty. Not physical, although he had punched or smacked a few of the slaves if they needed a wakeup call; nastier in a verbal way. Running down the slaves, calling them the most horrible names. Once Funny-boy was singled out and the boy could see his neck veins almost popping out of the skin. The boy had shaken his head as Funny-boy looked like he was going to attack the Trainer. Demon-boy couldn't understand why the change from the first couple of days, especially since their meeting in the apartment. For three quarter moons, the Trainer had made them feel worthless and he could see the look of hopelessness on many of the slaves faces.

They finished their twenty laps, and all moved into the centre of the field to start stretching. They were all covered in mud up to their knees. One slave was covered head to toe as he had slipped and fallen over. The drizzle had stopped halfway through their first run of the day. The Trainer had arrived into their third lap and said nothing but joined the end of the pack and ran behind them. The Trainer did this sometimes to stretch his own legs. As they started to stretch, the Trainer's voice rang out.

"Once you have stretched, move your way over to the south building and I'll see you inside."

The Trainer walked off towards the large, barn-looking building on the south end of the training field. They had never been in it and all the slaves had wondered what the building was for. Its walls were wooden with many windows on its sides. It was almost as tall as the eating house and living quarters building, except it looked single storied. The roof looked like it was stone slate. At each end of the building was a stone chimney. The boy had asked the Smith why a building that size would have two large chimneys and not a central opening in the centre like all other Outlander buildings.

"They don't want the heat escaping, chimneys get rid of the smoke, but keep most of the heat still in the room."

This didn't make any sense to the boy. The slaves finished their stretches and moved towards the building. Two massive doors were now open, and the boys moved inside. The Trainer was moving around the building opening all the windows.

It was one large room with a solid dirt floor. Looking at his feet, the boy saw the dirt floor had been hard packed and was very firm. Once all the windows were open, he could see the large beams that supported the roof. This building was the same size as the eating house and sleeping rooms, but with no internal walls.

"Move to the far-left wall!"

The slaves moved to obey, and all lined up at the far wall.

Looking along the length of the space, he noticed that there were white painted rocks at regular intervals. Five of them. The first was in line with all the slaves. The second in a straight line from the first heading to the opposite wall, twenty paces away. The third rock was forty paces away. The fourth sixty paces and the last at the very end of the building, looked about eighty paces.

"Watch what I do," said the Trainer.

He sprinted off down the hall and stopped at the line at the first rock, bent down and touched the ground. He then rose and sprinted back to the line of slaves, slowing down to touch the ground at the slave's feet before turning around and sprinting down to the rock at the 40-pace mark. Once again, he touched the ground, then turned and sprinted back to the slaves. He repeated this until he had made his way down the length of the building, stopping at every painted rock before sprinting back. Once he had finished, he was breathing heavily.

"Red group, line up on the first rock," the Trainer yelled.

The slaves had been put into two groups last quarter moon. Half of them now had a leather strap around their wrists painted in Red. The other half including Demon-boy, had a leather strap painted black attached to their wrists.

Red group lined up shoulder to shoulder on the line of the first rock.

"Go!" yelled the Trainer.

They set off at a sprint, bending down at the first rock before turning and sprinting back to the original line.

"Make sure your hand touches the ground," yelled the Trainer.

The first group took only a couple of minutes to complete what the Trainer had done. Red group were all breathing hard when they reached the line.

"Black group line up," said the Trainer as he stood on the side line.

Black group moved to line up. Funny-boy was beside the boy on his left shoulder.

"GO!"

Black group sprinted off. As they reached down, the boy bent down and slapped the ground, then turned and sprinted back. He reached the line where red group where trying to suck in air, turned and slapped the ground, then took off again towards the second mark. By the time Black group had reached the final mark, the boy's lungs were screaming. He reached the ground and turned.

"Come on Demon-boy, you're making us look bad!" Funny-boy half-whispered.

The boy turned and sprinted as fast as he could back to the original line. Funny-boy was at his shoulder just behind him. They reached the line and bent over, sucking air into their lungs.

"Hurts doesn't it, pit-rats! This is to get you used to the fighting, which can sometimes be stop-start. Little periods of rest and then explosive action that leaves you breathless."

The red group had got their wind back and the black group was still sucking in air.

"Red group, Go!"

The red group took off again. In total that morning, both groups completed ten laps of these new runs. At the end, all the slaves were breathing hard, legs aching and quite a few of them feeling dizzy. Two of the slaves had even vomited.

"Right, pit rats. You have an hour for breaking your fast this morning. Get some food, then get your ugly faces back here. Here's some advice, do not eat too much!" the Trainer said with a grin. The Trainer looked around the group, then left to get his own breakfast.

The slaves didn't move for a few minutes. Some stood, but most of them lay on the ground trying to catch their breath.

"What the hell is his problem?" Funny-boy said.

The slaves around him smiled. Funny-boy turned to the boy.

"He was hard but fair for the first few days, now he is just as much a bastard as the bastard masters," Funny-boy said with feeling.

Some of the slaves laughed and most of the others had a smile on their face. Some of the tension eased as the slaves picked themselves up from the ground.

"We better get some food. Bastard-face Trainer will no doubt do more of this shit latter on." Said Bulldog-boy

Funny-boy laughed loud. "Bastard-face," Funny-boy repeated.

The name was taken up around the hall by the other slaves. Bulldog-boy has just given the Trainer a nickname and knew that it would stick. They all moved outside and made their way to the eating room. The sun had come out, but the day was overcast. At least, it was not raining any more. Funny-boy walked beside the boy.

"Is he trying to get us to hate him? Because it's working," said Funny-boy.

"Must be, either way by the time we actually hit the pits, we will be very fit and strong."

"True," replied Funny-boy.

They approached the eating hut looking forward to breaking their fast. It was later than the time that they would normally have breakfast. It was already near midmorning. The boy looked at the sky briefly, then made his way into the food hall. He would have to ask the Smith tonight what the Trainer's problem was, he thought to himself as he lined up for food.

After they had broken their fast, they completed ten more laps of the new running exercise that Funny-boy had named Hell-runs. Most of the slaves struggled to finish the ten hell runs. Falling to the side lines struggling to breath. This earned them a dressing down and a few hard whacks around the head from the Bastard-face.

The half that had completely finished, then collapsed on the ground, sucking in a lung full of air. The Demon-boy, Bulldog-boy and Funny-boy had struggled just like the other slaves but still managed to finish. This had been the most intense training that they had done so far, even though the last half-moon period had been hard, today's work made the previous half-moon period look like a casual stroll.

"Go through a full set of stretches rats, then we are off to the left of the training field. Those who are not there soon enough, will feel the masters whip."

The slaves looked shocked. The whip was used in the slave camp, and many had seen it or even felt it upon their back. So far, they hadn't seen the whip being used in the training camp. Even the boy couldn't believe it. He had never felt the whip on his back but had seen it many times. Other slaves had described what it felt like, and it's an experience the boy didn't want to experience. He stood and made his way to where the Trainer said to meet.

"Where you going Demon-boy?" he heard Funny-boy say.

"I'll stretch once I'm where we are supposed to be. I'm not feeling that whip."

"Good idea. C'mon black group, let's go," said Funny-boy.

The black group all rose and followed the Funny-boy and Demon-boy out the door. A lot of Black group had started to follow the ideas and advice of the two more and more over the last quarter-moon. With them being the two fittest and strongest, it seemed a good idea to listen to what they said. Some of the red group also followed.

"I'll stretch where I want to," said a slave that had earned the name Grumpy-boy.

The slaves around him who often followed his lead agreed. They continued their stretches in the large hall.

The large group of slaves were finishing up their stretches as the Trainer and two of the masters arrived. The master known as Violent-man was holding a whip and a grin.

The slaves all remained on the ground looking up at the masters and the Trainer.

"We all here?" asked the Trainer.

One of the masters, one that the boy didn't know, pointed in the direction of the hall.

Walking slowly over from the building was Grumpy and four of the other slaves. When they saw the Trainer and the masters, they started running. They were on time, but the boy didn't think that would matter.

As the five slaves arrived, Violent-man turned to the Trainer. "Object lesson?"

The Trainer didn't want to agree but knew the advice of the blacksmith was solid. He saw the look of dread on the five slaves. He looked at the two masters and slowly nodded.

The two masters grabbed Grumpy.

"I was on time Trainer, I was!" he half-yelled as they dragged his shirt off him. The master that the boy didn't recognise, stood in front of the slave. He held his two arms. Violent-man uncoiled his whip.

"Let pain be your friend rat," he said as he sent the whip against the slave.

The slave howled as the whip landed, the feeling of intense burning traveling across his back. Five strokes in all, he received. As the Violent-man finished, the slave known as Grumpy dropped to the ground sobbing.

Funny-boy looked away. He didn't like Grumpy but still didn't want to see him whipped. The masters lined up another of the group and repeated the whipping. Funny-boy looked across to his new friend and saw the look in his eyes. The anger, the hate and it looked like the Demon-boy was going to say something or do something stupid. The Funny-boy took a risk and whispered.

"Don't. Do you want to be next?"

The words were like a bucket of cold water being thrown over him. His emotions shrunk and realisation hit him. He looked away, calming himself. If the five of them had followed his lead, they would not be getting punished now.

Once it was completed, all five of the slaves where lying on the ground. A few of them sobbing, shaking and in pain. The masters looked at the other slaves, with huge grins on their faces.

"Pain is your friend rats," they said before turning and leaving. The Trainer stepped back up. He pointed to a group of five slaves from red group.

"You five, help them back to their quarters. Put cold water on their backs and once you have dried it, smother their wounds in honey, then return here."

The five slaves jumped and helped the five whipped slaves to their feet. Half-carrying and half-dragging the wounded back to their sleeping quarters.

"Black group. Behind you, you will see some shovels, grab one each and follow me."

Just like Funny-boy had said, there was a large pile of shovels. Black group picked up a shovel each and followed. When they got to the Trainer, they saw large circles painted on the grass with white paint. There were nine circles in all painted into the grass. Each circle was roughly the size of the smithy. Between each circle was a space of roughly ten paces.

"Time to dig rats. By the end of the day, these all need to be dug to the depth of my shoulders. Black group will dig, Red group will get barrows to cart away the dirt and dump it in a pile left of the main gate. After a while the two groups will change."

The Trainer turned and left, knowing he would not have to supervise. The object lesson would be in the back of their minds. He turned and walked towards the smithy.

For the rest of the day, the slaves dug and moved dirt. Sweating through the afternoon, taking it in shifts to either dig or load up the barrows to pile it near the main gate. It took them all afternoon and past their normal dinner time to complete the nine circles to the required depth. The slaves knew exactly what the pits where going to be used for.

The five slaves that had been whipped did not returned to work and when the five that had helped them back returned, they said nothing and just got straight back into work. When the Trainer returned, the slaves had just downed tools and where standing back looking at their work. Nine round pits were now dug between the storage shed and the training field.

"Does not look too bad rats. Let's see," he said as he jumped down into the first pit.

Its walls where straight and slightly rounded off at the bottom. The floor of the pit perfectly flat. The Trainer nodded as the pit was to the correct depth. His shoulder the same height as the top of the walls. He jumped out and stood into every hole checking them.

"Well rats, you have done something correctly for a change."

The relief that washed through the slaves could almost be seen as shoulders relaxed.

"Pack up the tools and put them next to the pile of dirt near the main gate. Then go grab yourself some dinner."

As the slaves slowly ate their dinner of roast vegetables with one slice of roast meat each, the Trainer walked in.

"Now what does the Bastard-face want?" whispered the boy, as the Trainer stood where all the slaves could see him.

"Tomorrow is seventh day and marks the first three quarter moons that you have all been here."

He looked around at all the slaves before continuing

"The five rats that received punishment have been taken

away. They all have infections from the whip and will mostly likely die," said the Trainer.

It was a lie as they were heading back to the original slave camps that they came from, but the slaves didn't need to know that. Most of the slaves looked in horror, their mouths open. Other slaves just looked at their food, shaking their head. Only two slaves didn't look upset or shocked. Demon-boy and his two friends looked at the Trainer in anger. It's the second time that he had seen such looks from the boy. He'd best say something to him when he got him alone.

"As its the seventh day tomorrow, you are all given a day off."

Once again, the shock ran through the room, but it was a pleasant shock, a shock of happy surprise.

"My advice is to run a couple of laps in the morning to stretch your legs, then rest up for the day. On first day of next quarter moon, the real work begins."

"Real work?" he heard a voice say.

The Trainer spun but didn't know where the voice came from. He could press and find the culprit, but after the whipping, he didn't feel another "Object Lesson' was needed.

"Yes, the real work. Next quarter moon, you hit the pits! That's right rats, it's time to see how you fight."

The seventh day for the slaves was restful and a welcome break. After completing a few laps at a leisurely pace around the track, they all headed for a large breakfast. It was the normal porridge, but they all had second helpings.

The day was then spent lying in the sun and talking, or for some resting in their cells. It was a warm spring day with only a few clouds in the sky and as the boy lay down on the grass of the practise field, he looked up watching the clouds. He had spent the morning chatting to Funny-boy and some of the other slaves. More talk in a morning than all of the other slaves had experienced in the last three quarter moons. The big topic of conversation was, of course, the slaves that were whipped. The number of slaves was now down to seventy-nine from the one hundred. A few had been taken away with serious injuries from falls, some because they were not fit enough or willing enough to train, and of course, the five whipped slaves from yesterday. The slave that was murdered on the first day was never spoken of.

As the boy felt the breeze on his legs, he closed his eyes. He had spoken briefly to the Smith last night of the whippings. He had only reminded him that he was a slave and to continue working as hard as he can. He had also spoken a warning.

"Trainer said you have been giving him some angry looks, boy."

The boy looked guiltily at the Smith.

"If the Trainer would have been another of the masters, you would have been whipped too. I'm not saying do not hate the bastards, boy. They deserve your hate, just don't show it so openly on your face. Hold it in here, boy. Just like I have shown you" he said tapping his chest.

He had told Funny-boy of the conversation earlier that morning.

"Smith is right, you and I need to watch it. Bulldog-boy of course does not. He is so ugly no one can tell what he is thinking," said Funny-boy.

After Demon-boy stopped chuckling, he agreed and promised himself to hold his anger in check, no matter what was thrown at him. It was getting harder, he knew and understood that, but his anger had grown from what it was in the slave camp. Perhaps not being under the constant eyes of the masters had made him reckless. He needed to work on that. He spent the rest of the afternoon dozing in the sun before returning for the evening meal. After the meal, he made his way to bed. He knew tomorrow was going to be hard and was not looking forward to being thrown in the pit. He prayed not to be thrown into the pit against someone he liked. As he drifted off to sleep, he had the advice of the Smith in his head.

"Anger is a gift boy but keep it inside and let it drive you."

Good advice, he thought as he drifted off to sleep.

Chapter Seven

The next morning, they proceeded as expected; laps of the field followed by stretching, then into the large barn for more hell runs as Funny-boy called them. Once again, after ten of these hell runs, the slaves were left gasping for air and lying on the dirt-compacted floor. They were all trying to catch their breath when the Trainer shouted.

"Everyone up and make your way to the pits!"

With some internal groans, they got up and made their way to the holes that they had dug. The Trainer was waiting and had a sour look his face, so the slaves half walked, and half ran to get there. Once they had assembled, he told them to sit. They spread themselves around the first pit and sat. Some knelt at the back to get a better view; all still breathing hard.

"After a full moon cycle of fitness training, it's time to see how well you all fight. I'll pair you up and you will jump into the pit. The fight is over when the loser can no longer stand, or when I call hold."

The Trainer looked around the group and pointed out a

large slave from the red group. "You, jump in," he said as he scanned the group. Looking at the boy straight in the eye, he pointed, "You, in the pit."

The boy stood up and made his way to the front. The other slave from the red group had already jumped down and was loosening up his arms and legs. The boy got to the edge and jumped down. He just stood there looking at the other slave. The other slave was slightly taller than him but was slimmer. The boy was not nervous or scared. To be honest, he didn't really feel anything. He was getting himself ready when the Trainer shouted, "Fight!"

The slave ran at the boy throwing a right punch, wide and fast. The boy ducked and, on his way, up, punched the slave in the gut as hard as he could. It was like hitting concrete, the slave's stomach was solid muscle and if the slave felt the punch, he didn't show it. The slave followed up with a right elbow that connected with the boy's head, then turned and a left cross also connected with the boy's face. Blood flew from his nose and as he was off balance. He collapsed and hit the ground. He got up straight away and almost copped a knee in the face. The boy charged and tackled the slave around the midsection, picking him up and slamming him back into the ground. The slave had the wind knocked out of him. The boy jumped onto the slave's chest and started throwing blows onto the slave's face. There was no grace to the punches, just solid blows that rained down. The slave was not fighting back, but the boy kept going.

"HOLD!" the Trainer shouted.

The boy stopped, he got off the slave's chest and stepped back.

"Out. Next pair in," he said pointing at two slaves.

The boy sat down next to the slave that he had fought after helping him from the pit. Both had blood on their faces.

The slave looked over at the boy and nodded to him. Two by two's, all of the slaves got their turn in the pit. The boy watched with disinterest as the fights happened. The only fight he truly paid attention to was the fight of his friend Funny-boy.

Funny-boy was facing the second largest slave in the group, one not much shorter than himself. The fight was over quickly. The slave from Red group threw a haymaker of a left hand. Funny-boy stepped into the slave and grabbed the front of his shirt. He pulled him into a sickening head butt that exploded the slave's nose. As the slave stepped back, Funny-boy finished him with a fast right hook that knocked the slave off his feet. Funny-boy looked up at the boy and smiled. They got down and helped the still form, lifting him over his shoulder and throwing him up on the lip of the pit.

The boy was smiling and not paying attention, as the Trainer picked the last slave to get into the pit. However, since the slave total number was seventy-nine, there was no one for him to face.

"You," the Trainer said pointing at the boy. "You're up again, get in the pit."

The boy looked angry but remembered the Smith's advice and tried to calm himself. As he got to his feet, he heard Funny-boy whisper

"Picture one of the masters you're facing, not a slave."

As the boy climbed down into the pit for a second time, he looked at the second slave. Another slave that he had never spoken to, only seen. The slave had kept himself to himself and rarely spoke to anyone. He was short but very stocky with thick legs and wide shoulders. He was 4–5 inches shorter than the boy. The slave had a smile on his face. Remembering the advice that Funny-boy had whispered, he made himself ready.

"Fight!" yelled the Trainer.

The boy ran at the slave as fast as he could and threw a quick right punch at the slave's head, but the slave's head was not there. The slave had anticipated it and ducked completely under the punch. The boy spun around straight into a straight left, followed by a straight right. The boy felt the left explode into his face but didn't feel the right. He had already been knocked unconscious. When he came around, Funny-boy was sitting by him on the right, with the slave that had beaten him sitting on his left.

The Trainer was speaking. "You rats really need some instructions, that's for sure. Everyone over to the track, complete ten laps at a good pace, then return here. GO!"

The slaves got up and ran to the track. As the boy went to get up, the Trainer singled him out. "Not him, he is still too wobbly."

Funny-boy and the slave that had beaten him, left him there and joined the others. Once all the slaves were out of earshot, the Trainer started to speak. "Well, you got knocked senseless then, didn't you?"

The boy just nodded.

"Do you know why I made you fight twice?"

The boy shook his head.

"To give you more practise than the others. I said I would help where I can. You may not believe it, but I push you harder to make you harder, to give more experience. Learn from today, in particular that second fight. You rushed in like an idiot. Your first fight was okay, you moved, and you thought, then struck. Your second fight was pathetic."

"That slave hits hard!" replied the boy.

"Yes, he does, he has good technique and always seems in balance. When he fights next, watch him and try to learn. Speak to him tonight, ask questions."

The boy's head was starting to clear but he stayed sitting.

"Remember boy, you only have spring and summer to learn. Next winter, you are in the pit for real, facing opponents that will try and destroy you. I watched you today during the other fights. Your mind is wandering and not paying attention."

The boy looked up at the Trainer.

"Watch ALL of the fights, the techniques and the moves that the other slaves use. Then, when you face them, you will know of their strengths and their weaknesses."

"I will, Trainer, thank you."

The Trainer smiled a rare smile, then his face returned quickly to coldness when he saw the slaves returning to the pits, their laps completed.

"Right. Another fight in the pit each, then it's back to the big barn for what some of you call hell runs.

The slaves all sighed, privately of course. That afternoon, they all fought again. Funny-boy destroyed his opponent again, so did the slave the boy had faced and he had been knocked out by. This time, the boy watched all the fights, paying attention to all the slaves and how they moved. When it was his time again in the pit, he watched his opponent climb down. He was the same size as the boy, the boy had seen him in his first fight and watched him win. He was quick and vicious.

"Fight!" yelled the Trainer.

The boy half ran at his opponent and his opponent did the same. When they reached each other, they started trading punches, standing toe to toe, some connecting and some not. The boy tried to stay calm, yet at the same time, picturing the slave as one of the masters. He received a couple of good whacks to head but had also scored a couple of good hits to his opponent as well. He changed his tactic and ducked his head; the slave threw a fast-left hander. As he ducked, he punched the slave in the side a few inches down from his armpit. The Slave breathed, washed out. As he came out, the boy threw an over the top right that connected squarely. The other slave hit the ground. The boy stepped back thinking that he had won, but as he stepped back, the slave pushed himself off the ground and threw an uppercut in the boy's groin. It dropped him and he sank to the ground holding his balls, eyes watering.

"Hold!" said the Trainer. "There is a lesson there for all of you. It's the pit! Anything goes, no rules. The only rule is to be the last one standing."

The boy and his opponent got out of the pit as the next two jumped in. He sat down next to Funny-boy. "How are the balls?" Funny-boy said, smiling. The boy said nothing. More intent on wanting his stomach to stop heaving.

The rest of the day was taken up by another set of hell runs before stretching. The slaves all returned to the food hall bruised and battered, tired and exhausted, sore and some of them swollen. They slumped to eat, and no words were spoken. The boy ate mechanically and slowly. His jaw hurt so he took his time, and not looking forward to tomorrow at all.

"How were the first fights today?" asked the Smith.

He had been shaping wooden training axes all day, which was not a hard job but a tedious one. The welcome relief of the Trainer walking in, clear on the Smith's face.

"Interesting, Smith".

"Interesting in which way?"

"There are some slaves with good potential. I saw ten to fifteen that should do well in the pits once they've had their training."

"And the boy, is he in this group of slaves with potential?"

"No. No, he is not, which is why I am here."

The Smith put down the wooden axe that he was finishing with sandpaper.

"He can't fight?"

"He is too angry and rushes in like a fool. His first fight was okay, and you could see him thinking before striking out; he won. His second fight, he rushed in like a mad idiot and got knocked out. I gave him some quiet words to consider and thought that they hit home when he had his third fight. He had some good strikes and then let himself get surprised."

"Which is why he is being trained. I know the boy has aggression and have heard of the fights that he had as a slave."

"It's hard to put into words. He has aggression, yes. When his blood is up, he just rushes in, no defence or offence, just anger. He needs to harness that anger and focus it, otherwise he will die in the pit and quickly."

"It is said that you were pretty aggressive in the cages and full of rage yourself, Trainer."

"I was, but I didn't let the anger make decisions for me, I focused it."

"Then, we will have to teach the boy," replied the Smith.

"I can't. The masters are already becoming suspicious. They questioned why the boy didn't run some laps today. I explained that he had just been knocked out and was still dizzy. I don't think that they believed me. If they guess I know the boy, he or possibly I will not survive."

"I'll have more words with him."

"Try and convince him to use his anger, to channel it. Otherwise, trust me Smith, he will die in his first death bout."

The Trainer left the smithy. The Smith returned to his

sanding whilst he thought of ways to approach the problem of the boy's anger.

Over the next quarter moon, the slaves got used to their new routine. Mornings consisted of running around the track followed by hell runs in the barn. After breaking their fast, more hell runs followed by heavy work with the rocks.

The afternoons saw the slaves fighting in the pit. The Trainer watched the fights less and less as he started teaching small groups different techniques of hand to hand combat. Showing the slaves how to punch from their legs, protect themselves and other small dirty tricks that would help them in the pit.

Often the Trainer would be working with five to ten slaves showing them these techniques whilst the other slaves all took turns in the pits. All nine pits had slaves bashing at each other. As their skill slowly improved over the quarter moon, less and less injuries were happening. The slaves still returned to their beds with bruises and sore bodies, but nothing of the injuries that had plagued the first two days in the pit.

The boy was with six other members of the Black group working with the Trainer. He was demonstrating with a slave. The slave had thrown a punch as instructed by the Trainer. The Trainer stepped to the inside of the punch and stepped into the Slave, his elbow crashing into the slave's throat, dropping him."

"See? Work around your opponent, around their punches and kicks."

The slaves looked confused.

"If a huge bull is running at you, do you charge at the bull head on or do you step aside?"

The analogy was a good one and the slaves understood what he was talking about.

"Back to the pits and practise what I have been teaching you."

The Trainer turned to the other slaves. "NEXT GROUP!" he yelled.

As the boy walked back to the pits, his thoughts ran back to his conversation with the Smith after dinner last night.

"Trainer has told me that you are charging like a mad bull, boy."

"Yes, he told me as well."

"You need to listen to him, boy. Rage and anger are good, but it needs to be focused. Don't let it control you."

"How do I do that? I need that anger in the pits. You and Funny-boy said, 'Anger is a gift'."

"It is, but not wild anger, not uncontrolled anger."

"How do I use my anger like you have been telling me, but still stay in control? It makes no sense."

The boy was not usually argumentative, and the Smith was a little surprised. The Smith racked his brain to find a way to explain it.

"Think of the bull, boy. When his blood is up, he is pure rage. He is using his strength and size to bluster and bellow, pacing the ground and then rushing in."

The boy nodded.

"Now think of the snow weasel. We had plenty of them at the slave camp."

"Yes, we did, vicious little bastards."

The Smith smiled, "Yes, they are."

"Did you ever see the way that they took down a bigger foe?"

"Yes, Smith, I once saw a snow weasel take down a giant hare, five times its own size."

"How did it do it?" the Smith asked.

The boy thought back to the memory. It had fascinated him at the time.

"He charged at the rabbit; the rabbit stood its ground. The snow weasel at the last second, swerved and ran to the side of the rabbit, jumping on its back before the rabbit could turn to face it. It then latched on to the rabbit's throat and held on, not letting go. The rabbit ran but the weasel just hung on, tearing away at the throat. Eventually, he stopped and fell to the ground. The weasel continued to maul it. It was like…"

"Controlled rage?"

"Yes, that is exactly how it seemed. The weasel was vicious and looked crazed, yet it had method to what it was doing."

"Exactly. The weasel is the best example. Start trying to be the snow weasel when you are in the pit. Focus that rage and let the body do what it is being trained to do."

The boy understood some of what both the Trainer and Smith had been trying to tell him. He would have to put it to practise.

"Gather around. We will finish off the day with a few fights. You have all had two fights today, so we will test your stamina. The winners will gather on my right, the losers on my left. First two in." He had pointed to the closest two slaves. Once the slaves had dropped into the pit, the Trainer yelled, "Fight!"

The two slaves went at each other. You could see the improvement already, and even though they threw punches and kicks, there seemed to be a little more control. The fight was over quickly with one of the slaves tripping the other with a leg sweep, then diving on him, raining blows until the Trainer yelled stop.

It was not long before the boy was back in the pit. He was

facing the same youth from his very second fight, a quarter moon ago. The slave had beaten him by kicking him in the balls. He had become a favourite of the other slaves for being so ruthless in the pit. The boy had already had two fights today and had lost them. He was still trying to find a good balance between the rage and keeping control, trying to be like the snow weasel. He had almost found the balance in the second fight but fell to a lucky punch. He was determined to beat this slave and looked at his smug look. He could feel the anger building and blood pulse start to quicken.

"Fight!"

The slave ran at him, jumping in the air and aiming a knee to his head. The boy stepped to the side and punched for the slave's groin as he flew past. The punch connected and the boy stepped back as the slave landed and threw a punch at him. Once the punch fell short, the boy stepped in, faking a left jab then connecting with a right cross that slammed into the slave's right eye. The punch to the groin had slowed the slave but didn't stop him. The slave returned a kick to the boy's midsection, which the boy stepped away from, stepping into the slave again. His left hand grabbing the slave by the throat and his right-hand raining down blows to the slave's head. The slave punched and kicked the boy, but he ignored it like the weasel, he had locked on and was not letting go. He felt a punch to his groin that dropped him, but he still didn't let go of the slave's throat. On the way down to the ground, the boy continued to punch with his right hand. Time and time again, he punched the same spot. Within moments, he was on the ground straddling the other slave, left hand still around the throat restricting his breathing whilst his right hand continues to pummel the face. The boy could feel his adrenaline sing.

"Hold!" yelled the Trainer.

The boy stopped and looked down. The slave was unconscious and his face a bloody mess. He stepped off him and stood. He could see the Trainer trying to hide a smile and when he looked over at Funny-boy, he could see there was a grin so big, it had hidden the rest of his face. Another slave jumped into help and between them, they lifted the unconscious slave out of the pit. The boy then joined the other winners on the right of the Trainer. When he sat down, he felt a hand slap him on the shoulder. He turned to see Silent-boy smiling at him. He grinned back and felt a weight lift off his shoulders. None of the other slaves would ever know how important that last fight was to the boy. He needed to win, he needed to learn how to control his anger. He now knew how.

The other fights continued until everyone had fought and were he stood to the left of the Trainer or the right, depending on the outcome of the fight.

"Round two," the Trainer said smiling.

"The losers sit around the southern side of the pit." He then looked at the winners. He pointed at two slaves in the winners' zone. "You two, back in."

The slaves that were pointed out, got back into the pit. They fought quickly until one was the winner. As with the first round, the winner joined the Trainer and stood on his right side. The loser who had fallen to a lucky punch had come around quickly and joined the other losers, sitting on the ground.

More fights happened and were watched. Funny-boy as was his way, won easily overpowering the other slave. Silent-boy won with a great display of nimbleness as he managed to get on the inside of a strong slave and deliver a devastating uppercut, lifting the youth from his feet.

The boy was up next and got back into the ring. He was

facing a slave he didn't know well. He hadn't yet faced him in the pit. The slave was the same size as the boy.

"Fight."

Being in control of his rage, the boy made his way toward the slave as he ran at him. He dodged a kick and then ducked under a flying left hand. On his way up, he sent a quick left hook to the slave's chin. It connected, everyone heard a large crack and the slave dropped. He didn't get back up.

"Hold."

Once again, another slave helped him with the unconscious body. They got him to the losers' side of the pit and lay him down. He was breathing but out cold. One of the other slaves mentioned that he may have a broken jaw. The boy joined the other winners with a blank stare on his face. For the rest of the afternoon, the slaves were whittled down. The boy had fought and won four times in total. The light was starting to fade as there was only four of them

Standing at the Trainers right side were only four slaves, Silent-boy, Funny-boy, Longarm-boy and the boy among them. As the sun started to drop, the Trainer turned back to the slaves.

"The losers can finish with 10 laps of the track. Once you have done that, stretch and get some food." As the losers got up, he turned to the four. "Go and clean yourselves up, grab some food but make it a very small meal. The four of you are fighting tonight in the Chief's hall in front of the masters." With that, Trainer turned and left.

"In front of the masters?" one slave said.

"That's what we do remember? We are slaves, entertainment for the Outlander bastards," said Funny-boy.

The Trainer came to collect them from the food hall. Word had spread quickly amongst the other slaves that the four of them would be fighting in the Chief's hall. None of the other slaves were jealous, and thankful that they hadn't got any further. The four followed the Trainer out towards the gate. The Smith had fallen in beside the Trainer and they talked slowly together. The Smith hadn't looked at the boy or acknowledged him.

Funny-boy walked beside him, his face calm. Looking behind him, he saw Silent-boy who had a grin across his face. The boy was starting to think that he was crazy. The other slave who some called Longarm-boy, walked in silence with concern clearly on his face. They walked out of the gate and all of them were a little unnerved. The camp with its wooden walls had become their world over the last full moon. Stepping through the gate had made them all a little uneasy.

"Feels weird, eh?" commented Funny-boy, describing what the four slaves felt.

"Quiet," said the Trainer. " Do I need to remind you that we will be in front of the masters? They will beat you, whip you or even kill you, if you behave in a manner they don't like. I may be a little slack in the training ground but remember that you are slaves. The Outlanders will not hesitate to do whatever they feel like doing. Keep you mouths shut and concentrate on fighting at your best."

The Smith also added some cautionary words. "Remember, the Outlanders are unpredictable. Be ready for anything and obey without question."

The boy saw the Trainer nod at the words of the Smith.

They walked through the settlement and could already hear the noise from the Chief's hall. It sounded like the Outlanders were already drunk, and they were. As they approached the front entrance, the two massive doors were opened for them.

Walking in, the noise hit their senses first, followed by the smell. Yelling, laughter and conversation assaulted their ears. The smell was unreal but not expected. The smell of stale drink, stale unwashed bodies and roasting meat all rolled into a sickly, sweet smell. The hall was well lit with small fires in metal brackets, scattered all over the place.

As they approached the front of the hall, the Chief stood up from his chair, a large wooden chair that had some sort of animal skin thrown over it. He raised his hands for silence and the noise started to cease. The Outlanders were all watching the procession that halted below the steps of the Chief. The Chief's voice boomed out.

"You all remember last winter; we freed this man from being a slave. He became our trainer of pit rats and boasted a better way to train the pit rats. We listened to his proposals and we laughed."

The crowd of Outlanders laughed and whooped.

"But I gave him a chance to prove his words and gave him two summers to prove himself right and us wrong."

The laughter died down as all the Outlanders listened for what was coming next.

"I have paid many coins and you all have provided labour to build a new training camp. We now get to see a little of what my coin and your sweat has paid for."

The room erupted. Outlanders liked fighting over everything else and you could see the look on all of the Outlanders that looked forward to watching the pit rats fight.

"Clear a space in the middle of the hall and let's see if these pit-rats can entertain us."

A space was quickly cleared. The space was the same size of a standard pit but ringed by warriors with shields and not a hole in the ground.

The Chief pointed to Funny-boy and Silent-boy.

"Those two first."

The Trainer told them to remove their shirts. He then whispered to both of them.

"Fight hard and fight to win."

The two slaves entered the ring as the Smith and the Trainer stepped up and back onto a low bench, so they could watch. The Smith had grabbed a jug of spirits off an empty table along with two cups. He poured himself and the Trainer a drink. He caught the boy looking at him. He shook his head and the boy got the meaning straight away.

Funny-boy and Silent-boy loosened up their arms. The crowd was chanting but the slaves hadn't yet started fighting.

"What are you waiting for rats, get to it!" yelled Son-of-Angry-man, who was beside his father.

The boy knew they were waiting for the Trainer to yell out for them to start. The two slaves in the ring rushed at each other. Straight away, the boy noticed the savagery was next level. Almost as if they had been holding back in the practise pits. Both ducked, weaved and punched with great strength. The fight had just started and already both slaves had blood streaming off their face.

It was an interesting fight with Silent-boy not giving any ground and the fight was furious. There was no other way to describe it. It couldn't last forever and as Funny-boy started to get the better of him, Silent-boy had landed two very quick punches to the same spot, just below Funny-boy's left eye. It managed to drop Funny-boy to the ground. Silent-boy launched on top of him and continued to punch him. Left and rights coming as fast and hard as he could. The crowd was screaming its approval. Silent-boy stopped when he realised Funny-boy was not fighting back. He stood and stepped back. One of the warriors lifted his hand as the winner. Silent-boy was panting trying to catch his breath and watching intently with concern at Funny-boy. Two warriors jumped past the shields and lifted Funny-boy. They carried him to where the Trainer stood on a bench and dropped him on the floor. Silent-boy was led from the circle and handed a mug of drink. He skulled it and received a massive roar from the assembled warriors. The atmosphere sickened the Smith. This was not sport and although he had enjoyed the occasional fight in his younger days, it was nothing like this. He speedily drank trying to numb his disgust. He knew the boy was up next and was truly worried for him. He leaned in as he saw the boy led to the ring.

"How well will the boy do?" he asked the Trainer.

"He should be fine; he has made some progress today."

As the last two slaves took off their shirts, the Chief once again stood and addressed the crowd.

"How was that, my warriors?"

The crowd roared once again their approval.

"Well, we have something special for the last bout. You all remember my brother in-law that was killed in the raid in DuNoor many seasons ago?" The crowd nodded and agreed all remembering the warrior that had been unlucky and died in the raid.

"Shit!" the Smith said. The Trainer only nodded in agreement.

"On my left, may I present the killer of my brother in-law, the slave that we named as Demon-child."

The crowd went berserk. Booing and yelling insults at the boy.

"He is one of the pit-rats and will fight to win us more coin."

The Chief looked at the other slave.

"What do the other slaves call you pit rat?

He had looked at the ground before looking up at the Chief. "I am a slave, I have no name, master."

"Well slave, my son has an offer for you to make things interesting."

Son-of-Angry-man stepped forward. "Slave, if you beat the Demon-child, you will no longer be a slave."

A look of death came on Longarm-boy's face as his back grew straighter and he stood a little straighter. Freedom was the dream of every slave. He eyed the boy with malice. Longarm-boy had already beaten the boy during the last time they faced each other.

"But just to add more spice to the bout and spice to the wagers…," his voice trailed off as the crowd all laughed. "In a few quarter moons, my warriors start the raiding season and what kind of Chief would I be if I didn't give the best entertainment to my warriors?"

The crowd roared with approval again as the slaves in the ring stepped from foot to foot, waiting for the beginning of the bout.

"To give the bout some flavour, the fight will be a death bout."

The room roared so much the Smith thought the roof would come off. He looked with fear at the boy he had befriended only a few full moons ago. The relationship had grown until now, he considered the boy to be family. The Trainer looked on with a sick feeling to stomach. The Smith had mentioned earlier that they should be ready for anything. The Trainer knew this was the sick type of twist that the Outlanders enjoyed giving to slaves. He turned to look at the Smith with concern in his eyes also. The Smith was watching the boy and didn't take his eyes of him.

The boy was lost in his own world of fear. He had heard the words death bout and his stomach had sunk, his heart jumping into his throat. He worked to calm himself and bring his emotions under control. He looked over his shoulder to the Son-of-Angry-man; hatred etched on his features. He turned back to the slave, not seeing Long-arm but only seeing Son-of-Angry-man. He felt his pulse quicken and his anger start to rise. One phrase flashed in his mind – snow weasel.

"Fight!" yelled the Chief.

Long-arm moved quickly to close the gap and, in an instant, the two slaves were toe to toe trading punches. They moved fast, ducking, weaving and throwing punches, elbows and kicks where they could while the crowd around them cheered them. The boy was trying his best to get the better of Son-of-Angry-man. He didn't see Long-arm through the mists of his rage. Long-arm was connecting more punches because of his reach and the fight would only have one conclusion if it continued like this.

"Snow weasel!"

The word whispered through the boy's mind. He ducked a punch and threw a right towards the ribs of Long-arm connecting well. He dodged another punch and threw another to the same spot on Long-arm's side. Again, and again, he punched the ribs in the same spot, as hard as he could, dodging incoming punches or trying his best to shrug them off when they connected. Finally, he heard a crack as the ribs finally gave way; Long-arm screamed. He threw a quick combination of left and rights, which the boy sidestepped and dodged. As Long-arm turned to catch the boy, the boy launched and got both of his hands around Long-arm's throat. He kneed him twice in quick succession into the groin. As Long-arm started to drop, the boy went with him. One hand still on his throat as the right hand started to pommel Long-arm's face.

"The Snow Weasel!" he heard the Smith's voice in his head

He had used this move before and as the two slaves crashed to the ground, the boy kept the punches coming fast and throwing them with all of his strength. His left hand choking Long-arm and his right trying his best to break his face. Long-arm was turning blue in the face with lack of air, but the boy didn't notice. The boy was now screaming as he punched and punched, what he saw as the face of Son-of-Angry-man. He didn't see Long-arm's legs stop thrashing; he didn't see the light from Long-arm's eyes disappear. All he saw was the face of Son-of-Angry-man and continued to beat down with all of the energy he had.

He hadn't noticed some of crowd of warriors had stopped and were now silent, or nor did he notice the more blood thirsty cheer louder. He didn't see the look of sadness on the Smith's face.

"Hold!" the Trainer yelled finally.

But Demon-boy didn't hear him. He just continued to smash the no longer breathing face.

The Chief and his son looked down at the slave that was enraged, not understanding where this rage was coming for. The son smiled, but the father wondered what they were creating.

The boy didn't see the warrior walk up behind him or see him draw his axe from his belt. All he knew was the world went black as the warrior cracked him across the back of his head with the flat of his axe blade.

As the limp form was dragged off Long-arm, it was clear to see there was nothing left of his face. It was blood and flesh with nothing left to resemble the face of the slave it had been.

The limp form of the boy was thrown into one of the cells above the food hall. His door was locked as he lay in darkness on the pallet that he had been dumped on. Funny-boy and Silent-boy had followed the warriors and watched the boy get thrown into a cell. After the warriors left, Funny-boy turned to Silent-boy.

"I guess he lives with us now, and not the Smith?"

Silent-boy shrugged. "You will have to tell me why they call him the Demon-child."

As they had left, some of the warriors had been chanting Demon-child as the boy's limp form was carried from the Chief's hall. Funny-boy sat down against the wall outside the cell that the boy now laid in. Silent-boy sat beside him and listened to the tale of how the boy got the name. Bulldog-boy had joined them to check on what had gone down. He sat opposite the two and listened as Funny-boy recounted the tail of how his friend had become to be known as the Demon-child.

The Smith sat outside his quarters with a jug of spirits in his hand. He was sick to the stomach and worried for the boy.

"He never showed that sort of rage before in the pits," said the Trainer as he sipped on his jug.

"It's come from somewhere, although I hardly blame you, Trainer."

"I should have seen this coming and picked another to fight tonight."

"No. Even if the boy hadn't been selected, the bastard-masters would have found a way for him to fight tonight."

"He has anger, but I have never seen that depth of anger in anyone," said the Trainer. "And, why do they call him Demon-Child?"

The Smith looked over to the Trainer and if he hadn't

been half drunk, he probably would have said nothing. However, he was half drunk and sat there telling him all that he knew of the boy and why they call him Demon-child. They sat together late into the moon light discussing the boy, drinking and trying to make sense of what to do. The boy would not survive long in the pit with that rage, if the masters don't kill him first.

As the drinking continued in the Chief's hall, the Chief sat in his chair, jug in hand slowly sipping. His son was sitting on the steps in front of him.

"That was glorious to see father, he will earn you much coin."

The Chief smiled but said nothing.

His son continued. "Already, you can clearly see the standard of fighting is better than last year."

"You were not a fan of the idea if I recall, son!"

"No, I was not, which shows how wrong I was."

The Chief laughed; it was not often his son admitting being wrong.

"Yes, they will provide me with better coin next winter. What did you think of the Demon-child?"

"A mad dog that one, father."

"Yes. The Trainer said he had been progressing okay and had never seen that type of rage before. Do you think, son, we should allow him to get to the death bouts? I don't trust that demon with a weapon in his hands."

"You're not scared of him, father? He is just a child."

"Children grow boy. One day, you will turn around and a fully grown man will be standing before you, mad as a dog with a sword in is hand."

The words were not having any effect on the son and not convincing him at all.

"Keep him fighting, father. You still have a couple of summers before he gets to death bout age. Keep an eye on him and if he is still a concern, kill him."

"Probably a good idea. Either way, I look forward to throwing the Demon-child at Chief Erak's pit-rats next winter."

The son laughed as he stood up. "Yes, I look forward to that too, father."

Chapter Eight

The boy woke with a pounding headache. He was on a bed that felt unusual. He rolled onto his back and opened his eyes. Light was streaming through the window and he saw straight away that he was lying on a pallet in one of the barrack cells. Why was he here?

The door was open and not locked. His head continued to pound as he felt every heartbeat pulse through his head. He felt some uncomfortableness coming from the top of his head and he moved his hand to his head and felt the lump. He pressed down on it, which was a stupid thing to do, as the fresh pain that ripped through him made him yelp. Within minutes of him yelping, Funny-boy and Bulldog-boy had entered the cell. They both came in and sat down on the pallet on the opposite wall to the boy's pallet. The boy looked to them. Funny-boy for once not smiling, just looking at the boy in what could only be wonder. Bulldog-boy had a half grin on his face. The boy's memories flickered to the previous night and what had happened. He felt sick to the stomach and looked for water, grasping at the side table. Bulldog-boy threw him a water skin, which landed on the boy's stomach. He took a deep drink of water before lying back down on the pallet.

Funny-boy was the first to speak. "Remind me never to piss you off, Demon-boy."

Bulldog-boy laughed his sick little laugh. The boy just shook his head. He couldn't put into words what was going on in his head, or what was in his heart.

"Long arm-boy?" said Demon-boy with a questioning tone. Knowing the answer as soon as the words crossed his lips.

"Dead," replied Funny-boy.

He shook a little. Breathing deeply, before he uttered the only words he could think to say.

"I'm sorry."

"For what? The Bastard-masters are the ones that turned it into a death bout! You didn't choose to kill; you had no choice!" said Bulldog-boy.

"Feels like my fault," replied Demon-boy.

"It's not your fault. Although, I was surprised in the manner you did it. That's why I hope I never piss you off!" said Funny-boy.

The boy was in too much pain to laugh at the joke. He lay on the bed looking at the wooden beams holding on the roof. "I am a killer!" he said quietly.

"Which is what they are training us to be!" said Funny-boy.

"True, so very true," replied Bulldog-boy.

It was at that moment the Trainer appeared at the door.

"This one needs his rest," said Trainer.

Funny-boy and Bulldog-boy got up. Both clapped him on the shoulders before leaving. The boy looked at the Trainer. He held back his feelings of devastation of what he had done.

"So, you have killed your first opponent in the pit,"

Trainer said as he sat down on the bed that had been vacated by his two fellow slaves.

"I hate it!"

"I admit, I was shocked a little to see you in your blood rage. As the other two said, you are being trained to do just that."

"You were listening?"

"Yes, it's a bad habit that I have picked up. They are right, you should not lie here and feel sorry for yourself. You are being trained to kill, and I realise that now I'm looking at you what that actually means is just being realised. Am I right?"

"Yes Trainer, you are."

"You are finally grasping the reality of what a pit-rat does?"

"Yes."

"Good. Now you are under no illusion as to what your life has in store for you."

The boy looked back at the ceiling, wanting this conversation to be over. He was trying to push the flashbacks of last night's fight out of his mind and not doing a particularly good job of it.

"Today is a day of rest. Since the masters will be too hung over to come and check, I have given the day off to all the slaves. It is 7th day after all." The Trainer got up. "Stay here and rest. When you are ready go and wash yourself and then get some food."

One last thing occurred to the boy. "Why am I here? And not in the apartment?"

"The masters have said that you will fight better being in a cell, and not pampered in a luxury apartment with the Smith."

"They are punishing me?"

"No," said the Trainer, with a smile on his face. "They are

trying to break you. They want you weak, unable to fight so you die in the pits. So far, you have not showed any sign of breaking, have you?"

"I suppose not."

"Why?"

"Not sure," replied the boy, with honestly.

"What they don't realise is they are actually making you stronger."

"Stronger?"

"Yes, stronger. What were you feeling when the Chief announced it to be a death bout?"

The boy thought about it. It was hard to think of what he was feeling at the time, without feeling the emotions of what he had done. The memory was too strong in his mind.

"I was pissed off. It felt like the world was against me and they had made the deal with Long-arm because they wanted me to die."

"And they did, that is no doubt what they had in mind. Then, you took that anger out on Long-arm."

The boy squirmed in a physical sense and an emotional one.

"I'll leave you to your rest. Trust me in what I am about to say. You always remember the first opponent you kill in the pit. All the food or money in the world, will not make you remember the 2nd, or the 3rd. Work your way through it, then when you're ready, go and talk to the Smith. I'm sure having dinner with him every now and then will be allowed."

As the Trainer left, the boy felt ashamed. Ashamed for Long-arm's death in the pit. He closed his eyes once more.

The rest of the season went quickly. Demon-boy slowly healing from what he had done to Longarm-boy. It took a while to move through the emotions he felt. His two friends did their best to help him through it, unfortunately this caused some tension. Demon-boy needed to work through it at his own pace in his own way. He was snappy and almost surly towards his friends. He knew it was unreasonable but could not help it. The tension came to a head when Bulldog-boy and Demon-boy were facing off in the pit. Bulldog-boy had a habit of letting his mouth run. They were just about to fight when he opened his mouth.

"So how long are you going to sulk for?" said Bulldog-boy

Demon-boy looked at him and slowly walked forward. Trainer was talking to some of the other slaves and was not watching what happened.

"Well? Perhaps we start calling you Cry-boy?" said Bulldog-boy

Demon-boy's answer was exploding into action and punching him as hard as he could in the face, connecting with his nose. Bulldog-boy was not expecting it, Trainer had not said to start yet. As his nose broke, spurting blood all over his face, he started throwing punches of his own. The both stood toe to toe throwing punches. There was no strategy, no grace, method to what they were doing. Trainer turned to see the two of them brawling. He was about to stop it when Funny-boy came up to him

"Let them finish, it may be what he needs" said Funny-boy

The two continued trading punches, as hard and as fast as they could. Both of them had bloody faces and were quickly running out of steam. Bulldog-boy started working on his friend's body, trying to hit with as much power as he could. Demon-boy was trying to destroy his friends face, angry now.

Before long they both stopped and stepped back. Both out of energy. Demon-boy's body hurt, his face a bloody mess. Bulldog-boy, apart from having a broken nose, also was not recognisable, his face a bloody pulp. Still he managed to speak.

"You done? Or should someone else get down here and fight you? Perhaps once you have fought all your friends you have in this world you will start to think clearly." Said Bulldog-boy

Demon-boy stood there, bleeding and trying to catch his breathe. Saying nothing. Bulldog-boy took a step forward and continued.

"Perhaps breaking my nose is not enough. Perhaps you want to hurt the Smith as well, or perhaps Funny-boy." Said Bulldog-boy

The words started to eat away at Demon-boy. They punched through the rage and emotions he had been feeling. The beginning of shame started to take root in his heart when he realised, he had been trying to hurt his friend. Bulldog-boy started getting out of the pit. Once up he looked back down.

"Think about it Demon-child" said Bulldog-boy, knowing calling him what the masters did, would get his attention.

"Are you scum like them, or are you a pit-rat? Are you our brother or are you a bastard outlander? A brother of ours would not want to hurt us! Now wake up, stop feeling sorry for yourself or fuck off!"

With that Bulldog-boy stalked off to clean himself up. Demon-boy stood in the pit feeling ashamed. He slowly got out and headed to the smithy. Changing his mind, he spun and started heading to the far end of the field to be alone. Bulldog-boy's words although harsh, were true. He had needed to hear them. But hearing them and liking what he heard was two very different things. He reached the far end of the field and sat down, looking at his feet. He was carrying his tunic in his hand and used this to clean away some of the blood falling from his face. He sat there until night had fallen. He got himself up and moved to the water barrel outside of the smithy. Once his face had been cleaned of the blood, he went straight to his cell. He did not stop for a meal in the eating hall, just went to his cell and laid on his bed. He closed his eyes and the words that had been said echoed around his mind. The tears ran down his cheek on how he had been treating his friends. He realised how wrong he was, the thought the last thing in his mind as he fell asleep.

The next morning, he was up early again, standing on the field listening to the birds. He slept well and woke refreshed. He made his way down to the training field in the hope his two friends would be there. It seemed ages before they finally arrived. He felt fear as he heard Funny-boy and Bulldog-boy talking quietly as they approached. He was looking the other way and was too scared to turn around and face them. He looked at the ground as he heard their voices grow louder as they approached. He had his eyes shut when they reached him. He said nothing and was waiting for them to speak first. He felt a hand whack down on his shoulder. He opened his eyes and looked straight into Bulldog-boys smiling face.

"Morning. So, have you decided? Are you our friend and fellow pit-rat?" said Bulldog-boy

"I am your brother," replied Demon-boy in whisper.

Bulldog-boys smile grew larger. "See. Best way to deal with him is to pound his face."

Funny-boy roared with laughter and also laid his hand on Demon-boy's shoulder.

"Welcome back Handsome-face," said Funny-boy.

Bulldog-boy laughed loudly. He patted Demon-boy on the shoulder and moved away.

Funny-boy gave Demon-boy's shoulder a squeeze and also moved away. Demon-boy wanted to apologise but the words wouldn't come out. He tried to gather the courage but the words stuck in his throat. Finally, he managed to speak.

"I was wrong."

"We know that arse-face," said Bulldog-boy, setting Funny-boy to laughing again.

Even Demon-boy smiled. It hurt his face, but he smiled.

"Next time you have a mood, Funny-boy has offered to get in the pit with you," said Bulldog-boy.

Realising that they were both passing off the incident and joking about it, he decided to join in now.

"At least he can throw a decent punch, Broken-nose," said Demon-boy.

Bulldog-boy smiled and Funny-boy laughed again.

"See. Punch him in the head a few times and he is back to normal," said Bulldog-boy.

The others started arriving and nothing more was said. Although he appreciated his brother slaves, his friends, he never before truly appreciated the bond they had. He would not again test that bond. As all the other pit-rats arrived, some cracking jokes at his expense, he knew at some stage he would apologise to his friends properly. But today he basked in their warmth of friendship, their jokes and the brotherhood. Tomorrow or perhaps the next day, he would open up and apologise.

The two seasons had passed quickly for the slaves in the training camp. The seasons coming and going, bringing snow, then taking it away. The summer just gone had been warmer than anyone could remember and the slaves that were training for the pit, had sweated and slogged through the heat. Losing what little body fat that they had gained during winter.

Of the one hundred five slaves that had arrived at the training camp, sixty-eight remained. Some having been killed by 'Object Lessons' at the hands of the masters for not performing in their training. A few had died from injuries during training, but most had died from the illness that spread through the training barracks last winter. A sickness that spread through the training camp quickly, swelling the throats of those that caught it, suffocating them in their sleep. It was as the Smith had said "A bastard of a way to go!"

The remaining pit-rats that had survived, now some got a cell to themselves and no longer had to share. They were still locked in at night by the masters but having a cell to yourself was a further luxury for the pit-rats.

The first two seasons at the training camp had followed the same routine mostly. Up early and meeting his two friends at the training field. Then the day was spent lifting rocks, running around the track, hell runs, stretching and more time in the pits. Demon-boy had got to know a lot more of the other pit-rats and had become friendly with most, but still was only close to his two friends.

Over the last season Demon-boy had become a "Good little fighter" as trainer had described him. He had learned everything the Trainer could teach and the Trainer getting a glimpse of his future speed and power that was just starting shine through.

That day, Demon-boy was facing off in the pit against Funny-boy. Even though they were friends, it was still highly competitive, and they fought with the intensity of a real pit fight. The only difference was they would fight until one of them hit the ground. It was something all of the slaves had adopted in the recent year. Fighting until someone was on the ground, then stepping back. They were here to train, not maim their fellow slaves. If the masters were looking on, naturally this unspoken rule was forgotten about. The Trainer had said nothing when the slaves first started this and silently agreed that less injuries would further their training for now. It was still full contact but no more jumping on top of your opponent when he was down and finishing him off.

When the Trainer had passed this info on to the Smith, the Smith had smiled. "Good," was all he said.

"Yes, Smith. I'm actually quite impressed."

"Will it affect their training at all, do you think? The loss of full contact?"

"No, Smith. The training fights are still full contact, they just don't jump on top of them once their opponent is on the ground and beat the shit out of him."

Funny-boy stepped right, then sent a fast right cross. The boy saw the move coming and stepped into Funny-boy's left side, throwing a wicked fast right into his side. He struck and almost broke his hand. Funny-boys torso, along with the rest of his body, was solid muscle from the last two summers of training. Demon-boy stepped back as a left-right combination came at him. Funny-boy was stronger and extremely fast, but the boy was faster. In fact, over the last summer, all the slaves had come to realise none were faster than Demon-boy, apart from Bulldog-boy when his blood was up. The boy had used that speed in all of his training fights.

As he stepped back, the boy sent a thundering right kick to the knee of Funny-boy but missed when Funny-boy stepped into the kick and sent a right hook into the chin of the boy. The boy flew back landed on his backside, but using the momentum, rolled backwards, coming once more to his feet. His chin hurt but the boy knew that his opponent had pulled the punch. If that had landed at full strength, the boy would have been knocked out with a possible broken jaw.

He moved in quickly to Funny-boy, who went to grab him but Demon-boy ducked under his reaching arms. He stuck his leg behind the legs of Funny-boy, then pushed with all his weight hoping to trip the larger slave onto his back. Funny-boy instead held himself upright and sent an elbow into the side of the boy's head. This rocked him and made him groggy. He stepped back to give himself room but Funny-boy followed him to finish it. As Funny-boy rushed in, the boy sent a palm straight into the nose of Funny-boy with all his speed and strength. It smacked and spurted blood all over Funny-boy's face. The boy followed up with two good punches to the face, then stepped back. He didn't step back quick enough, Funny-boy grabbed him and pulled him into a sickening head butt, knocking the boy out. When he came round, he was being helped from the pit.

Funny-boy was already standing out of the pit washing his face with cold water before holding a cloth to his bloody nose.

The boy picked himself up and walked over to Funny-boy. "Is it broken, Funny?"

"No."

"Shame. I really want to start calling you 'Broken-nose.'"

Funny-boy smiled. "So bloody annoying fighting you, you move so dam quickly! It's like chasing a bird around the food hall and not being able to get it," said Funny-boy with feeling.

"That's the point. Still was not fast enough and you still knocked me on my arse."

"Fast enough. Your first proper pit fights are this winter, yes?"

"Yes," replied the boy with feeling.

"Well, I had seven fights last winter and I can tell you now, from what I saw, no one will be as quick as you. Make sure you use it."

The boy looked at Funny-boy. He had grown larger over the last two summers, if that was possible. He was as tall as most of the Outlanders, even though he was only in his sixteenth year. If he kept growing, he would be bigger than all of them. He had become a favourite of the masters and apparently, had won them much coin. Not only was he huge and strong, he was also incredibly fast. Just not as fast Demon-boy!

"Here is one that is faster than both of us," said Funny-boy.

The boy looked behind him and saw Bulldog-boy approaching. Bulldog-boy hadn't grown in height over the last two summers and was now a lot shorter than the Demon-boy, but his body was not only well muscled, but his shoulders and arms had continued to grow. He was looking more and more like a Bulldog every season. He was fit as the Demon-boy, stronger and to the annoyance of the boy, punched and fought faster than the boy when his blood was up. Which thankfully was not often. Bulldog-boy had good control of his emotions.

"How was the fight, Sunshine?" asked the boy.

Funny-boy laughed, then cursed as his nose started bleeding again. Bulldog-boy scowled at the boy. "Fine. Trainer said we are needed in the barn for more hell runs."

Even though over the last two summers, they had spent

more and more time in the practise pits, they were run off their feet most days to keep up their fitness.

"Well, we better not keep the Bastard-face Trainer waiting then," said Demon-boy.

Funny-boy and the boy laughed, while Bulldog-boy just smiled. Bulldog-boy only laughed at things in life that you were not supposed to laugh at. He had a sick sense of humour.

The wagon moved along the track, swishing through the mud and snow on the track. The snow coming down gently as the boy and five other pit-rats sat in the back with thick blankets around them. Winter had arrived only two quarter moons before and had arrived harshly. The masters had arrived back from their raid's late autumn. Now that they were back, it was a time of drinking, celebrating and, of course, the start of the pit fight season.

The boy had been expecting this all summer. Knowing he was now fifteen seasons of age; he would soon start the real pit fights. He had known this is where he had been heading, although he hadn't fully appreciated or understood the truth until the death of Long-arm. The memories no longer held as much pain as they once did, but it still saddened him. Funny-boy and Bulldog-boy had done much work to prepare him for his first fights in the pit. Using their own experience to teach the boy what to expect. Of course, his two friends were not with him for this day.

They had left the training camp that morning, heading to another Outlander settlement further inland called Erak. A stronghold in the mountains, two days by horse and wagon from Hurarock where their training camp was. One of the masters, the one they nicknamed 'No-hair', was driving the wagon with another called Sour-face on horseback behind them. The pit rats where chained to the wagon and although a little cramped, they were warm enough and not uncomfortable. The boy watched the scenery as they left the seaside settlement town of Hurarock behind and travelled inland. Chief Hura and his warriors had left a day ahead of them to reach Erak first and no doubt to start drinking as soon as possible. The Outlanders enjoyed a drink almost as they enjoyed watching slaves beat on each other or raiding!

The boy looked at the other faces in the wagon. He knew all of them from seasons in the training camp. Across from him was Moody-boy. A youth the same age as himself and, of course, this was his first time heading off to fight in the pits as well. He had earned his nickname by always complaining and never being happy with anything. He was surly and the only time that the boy had seen him smile, was when he was in the pit and managed to pull off a well-planned move. He was of slighter build than the others in the wagon, but he made up for size by being what the Smith described as 'a sneaky little bastard'. He was a solid little fighter in the pit, but the boy was unsure how he would handle himself in the real thing. Next to him was Empty-boy. The second largest slave in the training camp and almost as big and strong as Funny-boy! The difference was he had somehow damaged his brain when he was a child. He never spoke and was not very smart. Even if he took a beating from the masters, which he had many times, because he didn't understand what they wanted, he never showed pain or cried out. He just silently got back up with no expression on his face. He did okay in the pits because as far as the others could make out, he felt no pain. This was his second season of pit fights.

Sitting to the boy's right was Stomach-boy. Named for

having an empty hole where most people had a stomach. He ate more than all the others in the camp but never seemed to put on weight. He was as tall as the boy was and had the same build. Like Empty-boy, this was his second winter fighting in the pits. The boy had faced him multiple times in the practise pits and had beaten him on many occasions. He was a solid fighter but as the Smith had said, 'nothing special'.

He didn't need to look to the back of the wagon to know who was sitting there; Sick-boy. He had earned that name as all the other slaves were convinced that he was sick in the head. He enjoyed inflicting pain and that was evident in the way he fought, taking his time to make an opponent hurt as much as possible. He had jet black hair and even though only sixteen, a thick slave's beard was already covering his face. The boy respected him but had no direct bond like some of the other slaves. This was due to the fact that Sick-boy had been a good friend of Long-arm. The boy and he had never spoken of what happened, but the boy was certain Sick-boy was not at all happy with him. Whenever he was around, Sick-boy stared at him with anger in his eyes. He was also a one summer veteran to the pit fights. He had become a favourite of the masters due to his habit of tormenting his opponents.

The wagon rumbled on as the sun started to go down. Soon, they would stop for the night before continuing on tomorrow.

They arrived after lunch on the second day. Erak was a mountain stronghold that had been dug into the side of a hill. It was only half the size of Hurarock but had mighty stone walls surrounding it. It sat halfway up a small hill with large stonewalls and fields of wheat and other grains stretching for miles, all of which lay barren now as it was winter. They had followed the dirt road winding through these fields, through the gate and soon as they had crossed the gatehouse, the wagon hit cobbles. The streets were all paved. The boy took great interest in the small town. Children ran everywhere playing games and yelling. The buildings were all stone with slate roofs, with no wood construction anywhere to be seen. Even though it was midday and the sun was high in the sky, the entire town was sitting in the shadow of the mountain range that it sat beside. The boy couldn't help but think how far the sea was away from Erak, considering the Outlanders live to raid. He was brought back to reality when the wagon stopped.

"Out, pit-rats."

The slaves looked up and noticed that they were outside a huge building of stone. The stone was of the same grey dull stone as the other buildings except the corners and the main doorway. Here the rock was dull and black. The slaves didn't get a chance to get a good look at the building as they were unchained and lead to a side door further along the building. They were led into a small room with stone walls, no windows and another door leading to the main hall. The master led them I and threw a bag at their feet.

"Food and water in there! Rest here and someone will come for you. "Fight well, pit-rat scum" the master said, then left the building.

They saw the door leading outside closed shut, then heard someone locking it. The boy looked around the room. It was empty apart from two candle holders on the walls with candles burning brightly to light the small room. The slaves all sat against the wall and took a light meal for their lunch. The bag had contained some bread, an apple each and some water skins. The slaves lost in their own minds said nothing and just sat there staring at the walls.

It was some time before the inner door to the main hall opened and voices from the main hall got instantly louder.

Food had been brought to the slaves earlier. A basic broth with some meat floating in it. The boy didn't recognise the meat but didn't care. After they had eaten, the slaves all started stretching and doing basic exercisers to warm up their bodies. Sick-boy sat on the ground muttering to himself while he punched the stone wall. The boy had seen Bulldog-boy do this and knew it was a way that they got themselves worked up before a fight.

All of them stood and followed a warrior they had never seen before into the bright light of the main hall. The main hall was much bigger than the Chief's hall at Hurarock. To the right of the door, they entered was table filled with food, and beside it large barrels of drink. Barrels so large that they were taller than the tallest man. Some people were gathered around the food, getting a tiny bit of food or drink before the fights started. The opposite side of the hall held stone steps that started at the floor and stepped up all the way to the high ceiling. Sitting on these steps was hundreds of people. All yelling themselves hoarse as the slaves were brought in. On the left of the entrance, they had come through was an elevated stone floor area. On this was a long table filled with food; and sitting at that table were twelve people including Chief Hura and his son affectionately known as Son-of-Angry-man. No doubt, the Chief of this stronghold was sitting there as well, as the raised floor gave them an excellent view of what sat in the middle of the main hall. The pit! As deep as the practise pits, but the side walls where lined with stone. The floor looked like it was also made of stone, but with dirt thrown over the top. Old blood stains soaked the stone walls of the pit. Sitting on the opposite side of the pit were the five other slaves that the pit-rats would face.

They were sat on the floor facing their opponents. They

all looked at the ground and kept their heads down. The Chief of Erak stood and addressed the cheering crowds.

"First fight of the season has arrived, my people." The assembled crowd cheered. "My Brother of the blood, Chief Hura has brought some of his pit-rats to do battle. We have had good food, fine ale and now we shall have fine entertainment." The crowd cheered loudly again. "Let the fights and wagering begin!" the Chief shouted.

The boy saw one of the warriors of Erak clip Sick-boy across the head. Sick-boy got up and jumped down into the pit. The boy was watching and had to raise his head to see in the pit.

"Don't, lower your head and look at the floor," whispered Stomach-boy.

The boy heard the warning in his voice and quickly looked at the floor.

"We are not allowed to watch the fights. Just look at the ground until you are slapped on the head, then you get into the pit for your turn."

Stomach got a slap for speaking.

"No talking," said the warrior from Erak.

The boy sat there and had to listen to the roaring of the crowd, not knowing what was going on. The only thing that he could see was his feet, as he sat on the stone floor, knees up into his chest, arms around his legs and his head between his legs. He had been tempted to sneak a look but heard again the advice of the Trainer who had been left behind.

"If the other slaves warn you, listen!"

He took the advice of Stomach-boy seriously. He was nervously waiting for his time in the pit when he heard the Chief of Erak's voice boom out once again.

Demon-boy was lost in his own apprehension and time flowed quickly whilst his fellow pit-rats were in the pit.

"That is the first four fights, my people. Refresh your drinks, grab some food and we will start the final match."

He could hear lots of the sitting crowd rush to the doors to relieve themselves outside or run over to the food table to grab more drink. They rushed past him and more than one kicked him on their way past. He could feel his anger rise but held it in check. Plenty of time in the pit to unleash.

No, no, he told himself. Not to unleash. Stay calm, focused, and controlled. He breathed deeply and tried to keep his anger in check.

After a short time, the Chief's voice boomed once more.

"Take your seats. The last fight is about to start."

The boy heard stamping of booted feet as the crowd rushed back to their positions or their seats.

"We have something special for the last fight."

The boy sighed. Shit, bastard masters.

"Chief Hura and I have been placing some friendly wagers."

The crowd roared with laughter.

"However, on this night, we have wagered on the total outcome of all the fights. The wager that more of his pit-rats would emerge in victory than mine! The bet was 250 silver coins."

The crowd erupted with cheering again. The boy did not register the amount of 250 silver coins, he had no understanding of coins, but by the way the crowd cheered it must have been a large amount.

"As you know, the score is currently two wins each. Here is my question to my brother of the blood from Hurarock." The room went silent as the crowd waited for their leader to speak. "For this final bout, do you have the nerve to raise the amount to 500 silver pieces?"

The crowd erupted again in cheering, most of the crowd

indeed on their feet. Not that the boy could see but the Master, this Angry-man just laughed. His son beside him also laughed. Chief Hura stood to address the crowd.

"You want, my friend, to double the bet?"

"Yes. If you have the courage!"

Everyone in the room laughed, including the Chief Hura and his retainers.

"Let me see first who the pit-rat is that is left to fight for me and my silver coin."

The boy was slapped on the head and as he stood and turned to face the Chief Hura, the crowd quietened down to hear what the visiting Chief would say. The boy finally looked up at the Angry-man, the Chief of Hurarock. The Chief showed surprise but hid it well. He hadn't realised Demon-boy was fighting. The boy knew in an instant that the Chief was surprised. The Chief looked at him, questioning. The boy looked at the Chief in the eyes, and not sure why at the time, he nodded once. The Chief and his son smiled.

"I'll take that wager!" shouted Chief Hura.

The crowd cheered and sat themselves down. As the boy went to turn around and get in the pit, he caught a look from Son-of-Angry-man. The son drew his finger slowly across his throat. The meaning was simple. Either win or you die.

The boy jumped down onto the pit, landing cleanly on his feet. He looked across at his foe for the first time. The slave was taller than the boy by two inches, slim and muscled. The slave stretched his arms whilst staring at the boy. The boy didn't stretch, he just stood staring at the slave, the only movement was his chest from his breathing and the flexing of his arms as his fists opened and closed.

"So, who is this slave of yours, Chief Erak?"

"Third season in the pit and last winter was undefeated. The other slaves call him Ice- head. Next summer, he turns eighteen and will be fighting in death bouts. We look forward to it."

The Chief Erak was smiling, pleased at the little trick that he had just pulled. Goading Chief Hura into upping the wager but when he looked across, Chief Hura was smiling.

"And your slave?"

"WE call him the Demon-child and it's his first time in the pit," he said with a quiet smile.

Son-of-Angry-man roared laughing at what his father had said.

Chief Erak didn't miss the emphasis put on the word 'We'.

"Why do you call him that?"

"He killed my brother-in-law, when he was being taken in a raid."

"I met your brother-in-law, no offence my brother but he was not exactly a good warrior."

Smiling, Chief Hura resounded. "The Demon-child was only five summers old, when he killed him!"

Chief Erak blew out slowly.

"He also killed another slave in a training bout. I'm confident that he will do okay."

Chief Erak was not as confident now, but he stood and shouted in a clear voice, "FIGHT!"

As he heard the word 'fight', the Demon-boy rushed into action. The Demon-boy had whispered the same word over and over again to himself, whilst he was waiting to start; 'snow weasel'.

The other slave was a little slower off the mark and by the time that they reached each other, Demon-boy was a blur of movement. He stepped to the left and thundered a quick right hand to the face of the other slave, connecting to the left eye. He stepped back in time to dodge a fast counter punch. He ducked and weaved, dodging everything the other slave could throw at him. The other slave was getting frustrated and threw a kick at the boy to push him back. Using a trick that he learnt from Funny-boy, he stepped in and grabbed the throat of the other slave, pulling him into a crashing head butt that smashed the nose of the other slave. As the other slave took a step a back, he followed him, not willing to let him escape. He nailed his nose again with a swift left and followed up with a right as fast as he could. The punch exploding against the side of the slave's head! The taller slave was groggy now, but still standing. He tried to come forward but lost his opponent. He didn't see the boy had crouched down. The boy surged up and connected with a mighty left uppercut, then a solid right that turned all the lights off for the other slave. The boy stepped back and let the slave fall flat on his face.

The crowd cheered loudly; Demon-boy couldn't hear anything at all including his own thoughts. The boy climbed out of the pit. He stood, then looked to his Chief and once again, he didn't know why he did it, he bowed in respect to his Chief. Then he sat back down with his fellow pit-rats. As he sat looking at the floor, relief washed over him, and with the relief creeped a smile. He had won his first bout.

Chapter Nine

Winter arrived again and the Demon-boy sat looking at the setting sun. He thought back over the last three summers of hand to hand fighting in the pits. Many fights that had blurred into one mass of violence. He could no longer separate the individual fights or their details. He thought back over the training he had pushed through, the exhaustion and the pain of every day spent training. He took a sip from the clay jug that was filled with spirits, feeling the warmth of the liquid slowly creep down his throat and spread throughout his chest. He thought back to traveling through the Outlander County for fights. Some pits were close by, being only a day or two away. Others were many days away and the only way to get to them all, was a tour of many days sitting in the wagon, fighting at one settlement, then moving on the next day and then the next, a constant traveling that left the boy far too much time to think. The last tour before winters end, they had been on the road for full moon cycle, with the six fights making the boy feel more exhausted than any of the training that he'd received. He arrived back at Hurarock bruised, more tired than he had ever been, and resentful. Always resentful! His anger and resentment had grown over the last three summers as he said goodbye to slaves who went away to fight but never returned. As a boy, he had almost been accepting of the life as a slave, after all, he couldn't remember any other life. However now, as a teenager his anger had been unleashed. He'd had learnt some measure of control over his emotions, but they were always still there. Sitting beneath the surface ready to explode.

He took another sip, then with his left hand, rubbed his right shoulder. It still hurt from the early day's training where Funny-boy had whacked him with a practise maul. At the beginning of spring, the boy had been included in the weapon training with the others that had already reached death bout age. He accepted the tuition with weapons like he had accepted everything else in his life, determined to master it and stubbornly not giving up.

The number of pit rats had once again dwindled, many dying in the pit. Of the original one hundred or so, now only Twenty-eight slaves lived and trained in the camp and because of this, the camp often felt empty.

As Demon-boy was one of the youngest in the camp, he was one of the last to reach death bout age. Funny-boy and Bulldog-boy continued to pass on their experience gained in the death bouts.

Demon-boy was taking one last sip when he heard someone approaching.

"A fine night, boy," said the Smith, leaning up against the wall of the smithy beside the boy.

"Aye, it is," said Demon-boy.

Demon-boy stood with his own jug in hand, slowly sipping the fiery spirit that was in abundance in the Outlander settlement and somehow the Smith regularly got his hands on a few jugs. Summers ago, the biggest pleasure for the slaves was being fed the occasional piece of meat and that happened very rarely, usually only when a pit fight had gone extremely well for the masters.

Now however, the Trainer and the Smith had got access to a limited supply of Firemer. The strong spirit that was brewed in Hura, not enough to get the slaves all drunk every night, but enough that on the occasional evening, they all shared a cup together.

"Have you heard the news, boy?"

"What news?"

"A new intake of slaves is arriving in the morning."

"More pit rats?"

"Yep. Now that you and the other lads are in death bouts and there are not many of you left, the bastard-masters no doubt want to start training more to fill the ranks."

"I'm not yet in the death bouts, Smith!" he whispered.

"No, but you will be this winter. Are you ready?"

"No, maybe I'll just lie down and die in the first one?"

The Smith chuckled. He knew the boy was joking as the boy was too stubborn to die that way. "It's been done before!"

Demon-boy thought back to a summer ago when another pit rat had got into the ring for his first death bout. Instead of fighting, he smiled, threw down his weapon and charged his opponent. He had his throat sliced and as he fell over bleeding out, he laughed. The boy hadn't seen it but had heard about it from the other slaves that were there.

"I remember. The bastard–masters were not happy. The next five days of training were the worst I have ever had."

"Trainer got the worst of it!" said the Smith quietly.

The masters had blamed the Trainer and he had been beaten badly. He had lost his left eye in the beating and it had taken many full moons before he could resume training the slaves."

"They arrive tomorrow?"

"So, I heard."

"I hope like hell that doesn't mean that we have to share cells again!"

They both smiled. All of the pit-rats had got used to having their own cells and got used to the limited number of slaves now housed in the camp.

"You will have to see. How was weapons training today?"

"Good. I'm starting to get a feel for the weapons."

"Trainer said you are really coming to terms with the hand axe!"

"I suppose I am. I enjoy the short sword work, but the hand axe just seems more…" his words trailed off.

"Natural?"

"Kind of. Just feels comfortable in my hand."

"You are training with a dagger in your offhand and not a shield?"

"Yes, did Trainer tell you that as well?"

"Yes, he did."

The boy looked at the Smith, unsure where the conversation was going.

"You going to give me a lecture on not using a shield as well?"

The Smith laughed out loud that made the boy smile.

"No. I have given you enough lectures over the years, I doubt you want another from me."

"No, I do not."

"Although instead of the dagger, why not use a short sword in your offhand?"

"I would get myself tangled up!"

"Not if you practise. Short sword will give you advantage over the dagger and give you more reach."

The boy had thought about it before but couldn't see how to move cleanly with it and not get himself all tangled up.

"We will see," he replied.

"Well boy, I better get myself to bed. If there are new arrivals, I'll have more work tomorrow, mark my word."

As the Smith walked off, the boy returned to watch the last of the sun disappear behind the mountains. The Smith had become so much more than a simple blacksmith in the camp. He had somehow managed to dip his hand into every barrel as he called it. He was now supervising most of the training camp and the slaves, organising the work in a more efficient manner. Apart from the training of the slaves that was still the area of the Trainer, Smith's word was finally in all other aspects of the training camp. The masters said nothing when they saw how efficient the camp had become. With the help of the Smith, the Cook and her small staff had planted a garden in the middle of the training field which was mainly wasted land. The slaves ran around the outside of it and didn't really use the inner field itself apart from stretching. The stretching could be done anywhere.

The inner field was planted with potatoes and other starchy vegetables. The cook's helpers had also ripped down the nearest storage shed to the wall, to the left of the gate as you walked in. In its place, there was now a large herb garden that also grew some lettuce and other vegetables in the summer. The camp over the last six summers had changed, the boy reflected as he took one last sip of the jug. Then, he turned and made his way to the barrack cells.

Demon-boy ducked under a thrust that was coming for his head fast by the double-handed wooden axe held by Funny-boy. He came round with his axe, aiming at the thigh of Funny-boy, which connected. He pivoted away using his offhand wooden short sword to brush off the large axe as it came down to try and catch him. The boy almost faster than the eye could see, completing a full circle before bringing his reverse end of the axe crashing into Funny-boy's arm pit.

"Killing stroke!" yelled the Trainer.

Both slaves stepped back from each other, a slight sweat upon them. Funny-boy was blowing a little heavier as he reached under his armpit to massage where he had been whacked.

"You know how fast he is! Why did you step into range to let him catch you like that?" the Trainer said from the top of the pit, looking down at Funny-boy.

Funny-boy just shrugged and got out of the pit.

"Next pair in!" Trainer shouted.

Funny-boy nodded and climbed out of the pit, as the other two jumped in. Demon-boy handed him a water skin with a small smile.

"You move too bloody fast," said Funny-boy, between gasps.

Demon-boy said nothing.

"Using a short sword in your off hand is a good move. More reach than that dagger and you use it well," replied Funny-boy.

Demon-boy had struggled for the last two quarter moons to get used to having a short sword in his hand but it was starting to feel more natural.

"It still feels weird."

"Bullshit, you use it well. It certainly makes a difference."

Demon-boy sat down watching the other pair circle. He

won most of his practise bouts against Funny-boy. His strength and size counting for little when the pair were fighting with weapons. Demon-boy's speed was amazing, and he used it to great effect.

"One more quarter moon, Demon and you are in the pit for real. You ready?"

"Aye. Let's just hope whoever I face is as slow and clumsy as you."

Funny-boy laughed. He'd watched with pleasure as Demon-boy matured. He was not so silent, not so distant, and now joined in with the banter of his two closest friends. He still had a focused anger behind his eyes but had learnt to control himself.

They both heard shouting from the training field and stood up to watch.

The new arrivals had arrived at first light today and Bulldog-boy had been tasked with the first day of training for the new arrivals. In all forty new slaves had arrived. The Smith had made the new arrivals all share a barrack room, the older pit-rats still got a room to themselves.

"Were we ever that young?" commented Demon-boy.

"You were. A baby straight from the teat when you arrived. Looks like Bulldog-boy is enjoying himself."

Demon-boy looked over to where Bulldog-boy was running behind the pack of new arrivals as they ran around the track. He was yelling at them and letting the world know how useless they were. If any of them fell back from the main pack, they would feel a whack on their legs from the short wooden sword that he carried in his hand.

"My turn tomorrow apparently," muttered Funny-boy.

"Really?"

"Yes. The senior pit-rats will take it in turns to spend a day training the new arrivals. I'm sure you will get a turn."

"I hope not. I need more practise before next quarter moon."

The winter had arrived three days before with a flurry of snow that had landed on the ground. It would get worse in the next full moon. With winter here, Demon-boy's time to enter death bouts had also arrived.

The quarter moon had gone swiftly with less focus on physical training and more time in the pit. Demon-boy had got used to using a short sword in his offhand and knew it complimented his hand axe much better than a dagger.

He had a day off to train the new slaves. An amusing experience if one could call it that. He didn't yell at the new arrivals as all the other senior pit rats had, just stared with a focused intensity that he thought may have scared them more. They never slacked under him, even though he very rarely hit the new arrivals or vented on them in any way. He still remembered the look of shock and fear on their faces when the Trainer had introduced him as Demon-boy. He smiled at the memory.

He was wearing many welts and bruises from his practise bouts two days ago. All of the punishment coming from his last two fights he'd had with Bulldog-boy. Bulldog-boy was stronger and, in some instances, just as fast as Demon-boy. Bulldog-boy also used two weapons in the pit, although he favoured two hand axes. He was fast, strong and would win more often than not. However, during their last two practise bouts, Demon-boy got the better of him. He looked over at Bulldog-boy who was sitting straight across from him in the wagon. Bulldog-boy was asleep, another skill he excelled at. In the end he had never said the words that he thought needed to be said. He never apologised to his two friends, but somehow it did not seem to matter. They were closer than ever.

Sitting either side of his friend were two other slaves. Slaves that he had got to know over the last five summers and respected but was not close to as he was his other two friends; Firehead-boy on the left of Bulldog-boy, who had flaming red hair and a temper to match. As a youth, he would pick a fight at anything but since he had grown into manhood, he had mellowed somewhat. He still had his temper, but it never usually got the better of him. Firehead-boy was twenty summers and the oldest in the camp. Of average size height and width, but like all the other pit-rats, was ripped muscle from all the training.

On the other side of his friend was, of course, Sick-boy. Sick-boy now shaved his thick beard with a knife most days but left the hair above his lip and the bottom of his chin continue to grow. Sick-boy and Demon-boy had still not grown close. In fact, Sick-boy was close to no one in the camp. He stuck to himself and preferred to enjoy it that way.

"It's not very often that we get to travel together," whispered Funny-boy, from his left shoulder.

It was true. Demon-boy could count on one hand the times all three of them had got to travel together for fights. He was not sure how the bastard-masters went about choosing who was fighting. There seemed to be no pattern that he could work out.

"No, it's not, and I'm not unhappy about it"

Funny-boy smiled and went back to watching the scenery. They still were not allowed to speak, and even though they were no longer chained to the wagons, the masters trusted them enough now, they knew not to push boundaries. Demon-boy smiled as he realised none of them would ever think about trying to escape. It was never a thought that crossed their mind. They knew too well; they would not get far.

They had been in this wagon for three days now and although boring, Demon-boy found it to be very peaceful. A good time to clear one's mind before the pit. This trip saw the five pit-rats traveling once again to the capital of the province of Pulnuk, the neighbouring province to the one they lived in. The largest city on in the Outlander nation! All of the pit-rats had fought here before. In fact, it is where Bulldog-boy had won the finals of the knockout tournament. A large competition that was held every summer cycle before the spring arrived. All provinces entering their best fighter, and then one by one, the pit-rats where knocked out until only two slaves where left. Bulldog-boy had reached and won the final. He received no reward of course; he was a slave, but he certainly let none of the other slaves forget his win. In fact, he mentioned it at least once a day, much to the amusement of Funny-boy and Demon-boy, and the annoyance of most of the other slaves.

All five of the pit-rats from Hura sat in a cold room with only two lamps hanging from the wall. They had arrived that afternoon and been shoved straight away into this room off the main hall. Unlike other fights, they would be led one at a time to the pit before being returned. Two of the pit-rats had already won their fights, Sick-boy and Funny-boy had been out there longer than normal, before being brought back. They both sat against the wall drinking from water skins. Funny-boy was still breathing heavily from his bout, whilst Sick-boy nursed a cut to his ribs, holding a wet cloth against it.

Firehead-boy was currently in the pit. You could never tell by the noise coming from the main hall who had won and who hadn't, so pit-rats tried to block out the noise. That is what Demon-boy was doing as he was up next. All of a sudden, the crowd raised their voices louder than normal, and they all knew the fight was over. They waited for the door, but Firehead-boy didn't enter. After some time, a warrior came through and yelled, "Next up!"

Demon-boy climbed to his feet, trying not to think of where Firehead-boy was, both of his weapons in belt around his waist. He had short trousers on but was shirtless as this was the rules of the pit. The slaves wore leather guards on each wrist that had been stained black in the colour of the Hura Province. He walked to the door and then he heard Funny-boy.

"End it quickly. They try to draw out the fight and trust me, they are somehow fitter than we are!"

Demon-boy nodded his thanks, then walked out of the room. Once again, his senses were assaulted from the sights and sounds. The noise of yelling voices, claiming money they had won and bragged about. Heat from the fire pits that surrounded the great hall, heating the room to a comfortable temperature for watching, but an uncomfortable heat to fight in. He didn't need to look up as he had been here before. The pit was surrounded by wooden seating, a tiered seating that went all the way to the top off the walls. A grandstand system surrounded the pit and allowed more than a thousand Outlanders to watch with joy as slaves hacked each other to pieces! He knew without looking where Chief Hura would be sitting. He was always in the front row with whatever Chief ruled this province. His bastard son sitting beside him.

'Snow-Weasel'

He whispered to himself to calm his thoughts as he jumped down into the pit. The youth opposite him was slightly shorter than him but the same size in every other aspect. He noticed the youth's black eyes glaring at him, eyes staring out amongst his long black hair. He had a powerful chest and looked older than even Firehead-boy. He held a short sword in one hand and in the other, a small round buckler shield.

Both of the pit-rats stared each other down, lost to their own thoughts, whilst they waited for the word for them to begin.

"FIGHT!" screamed the Chief of Pulnuk.

'Snow-weasel' was the only thought that crossed his mind as his body lurched into motion. His opponent had reacted faster and came in first with his shield, his sword trailing and ready to swing. Demon-boy had already planned his first move and the crowd went deathly silent as his opponent stopped mid step and only halfway across the pit, Demon-boy's hand axe buried in his face. Before his opponent could fall, he had followed up with all his speed and pulled the axe free, blood from his opponent's face covering him in the process, before swinging on his heal and slashing the pit-rat's throat with his sword. He stepped back as the body fell to the floor of the pit. Lifeless! The fight lasting seconds, the way he had planned it.

The silence ended with an explosion of screaming voices, as the warriors all stood and cheered. The boy didn't notice the cheers, and if he did, he would not have cared. He tucked his weapons back into his belt and climbed out of the pit. Following on from what he started three summers ago, he presented himself to his Chief, stood a few metres away, and bowed. Son-of-Angry-man was laughing and yelling with the rest of the crowd, Angry-man, Chief of Hura just smiled a cold smile as his pit-rat stood from the bow and walked back to the side room.

"You are back bloody quick," said Funny-boy, as he jumped to his feet and ran across to him.

"Yep."

"What the hell happened?"

He said nothing at first, slumping against the wall and letting himself fall into a sitting position. He took a drink from a water skin and waited for the adrenalin to work its way through his system. Finally, after a while, he turned to the others.

"You're not happy that I survived my first death bout?" even as he said the words, it allowed the realisation of what he had said sink in. He had survived his first death bout. Relief flowing through him and a smile on his face.

Funny-boy reached him and squatted down.

"Why are you smiling, what happened?"

"I threw my axe!" was all he said, laughing aloud.

"Say no more, I want to hear this when I get back," said Bulldog-boy, as he left the room and was escorted to the main hall.

Sitting in the wagon with blankets wrapped around them, all of the slaves sat warm, comfortable and a little drunk. After all of them had won their death bouts, Chief Hura's son had given two jugs each of Firemer spirit to each of the pit-rats. Firehead-boy had taken some nasty cuts to his gut, but the cuts had been stitched and smeared with honey to stop infection. The morning that they left Pulnuk, they had eaten a good lunch sitting in the wagon and with nothing else to do, had started drinking. Snow was coming down hard and the wind was blowing, but they were not bothered.

"You threw your axe?" asked Bulldog-boy.

"Yes. The slave came at me and I just threw my axe at him as hard as I could."

"It connected?" said Sick-boy.

Which was a surprise, he never joined in any conversations.

"Yes. The axe got buried in his face."

They all laughed.

"Dangerous move," replied Firehead-boy.

"He died straight away?" mentioned Sick-boy.

"Not sure, but once I pulled my axe out, I cut his throat with my sword to be sure. Then he fell over!"

They all laughed again. Dying slaves was not usually a laughing matter, not something the pit-rats would ever make a joke of, but none of them apart from Demon-boy had been drunk before and they all got a little carried away. Demon-boy turned to Sick-boy.

"You should drink more often Sick-boy. Your actually not bad company when you're drunk."

They all waited for Sick-boy to say some violent comment or react badly like he always did, but his reply had them all laughing again.

"Yes, I should. I find you a more agreeable person too, and the more I drink, the prettier you get."

Their laughter died as they heard galloping horses. They wrapped their blankets around them tighter, hid their jugs and remained silent. Within minutes, Chief Hura, his son and some of his warriors had caught up. They slowed as they got to the wagon and the Chief rode beside it in silence, staring at Demon-boy before finally speaking.

"That is the first time in living memory that all pit-rats from one Chief have won all their fights." His words were even and cold. The slaves kept their head down. This Chief was not known among the slaves as 'Angry-man' for nothing. Which is why they were all completely shocked when he continued.

"Well done. You all fought well. Enjoy the jugs of spirits

that my son has given you." That was all he said before he rode off, his son and warriors following. They all remained quiet not quite knowing what to make of the compliment. It was Firehead-boy that broke the silence

"Bugger me."

They all giggled.

"Can I?" replied Funny-boy.

They all roared with laughter again. As they laughed, Demon-boy passed his jug up to the driver. The Driver, the warrior they had called No-nose, as he had lost most of his nose to some sharp weapon summers before, looked at him.

Slowly, the warrior took the jug and took a long sip of the half empty jug. He went to pass it back, but the boy told him to keep it. The warrior nodded his thanks and flicked the reins, driving the large wagon horses to speed up. Thinking back to some advice the Smith had given him a summer ago.

"Not all the bastard-masters are the same. Don't paint them all with the same brush boy, you never know when you will need a friend amongst them!"

Demon-boy opened his second jug and took a sip. The others still gigging at some off-colour story Funny-boy had broken into. They rode through the snow laughing and drinking.

The masters had slowed their horses to a walk to give the horses a chance to catch their breath. They had been riding hard all morning and the morning fog of the ale and spirits that they had drunk last night, slowly clearing. Chief Hura, his son and five other warriors chatted slowly as they walked.

"Why did you give away ten jugs of Firemer to the pit-rats?" Chief asked.

It was not said with anger, or acceptance. More a calculating question.

"They won me a lot of silver, father. I was feeling generous!"

"You are not well known for kind treatment of slaves. I have lost count of how many you have killed."

"They are slaves, father! They live or die on our whim!"

"Which is why I ask you, why give away spirits to them?"

"Was it not you, father, who taught me to keep the slaves off balance? To keep them guessing at all times! To never have them get relaxed or able to predict what you will do!"

"I taught you that, yes."

"Well then. They know that I will beat them or kill them if I feel like it, or if they anger at me or even look at me in the wrong way. The rare act of giving them something, would that not throw them of balance the most?"

Chief Hura was impressed. Although his son had grown into a great warrior, strong, fast, and ruthless, he had doubted his ability to lead because of his inability to think. This was a time he had seen his son do something that showed intelligence.

"Yes. I taught you all that. So, were you playing with them?"

"No. As I said they won me much coin."

"How much did you win?"

"Eight hundred silver coins," the son replied, with a smile on his face.

The Chief smiled to himself. He had won five hundred silver coins as he doubted some of his pit-rats to win. His doubts stopping him from wagering too much. "A tidy sum. It was a worthy wager."

"And you father? How much did you win?"

"You know how much."

The son laughed, knowing he had won more than his father.

"You doubted our pit-rats?"

"Only one of them. I expected and had hoped for the Demon-child to die in is first death bout!"

"And what a fight it was!" he spoke loudly.

The other warriors cheered. They followed the lead of the Chief's son and had bet on the outcome. Even though they didn't win as much as the Chief or his son, they had less to wager after all, they still rode with their coin pouches full of silver.

The son continued. "I have never seen a warrior move so fast. It was over in seconds!"

"Yes, not what I expected. Although the axe throw was a good one."

"It was a perfect throw, father. Don't mistake me, I hate the slave I do, and have enjoyed beating him when he lived at the work camp. But he has made me plenty of coin last season and I expect to make a lot more this season."

"I expected him to die. How many obstacles have we put in his way?"

"Many. I sometimes think you spend too much time worrying about him. He will live, or he may die. Either way, we can make coin and pride of his wins."

The Chief knew his son was right. The Demon-child had always held himself straight, He knew how to hold himself and be submissive when the masters were around but there was something in the boy's looks, fire behind the boy's eyes that no other slave had. It was something the Chief didn't like. The Chief had watched him once when the boy thought no one else was around. He had snuck into the indoor training barn one morning, climbing up into the dark of the barn's rafters, where he would not be seen. He had told no one as the thought of the Chief of the province sneaking into one of his own buildings, would be a grand joke and leave all of his men laughing.

He had watched the training for two hours and in particular, watched and kept his eyes on the Demon-child and the way he trained. Strong, fast, and fitter than all the others. A pride of who he was that could be seen from every action he did. A pride that flowed through his veins and even affected the other slaves. When he was around the other slaves, they fed off his energy, fed off his work ethic and most of all, fed off his confidence. Whether the Trainer or in fact the Demon-child knew, he was leading these slaves and they were following. This was a concern if he chooses to rebel, the others would follow without a second thought, and that was dangerous.

He was not worried about the slaves rebelling. He had four thousand warriors in this settlement alone and they would not pose a problem. He was not even worried about the waste of coin. The training camp would come to if he had all the slaves slaughtered. He had won so many more coins in the last three summers that the training camp had paid for itself many times over already. He was worried, he did just not know why.

"If he worries you that much, father, kill him. Call it another object lesson!"

Even though his son had shown some insight in being generous towards the slaves, once again in that one comment, he once again proved he hadn't thought the situation through. Yes, he could kill the boy, but he knew the rest of the slaves would not train as hard or fight as hard if he was not there. It was the power of the Demon-boy that no one else saw, his ability to draw to himself other men and lead them, an ability that came naturally and was done in a non-conscious manner, the boy doing it without knowing what he was doing. A natural leader.

"He certainly is a demon in that pit," the Chief finally said.

The warriors all agreed, laughing with each other. The Chief continued to think on it, realising his son was actually right, another object lesson was needed. Something to break the boy, not kill him.

Chapter Ten

The first season of death bouts went quickly for Demon-boy. Trainer had been correct when he said, "you will never forget your first death bout, but all the silver in the world will not make you remember the face of your opponents of the second or third."

All of his fights blurring into one single image of violence and death. He could remember certain parts of his fights, especially if an opponent completed a move that could be learned from. His natural speed and aggression leading him to win his fights, time and time again out classing all of his opponents. That is not to say he remained untouched by his opponents. Fighting in death bouts was dangerous, there had been many times that he received cuts and bruises. He had become a favourite of the Outlanders in the settlements that he had visited, but his own masters always showing bitter contempt for him, no matter how much silver he won them. Demon-boy no longer cared and nursed his hate, telling himself he would kill the masters one day, especially Chief Hura. Of course, his three friends nursed the same hate, but apart from Bulldog-boy, none with the same intensity of Demon-boy. They all joked of killing the masters one day. For Demon-boy, it was no joke, no dream. It was a need, a goal and nothing to joke about. He kept these feelings to himself mostly and although his friends knew of the face value of his hate, they would not guess at how deep it went.

"No boy, never ever turn around like that. You are taking your eye off your opponent and leaving yourself vulnerable," said Demon-boy.

He was in the pits with one of the younger pit-rats sharing his knowledge. Demon-boy was an efficient fighter, but as he himself admitted, not a great teacher.

"I have seen you spin like that!" said the young pit-rat.

"Yes, you have. If you watched closely, it is always after an attack that has left the opponent off balanced or stunned. Also, watch my head. It turns quicker than my body, so when my weapon comes around, I am looking at the place that I am going to strike."

The young pit-rat nodded, but not fully understanding.

"I'll help demonstrate!" said Bulldog-boy as he jumped into the pit holding his two wooden practise hand axes.

Demon-boy nodded, and the young pit-rat jumped out and joined the other younger slaves to watch. As Bull-dog boy and Demon-boy faced off, other slaves joined to watch. The two were the fastest in the camp when it comes to weapon work, their fights were always great displays.

"Loser gives the winner a foot rub?" said Bulldog-boy with a grin on his face.

Demon-boy smiled and launched his attack, exploding into action. He led with his left-hand sword coming in high aiming for the head. It was almost blocked by an axe, but Demon-boy pulled back quickly, then came under and up with his own wooden axe, aiming for the chin of Bulldog-boy.

Bulldog-boy smiling and stepping to his right foot then spinning to his left, his axe coming around very quickly aiming for the knee. Demon-boy was not there but had continued forward as his right-hand axe rose in the air, also stepping to his left and steeping out of range. The crowd that had gathered watching in awe as the two stalked each other across the pit, stepping slowly before exploding into action. The two had faced each other many times and now that Demon-boy knew not to let Bulldog-boy get too angry, which seemed to increase his speed and velocity, allowing him to win easily. Bulldog-boy tried something new. However, he launched his right-hand axe with all of his power, hurling it straight at Demon-boy's head. The axe flew straight and Demon-boy only just got out of the way. Bulldog-boy, however, hadn't waited and followed the thrown axe with all the explosive speed that he could. Bulldog-boy had swapped his other axe to his right hand and came round in wide circle to catch Demon-boy, who was still a bit off balance and almost caught him; almost. Demon-boy had stepped to his right foot like Bulldog-boy had done before, but in a whirl of speed almost too quick for the eye of the watchers, swung to his left and came round full circle. He stopped his wooden sword just in time to slow it as it hit the back of Bulldog-boy's neck.

"Killing blow," said Silent-boy who was also watching.

The pit rats cheered as the two in the pit caught their breath. Bulldog-boy stood back and smiled.

"I keep forgetting how fast you are!" he said.

Demon-boy put his weapons into his side rope belt and also smiled.

"Almost caught me with that throw!" he replied.

Bulldog-boy walked across and picked up the axe that he had thrown, wiping dirt from the wooden blade.

"If I had been faster off the mark, I would have caught you. Next time."

They both laughed as they got out of the pit.

"You see boy? My head always turned faster than my body," said Demon-boy to the young pit-rat he had been training.

"Yes, I saw it. You moved so fast!" he replied.

"You too can have the same speed, you just have to train and develop it," said Demon-boy.

The other slaves all went back to their training as the Smith hobbled over. Bulldog-boy and Demon-boy talking as the Smith reached them.

"Demon-boy, Bulldog-boy," the Smith said, in greeting.

"Smith. Everything okay?" replied Bulldog-boy.

"No. It's not."

Both of the pit-rats looked at the Smith and noticing the look of concern on his face.

"What the matter?" asked Demon-boy.

The Smith looked at the ground for a second before looking up and staring at Demon-boy.

"The bastard-masters want to see you, now."

"Me?" replied Demon-boy.

"What has he done wrong?" said Bulldog-boy.

"Nothing as far as I know, which worries me," replied the Smith.

Demon-boy looked over at the other pit-rats training. Funny-boy was taking the younger slaves through fight training in one of the pits.

"Now means now, boy. No time to brood. Let's go!"

"I'll see you after!" said Bulldog-boy as he clapped Demon-boy on the shoulder.

Demon-boy fell in behind the Smith as they walked to the gate. Many thoughts running through his head, wondering what he had done wrong this time. Although the bastard-masters never needed an excuse or a reason for doing anything. They passed through the gate and walked through the settlement of Hura, the Outlanders ignoring the two as they walked in silence. They were almost at the doors when the Smith finally spoke.

"I have no idea of what they want. Just watch that temper of yours and stay calm. Remember what I have taught you about new situations."

"Expect the best but prepare for the worst!" replied Demon-boy instinctively.

The Smith looked over and smiled. "Correct. Come on, let's get this over with."

The Smith and Demon-boy stood at attention in front of the main table as Chief Hura, his son and a few trusted warriors finished their lunch. Chief Hura looked over at the pair, smiling he spoke first.

"Always on time, Smith," he said, while looking at Demon-boy.

"Yes, master. You asked for this pit-rat, so I brought him."

The talking round the table got quieter as the Chief went on. "The season has gone well, Smith. Many fights have been won with very few losses. Even the Demon-child here has won all of his fights!"

"Yes, master, it has been a good season," said the Smith.

Demon-boy was trying to empty his head and heart of the anger that he felt whenever around these bastards.

"The season is not quite over yet, Smith. We have one more round left, in the capital settlement of Pulnuk Province."

The Smith looked at the master now with a questioning

look in his face. The Chief knew what he was thinking as they had recently had a round of bouts there.

"You will also recall that last year, one of our pit-rats won the end of summers competition at Pulnuk!"

"Yes, master. I remember well."

Son-of-Angry-man jumped in. "We have to defend the title that we won, Smith and this end of summers is special which is why the Demon-child is here!"

All of the table laughed loudly whilst the Chief smiled. Smith no longer looked confused and Demon-boy kept looking at the ground, least his emotion got the better of him.

Chief Hura took his eyes off the boy and turned his attention to the Smith.

"That's right, Smith. The Demon-child here will represent us this end of summers winter bouts. He has had a good season, has he not?"

"Yes, master, he has and will fight well. He is quick with his fists and as you recall that he won many fights before he started his armed death bouts!"

"Oh, I remember Smith, but as my son said this end of summers is special."

The table laughed again.

"In what way are they special, master?" said the Smith.

"This end of summer bouts will be different. At the request of a few of the other chiefs, the bouts will be with weapons!"

The Smith took this in and knew the boy would do okay.

"The slave here will win many fights for you, master. He will do well in fights to first blood as he does when in death bouts."

"Good to hear, Smith. Considering the competition this end of summer is all death bouts!"

The table laughed and cheered as the Smith looked

puzzled and Demon-boy stared at the ground, his anger making him breathe faster.

"Death bouts master? I was told that the end of summers competition has always been unarmed? Is this not a waste of pit-rats?" asked the Smith.

"Every once in a while, they can be death bouts! How do you think the Trainer won his freedom? And why do I care if we waste slaves, Smith?"

The Smith quickly looked over at the boy. The boy's breathing was fast, and he could see the boy's veins throbbing in his arms and neck. He could say nothing, as it would draw attention to the boy's anger, which would be dangerous for both of them. The boy was holding himself in check, so the Smith turned his attention back to the masters. "Will you offer the boy here his freedom if he wins this?" enquired the Smith.

The table laughed again. "No. Made that mistake before and look how that turned out! Lost my best pit-rat, although he trains the slaves well.," said the Chief.

The table laughed again. The Chief looked over at Demon-boy again before speaking. "Well Demon-child, you think you can win a few fights in the same day?" asked the Chief.

Demon-boy exhaled trying to get control of himself before finally speaking. "Yes, master."

"Not that you have any choice," said Son-of-Angry-man.

"I will make you a deal, Demon-child," said the Chief.

Demon-boy knew as well as the Smith that it would not be a fair deal. Smith looked at the ground along with Demon-boy, both knew the masters would make it harder, they always did.

"If you win all of your fights and defend our province's title of having the best pit-rat, all pit-rats will go back to having seventh-day off training and work. This will never change. On my word and the word of my son."

Both the Smith and the boy knew this was a lie. The master's word was worth pig shit, but of course, neither of them could say this. It was the Smith that spoke first. "A worthy goal, masters."

"We have not finished yet, Smith!" said Son-of-Angry-man.

"No. Perhaps a little more motivation is needed for the Demon-child to fight his best and not just lay down and die, like others have in the past. If you lose the Smith here dies along with ten other pit-rats of my son's choosing."

Demon-boy looked up, losing control for just a moment. The look of hate on his face open and for all to see. The Smith saw the look and knew there was nothing he could do.

Son-of-Angry-man moved, first standing and jumping the table. He was at the boy quickly, grabbing the boy by the throat with his left hand. His right hand grabbing the wooden baton. The Smith looked at the ground knowing if he intervened, they would both die.

"You NEVER look at a master like that, Demon-child! Perhaps my son needs to remind you of your place, Slave!" said the Chief.

The Son-of-Angry-man smiled as he brought the baton down as hard as he could, smashing it into the right side of the boy's jaw. The boy dropped as the Chief's son let go of his throat.

"Know your place, slave! You are nothing!" said Son-of-Angry-man as he laid into the boy, smashing the baton into his mid-section over and over again.

Demon-boy tried to cover up but to no avail, as the master beat him.

"Enough son, he needs to be able to fight," said the Chief.

The Chief's son kicked him once in the stomach as he replaced his baton. He straightened his tunic and returned to where he had been sitting.

The Smith risked a quick look to his right, seeing the boy slowly start to pick himself up. The boy had a trickle of blood coming from the corner of his mouth. He held his ribs as he slowly started to stand. Once he had stood, he kept his head to the ground. He was still holding his side and was slightly bent at the waist, leaning to his left.

"You are not teaching the pit-rats their place, Smith. You need to work on that," said the Chief.

"Yes, master," replied the Smith, masking all of his own anger

"Take him back to the camp and make sure he is fit and well for training. We leave for Pulnuk in eight days," said the Chief.

"Your will, master," the Smith replied.

The Smith turned to leave with the boy following behind, walking slowly as his body ached with the pain of the beating.

"You better make sure he wins, Smith, would hate to have to hang you," said the Son-of-Angry-man. The table all laughed again.

"What have I told you, boy? Do you want them to hang you?" said the Smith, as they walked slowly back to the training camp.

The boy said nothing, breathing through the pain, angry still written all over his face.

"Say something, boy!"

Demon-boy said nothing, just looked straight ahead as he continued his painful walk towards the camp.

"You do realise that they could have killed us both for your own stupid mistake? No, you didn't realise that as you were only thinking of yourself and your own anger! We are slaves! Now and always! If you do not like that, then perhaps just wait until you are alone and end it!"

Still the boy said nothing. They arrived at the main gate of the training camp and went their separate ways. Smith went off on some errand, Demon-boy returned to his rooms to rest. His jaw hurt and he knew he was going to lose a tooth, he could move it with his tongue but thankfully, the tooth didn't hurt. His jaw did and he was surprised that it was not broken. Reaching his room, he laid back on his bed, pulling his blanket over himself. He had only been lying down for a few minutes when Bulldog-boy arrived, sitting down on the opposite bed.

"What happened?"

"A beating!"

"What did you do?"

"Masters didn't like the way I looked at them!"

"And that's all?"

"No. In eight days, I am off to Pulnuk to defend the title that you won last summers end."

"Is that all? I am sure you will do well. You are surprisingly good with your fists as I remember. It's not exactly a death sentence, is it?"

"It's not unarmed. This year, it is death bouts!"

"Fuck!" Bulldog-boy said, with feeling.

"Exactly, but there is more."

Bulldog-boy looked up.

"If I lose, the bastard-masters will hang the Smith and ten of the pit-rats!"

Bulldog-boy shook his head and continued to look at the floor.

"They hate you so much, don't they?"

"Yes. I guess I better fight at my best."

Demon-boy reached into his own mouth and gripped the tooth that he had been playing with. He twisted it and the tooth came away. He threw it on the floor and spat blood onto the floor at the same time. He reached for his water skin that was on the floor, pulling the stopper and taking a large drink.

Bulldog-boy stood. "Yes. I would suggest training hard for the next few days but give yourself a couple of days to recover and relax before you leave."

Demon-boy nodded.

"I'll get back to it. Smith is in a bad mood and I can't deal with him yelling at me today!"

As Bulldog-boy left, Demon-boy lay back down and closed his eyes. He hadn't meant to endanger the Smith. He would have to apologise but for now, he needed rest.

The eight days had gone far too quickly. The Smith had overseen Demon-boy's training personally. He had him doing mainly speed training with practise bouts in the late afternoon. They hadn't exchanged many words and Demon-boy hadn't yet apologised. In fact, the boy had said barely anything. The conversations were all one way, with the Smith ordering him through his workload for six days. His body no longer hurt from the beating, which meant nothing had been broken. He had a lovely dark bruise that was starting to change to purple on the side of his face from where the baton had hit. He also had a few dark bruises on his left side. He was then given two days to recover where he spent his mornings stretching after light runs, then resting up and watching the other pit-rats train. He had a few conversations with Funny-boy and Bulldog-boy but was mainly left to himself. He spent the time clearing his head and preparing for the bouts that he was about to enter. He wanted to sit the Smith down and have the conversation to say the things that needed to be said, but the Smith was always busy. Hopefully, he would get the chance to say sorry after he won the bouts. The thought echoing through his mind.

Demon-boy looked around the large crowd as they all yelled and cheered, the combatants currently in the pit. He was nursing a tiny cut to his left side, holding a cloth up to it. He had been a little careless in his first bout and let a sword thrust through his defences. He had managed to move at the last second, so the sword didn't go into him too deeply. The fight had been furious and amazingly fast. Demon-boy was surprised how quick his first opponent had been. Not as fast as himself, but certainly fast enough to surprise him. He had finished his opponent with a move taught to him from Sick-boy. Using his off-hand sword, he had tangled up his opponent's weapon for a brief moment, tying up his weapon arm. Then when his opponent threw his shield at Demon-boy's head, he ducked and brought his axe up between the pit-rat's legs, cutting into the opponent's groin and going in deep. As the pit-rat dropped his own sword and started to drop towards the ground, he stabbed his own sword into the opponent's neck. It was a bloody finish and earned a massive roar from all the attending Outlanders.

He looked up around the large drinking hall of the Chief of Pulnuk. He had been here a few times but never seen as many Outlander bastards crammed in. He, of course, was sitting on the stone floor at his own master's feet, as were all of the pit-rats. The chiefs of all provinces sitting in the front rows of the tiered stone seating, their slaves at their feet, the pit-rats weapons held by the host on a large table to the side of the pit. Demon-boy had a water skin next to him and had some time to recover before the next round. He tried to watch the other combatants, to get a sense of who he would face and how good they were but couldn't see a lot of the fight from his position on the floor.

A large roar grabbed his attention as his mind had started to wander. He felt a smack on his head.

"You are up, slave! Don't die!" said Son-of-Angry-man loudly.

He stood and without looking at the masters, walked to the table that held his weapons. He picked his weapons up and walked to the edge of the pit. Chief's Hura's province was announced, and a huge cheer went around the hall. Demon-boy looked around the hall, seeing all the Outlanders cheering. He had become a favourite over the last couple of summers in the pit and he hated it. If the outcome was not so important, he would be happy to drop his weapons and let himself be hacked down. Unfortunately, it was not an option. The thought stirring his anger as he jumped down into the pit and landing softly on his feet. He didn't notice his opponent do the same and as he looked up, got his first look at his opponent. The slave was huge! Almost the same size as Funny-boy but his skin was a pale white, the same complexion of the Outlanders. In fact, his opponent looked like an Outlander. Demon-boy didn't care why he was in the pit or what he had done wrong to be sold into slavery. The only thought in his mind was he gets to kill an Outlander and he smiled. The other pit-rat swung his massive two-handed axe in circles to warm up his shoulders whilst Demon-boy stood stock still, staring with all his anger, hatred and despise at the

Outlander in front of him. He was waiting on the word from Chief Pulnuk to start when an evil little thought crossed his mind. He smiled, perhaps he could disappoint the bastard-masters in a different way.

"FIGHT!" yelled Chief Pulnuk.

As always, he exploded into action. Faster than it looked possible, he sprinted across the pit. The pit-rat was just bringing his axe around to block but was too slow, as he lunged his sword, scoring a cut across the inside of the pit-rat's neck. His aim had been slightly off, and he missed the main vein in the neck that he had been aiming for. Before the massive axe swung round to take him, Demon-boy rolled out of the way to his left before returning to his feet. A tumbler roll that was now taught in the training camp as a good way to get out of trouble, Bulldog-boy would be proud. He didn't stop but once again with a speed that amazed everyone, exploded back into range of that massive axe. He feinted this time with his axe and let his opponent block it, with his left-hand sword coming close to his body and lunging for the pit-rat's eye. The pit-rat took the bait of the double feint and raised the axe haft to block the blow. Demon-boy pivoted on his left foot, his hand axe in his right hand coming around fast. The pit-rat was too slow and didn't see the axe coming as it came around and severed his right hand. With a scream, he dropped his massive axe and held the stump trying to stop the bleeding. Demon-boy took a few steps back and dropped his weapons. He then jumped back into a tumblers forward roll, coming up onto his feet with his opponent's massive axe in his hands. It was heavy and the weight almost threw Demon-boy off balance as he regained his feet. The large pit-rat was on his knees looking at his hand, lying on the ground in front of him. Demon-boy raised the axe high in the air and held it for a second, before bringing it down with all the strength that he had. The axe fell straight onto the back of the pit-rat's neck, decapitating him instantly. The Outlanders watching all roared their approval as Demon-boy threw down the large axe. He returned to gather his own weapons and as two large Outlanders jumped into the pit to remove the body, he jumped out. He took his weapons to the table, then returned to sit at the feet of Chief Hura. He didn't bow as he once started doing or look at him at all. Just sat and drained his water skin.

"I hope that neck thrust was not meant to end the fight in a boring way, slave!" said Chief Hura.

The words sending a slight chill through the mind of Demon-boy. He knew! The chief knew he was trying to make a mockery of the fights.

"Would hate to have to hang the Smith with you watching, Slave!" said Son-of-Angry-man.

Demon-boy kept his head down and said nothing.

"You have reached the finals, slave. One step closer to keeping the Smith alive," said Chief Hura.

"Brothers, we have reached the finals!" yelled Chief Pulnuk. The roar echoed off the wooden rafters. "What a final bout we have for you all. We have seen some great bouts, had some fine drink and fine food. Now, we are ready to see if Chief Hura can take the title two end of summers in a row!"

The crowd roared again as Son-of-Angry-man stood and raised his hands in the air, being a little bit more of an attention seeker than his father, he enjoyed being centre stage. His father just smiled and looked down at the Demon-boy at his feet. Could he win this last bout? Chief Hura would make many silver coins if he did. Unlike other bouts throughout the season, the rules on bets was stricter. All bets had to be made before the competition started, and you could only bet on one slave to win the entire competition. No bets were allowed after the first fight started; all bets were written down. The Outlanders had introduced this long form of gambling many seasons ago to prolong the betting and build anticipation. Chief Hura was sure that some of the lower ranked warriors still exchanged a few coins on individual fights, but none of the higher ranks did and certainly not the chiefs. Also, the odds were fixed and ran by Chief Pulnuk. Chief Hura knew this was a way he could make money, although his fellow Chief said it was a way to keep things even. All odds where five-to-one. Chief Hura had bet a thousand silver coins on his pit-rat which means if the Demon-child won; he would get back five thousand silver coins plus his original one-thousand. He thought of something and turned to his son

"How much did you bet on the Demon-child?"

"Two thousand coins, father!"

"That much? That's most of the profit from last season!"

"Yes. I am confident the slave would win, you gave him a good incentive after all."

Demon-boy sitting at their feet overheard this. He would have liked nothing better than to lose this final fight but couldn't with the life of the Smith riding on it. The only way he could show his contempt was by ending the fight as quick as possible, to end the contest and the enjoyment of it as fast as he could. Robbing the Outlanders of a drawn-out battle. Bulldog-boy had told him the final he had won last year, although it was unarmed, had lasted for twenty minutes before he finally won. His memory went back to the way he had won the first death bout that he had ever fought in at the beginning of the season. He had thrown his axe at the start of the fight, ending it before it had even started. He smiled.

"From the province of Hurarock, I give you Chief Hura's entry!" yelled Chief Pulnuk.

Demon-boy stood and walked again to the table, grabbing his weapons before jumping down into the pit. He walked to the opposite side and stood facing his own masters, as was customary, and looked at the ground planning his opening move.

"Representing my province and trying to win the title back for Pulnuk, I give you my pit-rat!" he yelled once again.

The roar was the loudest yet but Demon-boy blocked it out. He watched the pit-rat jump down and a memory was triggered as he saw the blonde hair tied up in a warrior's tail flow through the air. He looked into the cruel eyes and instantly recognised who he was facing. Chief Hura had sold this slave to Chief Pulnuk a few seasons ago and it had been many summers since he had been the sport of this slave and his friends. It had been many summers since he had first fought back and won over this cruel slave and his friends. The pit-rat was smiling at him in the evilest of ways, malice dripping from him. He was a few inches taller than Demon-boy, and his body was well muscled and lean. He carried a short sword in his right hand and a large knife in his left. He also stood statue still, looking forward to fighting the slave that had made his life difficult, had been the reason for him being sold to be used in the pit.

Chief Hura and his son were also smiling, they couldn't have planned it better if they had tried. They watched the rage in Demon-boy rise and saw the madness in his eyes and celebrated it. They knew he would fight to win and not doing anything, unpredictable.

"FIGHT!" yelled Chief Pulnuk.

Both of the pit-rats exploded into action. Demon-boy was faster, but it mattered not as their weapons rang out with attack and block, both using all the skill they could to hurt each other. The opening move he had planned, now forgotten as he engaged his old enemy. The Outlanders watching, yelled with excitement as the two finalists attacked each other with a speed and violence not yet witnessed yet at this competition. Demon-boy blocked a sword blow on his offhand sword and pivoted off his left foot, circling around to his right to bring his axe around. The other pit-rat's sword was waiting for the axe and as the sword blocked the blow, his large knife came over the top aiming for Demon-boy's throat. It narrowly missed as Demon-boy disengaged and took a step back. Once the knife went past, he swung a blow at the pit-rats wrist with his axe that missed as the pit-rat stepped back himself. The cruel pit-rat was smiling which enraged Demon-boy all the more. His attacks became clumsier and his skill started to drop as his frustrations mounted. He was faster than the other pit-rat, his previous tormentor but the pit-rat was more skilled and used that skill well. He tried to calm himself and think of the snow-weasel, but nothing he did worked. His frustrations clearly on show as he couldn't land a hit! He stepped back from the latest attempt but took a knife cut to his left bicep. It was not deep, but blood flowed freely. He knew that his sword arm would lose its power before long and he would be down to just his axe. The fight continued for ten minutes, strike, counter strike, block, step back and then step into re-engage. Both pit-rats were superbly fit, but stamina and strength in a fight as furious as this would only last so long. As Demon-boy stepped back from his last attack, the other pit-rat exploded towards him, bringing both his weapons forward in parallel thrust towards his chest. A mistake, as Demon-boy blocked with both his weapons, driving the pit-rat's weapons out wide and then stepping in to deliver a vicious head butt that broke the nose of his old tormentor. As the pit-rat was stunned from the damage to his nose, Demon-boy pulled his axe back and high, then swung down, burying his hand axe halfway into the top of his opponent's head! The pit-rat looked blankly as he fell backwards dead. The Outlanders that had bet on the Demon-boy were on their feet roaring as loud as they could! Demon-boy didn't stop there however, his rage had taken control and he followed his old tormentor to the ground. He changed his sword to his right hand and started raining down blows on the face of his old tormentor. Again, and again, the sword struck dead flesh as he took out all his frustration and anger of the masters on this corpse. He heard another roar and didn't realise that it was coming from his own throat, as he continued to rain down the blows. He didn't hear the command to stop from his own master, nor did he hear the feet of three warriors jump into the pit behind him. One warrior on each arm and one behind him putting him in a headlock to drag him off the body. He was still screaming and kicking his legs as they dragged him to the other side of the pit. Son-of-Angry-man stepped forward and jumped into the pit. Drawing his hand axe, he spun it and hit Demon-boy with the flat side of it, knocking him out instantly.

When he came around, he was in a room that he had never been in before. It was a small stone-walled room with a stone floor and no windows. It was cold but was well light from many candles burning on the walls. He was lying on the cold stone floor with his arms outstretched in front of him, his hands tied to rope that was tightly secured to iron rings on the floor. He couldn't move his legs so assumed his legs were also tied to the floor. Standing in front of him was Chief Hura, his son and Chief Pulnuk.

"He is awake," said Son-of-Angry-man.

"Congratulations on winning the end of summers competition, slave! You have saved the life of the Smith," said Chief Hura.

Demon-boy looked up at the masters, the question on his lips remaining on his lips as his head throb.

"You may have won but your disrespect for Chief Pulnuk cannot go unpunished!" said Chief Hura

Without thinking Demon-boy spoke. "I am to be punished. I just won!"

"Yes. Think of it as an object lesson," said Son-of Angry-man.

"A fucking object lesson?" said the boy, caution now thrown to the wind.

He saw Chief Pulnuk nod.

The pain erupted across his bare back as the whip landed. The burning sensation hitting the nerve endings in his spine, making the Demon-boy howl with pain. He was about to scream more abuse when a second slash landed. He saw the smile on Son-of Angry-man's face, a look of anger on Chief Hura and a blank look on Chief Pulnuk's face. Over and over again, the whip landed on his bare back, slowly turning his back into a canvas of whip marks. The pain finally bringing something to Demon-boy that he had thought he had lost all those summers before, tears. He cried, screamed, and howled his way through the twenty-five lashes. At first, he had kicked his arms and legs trying to get free of the pain, but as the warrior behind him completed his twenty-fourth lash, Demon-boy had blacked out from the pain.

"Wrap him in a blanket and tie him in the back of the wagon in the barn for now!" said Chief Hura.

He took Chief Pulnuk's hand in a warrior's grip. "My

apologies for my slave not showing the correct amount of respect in the pit, brother-chief."

"No apology is necessary. It was still a grand fight and well worth watching. That pit-rat of yours is one of the best I have seen," said Chief Pulnuk.

"He may be good in the pit but after all these summers, he still has not learnt his place."

Chief Pulnuk laughed as he led the others back to the drinking hall to continue the end of season celebration.

The winter season was over. Demon-boy had completed his first season of death bouts and survived. He had been cut a few times in his first season, all of the scars on his chest, gut, and arms. In nine death bouts, nine dead slaves had fallen at his feet, then a further three wins at the end of summers competition that he had won.

This winter season had been hugely successful for Chief Hura. The training camp that Trainer had asked for was proving its worth. He had won so much more than the amount of coin that the training camp had cost. His biggest win was when Demon-boy won the contest at Pulnuk. Some of the other chiefs had even constructed their own training camps on seeing how good his pit-rats fought. It was a compliment and Chief Hura admitted to himself at least, that Trainer was right. With spring here, his warriors were looking forward to the coming raid season. The Chief was also looking forward to the summer raids and had a little to do before summer. His ships had been maintained during the winter, being dragged up into the beach above the waterline, large tents set up around them, and the warriors and ship wrights working on them throughout the cold full moons. There was only one task that needed to be completed. A task that he had passed to his son, a task that his son would relish in.

Demon-boy had taken a few quarter moons of healing before he could start training again. On arriving back from Pulnuk, the Smith had tended to his back wounds, smearing them in honey and covering them in wet damp clothes to draw away the heat. This fortunately gave him the chance to speak to the Smith.

"I am sorry, Smith," said Demon-boy.

"For what boy?"

"For my anger before I left for the end of season fights. I risked not only my life but also yours as well. You were right, my anger clouded my judgement. I am sorry!" said Demon-boy.

The smith stopped applying the honey to his back and looked at the back of the boy's head. True he had been angry then, and other times when the boy's attitude endangered himself and others. But he understood where the anger came from.

"Thank you boy. I know where your anger comes from, truly I do," the Smith replied after some time.

"You do?"

"Yes. I do. Every step of the way the bastards have thrown obstacles in your way, made it harder or generally made life as difficult as possible."

"Yes" is all the boy said.

"But you have made it through, somehow survived. You still need to learn to think sometimes and you are still not in control of your emotions. In fact, I am not sure you will ever be totally in control of your emotions. Don't get me wrong boy, you have come a long way to being in control."

Demon-boy said nothing. Just listened.

"The world has been against you from the time you were taken. The bastards have made your life a living hell since you were taken. But boy, you are still here. You are still breathing yes?" said the Smith.

'Yes, I am Smith" he replied.

"I do not think I could have stayed in control if they threw at me, everything they have thrown at you," said the Smith.

"Then why have you been so tough on me? Why have you spent so much effort on trying to get me to control myself when you admit you could not do the same?" he said with feeling.

"Because you are stronger than me boy. You have more potential than me. You are better than me," said the Smith.

Demon-boy turned himself over to look at the smith. He said nothing, just looked at his mentor, his father, his mother and his friend. Tears started to well up in his eyes.

"You can be more than I ever was boy, but first you have to make dam sure the bastards do not kill you. Yes, you have a very slim chance of ever getting out of here boy, but that does not mean you have no chance at all."

Demon-boy lay back down on his stomach, to hide the tears that were rolling down his face. The Smith continued to apply honey to the whip marks. Nothing more was said as the Smith finished up. He wrapped wet cloth around the boy and stood up. He got to the door and then turned.

"Thank you for saying sorry boy. I just wish for you all the things I could not have. I wish for you want for you to be what I could not be," said the Smith.

With that he left Demon-boy.

It had been a painful few quarter moons of lying on his front on his bed. He had many visits from his two friends where he got to tell them of all that had happened, including the whipping that he had received. His two friends doing all they could in the evening to lift his spirits but to no avail. He was in too much pain, and his hatred for the bastard-masters still strong and in the front of his mind. Trainer had also had long chats with him, trying to calm him. This was also of no use. Smith and Trainer had decided that time would bring him back to his old self. They guessed wrong that he would calm down. The pit-rats were lingering over a large breakfast. The end of the winter season had arrived and since the season had gone so well, Trainer had given the pit-rats a few days off before he would implement a new training plan that he had been working on with the Smith. All of the pit-rats from the new arrivals to seniors all sat in the meal room, enjoying an easy breakfast. Trainer was having a meal in the corner with the Smith, talking amongst themselves, when Son-of-Angry-man walked in with three of his warriors.

"On your feet, you pit-rat scum," spoke the master, louder enough to travel over the food hall.

The slaves all jumped to their feet, dropping spoons and bowls on the tables. Trainer had stood as soon as the masters had entered. He had walked over to Son-of-Angry-man and reached him quickly.

"Master, how can I help?"

Once again speaking loudly so his voice would carry, Son-of-Angry-man barked out his orders.

"New training today! All slaves out on the field, NOW!"

"Master, I have given the slaves a few days off."

He didn't finish as one of the warriors reached forward

and backhanded the Trainer. The strike connected with a loud whack. Most of the slaves bowed their heads, realising how dangerous this situation had become in a heartbeat! Most of the slaves, apart from a few of the more senior slaves, automatically bowed their heads and looked at the ground. The senior slaves looked on, as did Demon-boy and his two friends.

"Don't question me, slave!" Son-of-Angry-man screamed at the Trainer.

Trainer had accepted the hit but hadn't fallen. He was a veteran pit fighter after all and was used to being hit.

"Master, when I was given the job of Trainer, I was told nothing would interfere with my methods."

"You questioning me, scum?"

"As a free man, it is my right."

The warriors surrounding Son-of-Angry-man hands rested on their weapons. The Smith saw what was happening but unfortunately no one else did. The Trainer certainly didn't.

"Who said you are free?"

"Your father did when he freed me!"

The Son-of-Angry-man smiled. The warriors at his side laughed. Before Trainer could react, two of the warriors leaped, grabbing his arms and holding him.

"What is this? Is this how you treat free men?" yelled Trainer.

Son-of-Angry-man pulled his axe, the shining silver one that the Smith had made and thrust it towards the Trainer, striking the Trainer in the face. A cut opened above the Trainer's missing left eye; blood began to poor. The Son-of-Angry-man stepped back. His five warriors drew their weapons and laid into the Trainer. Cutting and slashing as the Trainer's body hit the ground. Although most of the slaves were looking at the ground, they had heard the exchange and briefly looked up. The warriors continued and with every cut, every slice, slowly took a piece of the Trainers life. Son-of-Angry-man grinned at the pit-rats. Most of the newer slaves were trembling. The ones not trembling were looking at the ground, not willing to watch, least the wrath of the masters fall on them. Demon-boy, however, felt the anger once again creeping through his veins as he listened to the exchange. In the first few words of exchange without realising, he moved around the table that he had been sitting at, taken a few steps toward the warriors. As the warriors had started their attack, his rage surged and threatened to explode, his heartbeat in his ear was the only thing he could hear. Veins in his throat throbbing with the adrenalin now surging through him and it was clear to those of the senior slaves, he was about to do something foolish. All of the senior slaves moved behind him, foolish or not, they would follow him. The underlying hold Demon-boy had over the other senior pit-rats, overtly showing itself for the first time. The Smith saw this and when Demon-boy looked at the Smith, the Smith shook his head, trying to tell the boy 'NO! Stop!' The Smith's nodding would not hold him. As Demon-boy moved forward with the rage all over his face, the Smith was trying to get his attention and failing. The Smith knew that if the boy attacked, most of the other slaves would follow his lead. It would only take a word from the boy and they would all rush in. Funny-boy had seen the Smith, however, and stepped beside Demon-boy and grabbed one arm, Bulldog-boy grabbing the other arm and pulling him back.

Son-of-Angry-man saw this and laughed harder.

"He dies," Demon-boy said to the others quietly.

The Trainer was now a pile of bloody meat and

unrecognisable as the person he had been and yet the warriors continued to hack and slice their weapons.

"Yes, but not now, without weapons, trust in the Smith," Bulldog-boy muttered.

Demon-boy only just heard his friend. His heart was pounding and he focused on one thing only, the death of the masters.

The warriors stepped back from their frenzy. They were breathing hard.

They smiled at all the slaves and then turned around and walked back out the door. Son-of-Angry-man looked at the slaves once again and then also left.

Funny-boy and Bulldog-boy were struggling to hold Demon-boy as he renewed his attempts to get free. Pulled and pushed, but with his two friends either side of him, there was no way he could move. Smith appeared quickly in front of the pair and slapped him, hard.

"Control yourself boy, or you will join him."

The slap did nothing. He continued to struggle. The Smith slapped him again, harder with all his strength. "The lives of the pit-rats and your friends rely on you," said Smith.

The slap and the words broke through the mist of rage. For a moment, the boy stared into the Smith's eyes, hearing his heartbeat, hearing it slow as he started to calm himself. Finally, the boy fell to the ground as his two friends let go of him.

"Make sure he goes nowhere," the Smith told them.

They both nodded as the Smith called out other slaves. He ordered three of the more senior slaves to clear the mess and wrap up the body into a sheet, they acknowledged him and set to work without question. Grabbing four of the other senior slaves, he told them to go outside and grab shovels, then to go over to the far-right corner of the training field past the track. Next to the fence, they were to dig the grave. The Smith then left the food hall and walked outside to check if the masters had gone. Once he was outside, he saw that Son-of-Angry-man and his murderers were not alone. One hundred warriors with all of their weapons waited by the gate. They had planned this and expected rioting. There was no reason to it. He quickly returning to the food hall, he found all his instructions had been carried out. The body, or what was left of it, was wrapped in a bed sheet. A bed sheet that was quickly turning red from all the blood that was still pouring from the former body of the Trainer. Reaching Demon-boy, he saw that he was still fuming and hadn't gotten himself fully under control and it would only take a small spark to ignite him. His two friends were sitting with him on the bench, talking to themselves.

"You three, go to your cells and wait. Calm him down and do not come out."

"He needs to die," said Demon-boy, between clenched teeth.

"Perhaps one day he will, but not today."

"Why not today? You have the key to the weapons shed," said Funny-boy.

"Because outside, standing at the gate, is the bastard master with one hundred of his warriors, all armed and waiting for just a stupid move as that," the Smith said louder than he wanted to. "Just get yourselves hidden away and calm him down. Throw a bucket of cold water on him if you have to.

Two of the slaves picked up the bloody package and left with it, heading to the grave that was being dug. Other senior slaves were cleaning the blood from the wooden floors, whilst some of the other slaves helped the kitchen slaves clear the tables. The bulk of the slaves had headed upstairs and were sitting in their cells as the Smith had instructed them too.

Later as the some of the slaves filled in the grave, the Smith stood watch. Trying to work out in his head why Trainer had been an object lesson. Clearly, it was aimed at the boy, but why? The boy had worked hard, fought well, and won much coin for the masters. Trainer had also proven that his ideas of this training camp were paying off. A waste of life, the Smith screamed internally to himself, a dam waste of a good life.

"Smith," called a warrior that had walked up from the gate.

Calming himself, he slowly turned around. "Yes, master."

"The Chief wants you to attend him at sundown," said the warrior.

Smith said nothing just nodded and the warrior walked away.

"Now, what the hell is going to happen?"

"I am going to kill that bastard-master!" said Demon-boy, as he breathed long, slow breaths.

The three of them had returned to Funny-boy's cell.

"He needs to die, but Smith is right. Not now, we need to wait!" said Bulldog-boy.

"We?" replied Demon-boy.

"Yes, we," said Funny-boy.

He looked over at his two friends that were sitting across on the second bed.

"Before we do anything, we need to think. It's no good rushing off full of anger, we will just get ourselves killed. The

Smith has been teaching you tactics, use them," said Bulldog-boy.

He thought back to all the evening meals and conversations, trying to find something the Smith had said or taught him that would help now. Nothing came to mind.

Funny-boy stood up straight. "We cannot just sit here doing nothing," he said.

"We have no choice at this moment. Well Demon-boy, what do you think?" said Bulldog-boy.

He cracked an evil half smile and looked at his two friends. "Smith always said sometimes the best way to tackle an enemy, was by doing what the enemy least expected. Sometimes you do nothing"

Smith walked through the township with the warrior by his side. He was still disturbed by the murder of Trainer and was trying to clear his mind before his meeting with the Chief. As they walked through the settlement towards the Chief's hall, he tried to block out his feelings and think with his mind.

They reached the hall and strode the steps to the main door, Smith trying to keep up but lagging behind because of his limp. They walked in and the hall was virtually empty. Apart from ten or so warriors sitting at a bench and table, drinking, and eating, the only people in the hall was the Chief and his bastard son, sitting at their own table indulging. The warrior sat down with his mates whilst the Smith shuffled forward and stood a few metres from the table. He continued to stand and said nothing, whilst the Chief and his son ate and chatted. By the time they had finished their meal, his leg was sore. Judging it was the right time, he finally addressed the master, staying as calm as he could.

"Master, you asked for me."

The Chief looked at him as he sipped his ale, then finally spoke. "I hear you have been running the training camp with great efficiency over the last season." It was a statement and not a question.

"Is there any end to your many talents, Smith?" cracked Son-of-Angry-man with a smile.

"As you know, Masters, I was a sergeant with soldiers under me and am well used to organising a workforce."

Chief looked at him with an unreadable expression. The Smith thought he had learnt to read the Chief but on this occasion was proved wrong.

"Since our Trainer has had such a terrible accident, I think it would be best for you to take over all training of the slaves for now. You have trained men before as a sergeant?"

An accident thought the Smith to himself. He had to control an angry retort. Now was not the time to question. "Yes, master, I have trained men."

"Well from what I have heard, a lot of our new training practises that the Trainer was using, came from you! Is this correct?"

Where the hell had he heard that from? Not even the slaves knew that. Demon-boy did but would not have told his two friends.

"Well, Smith?" snapped Son-of-Angry-man.

"Some, masters. Trainer and I had discussed ideas on how to train men."

"Some?" said the Chief, as he took another drink.

"Don't hold back now, Smith. It would not be safe right at this moment to hold back information from us," said Son-of-Angry-man, tapping his hand axe.

The Chief continued. "The hell runs as the slaves call

them, the running with barrows of rocks are all your ideas, yes?"

"Yes, master, they are."

"There we go, Smith. Since they were your ideas, then you will replace the Trainer quite easily, I would imagine. Since you are such a capable man, you will have no problems running the training camp as well."

The Smith said nothing. He would not have any time for any blacksmith duties, but then there was less and less work for the smithy these days. The work there was could be handled by Quick, his apprentice of these last five summers.

"Yes, master. I can handle both duties. My apprentice is ready to take over any blacksmith duties."

"Your apprentice is dead, Smith!"

The Smith's eyes widened, and his anger almost got the better of him. He calmed himself.

"How?"

"My son here caught him trying to escape at sunset. He was executed."

Both the Chief and his son watched for any reaction, but the Smith remained calm and unreadable.

"Who will run the smithy, masters?"

"What smithy? At first light tomorrow morning, my warriors will pull the smithy building down, brick by brick. You have done good work and we have more than enough weapons for the pit-rats and my warriors to use. My weapons room is packed with all of your fine work. It will be seasons before I need more made"

"You are pulling apart the smithy, master? Where will I sleep?"

Son-of angry-man answered. "A good trainer will sleep with this those he trains in order to keep an eye on them, don't you think, Smith? Close enough to keep the slaves in line and stop them from doing something stupid. You can have a cell in the barracks!"

"Yes, I think the training camp was a little too luxurious, you are slaves and I have not enjoyed seeing an element of pride surface in certain slaves," relied the Chief.

Smith was finding it harder and harder to stay calm, but if he didn't, it would be his life.

"Also," the Chief continued, "all non-practise weapons have been removed from the storage in my training camp and locked away here in the settlement."

This clearly shocked the Smith and the shock registering on his face. The masters smiled.

"Why, Masters?"

"Why, Smith? Well, we would not want our slaves to have access to weapons as they may turn on us, would we? They will be returned to the pit-rats before each fight."

Smith had underestimated the Outlanders. The Chief was right, he and the other slaves had become too complacent and used to the luxury that they now lived in.

"The Trainer had become soft on the slaves, Smith, I would not like to see you make the same mistakes," said the Chief.

"Is there anything else, masters? I have a lot to organise."

"No, Smith. Work those slaves harder than Trainer did. I would hate to have to take away the cooking staff and the good food that goes along with them," said the Chief.

Smith knew it was not an idle threat and looked at the two masters.

"Go then, Smith. No more rest days, get those slaves training."

The Smith said nothing just backed away, then left. The warrior that had escorted him, joined him, and walked beside him back through the settlement. The Smith looked at the warrior with him. The slaves had named him No-nose. He was one of the better masters, in the fact that he didn't look for any reason to beat them.

"Your world may look like it is collapsing but trust me! Things can get a whole lot worse. Mind yourself and be careful," said No-nose.

"I do not understand master. The camp had given good results."

"It has Smith," replied No-nose.

"Then why is the chief so intent on destroying all the hard work? Does he not like the amount of coin he has won of all the pit-rats?" said the Smith.

"I do not know smith. All I know is he hates the Demon-child. I will say no more," said No-nose.

"Thank you, master," said the Smith.

No-nose nodded. Normally he would not question any master, but No-nose was reasonable, intelligent even. The Smith nodded back and they continued to walk. The slave's world had been turned upside down and the Smith was angry at himself. He had become too complacent and hadn't seen this coming. He would not make that mistake again and if he could help it, none of the other slaves would either.

The next morning, well before the sun had come up, a loud banging woke all the pit-rats from their sleep. Chucking on their training clothing, they ran down to the food hall. All of them assembled into the warm room. The fires had been lit at both ends of the hall and candles had been also lit. Standing in the middle of the eating hall with a large pot in one hand, a large wooden spoon in the other stood the Smith.

"All take a seat," he said loudly.

The pit-rats all hurried to obey, sitting themselves quickly on the closest benches and tables. Demon-boy and his two friends had arrived and sat down at the back against the wall.

The Smith put down the pot and wooden spoon, then moved closer.

"Yesterday has happened and nothing we say or do, will change that."

He looked around to see his words were heard and understood. He saw blank faces from the younger slaves and a mixture of resignation and anger from the senior slaves. Looking across at Demon-boy's table, he saw the look on the three faces. Anger, pure anger. He would have to deal with that before they get themselves killed.

"Last night, I was made the new trainer."

Whispers broke out across the room.

"SILENCE!" he yelled. "I am the new trainer and I am also now officially in charge of this training camp. What I say, goes."

The Smith saw Demon-boy stand up and take a couple of steps forward. Shit, he thought to himself. Of all the times he could be assertive, he chooses now.

"You want us to forget about what happened yesterday, 'New-Trainer'?"

The Smith could feel the boy's rage, directed at him by a stare alone, let alone the scorn in his voice when he called him 'New Trainer'.

"No. Do not forget it! Keep it in the front of your minds at all times. Never forget what the Trainer has done, taught you, said to you. But most importantly, do not forget that Trainer died for all of YOU."

The boy went to continue but the Smith jumped in quickly.

"Never forget that as slaves, our lives are on a knife's edge.

We are slaves and the masters will always, always, look for any reason they can to kills us. All of us including myself, have forgotten this. Well, we have all just been reminded."

"Trainer was not a slave though, was he?" said Demon-boy.

"No boy, he was not. And that should make you realise how easy it is for the masters to kill whether you are a slave or not! Perhaps all of you will learn caution again! Perhaps you will learn your place again in this camp. Perhaps the death of Trainer will teach you to stay alive."

Even Demon-boy said nothing as the whole room thought on the words. But the Smith didn't give them time to think.

"Right. All of you on the practise field now. Ten laps at a slow pace before stretching, then I want to see twenty laps of a good pace. Now GO!"

All of the younger slaves jumped up and ran outside, heading for the training ground. The older slaves looked to Demon-boy, and when he nodded, they too headed outside.

"You three, sit back down," he said pointing at the troublesome threesome.

Demon-boy and his two friends sat down, and the Smith joined them.

"Now, what are you three planning?"

Demon-boy smiled before replying. 'What makes you think we are planning anything?"

"Because I know the three of you too well, now shut up and listen," he breathed and then continued. "Today at first light, the Smithy will be taken apart brick by brick and taken away."

"Why?" replied Bulldog-boy.

"I'm not sure, perhaps a reminder from the masters that our lives are in their hands. A lesson we have now been reminded of. Also, ALL of the iron weapons were taken away last night, leaving just the wooden practise weapons," the Smith said, seeing the shock on their faces.

So, they were planning something.

"Don't ever think the Outlander-bastards are stupid. They knew what they were doing when they provided us all with an object lesson."

"Object lesson?" muttered Funny-boy.

"Yes, object lesson. Don't the three of you see? It was planned and it was planned well. They knew exactly what they were going to do before they walked in here. They had already decided Trainer was to die. They had one hundred warriors waiting for slaves like yourselves to do something stupid. They know you cannot be trusted after what happened yesterday, so they have taken away all of the weapons."

Finally, Demon-boy spoke calmly. "Yes Smith, we were talking of taking action. Bloody hard now with no weapons however."

"Of course, you were planning something, I'm not stupid boy, and neither are the masters."

Bulldog-boy spoke up as if they couldn't trust the Smith, they could trust no one. "Smith. We talked last night. We can no longer live like this. We all know we are slaves! But all of us here have trained hard, we have fought hard and we win every fight earning the Chief much coin. We are stuck in this camp when we are not fighting. And now they are taking away the small luxuries we did have from us."

"You are slaves!" asked the Smith.

"Yes, we are, Smith," said Demon-boy, before continuing. "If our small amount of luxuries is now taken away from us, what have we got to fight for? Why should we fight? There is no incentive nor reason for us to fight. All we have left to us is to lie down in our next pit-fight and let ourselves be killed. That is the only way to hurt the masters!"

"Aye, it would piss them off a little, but then all your brother slaves would die," replied the Smith.

Funny-boy raised his hand to grab their attention. "What do we care if the master does kill us? We die in the ring or we die by the master's hands. Sorry Smith, but I don't care much anymore, and I am with Demon-boy on this. We cannot live like this anymore."

The Smith was afraid of this. He would have to talk them out of any action that they were thinking of doing. This defeated attitude was not what he expected at all.

"And what were you all planning? To get into the weapon shed, grab your weapons and take on the masters?"

The three slaves smiled back at the Smith.

"No, Smith. You taught me to do the last thing your enemy would expect. If we do not have our weapons, then what does it matter?"

The Smith sighed. Perhaps if he told them, they would have a little hope, rather than not just lie down and die. He made his decision quickly. "I have some weapons hidden," he said very quietly.

"You do?" the three of them almost shouted.

"Shhhh. Keep it down. Yes, last winter, I hid some weapons in the camp."

"Why?" asked Bulldog-boy.

"You all know that I cannot sleep sometimes, so I work late or get up early. Well over the last few seasons, I have made weapons that are of better quality than what you lads would normally use. I couldn't give them to you now, could I?"

"Where?" asked Demon-boy.

"No. I will not tell you, not for a while yet. Perhaps once you have thought your way through a decent plan of action and consulted me, I will tell you."

"What weapons are there?" asked Funny-boy.

"A mixture. Some personal weapons for you three and Trainer, even though he will not use them now. Also, some simple swords and knives."

"You want to know what we have planned?" asked Demon-boy.

"No. Not here, not now. I am convinced that within these walls, there is a spy. I'm not sure who it is but after yesterday, I am convinced. They knew our reactions too well and knew what to expect."

"When then?" said Bulldog-boy.

"When I want to know, I'll ask. Now the three of you better go and join the others. My advice, more than I have ever given you before, keep your heads down, your mouths shut and train like you have never trained before. For the whole summer, do nothing."

"The bastards are away during summer!" said Bulldog-boy.

"Like the advice you quoted back at me before, boy 'Do what the enemy least expects!'. That means training and doing nothing else."

The three nodded as they got up.

"Where is Quick?" asked Demon-boy

"Dead. He was caught escaping," said the Smith.

"Escaping, that's bullshit," replied Demon-boy.

"Of course, it is, another reason for you three to watch yourselves," Smith said.

They all nodded and left, running over to the practice field to catch up.

"So, cook, they had a meeting today. What was said?" asked the Chief.

"Smith told them to learn from Trainer's death and work harder, master!" replied the old cook.

"That was all? You would not lie to me would you, Cook?"

"No, master. He then explained he was trainer and sent them all out to the training fields."

"This is when the three pit-rats and the Smith had a little chat?"

"Yes, master. The three boys were planning something, but the Smith talked them out of it."

"What were they planning?"

"I'm am not sure, master. The boys never spoke of it. The Smith then told the boys he had weapons hidden somewhere and to do nothing over summer but train."

"Hidden weapons?" said the Chief, shock evident in his voice.

"Yes, master. He then told the three that you should always do what the enemy does not expect you to do, or something along those words."

"I know what it means, Cook. You have done well, keep it up. I want to hear anything that is said. And keep an eye on those three boys."

"Yes, master!" The Cook left and returned to her quarters in the settlement.

"Hidden weapons, father? You are going to kill them surely?" said his son.

"Of course, son, but I would rather wait until they spring their surprise, before springing one of my own. Let them think they have won before we pull the rug from under their feet."

"You are cruel, father," said the son, with a large laugh written across his face.

"Besides son, we have all summer before they will try something."

"True."

"I'll just make sure we leave a few extra warriors in back from the summer raiding."

"How many?"

"One ship worth."

"Fifty men?"

"Yes. Although I am tempted to leave a few more."

"Which ship?"

"I have not decided. We have a few full moons before the seas are ready for travel."

"I would rather have them all killed. This project of yours has taken you too much of your time away from the summer raiding as it is!"

"You do realise son, that the wagers I have won in the last three seasons of pit-fighting has made me more coin than any two of my ships combined in raids over the same period?"

The son scoffed. He knew it was true.

"Besides, you yourself said the raiding was getting less and less profitable as the summers roll on. The prices for slaves are down and the weaklings on the mainland's we raid, are learning to hide what little wealth they have. Perhaps winning our income on the pit-rats is the way of the future."

"Maybe, if you don't have to kill them all first."

The Chief laughed loudly. He smiled at his son, although he knew what was said was true.

Chapter Twelve

The summer of training had been the hardest for a long time. The boy was breathing harder as he finished his lap of the track. Bulldog-boy had taken his load of rocks in the barrow and taken off to complete his last circuit of the morning. The Smith was working them all harder than they had ever been worked before. He had implemented more exercises that would improve their stamina and also explosive speed. A speed they needed in the pits that was lacking before.

Demon-boy looked over at Funny-boy, also gasping for air and sitting on the ground. His friend was huge and had reached his full growth. He was now taller than even the Outlanders. His body had always been strong and heavily muscled, but now his body was harder with almost zero body fat. If there was any fat left on Funny-boy's body, it was hiding under his eyelids or in his groin. All of the slaves were the same. Demon-boy had reached his full height and now stood at six feet tall. Not as tall as Funny-boy who is close to seven feet, but certainly taller than Bulldog-boy's five and a half feet. Demon-boy's body had grown more muscled under the training of the Smith. He didn't think it was possible, but his chest, shoulders and arms had grown and now were large, balancing out his height.

As he watched Bulldog-boy lead the pack around the track, he realised there was only a few quarter moons left of summer and soon the Outlander-bastards would return from their raids.

The hate that he had for them had fuelled his training, as it had fuelled all of the other slaves. In the evenings, the Smith had continued his talks of tactics and strategy that he had learnt and experienced, but had included Funny-boy, Bulldog-boy and surprisingly Silent-boy. Silent-boy was a quiet, steady slave that didn't say much. But when he did, it showed a natural intelligence that was hiding behind those blue eyes. Silent-boy was Outlander himself and had grown up in the neighbouring country of Irik. He had been taken by the Outlanders when he was out with his county men fishing. His hate of the Outlanders was almost stronger than that of Demon-boy. He had been included in the evening talks with the Smith for a few reasons. He was superbly fit, strong and had shown that he was a good fighter. Also, the Smith admired his intelligence and calm. However, most importantly, he was included in the talks because not only did he know the land of the Outlander nation, but he was a sailor, knew the ways of the sea and how to sail on it. He was taller than Demon-boy and reached over six and a half feet tall. Slim muscle covered his body and his skin was a ghostly white, like all of the other Outlanders. He had been an original member of the first pit-rats that had arrived here but had never made many friends. He stuck to himself and preferred his own company. He was never rude and always spoke quietly with other pit-rats when engaging in conversation. And although he had been at the camp the same time as the others, he had never really bonded with Demon-boy and his two friends. Demon-boy remembered when that changed.

It was dark and Demon-boy and his two friends where standing over the grave of Trainer saying nothing, just lost in their thoughts. They didn't hear Silent-boy approach.

"Sorry to interrupt," was all he had said.

The three slaves turned quickly and watched as Silent-boy stood beside them, looking at the grave. He said nothing else, just lost in his own thoughts. The three stared at him for a while before going back to their silent thoughts, remembering Trainer. Demon-boy, of course, was the most emotionally charged. He had shared a bond with Trainer that none of the others, apart from Smith knew of. He remembered back to the first time that he met Trainer, all those summers ago in the slave ship as they stared across at each other. He had calmed Demon-boy with his eyes and head movements. Offering reassurance as best he could.

As the three of them made their way back to their cells, Silent-boy had followed. All of them moving into Demon-boy's cell and sitting down on the two beds. They hadn't realised that Silent-boy was following and were a little shocked when he entered the cell as well and sat next to Demon-boy on the bed. Funny-boy had reacted first.

"What do you want?" he said, with a little menace.

"When do we leave?" is all Silent-boy said in explanation.

"What do you mean 'when do we leave?'" asked Bulldog-boy.

"Who said we were leaving?" said Demon-boy.

Silent-boy looked across at the three of them, nothing showing in his face except the normal calm he radiated. "I am not staying. I will leave but it will not be alone. Of all the slaves here, you three are the most likely to try to escape." he said quietly.

"What makes you think we are going anywhere? If we were planning something, why would we take you?" said Funny-boy.

Silent-boy got up and moved to the cell door closing it, then returning to sit next on the bed again. "Because if you plan on leaving this land, you will need someone who knows how to sail a ship and knows the way of the ocean! You will need a guide to get you across the lands of these Outlander-bastards! I can do these things!"

The three looked at the slave. He then slowly told them of his story, and how he had been a fisherman braving the oceans to ply his trade. He had told them he was born and raised in Irik, the neighbouring country. "If I can get us to my homeland, we will be free!" he had told them.

"Why would we be free?" Demon-boy asked.

"Because my people do not keep slaves! Over the summers of my youth, many slaves from the Outlanders have reached my homeland, becoming free the moment they stepped over the border. It was a time of much celebration amongst my people when escaped slaves managed to get to my country. They are then looked after until they choose what they want to do, where they want to go."

The three had listened and listened well. The four of them talking long into the night. From that night on, he had been included in the evening talks with the Smith.

"Right. All grab a rock in each hand and line up!" yelled Smith.

They had all finished their circuits around the track. The barrows of rocks had been packed up in their usually place next to the large barn that they hadn't used much this summer. All of the slaves which now numbered sixty-one, grabbed a rock in each hand and lined up on the track. Smith had introduced this at the start of summer. It was a cross between the rock exercises and hell runs. Two painted rocks had been placed on the side of the track, fifteen paces apart. All of the slaves got into teams of three. Two would stand at one rock, the last member standing at the second painted rock. When the Smith yelled go, the first would explode into a sprint, running as fast as he could to the second painted rock. On reaching the line, the slave waiting would then sprint back to the first painted rock, with the waiting slave then taking off once the second slave had reached the line. It was a relay and it gave each slave about ten seconds rest before they had to sprint again. They did this so that each slave had completed twenty-five runs. It was gruelling and the Smith had made them focus on their take off speed, teaching them to react as quick as they could and explode into movement.

"Go!" yelled the Smith and the first line of slaves took off.

The Smith watched the slaves as they sprinted. He was happy with the progress of the slaves and knew they were now fitter than they ever been. He had made other changes as well. The afternoons were still used solely for combat training. However, he had given the two groups' time together in the pits, to let the experience of the senior slaves wash over onto the junior pit-rats. This helped in three ways! The more inexperienced pit-rats learnt valuable lessons, soaking up all the senior slaves could teach them. Secondly, it worked to bring ALL of the pit-rats to be drawn together into one group, and they worked better for it. Thirdly and most importantly, it had built on the natural leadership abilities of Demon-boy. A summer ago, most of the slaves had recognised Demon-boy's leadership on a subconscious level and would naturally jump at any request that he would make or listen to any advice he gave. Now all of the slaves were drawn to him, whether they realised it or not. The Smith knew that if Demon-boy asked them to rebel, they would! They reacted to his natural authority and even Demon-boy himself hadn't realised it. The Smith smiled and hoped the boy would not realise it for some time yet.

Once the new runs had been completed, Smith sent them all off for a light lunch. He watched all the slaves stretch before heading off to the food hall. He was a little proud of how they had all trained this summer and knew that the winter season was only a full moon away.

Life after the death of the Trainer had been difficult for the slaves and indeed, the Smith as well. The Smith had quickly established a new routine, loading up the slaves with new training to keep them focused and driven. The routine had worked.

Mornings spent working hard on new training methods that the Smith had discussed with the Trainer, but of course, the Trainer not implementing them.

The afternoons were focused on combat training, but the Smith had added one more hour of fitness before the slaves' sought out their evening meals. After their meals, the slaves had an hour or so of free time before they were once again locked in their cells, a rule the masters had brought back into effect after the death of the Trainer. He knew the four of the pit-rats he worked with were planning something but hadn't yet asked them what it was. He still hadn't found the spy he suspected was amongst them. It was clearly not one of the pit-rats, but he didn't rule it out. At first, he thought it was Sick-boy. But after watching him and even testing him quietly, ruled him out. Clearly, it was one of the cook's staff. All of them were slaves but lived outside in the main settlement. The cook and her five male slave helpers could be the only ones.

He just saw no evidence and couldn't prove it. He rubbed his head and went to join the slaves for evening meal.

That night, the Smith and the four slaves that had grown closer over the summer sat in the eating hall. The other slaves had gone to bed and the cook staff had left. Last year, the Smith had made a master key for the cells, so once the Masters had locked all the pit-rats in their cells and left, Smith had quietly let out the Demon-boy, Funny-boy, Bulldog-boy and Silent-boy. They had made their way down to the food hall and sat in the darkness with no candles burning.

"We have a plan!" said Bulldog-boy.

The other three nodding.

"Are you are going to tell me?" asked Smith.

"Yes," said Demon-boy.

"The bastard–masters will be back from their raids soon, so it better be quick," said the Smith.

"We want them back," replied Silent-boy.

The Smith had a look of confusion on his face and saw the four of them smiling.

"Yes. We want them back! You taught me to do what the enemy least expects. They would expect us to do something in the summer, with less warriors around. They would not expect anything during the winter, with them all returned," said Demon-boy.

"True, but that increases the risks," said Smith.

"We don't think so," said Funny-boy.

Smith listened as they outlined their plan. He watched as he listened noticing the four of them were together, acting as one and very motivated. The plan was indeed the last thing the Outlanders would expect, but it was extremely dangerous.

A gamble that relied on so many things falling into place! He listened as they finished talking. "It is risky, with many things which could go wrong."

"Attempting anything is risky!" said Bulldog-boy.

The Smith nodded his agreement. Then, asked the boys one finally question. "When?"

"Whenever the opportunity presents itself," replied Silent-boy.

The four pit-rats nodded as the Smith thought his way through their plan. He was trying to find fault with it but couldn't. Although it was risky and could see them all dead, it was as he had taught the boy, the last thing the Outlander-bastards would expect. Therefore, it had the best chance of working. He thought heavily before speaking.

"The chicken hut!" was all the Smith said.

They all looked at him with confusion on their faces. The chicken coop had been only put in at the end of last winter. The cook had asked for it as a way to get rid of food scraps and provide eggs.

"Before the chicken hut was built, I buried the weapons under it."

"The chicken hut?" said Bulldog-boy in surprise.

"Yes. In the main enclosure, not where they sleep at night but in their yard. If you dig down about three feet, you will find sacks. The weapons are in those sacks. Not enough for all the slaves but enough to carry out this plan."

The pit-rats all smiled.

"Although for this plan to work, I would suggest bring one more into the group in secret. One of the pit-rats that you can trust to get the job done. If any of you are missing, it would be noticed. You're all too well known to the masters. One of the others that you trust but is not well known by the masters."

"Sick-boy?" suggested Funny-boy.

"Yes," said Demon-boy.

Silent-boy nodded, then added his opinion. "Yes, but perhaps not tell him or bring him into the group at all. There is no reason he needs to be told. We could tell him at the last minute and he would carry out what needs to be done." Once again, his calm and quick mind making a worthy suggestion.

"Agreed," said the Smith.

"So, it is set then?" said Bulldog-boy.

"It would appear it is. Now we just wait for the bastard-masters to arrive back and the opportunity to present itself."

"How many are you taking?" asked the Smith.

"Just the senior pit-rats, the other slaves have not fought in the pit with weapons yet and we don't know if they could make it. The senior pit-rats are desperate enough to make it," said Demon-boy.

All five of them nodded. It was late and they had spoken longer than they had anticipated. They all left and quietly returned to their cells. The Smith locked them all in, then returned to his own bed. Laying in his bed, he thought over the plan that they had outlined and was impressed. So many things could go wrong. As he drifted off to sleep, he hoped he had the strength to get out with them.

The Outlanders had arrived back from their raid later in the summer than normal. All of their ships where heavily laden with plunder. It had been the most profitable season in many summers. The Outlander joining further south than normal, looking for un-raided seaside towns to sack. They had much coin, silver and gold, as well as expensive cups and other household items made from silver or gold. Their biggest plunder had been the three hundred slaves they captured. Young women that many of his warriors had claimed and would be used as personal slaves for sex or sold when they got back to the mainland. It made space on their ships limited, with every spare space taken up with sobbing women. The Chief hadn't taken any children this raid, there was none to be found in the three settlements that he had ransacked, which was odd.

He stood at the prow of his son's new ship, looking towards the beach they would draw up into. He was tired after the season of heavy fighting and knew in his mind that he didn't have many seasons of raiding left in him. He would then be like Chief Erak, staying home and entrusting the raids to others. The Chief knew his son would manage well enough.

"Almost home, father!" his son said, handing him a water skin that was filled with wine. They had found an entire cellar full of large barrels, filled with the red wine that was prized in the southern lands. It made a welcome change from ale and Firemer that they normal drank. The chief would quite like to be able to make wine, but unfortunately the lands of his people were just too cold.

'Yes, almost home. Been a good season!" his look far away.

"What do you think of, father? You look so far away again."

"The pit-rats, boy. I think I have come to a solution of sorts."

"And?" his son pressed.

"We will keep a few pit-rats, but I think it's time to shrink how many we have. We will still keep a training camp for them, but the numbers will not grow. I want to keep them to a more manageable number, say twenty or so."

"You will kill the Demon-boy?"

"No. I will put him into some impossible fights. If he wins, we will make a fortune. If he loses, we will be rid of him."

"Impossible fights, father?"

"Yes. I'll pit him against two in his first fight. If he wins, I will put him against three the next."

His son smiled. "He may yet win; he fights well for a slave."

His father looked at him. "Okay, he fights well in general."

"Yes, but eventually, he will be killed."

"And the other slaves?"

"All of the senior pit-rats with face the same. The younger ones that have not been with us for long will fight as normal."

"Just kill him, father. You have wasted too much energy on the Demon-boy. He is a slave!

The Chief smiled. "Yes, he is just a slave. However, I have found it entertaining to throw challenges in front of him. When he faced Erak's best pit-rat in the first death bout, I expected him to lose but he won, and I was amused. Seeing him in other death bouts amused me and hearing of his reaction to the death of the Trainer, also amused me."

"What has changed?"

"I am no longer amused. He will die in the pits this winter. Trust me on that!"

They both stood on the prow as the ship beached at the front of his settlement. The Chief had listened as the warriors were welcomed back by laughing and cheering. He looked over his people, seeing the joy as wives and children welcomed back the warriors, glad to see their husbands and fathers back safely. Returning home to these scenes of happiness never failed to please him. This raid had seen less losses of warriors than other raiding season for many summers. He looked over his people and saw an old woman standing against amongst the others. A slave that was hiding under a hood, and the

Chief knew exactly who it was and nodded to the cook. She must have something to report as she bowed back. He jumped down, accepting pats on the backs and hugs from his people. He made his way across to the cook, ignoring his people. He reached her quickly.

"Master, I know of their plans!"

Demon-boy sat on the stone floor as the crowd cheered the fighters. In the pit made of stone, fought Silent-boy. Once again, they were in Erak. Demon-boy had fought here many times before and had earned a reputation amongst Erak's warriors. His first death bout had been here, and the fight had been over in just a few seconds. Even though they were not supposed to watch, Demon-boy had put his heads between his knees, his arm covering what appeared to be his vision. Like other slaves, they had learnt to angle their head in such a way to still see the fight, but for it to appear they were not. A move Bulldog-boy had come up with and passed onto all the other slaves.

The fight hadn't been going long when Silent-boy got first blood, his sword scoring across the bicep of his opponent. Silent-boy preferred to fight with a longsword, as his people in Irik used. He was proficient with it and even though he had learnt to use other weapons, using a two-handed great sword was his preference. He fought calmly with no emotion showing on his face. His opponent lunged, his sword in his left hand towards Silent-boy's face. Silent-boy stepped to the left and smacked the other pit-rat in the face with the hilt of his sword knocking out two teeth of his opponent. He then stepped back as the opposing pit-rat swung a straight right with his fist, then followed up with a slashing left aiming for the throat of Silent-boy. Silent-boy stepped in avoiding the thrust and bringing his longsword up into the groin of the slave. The slave screamed and bent over. With silent detachment, Silent-boy swung his long blade in a full circle with all his strength, straight into the slaves throat, slicing it wide open. The slave dropped to the ground and bleed out very quickly.

The gathering warriors cheered at the move as the slave's head dropped to the ground. They continued to roar their approval as Silent-boy wiped his blade clean on the slaves back before getting out of the pit. He sat back down next to Demon-boy, who whispered loud enough just to be heard.

"Nicely done."

"Thank you. You expecting the Bastard-chief to have something in store for you?" he whispered back.

"Look across the pit, there are two slaves who have not fought yet and I am the only one that has not fought yet on our side!"

Silent-boy looked over. He hadn't noticed that the opposition slaves outnumbered them by one. He shook his head as Chief Erak's voice rang out across the hall.

"As always my brother in arms, Chief Hura has asked for a special bout."

The crowd roared again. Demon-boy received a slap to the head and stood before jumping down into the pit.

"We give to you one of the best pit-rats Chief Hura owns, we give you the Demon-child!"

At the mention of his name, the crowd once again cheered loudly, the sound vibrating off the stone floors.

"Against Demon-child, we will throw not one, but two pit-rats into the pit to face him."

The gathered warriors roared even louder. Demon-boy looked up as the two slaves joined him in the pit. Both were holding a small buckler shield in one hand, a short sword in the other. They were of equal height, slightly shorter than six feet, and covered in slim muscle which marked them for speed. The Chief of Erak had his own training camp now and it showed on the faces of these two slaves. He saw determination, hate and confidence in both of their faces. They slowly moved their arms limbering up as he stood still, waiting to explode into action.

"To make things interesting, I offer the following wager to my brother Chief."

The room went quiet, waiting to hear the wager. Outlanders lived to gamble, the bigger the wager, the more excitement they received from the contest.

"I offer the finest of my raiding ships and two thousand silver coins if I lose. If I win, he gives me ten of his prettiest slave girls and two thousand silver coins."

The crowd didn't cheer, just looked at Chief Hura to see what he would say. Chief Hura stood.

"I want more, brother. It's two against one and the wager does not reflect the odds," said Chief Hura before looking around the room. He looked at the Demon-boy standing in the pit, his back facing the Chief, which angered him. He looked at his son as his son had just whispered in his ear. He liked the idea and smiled.

"I would ask for this Chief Erak. If I win, you give me TWO of your finest ships and seven thousand silver coins."

It was a huge amount and was the biggest amount any chief had offered in wager. The room remind silent waiting on the rest of the wager.

"And what do I get if I win?" replied Chief Erak

"If you win, I will offer you ten of the youngest and prettiest slave girls I have, five thousand silver coins and lastly four of my best pit-rats to replace the two you have fighting tonight."

"Why would I need to replace them? If they win, they will be alive," said Chief Erak.

"Because if your two pit-rats win, I want them set free!" said Chief Hura.

The crowd was shocked. It was a massive wager and although Chief Erak could afford it, he had many silver coins after all, it would be a hard one to swallow. Chief Erak looked at his two pit-rats. Their faces showing their enthusiasm and he knew they would fight like demon's themselves to win their freedom.

Demon-boy sat there with rage written all over his face. He also knew the opposing two slaves would fight like demons to win their freedom. Silent-boy just shook his head in silence. All of the wagers he had been told of by the more experienced pit-rats in the training camp, never mentioned bets of this size. Although his friend had great skill, was strong and faster than any other warrior he had seen or heard of, against two slaves who could win their freedom, the fight could only end one way. He was worried for his friend.

"What say you, brother?" yelled Chief Hura, milking the moment.

"Bugger it, I accept."

The noise that erupted was deafening, even Demon-boy who was standing, lost in his own private rage, was shaken. He focused on the two pit-rats in front of them, they had huge evil smiles on their faces, and he knew he would not survive. For the first time in the pits, he lost his confidence. The other two pit-rats knew he was not confident and their smiles grew larger as their arms started limbering up more aggressively. He stood there waiting for his death. The cold feeling of final breath washing over him as he accepted his fate. He was ready to fight hard and die hard! Until some words came across from Silent-boy. Some words that he could only just hear because of the noise of the crowd.

"Disappoint them, snow weasel, rage and speed are your gift."

It was a dangerous move to pull and if anyone else had heard the words, Silent-boy would have been killed.

Demon-boy stood a little straighter, his eyes focused, the rage building again as he blocked out the roaring of the crowd. His sole focus, on the two pit rats before him.

"FIGHT!" yelled Chief Erak.

One of the pit-rats moved slightly to his right, the other slightly to the left. This was to block off his retreat. There was no room to move, so he did what Smith had trained him to do. He remembered the words of the Smith so clearly in this moment, as if he were standing beside him.

"Always do what the enemy least expects you to do."

The thought was running through his head as he charged the warrior on his right. Due to the new training the Smith had given all the slaves, he now could go from standing still to moving very quickly. As he rushed the warrior on his right, he jumped in the air to the right. As he moved towards the pit wall, his right leg found purchase and he pushed off with all his strength. This was the last thing anyone in the hall would have expected, and of course, the two pit-rats against him certainly didn't anticipate the move. Demon-boy had pushed himself up into the air over the shield of the pit-rat on the right. He had dived headfirst over this warrior, time slowing down as he lurched himself through the air. As he flew over this pit-rat, he slashed his short sword in his left hand down, slicing a huge cut on the warrior's shield arm. He spun in the air, landing on the ground on his shoulders, so he could fall forward into a tumblers roll, landing on his feet. He was facing away from the two slaves. He spun on his heal heading right, his hand axe leading the way. It narrowly missed the slave he had cut as the slave ducked, but as he continued to swivel, his short sword came up and stabbed into the shoulder of the pit rat. At the same time as the sword stabbed deeply into the pit-rats shoulder, his hand axe had continued to block the sword of the second fighter.

The first pit rat dropped his sword as the power fell from his arms when he pulled the sword from his shoulder. This pit rat fell to the ground on his hands and knees. The second pit rat had dodged the sword as it came at him and stepped back. Demon-boy didn't give him that luxury and followed up with a sword thrust to the face which was blocked by the fighter's shield. However, the fighter forgot briefly about the axe in Demon-boy's other hand which dropped and came out wide, under the shield, connecting with his knee. The fighter screamed as he felt his knee smashed into pieces. He still managed to swing his sword again at his head, missing closely as he ducked. On his way back up, he sliced the sword into the fighter's throat, pushing with all his strength until the sword went all the way through and came out the back of his neck. The slave dropped as his spinal cord was sliced apart. The sword dropped with the fighter. Demon-boy swung back to the other fighter who was just getting to his feet, reaching for his sword.

He ran over quickly stepping on the sword and kneeing the slave full in the face. He then stepped behind the fighter. Helping the slave to his feet while fending off weak punches, he managed to raise the fighter to a standing position. He looked at Chief Hura. He smiled coldly at the Chief as he slashed the throat of the slave with his axe. He let the body drop. The crowd was going wild, but he only heard the beat of his own heart and the rage in his own veins. He saw the other slave on the ground, choking slowly on his own blood.

Remembering his first fight in this ring and smiled as he drew his arm back and threw his axe. It sailed end over end before burying itself into the forehead of the fighter that was choking. The slave died instantly.

He walked over and grabbed his axe and his sword. He didn't even wipe them. As the crowd screamed his name, he drew himself out of the pit and without bowing, something he had always done, sat back down with his back to the Chief.

He chanced a look at Silent-boy, and saw he was trying hard not to laugh.

"Do you think they are disappointed?" he said before bowing his head and trying to breathe.

The fight had been over quickly.

As the gathered warriors continued to chant Demon-child over and over again, Chief Hura looked coldly at the pit-rat he had expected to die. Yes, he had just won the biggest wager that had ever been wagered on a pit-fight, but he no longer cared. He could still see the smile on the Demon-child's face as he had stared at the Chief and proceeded to slice the other slave's throat. He looked at his son who managed to speak over the noise around him. The son was about to speak when the father shook his head.

"When we get back tomorrow, kill the Smith. In a few days when that has sunk in, kill him in front of all the others," he said pointing at Demon-boy.

The son nodded slowly. "About time, father. This amusement of yours has gone on longer enough!"

The room continued to cheer and many bets across the hall were being collected.

"How is it that you never seem to win these bets I make with you?" said Chief Erak.

"Because I never expect to win!" replied Chief Hura.

"What price for this Demon-child?"

"None. He is not for sale."

"Name a price and I'll pay," pleaded Chief Erak.

"No. I have plans for that pit-rat."

Chief Erak saw the eyes of the Chief Hura and decided not to continue. It had been a surprising fight and even though he knew this Demon-child and had seen him fight before, he hadn't dreamed of him winning against two of his better fighters. It's not like he couldn't afford to pay the wager, it was his pride that was injured.

"What are your plans for the Demon-child if I cannot buy him then?" he said.

"I plan on killing him!"

Chapter Thirteen

Demon-boy had arrived back from Erak on sixth-day. He and the others were not given time to rest but put straight back into training on seventh day. The masters promise of pit-rats having seventh-day off if Demon-boy won the end of the year competition, a distant memory. Demon-boy and the Smith knew he would not keep his word. It was late afternoon two quarter moons after he had arrived back and all of the pit-rats were in the training pits, practising their moves; the older more experienced ones teaching the younger. The Smith had been called away to the main settlement just after lunch. Demon-boy watched Silent-boy as he was down in the pit, taking the youngest pit-rat through a mock fight. He had hoped to catch-up with his other two friends Bulldog-boy and Funny-boy, but they hadn't returned from their death bouts yet. They had left a few days before he got back, the bastard-masters traveling straight from Era and heading to the far north province of Icuk to watch their bouts. They were due back any day now.

He watched as Silent-boy whacked the younger youth on the back of the head.

"Remember to move! Your legs are not rooted to the ground, so move them," Silent-boy told the younger slave. "You need to remain fluid, always moving, never stopping for too long. If you do you become an easy target."

"Okay," the young slave nodded.

"Jump out and watch closely as I have a fight with someone else, watch how my body is either moving or waiting to move."

The young slave nodded and got out. Silent-boy had taken this younger slave under his wing a few full moons ago. The young slave no older than nine summers, was quiet and shy. He hadn't even earned a slave-name yet.

Another older pit-rat called Stonefist-boy jumped in. The two of them launched straight into a full contact fight. Demon-boy smiled as he also watched Silent-boy. Always moving and looking for a way to land hits on his opponent. He didn't have the strength of Funny-boy or the explosive speed of Bulldog-boy but had a higher level of skill than both. He walked away, heading towards the track. Another hour of running circuits and they would call an end to the training, heading for meals.

The Smith stood in front of the Angry-man and his son. He had been called away after lunch and told to report to the Chief at the beaches. Once there, he had been led to a stone building used for storing dried fish. Although empty, the smell of the smoked white meat still filled his nostrils. He stood in front of the Chief and his son, four other Outlander warriors standing behind him, guarding the closed door. Not that he would try to escape, with his limp he would not get far.

"I hear rumours, Smith. Rumours of a plan to escape!" said Angry-man.

The Smith's throat went tight, and he felt his stomach lurch. They bloody knew!

"Well, Smith? Nothing to say?" said Son-of Angry-man.

"I know nothing of a plan, master. I certainly have no plans to leave. How far would I get on this leg?"

Both the master and his son smiled.

"And still you lie to us!" said Angry-man.

His son also smiled and continued.

"Rumour has it you were going to steal one of our ships?"

All of the Outlanders laughed including Son-of Angry-man. Angry-man smiled a cold smile.

"We know everything, Smith. We know you have weapons hidden, although we do not know where. We know of certain slaves within our own settlement here that will try to help you get out. We know you were planning to run to our other beach settlement of Badwater, a settlement of five days on foot to the north to steal a boat and not try for one of the other boats, not one hundred paces from us. Very clever, Smith," said Angry-man.

The Smith tried not to show the shock. They knew everything.

"We know you were going to sail to the west first, before turning south to throw us off the scent and only take enough slaves to sail the boat."

The Smith breathing had increased, but his nerve held.

"I'm not sure who has been telling these lies, master. However, they are not true."

The warriors behind him laughed again.

"Your guilt is written all over your face, Smith. My father

had already decided your guilt before you were summoned to us!" said Son-of-Angry-man.

"If I am already guilty, why are we still talking..." his words abruptly cut off as two warriors grabbed and arm each and pulled them behind his back.

A third warrior moved and tied a rope around his wrists, securing them together tightly.

"Why are we still talking? Perhaps I wanted to see if you had the balls to admit it, slave."

"Master, you have been told lies," replied the Smith, between clenched teeth.

He knew to admit the truth would only endanger the pit-rats.

"I don't think so, Smith" said Angry-man as the Smith was pushed down into a wooden seat.

The master was taking off his topcoat and tunic as the Smith's legs where bound to the legs of the seat. "This would have gone so much better for you if you had told the truth. Now you will die, as painfully as we can do it, but not before you tell us of the hidden weapons and the pit-rats in on this plan of yours."

The Smith didn't fight but sat glaring at the master who now stood shirtless before him. As the first blow landed rocking his head back, he thought of the boy. He lifted his head again, glaring at the master. If he were going to be beaten, he would show no weakness. If they killed him, so be it.

The punches rained down, hitting his face, his chest and anywhere else that the master though he would get a reaction. The Smith stayed silent, sealing his lips through the pain, not uttering a single word, holding in the screams as agony moved through his body.

Demon-boy was eating his evening meal with Silent-boy when the doors to the food hall were flung open. His heart jumped in his chest expecting to see the bastard-masters but was relieved when he saw Funny-boy and Bulldog-boy walking fast towards him. His relief was short lived.

They came over fast and sat down opposite them.

"Smith is dead!" said Funny-boy, with a worried look on his face.

The words bounced off Demon-boy and he couldn't accept them. "What?" he replied.

"I said, Smith is dead," said Funny-boy again.

He felt his blood, pumping through his veins as he tried to remain calm.

"How? When?" asked Silent-boy.

Bulldog-boy spoke, telling all he knew. "Not sure. We arrived just now and as our wagon approached the settlement, we noticed a body hanging from a tree upside down. It was the Smith. He was naked and his body was bruised with burn marks all over his body. They tortured him before killing him."

Other pit-rats had gathered around the four of them and had heard the news. Whispers of conversations spread around the room until all of the pit-rats were now gathered around the four of them.

"Silence!" said Demon-boy loudly.

The room fell quiet. Demon-boy looked around at all the pit-rats. They all were waiting on him, he realised. Waiting for him to say or do something! When had he been thrust into this role?

"Masters will be here soon to lock us into our cells. Do nothing! Go to your cell and wait," he said.

"But…" said one of the younger pit-rats.

"No buts! Finish your meals, go to your cells and wait."

The slaves all moved instantly returning to their tables to finish their meals. Leaving the four to their conversations.

"What are we going to do?" whispered Bulldog-boy.

Demon-boy looked in turn at the three of his companions before speaking. "We are leaving! Tonight!"

His three companions nodded, and he saw in their face's determination and strength.

"What are we going to do?" asked Funny-boy.

"No, not here. We talk when it's safe. Do not forget Smith had the only spare key to the cells and always had it hidden on himself!"

"Not true," replied Silent-boy.

The others looked over at him looking for an explanation.

"He gave me another one a few quarter moons ago. Said he had made two but made me promise not to tell you all until the time was right. I would say that time is now right."

They all nodded.

"Once again, the Smith has provided for us," remarked Demon-boy.

The Angry-man and his son sat on the beach sharing a jug as the light completely faded from the sky.

"Why did he stick to his story? Why did he not admit it? We know he is not weak or lacked courage."

"I am not sure, son. He certainly died hard!"

"When do I kill the whelp?"

"Tomorrow, you can kill him, son. I am sure the news has reached the slaves by now. Give him a night to live with the death, then tomorrow afternoon you can give the other slaves another object lesson."

Son-of-Angry-man smiled. "I look forward to it, father!"

"Take fifty of our best warriors with you, fully armed. When the Demon-boy is cut down, the others may be shocked into action. If that happens cut them all down!"

"All of them?"

"Yes. All of them"

"The slaves will be locked into their cells by now. Do you think they will try something tonight, father?"

"No. We found the key the Smith had made. I doubt he made more than one. However, just in case, I have ordered a few hidden guards around the training camp for the night."

"How many, father?"

"Twenty hidden in various places around the camp, none of the pit-rats could get out without being seen!"

"Well, I better go get some food, father. Shall I bring you some back?"

"No, son. Send someone down later with some bread and another jug or two. I feel the need to relax under the stars tonight."

Son-of-Angry-man moved off towards the settlement and a hot meal. He looked forward to tomorrow and smiled to himself.

The four of them gathered in the food hall as they had done many times before. The only difference was Sick-boy was also with them. They had waited until they heard the main gate closed and had arisen. Silent-boy letting the four others out of their cell along with the younger slave that he had taken under his wing. The younger slave was now hiding on the porch with a dark blanket wrapped around himself, keeping a watch out for any sign of the masters.

"What are we doing? And how long have you had a way to get out of the cells?" demanded Sick-boy. He had also been let out of the cells by Silent-boy but had no idea why and was being his normal surly self.

"We are leaving. Tonight," said Demon-boy.

"To go where?"

Funny-boy saw the anger rising in Sick-boy and jumped into the conversation.

"We have been planning to leave for some time. Our plans are made, and we need your help. Or, you can stay here! It's up to you."

Sick-boy looked around at the others. "Why am I only being told now, then?"

"Because," said Demon-boy, before being cut off by Bulldog-boy.

"Because, we didn't trust you. Be honest, man! You do not exactly control that mouth of yours, do you?" said Bulldog-boy

"No. I do not," said Sick-boy, in his sullen manner.

"Exactly. We all have roles to play and we are now telling you yours if you want in!"

"I want in. I want out of this place. What I want to know is why we didn't escape during the summer when the bastard-masters were at sea? Why wait until now?"

"Too predictable," said Silent-boy.

"Yes. We needed to do it when the bastard-masters least expected it."

"After killing the Smith, they will expect something like this," said Sick-boy.

"Yes, they will. Which is why we go carefully but with speed," said Demon-boy.

"If you are in, you follow Demon-boy's lead or you can stay here, betray us and I'll kill you myself" said Bulldog-boy.

Demon-boy watched the face of Sick-boy, looking for any sign of betrayal. All he saw, however, was Sick-boy trying to conceal his excitement.

"I can do that. Once we are out of here however, I go my own way, as it has always been."

The four of them looked at Sick-boy and then nodded.

"Good. So, what's the plan?" replied Sick-boy.

Before Demon-boy could speak, the main doors opened a little and the lookout came running over. Beside him, ran a slave from the settlement. Demon-boy knew her face but had never spoken to her before.

"This lady surprised me!" the young slave said.

All five of them watched the slave as she made her way to the table. She was anywhere between forty and fifty summers of age. Her hair was a sandy blonde, with eyes of dark brown. She was attractive and had an air of calm around her. She was what the Smith would say 'Pleasing on the eye and soul'

"I have a message for you, Demon-boy," said the slave.

"I don't know you!" said Demon-boy.

"No, you don't. The Smith did and through him, I know you."

"How?" said Funny-boy.

"It's not important. I heard the cries of the Smith as they killed him," she said.

The look of sadness in her eyes could be seen.

Demon-boy's face went cold at the mention of the Smith.

"Don't point that anger at me, Demon-boy, I do not deserve it. I bring a message!"

"What message?" said Bulldog-boy.

"Towards the end, Smith was shouting the same thing over and over again. The masters would not know what it was as he was speaking in a language from across the sea, the language of my people!"

"What was his words?" asked Demon-boy.

"They know!" she said, before continuing. "He screamed it over and over again."

"Do you know what he meant by that?" said Funny-boy.

She shook her head.

"I do," replied Demon-boy.

"What does it mean?" said Sick-boy.

"It means the Outlanders know of our plan and we must change it!" said Silent-boy.

Demon-boy nodded before turning back to the woman. "How did you get in here?"

She smiled. "I have been in this camp a long time. At the back of your indoor training hall is a small hidden tunnel."

"What tunnel?" said Sick-boy, sounding shocked before he continued, "I have been over every part of this camp and would have found it!"

She smiled again. "You must be Sick-boy. Smith describes you well."

"I would have found the tunnel, there is nothing in the floor as I check every part of it!" exclaimed Sick-boy.

"Why would you check the training hall floor?" said Silent-boy.

The others nodded.

"For a way out," replied Sick-boy.

"Where does this tunnel lead?" said Demon-boy.

"It leads to the main cook house behind the mead hall of the Chief. It's not very big and you have to crouch to get through. The tunnel comes out in the basement storage room."

"The bastard masters will know about it," said Funny-boy.

"No. If they knew about it would have been filled in when

this camp was built. According to the older slaves that serve in the kitchen, it was built during the previous chief's reign. They do not believe he passed on the information to his son!"

"What was it used for?" said Sick-boy.

"It's not important. Why do we trust you?" said Demon-boy.

She smiled again. "He said you would say that when we spoke of you. He said if anything happened to him to tell you of the tunnel and if you did not believe me, to say the following word to you," she said.

"What word?" said Silent-boy.

"Corvin," was all she said.

In that one word, Demon-boy knew she was not a snitch for the masters. In that moment he knew of the connection between this woman and the Smith, judging by the look of love in her eyes, the connection was an intimate one.

"He must have trusted you," said Demon-boy.

"He did," she replied.

"Corvin? What the hell is that?" exclaimed Sick-boy.

The others looked to Demon-boy for an explanation.

"That was Smith's name. No master would ever know that, and he only let it slip once in front of me, when he was drunk. I trust you," said Demon-boy.

"Thank you. I best leave, I do not need to know what is happening. Whatever happens, Corvin thought highly of all of you. Well, all of you except Sick-boy, of course," she said.

Sick-boy shrugged his shoulders, not caring.

She turned and made her way to the door before turning and saying one further thing. "Also, I saw the cook leaving the mead hall before the Smith was summoned to the masters." She held the look of Demon-boy for a few seconds, then disappeared into the gloom. Demon-boy knew straight away who had betrayed them.

"So, what do we do?" asked the young slave that had stayed silent through the conversation.

Demon-boy thought about it. "We go to our backup plan!"

"What backup plan?" said Bulldog-boy.

"The plan Demon-boy and I came up with, in case the other one fell to pieces, as it just has!" replied Silent-boy.

Demon-boy looked over at the young slave. "Go back to keeping watch please."

The young slave nodded and rushed back outside as Demon-boy continued.

"Funny-boy, you go release the slaves and get them to assemble in here and make sure they are quiet. Tell them I ask them to do this. Bulldog-boy, take Sick-boy and go dig up the weapons and bring them here. Once you have the weapons, I want you Sick-boy to go through and investigate this tunnel. Go through it and make sure it comes out where she says it does. Silent-boy, go with Sick-boy. I'll stay here and explain a few things to the other pit-rats."

They all left quickly to do what needed to be done. As Demon-boy sat there with his own thoughts, he thought of the Smith. His rage inside hadn't died since he had been told of his death. It had sat beneath the surface, waiting hungrily for the opportunity to be venerated and he would get that opportunity. He felt tears forming and got angry at himself. Plenty of time for tears later. Now was the time for vengeance then escape.

All of the pit-rats had gathered in the food hall and were quietly seated. Demon-boy stood before them. He looked over at Funny-boy, who nodded his head in reassurance. He started to talk.

"As most of you know the Smith is dead!"

Murmuring started straight away.

He let the news sink in before continuing, "I am not sure why, but he was tortured and hung by the bastard-masters. He was a father to all of us. As I said, I don't know why, but what I do know is I am leaving. Those of you that wish to stay can, but myself and the three standing behind me will not stay in this place one moment more. It is time to get out of this shit place."

The pit-rats waited on his words, some with hope in their hearts, others not believing what they are hearing.

"If you are tired of this life, tired of the bastard-masters and are happy to risk life to escape, you are welcome to join us! It will not be easy; we will be on foot running in middle of winter. It will be cold and hard but if we make it, there is a freedom waiting for us that we have never known."

Demon-boy looked over the assembled pit-rats. Sixty-two young men that were all looking at him, nodding their heads, fire in their eyes. A young pit-rat known as Thickskull-boy stood.

"We will follow you, Demon-boy. Wherever you lead us we will follow!"

The other pit-rats all nodded enthusiastically and Demon-boy knew he would have to try and get them all out of here. He knew he had to prove their faith in him was not misplaced. He felt the weight of responsibility on his shoulders and said nothing further. Thankfully, Silent-boy stepped forward.

"Our plans have been made for a while. If we give you instructions, you must follow them. If you fail, you doom us all. We will not tell you all of our plans, that way if you are captured, you cannot tell the bastards what you do not know. It will not be easy and the risk of losing our lives is bloody high. However, follow us and there is a small chance of freedom."

More nodding and Demon-boy could see the pit-rats

where driven and motivated to follow. He added to what Silent-boy had said.

"If any of these three standing behind me ask you to do anything, do it. They speak with my voice."

Demon-boy looked to his three friends, seeing all the determination in their faces. He looked back and saw the same look on every one of the pit-rats before him. The time was now, and he would not waste this chance.

Son-of Angry-man left the mead hall. It had been a good session and as his vision began to clear in the fresh air, he made his way to his own sleeping quarters. His father hadn't joined in that evening and had left his son and his warriors to their drinking and feasting. As he made his way down the settlement main road, he laughed to himself. The Smith's death had been long overdue, as had the Demon-boy's death. That would be fixed tomorrow and he had already picked the warriors to accompany him. As he breathed in the fresh chill air, he thought back over the season of raiding. It had been a good raiding season with much loot and many slaves. Two of the prettier slave girls would be waiting for him in his rooms. His new ship had performed well, so well in fact, that his father had commissioned three more just like it.

He had enjoyed watching the Smith bleed and scream. The words he screamed; he didn't understand. Words he had never heard before in any language that he had heard before. It didn't bother him overly much as he walked into his home. Shutting the door behind him, he chucked his cloak on the chair in front of the fire that was slowly dying. The room was still warm as he headed for the bedroom in the back and his giant bed.

He got to his room and found candles burning but his bed empty. Usually this would anger him, and he would have headed straight out to find the slave girls. However, in his drunken state, he didn't care. He didn't even remove his trousers or shirt before collapsing on his bed. He landed on his back and closed his eyes. He was almost asleep when he felt a cold pressure against his throat. He tried to brush it away but failed. He opened his eyes and looked straight into the face of a pit-rat and a hand was clamped over his mouth. He tried to struggle but the hand that held him was strong.

"You think I would leave without first saying goodbye?" said a voice to his left.

He looked over and saw the Demon-child looking at him. Turning back to the other pit rat, he saw it was the dark one. Son-of-Angry-man continued to struggle but there was no way even if he was sober, he could have moved the massive hand from his mouth, let alone the knife from his throat.

"You killed Trainer, you killed Smith," said Funny-boy.

"And now we are here to kill you. Before you disappear into the darkness, I want you to think of your father's settlement, think of it as you know it. Then picture it in flames!" said Demon-boy.

"Very soon, the settlement of your father will be in flames and burnt to the ground!" said Funny-boy.

He looked over at the Demon-child and saw the look of determination in his face. He tried to speak but couldn't, the hand clamped over his mouth being too strong.

He looked at the Demon-child as he felt the pressure on his throat increase. As the knife sliced his throat, he felt the hot warm sensation of liquid running down over his neck. He knew it was his blood. He struggles some more to no avail. As the darkness slowly came for him he heard the Demon-child speak once more.

"When the light fades and the darkness comes, where do you hide when the Demon-child comes for you?"

The light went dark as his life faded and left him.

"Chief, my Chief!" one warrior shouted as he ran across the beach towards the Chief.

"What is it?" said the Chief.

"The training camp, my Chief, it's on fire!"

"What? What's on fire in the training camp?"

"The whole camp, my Chief. The whole training camp is on fire! Every building!"

Angry-man jumped up and started running. As he got to the settlement, he started shouting orders to the warriors waiting for him. "Gather all the men and find my son. Tell him to meet me at the camp!" he said, as he continued to run towards the training camp.

He could see the orange glow long before he reached the training camp gate. When he arrived, there was twenty other warriors with him, all of them had their weapons drawn. One of the warriors that had been waiting approached the Chief.

"My Chief. As you can see all of the buildings are well ablaze."

The warrior was correct. All of the buildings where engulfed by flames that climbed towards the sky. There was no way to put them out, all that could be done was watch them burn and make sure the flames didn't spread to the settlement.

"What happened?" shouted Angry-man at the warrior.

"I am not sure, my Chief! We heard someone yell fire and all ran to the camp when we saw the flames!"

"Was the gate open when you arrived?"

"No, my Chief! The gates were locked, and I had to send for someone to unlock it!"

"Where are the guards that were supposed to be watching it?" he screamed. As soon as he had said the words, five guards of the twenty he had appointed to stand guard, approached. "Well?" he said.

"We saw nothing, my Chief. The camp was all still and silent. All of a sudden flames erupted from the large training shed first, then within seconds the rest of the buildings took flame."

"You saw nothing?" he yelled.

"No, my Chief. We saw no one."

"And the slaves? Where the hell are the slaves? I doubt they set everything to the torch, then stayed there to be burnt alive."

Another warrior stepped forward. "None of the slaves left the main building, my Chief. No movement was seen from any of the guards."

"Someone must have seen something! Where the hell is my son?"

No one answered as no one knew. Then they heard the screams. "Fire, Fire, Fire," rang out through the settlement.

Angry-man swung to see flames coming from his drinking hall. Flames already spewing out the windows. He ran back to the settlement as warriors, slaves and children fought to fight the fires with buckets of water. Along with the drinking hall, it looked like another ten buildings had been set a light. His fury at the situation was easy to see on his face, and his warriors shrunk back from him.

"My Chief," said a voice approaching him. It was the warrior that he had sent to finds his son.

"Where is my son?"

"He is dead, my Chief! Someone killed him in his rooms."

"NOOOOOOOOOOOOOOOOOOOOO!" he screamed.

"Get every warrior we can spare from putting the fires out. The slaves are out here somewhere. FIND THEM."

"My Chief?" said the warrior who had found his son.

"Send two hundred warriors at full speed towards Badwater. Tell them to search every village and path between here and there. Send fifty warriors to every other sea settlement we have; they will be looking for a ship. Every other warrior is to help get these fires under control. And you," he said pointing at the warrior who had found his son. "Take me to my son!"

"Yes, my Chief."

All of the warriors moved quickly to carry out their instructions. Within heartbeats warriors and horses were sent out in all directions that lead to sea settlements.

The Chief had followed the warrior to his son's rooms. Upon entering the room, he straight away smelled the blood in the air and the shit from when his son's body had released its bowels. He got to his son's room and looked down at his son. His body lay on the bed, blood covering everything. Missing from the scene was his son's head. He looked over at his son's weapons belt that was hanging from the door. The hand axe the Smith had made for him gone.

"NOOOOOOOOOOOOOOOOOOOOOOOOOOOOO!" he screamed before drawing his knife and cutting the throat of the warrior that had accompanied him. He ran out of the room, heading outside.

"My Chief," yelled another warrior as he made his way outside.

"WHAT NOW!" yelled the Angry-man.

"Our ships on the beach, my Chief."

"What? They are gone!? I thought I gave orders that they were to be checked on, then guarded?"

"You did, my Chief, I was in that group you gave those orders to!"

"Well, spit it out!"

"The ships are all aflame, my Chief!" he said with his head facing the ground.

"How many?"

"All of them, my Chief!"

"ALL OF THEM? There are over thirty ships beached."

"Yes, my Chief. The warriors are trying to save what they can, but all of the ships are burning brightly," the warrior said.

The warrior looked up in time to see his own Chief stab him. The Chief's knife entering his heart. As the body dropped, Angry-man took off towards the beach. Arriving, he called out to one of his more trusted warriors.

"Mekak. What happened?"

"I'm not sure, my Chief! We were watching the ships and I swear, we saw no one go near the ships. All of a sudden, they burst into flames."

Angry-man grabbed the warrior by his shirt and held his knife to the warrior's throat. "I have just killed two of our warriors. Speak the truth!" he half yelled.

"I swear my Chief. No one approached or left the ships. Either by land or by the water."

Angry-man held his knife at the warrior's throat before finally taking it away.

"How the hell did they do so much damage?" said Angry-man.

The warrior knew better than to offer an answer.

"Find them for me, Mekak. You are my longest serving warrior and have never failed me, take control of the search for them."

"Yes, my Chief," he replied as he ran off.

Angry-man watched his ships burn from the inside out. Warriors tried their best to fight the flames with buckets of water, but it was a losing battle. He watched as the flames grew larger and larger. His breathing coming in short powerful gasps as his own fleet of raiding ships burned.

The warriors moved through the settlement that was in chaos. All of the Outlanders that lived there battled the flames to stop them before the whole settlement was lost. Some of the pit-rats had been caught and quickly killed. The bodies dragged before the Chief. He looked over every one of them and shook his head before yelling for the warriors to keep searching. In all fifteen pit-rats' bodies had been dragged before him. This left approximately fifty of them still on the run. The sun had started to rise over the settlement. He hadn't received messages from the seaside settlement that had ships, his warriors still out searching but sending messages back regularly.

As Angry-man started to get a look over his capital with the rising light, he could finally get an idea of the damage. Every building in the training camp had been burnt to the ground. His drinks hall had collapsed, the fire burning through the support timbers and roof. He had lost a quarter of his settlement to the flames and not to mention, all of his ships that had been beached had been lost to the flames. He strolled around the settlement surveying the damage. It would take him a full summer to rebuild the lost buildings. It would take him summers to replace the lost ships, but more importantly no amount of time would let him replace his lost son. He had found his son's head. It had been nailed to the same tree that the Smith was hung from. The Smith's body, of course, there was no sign of. He stood once again at the beach, watching the last burning embers of his ships. He wanted nothing more than to get his hands on the Demon-child, who he knew was responsible for all of this. He should have killed him. He kicked the Firemer jug at his feet, sending it rolling down the beach. He would move heaven and earth to get his hands on that little pit-rat, and if it were the last thing he did, he would see him die a slow and painful death. The thought a good one as the thought of revenge consumed him, but first he would have to find the little bastard.

Chapter Fourteen

The sun was starting to come up as morning was approaching fast. The night had been cold, just as the previous five nights had been cold. The slaves struggling to keep their feet warm as they had run through the snow throughout the night, resting only a few moments every so often to stretch and warm their feet and hands. Slaves didn't own socks, let alone boots and had to tear up rags and older clothing before wrapping their feet in them. Although used to the cold, none of the escaping slaves had been ready for the coldness of running through the bad weather of winter. Simple tasks like emptying their bladders becoming a nightmare. Some of the pit-rats had started urinating on their hands to keep them warm. The few that did tried to convince the others they should do the same, but the practise did not spread through the group.

They had stuck to the plan Silent-boy and Demon-boy had come up with, running at night through the worst of the cold and resting up during the day when it was warmer. The plan was a good one, but they faced many challenges moving through the cold nights. They had already lost five of the younger pit-rats through exhaustion and cold. A life of training and fighting had hardened them all and made them extremely fit, but it didn't matter how fit they were, fitness would not keep the cold from their bones. Of course, the younger and inexperienced pit-rats didn't have the same level of fitness and endurance the older ones did, and they suffered more. Demon-boy was impressed with the younger pit-rats that had made it this far. They never complained and even though they were close to the end of their endurance, they did their best to keep up. Of the senior pit-rats, only twenty-three had made it out, this included Demon-boy and his three friends. Forty-nine slaves on the run through the cold of winter. Food was an immediate problem; they had none. Thus far, they had survived on a small amount of food that they had taken with them, when they ran from the training camp. This was now gone. Their bodies with no fuel, running on empty and Demon-boy knew they couldn't go on.

They had left with only the weapons Smith had hidden, which hadn't been many. A few knives and short swords are all the slaves had. The only slaves to have decent weapons were Demon-boy and his three friends. The silver hand axe the Smith had made for son-of-angry man now hanging form Demon-boys belt. They had all grabbed their slave blankets as they left and had looped these around one shoulder and tied the other ends together to make a sort of rucksack. In the blanket was any spare clothing and of that, there was not much.

On their third night, they had come across the original slave camp that Demon-boy had grown up in. Demon-boy had explained the need to take a slight detour in order to secure more supplies.

"We are not going straight for the border?" asked Funny-boy.

"No. Demon-boy is taking us to his old slave camp which is not far," replied Silent-boy.

They had all stopped for a brief break to warm their hands and feet in any way they could and allow the younger ones to catch their breath. The four friends stood together on a small hill, overlooking a valley.

They couldn't see it but Demon-boy assured them that the camp was at the end of the valley. "It's at the end of this valley. I am not sure how many slaves are still there but if we can get in undetected, we should be able to pick up more food and hopefully more clothing."

"We do need more clothing. The cold is getting dangerous, especially for the younger ones," replied Silent-boy.

"How many masters?" asked Bulldog-boy.

"When I was there summers ago, there was only about fifteen!" said Demon-boy.

"We could take that many!" said Bulldog-boy.

"Yes, we could, but it would make much noise and wake the other slaves!" said Demon-boy.

"That's what we want, they can come with us!" said Funny-boy.

"No. They would slow us down and how many of them would be trained to fight like us?" said Silent-boy.

They all knew what he said make sense, but it was hard to swallow. The thought of leaving behind any slaves was hard.

Demon-boy saw the look of anguish on Funny-boy's face and replied, "He is right. When I was there, an old woman and young boys tended the fields. They would not last long out here!"

"So, we sneak in?" asked Bulldog-boy.

"If we have to. We get in, silently take out any guards, take what we need and be gone as quickly as we can," said Silent-boy.

Demon-boy nodded his head in agreement before continuing. "They have a large supply shed full of food, although most of it needs to be cooked which is no good to us. There should be however some smoked meat and bread that we can easily eat. There are no weapons shed but if we can take out the guards, we can take their weapons and more importantly their boots. If we are overrun by a patrol, we do not have enough weapons to fight them off."

They all agreed and discussed who was going in.

"We leave a few of the senior pit-rats with the young ones and take only the senior pit-rats that have proper weapons," said Silent-boy.

"How many is that?" asked Demon-boy.

"With us four, there is another five pit-rats with short swords or hand axes, nine in total," said Bulldog-boy.

"Should be enough. Will take us another hour to get there and it's only a few hours until sunrise. We need to get this done," said Demon-boy.

"I'll send Talk-boy with the younger ones. He can find a spot to lie up for the day. I'll also tell him to keep out scouts to guide us in," said Silent-boy.

"Agreed. Tell him somewhere very well hidden," said Demon-boy.

They got in easier than expected. There had been only two masters guarding the main gate that were taken out very quickly by Bull-dog boy who had approached the gate, acting like a drunk slave that had got lost. When the masters went to grab him, he killed them on the spot. The other guards of which there were only three, were killed in their sleep. Once no more masters could be found, Demon-boy changed his mind.

"Silent-boy, send someone for the other pit-rats they should not be far. Get them all back here and in this room," said Demon-boy.

Silent-boy nodded and left the shed.

"Why the change of plan?" asked Bulldog-boy.

"Might as well give everyone a chance to warm up," said Demon-boy.

Entering the camp brought back many memories for Demon-boy, some good and some bad. It was a little overwhelming and Demon-boy silently struggled with the emotions.

All the slaves in the camp had been asleep and Demon-boy resisted the urge to wake them, knowing so many would not help the situation. Instead, they had spent a reckless two hours gathering up any weapons, food, clothing, and blankets that they could find. Resisting the urge also to burn the place down. The pit-rats were all in the eating shed sorting themselves out and keeping warm when an old lady walked in and stared at them. The pit-rats knew she was a slave but still stood, unsure.

"Stand-down," said Demon-boy, as he approached the cook that he recognised. "Hello cook, it's been a very long time."

Cook looked at him, not recognising him.

"You do not recognise the 'Demon-Child'?" he said.

Light dawned in her eyes and she stepped forward into a hug from Demon-boy. "You are back, child?"

"Just stopping through. We needed some supplies on our way to the border."

She released him and stepped back. "You are escaping?"

"Yes."

"The Smith is with you?" she asked looking around. She then noticed the pain in Demon-boy's eyes. She knew what he was about to say before he said it.

"The masters hung him."

She nodded, lost in her own thoughts. "A great man the Smith was!"

"Yes."

"The guards are all dead?"

"Yes."

"Do not wake the others, they will want to join you and more numbers would not help." As always, she saw straight to the heart of the problem.

"Thank you, cook. Yes, we would like to take everyone but cannot risk it."

"There is not many of us here, twenty slaves in all."

"That's why there was only five guards?"

"Yes. The iron mine is mined out and we only have a few slaves left to tend the fields."

They were interrupted by Silent-boy. "Sorry to interrupt, ma'am. Demon-boy, we need to move. The sun will be rising soon. We need to move."

"I understand. Before you go, get into the old smithy. I see you are short on weapons; I think there may be a few hidden in there from when the Smith worked the forges," she said.

"Of course, he often couldn't sleep!" said Demon-boy.

She nodded knowingly. "Stay safe, my boy. Get out of this place." She squeezed his hand that she had been holding, then let go.

"I will, cook, and thank you. For everything you have done for me."

"No need to thank me my boy. Just get this lot to safety

and you will make this old woman happy and word will spread. The other slaves will be inspired." She then turned and returned to her bed.

They all piled out of the eating shed and headed for the gates, Demon-boy and his three friends smashed their way through the old smithy door. Whilst his three friends searched for weapons, Demon-boy went into the old Smith's quarters, his first time in there. They had carried candles from the eating shed and searched thoroughly.

"Nothing in here!" yelled Bulldog-boy.

"In here!" yelled back Demon-boy.

He had just pulled off the top of the wooden bed the Smith had slept on. Underneath was five large sacks, hidden in a small cavity dug into the earth. The others had come in and seen Demon-boy lifting the sacks out. They opened them and smiles spread over their faces. A total of six short swords, eight hand axes, ten large daggers and one large sack that held a massive two-handed long sword. Demon-boy drew out the sword and handed it to Silent-boy.

"You prefer to fight with something like this, I think!" he said smiling.

Silent-boy took the weapon and held it aloft, a smile spreading across his face. "Thank you!"

Demon-boy looked over at Funny-boy. "Don't worry my friend, we will find you a large axe, I am sure."

Taking the weapons, they left the camp and met up with the larger group. Weapons were handed out and now most of the senior pit-rats had weapons. Most of the younger pit-rats now had a knife at least, with a few of the better trained ones, five in all, having a weapon as well. Silent-boy being the one who had trained a lot of them, decided who got the weapons and who didn't. The group made its way to the border, it would not be long now before the sun was up and they had to still find somewhere to rest and eat.

The raid had been hugely successful and well worth the lost time. Apart from the weapons, more clothing and blankets were stolen so all pit-rats now had a second blanket, more clothing and also more importantly a good supply of food. If they were careful, the food would last five days at least. As they moved off at a steady run, Demon-boy had stopped and looked out over the camp. He spent a few minutes looking back over his past before turning to catch up with the others. They were running harder than normal to put as much distance as possible between themselves and the slave camp. Heading east towards the next province of Pulnuk, they ran silently, each slave fighting through his own fears, his own demons as their bodies protested at the pace.

The sun was just starting to light the sky on the sixth-day as Demon-boy and the others started to look for a place to hide for the duration of light. They had crossed the province border just before sunrise and didn't want to be caught during day. They were taking their rest as Silent-boy came slowly running in from his search.

"Found somewhere," he said.

"What's it like?" asked Demon-boy.

"Best one yet. Just up on that small hill that is covered in pine trees, is an overhang with a small cave under it, not to mention the ground under the overhang is dry with no snow!"

"Would it hide us all for two to three days?"

"Two to three days?" questioned Funny-boy.

"Yes. We need a couple of days rest. The younger ones are at the limits of their strength. We all need the rest," said Demon-boy.

"Not wise, Demon-boy. The Outlander-bastards could

catch up to us. When they find that slave camp and the dead warriors, they will guess our direction," said Silent-boy.

"Wise or not, we have no choice brother. We need at least two days' rest with some good food," replied Demon-boy looking at his three friends.

Bull-dog boy nodded his head in agreement. "He is right. We all need rest and good food. We should be able to hunt some small game. Could a fire be seen from this overhang?" he asked Silent-boy.

"No. If we burned a fire during the day, the smoke would be well hidden and couldn't be seen. We would need to place watchers, however."

Moving into the hills lead by Silent-boy, they arrived as the sunlight had risen. It was now full dawn as they reached the overhang. Silent-boy had been right, it was dry and hard to find. The small cave at the bottom of the overhang had a small entrance that you had to half bend to walk through, but once in there, was large enough and could accommodate most of them sleeping at once although it would be tight. The area of the overhang was large, sheltered from the wind and the snow. To the front of the overhang was thick forest.

Some of the pit rats went out into the surrounding bush to look for dry wood, then carried it back to stack under the overhang. Bull-dog boy had taken three of the more junior pit rats with him to hunt. The watchers were out and Silent-boy was keeping an eye on them. Demon-boy and Funny-boy were busy stacking rocks to the left of the overhang beside the entrance to the cave, building a small wall to hide the flames of the fire they needed. All of them were exhausted but went about their tasks with mechanical determination skill that all slaves possessed.

It was mid-morning when all the pit-rats had finished their tasks and could relax. Of the forty-nine pit-rats, four were on watch and apart from Demon-boy and his three friends, all of the rest had eaten some food and squeezed into the cave for some sleep. Bull-dog boy and his three young helpers had returned with a large female pig. Bull-dog boy had already guttered and skinned the animal that was now slowly roasting over the fire that had been built. Once the pit-rats had woken from their sleep, they would have their first hot meal since they escaped. The four friends talking quietly amongst themselves in front of the fire. The first time they had truly been warm since they had escaped. As they talked, Demon-boy looked at them one by one, thankful for the support and companionship the three had given him. He held his hands out to the flames and now finally had time to think back over the night of escape.

They had kept to the shadows as they crept around the camp making ready. Sick-boy and Silent-boy had returned from the tunnel with gifts. The storeroom at the other end of the tunnel had been used to store the Outlanders' supplier of Firemer. The spirit was called Firemer as it burned all the way down the drinkers' throat and because it was very flammable. They all returned through the tunnel on many trips to gather as much as they could.

Every building in the training camp had been prepped. The contents of the Firemer jugs poured over wooden beams and walls, soaking anything flammable. A small candle, cut off until it was no longer than a fingernail, was placed on the floor in a puddle of the spirit. The wick then lite. Every building in the camp had this.

All of the pit-rats had gathered in the storage room under the drink's hall with their blanket rolls of possessions, waiting for the word from Silent-boy to move as they listened to the drunken laughter of the Outlander-bastards above them. While they waited, Funny-boy and Demon-boy had followed an unfortunate slave that had come across them in the storage room. Quickly gagged, it was not hard to convince the slave to direct them to the target building, the home of Son-of-Angry-man. They quickly followed the slave to the building in question, then advised the slave to go hide. They had entered and came across the two slave girls. It was not hard to convince the two girls to go and hide for the night. There the friends hide for what seemed the entire night, hiding in the shadows of the room, patiently waiting.

Demon-boy didn't enjoy the killing of Son-of-Angry-man. This surprised him. It felt like closure and a small relief but hadn't taken away the pain of the Smith's death. Demon-boy had taken no joy from beheading the master and carried it out with the same emotion one would have gutting a fish.

They had carried out the deed and quickly returned to the storage room without being seen. Getting back, Demon-boy laid a hand on Silent-boy's shoulder in thanks, as all of the pit-rats were ready. Their possessions over their shoulders, two jugs of Firemer in their hands.

When they heard shouts from above, they knew that was the signal and all carefully made for the drinking hall up the stairs. They arrived to find two Outlanders sleeping in the corner, so drunk that thunder would not wake them. They set to work soaking all the main support beams of the drinking hall. A candle had been left burning in the basement storage room that they had just come from. The basement soaked with the rest of the flammable spirit. Once the drinking hall was taken care of, they then broke up into teams, spreading to parts of the settlement away from the training camp that was on fire. Some of the pit rats lit fires in homes, others went to the beach to add candles and Firemer in the bellies of the Outlanders' ships. They had to wade through cold water without being seen, but Sick-boy had promised it could be done and took seven other pit-rats to help him. They managed to slip into the water and silently wade over to the ships and get aboard without being seen. Once this had been done Sick-boy had taken off to dish out some justice to the cook that had betrayed their plans with some of the other pit-rats also searching out their own targets. The time the drinks hall exploded into flames, most of the escapees had already left the settlement, running off to the east. They had stopped briefly at the first foot hill they came to and looked back over where they had come from. The fires of the settlement lit up the sky and even at this distance, the fires from the Outlander ships could also be seen.

The plan had gone off well, apart from losing Sick-boy who had never returned to the group and also losing fifteen or so pit-rats, who were more focused on killing as many as they could and cared less about escaping. They had been lucky, very lucky!

"You need sleep, Demon-boy. Go get your head down and I'll take first watch," said Bulldog-boy.

Demon-boy didn't argue. He picked himself up and wrapped his blanket around him. Making his way into the cave, he found a spot and laid himself down. If he had ever been more exhausted, he couldn't remember. Yes, his life was full of hardships and hard training, but nothing compared to this. As he lay down and moved his blanket over himself, he tried to think of the next steps in their escape, but sleep took him, and he was dead to the world.

Three full days and two nights, they rested under the overhang. It was longer than Demon-boy wanted but the rest was needed, and all of the pit-rats were looking better for it.

They fed well on roasted pig for the first day and then fed well on roasted rabbits and a roasted venison from a doe they had managed to catch. Bulldog-boy and his helpers had also smoked some rabbit meat and venison, giving out parcels of smoked meat to all the pit-rats. This meat should last them a further two days. The comment was made by more than one of the slaves that this was the best they had ever eaten. Funny-boy and Demon-boy were eating some smoked venison at the time. Their eyes locked and they just smiled.

Once the sun went down on the third night, they left the overhang, moving slowly at first and then increasing their pace. It was just past midnight when they ran into their first patrol.

Silent-boy running slightly ahead of the others had spotted their fires and the bodies sleeping around them, the horses gathering what grass they could from the surrounding snow.

Silent-boy was waiting when the others had caught up. He told all of the pit-rats to stretch and warm themselves whilst creeping forward with Bulldog-boy, Funny-boy and Demon-boy to show them what he had seen.

"We can go around them; they are asleep with only a few watchers. They would not see us," said Funny-boy.

"Yes, but they would find our tracks in the snow and even if it snows again tonight, they have horses and could come across us during the day," said Bulldog-boy.

Demon-boy looked across at Silent-boy, the pit-rat he had come to rely on most and who was the unofficial second in charge of the pit rats.

"We have to take them. Sneak up and take out the guards, then take as many as we can whilst they are asleep," said Silent-boy.

"There is over seventy of them, we number forty-nine

with more than half of those too young and inexperienced in fighting," replied Bulldog-boy.

"We can't help the numbers! Besides, they have food and although you provided us with a good amount of meat, it will only last another few days. Right now, we have the element of surprise," said Silent-boy.

"Not to mention they are all wearing boots. We manage to kill them and we can get rid of these rags on our feet. I don't know about you lot, but I am sick of my feet being wet and cold!" said Bulldog-boy.

Funny-boy looked over at Demon-boy before whispering, "What do you think, Demon-boy? We go in?"

Demon-boy was thinking of one of the many battle stories that Smith had told him, one in particular that had caught his interest and had made him laugh when Smith told him of it. Looking at his companions he smiled, a smile so big the others couldn't help but snigger when they saw it.

"We go in, but with different goals. Listen up," Demon-boy said, then explained the plan of action.

Malak was woken by a war-cry from one of his warriors. Jumping to his feet, his weapons were already in his hands. He saw his warriors all on their feet scanning the darkness. The fires were out but by the moon light, he could see warriors moving through the night in the surrounding field they had camped in, searching for something.

"What is happening?" he yelled.

His second in command ran to him. "Malak, we have been attacked!"

"By who?" replied Malak.

"We think it's the runaway slaves."

"Slaves would not attack us. There are seventy of us, you idiot!" he replied, as he followed his second in command. He reached the furthest fire and saw the five bodies lying beside the fire, their throats cut and blood staining the snow. He looked at the bodies and noticed the weapons were gone as well as their boots. He growled low.

"There is more, Malak!" said his second in command, before leading him to all the bodies of the night guards he had placed.

"Five warriors dead by the fire and five-night guards dead as well?" he asked.

"Yes. They must have killed the guards first, before putting out our fires carefully and stealing a number of the horses and killing five others."

"OUR HORSES ARE DEAD?" screamed Malak.

"Twenty of them, yes. A further five stolen."

Malak was furious and started yelling out orders.

"I want five warriors out on their horse in every direction, the rest of us will pack up here and move towards the east. Those without horses are to walk two days to the south, the seaside settlement of Puta is there. Beg, borrow, or buy some horses and ride back with word to the Chief. He must be told we are on to them and need more men!"

All the warriors jumped to action, their gear and horses collected before they moved off. Malak's orders followed as they moved in different directions.

The unlucky warriors without horses grumbled as they set off on foot for the seaside settlement to the south. They were not unhappy for long, they were ambushed by pit-rats led by Funny-boy, quickly killed before being stripped of their clothing, weapons, boots and any other supplies they carried. As Funny-boy and the pit-rats moved off to catch up with the others, the dead warriors' skin was turning blue from the cold. Their naked flesh frosting quickly as blood drained from the bodies. The Chief would not be warned now, and Malak didn't realise that he was on his own. His warriors now numbering thirty-five, the escaped slaves not losing any.

The sun was up, although it was snowing. Malak and his men were moving slowly as the tracker in the group did his best to follow the slaves' tracks. Not easy as the footprints were slowly being filled up by the light snowfall. It would not be long before all traces would be gone. Malak's temper hadn't improved with the arrival of day. All of the group of riders that he had sent out, hadn't been seen since midnight. They had their orders, search the immediate area before meeting at the small village of Erath that was a half a day's ride ahead. He didn't know how far away the riders were, nor did he know that of the four groups he had sent out, only two remained. Two of the groups being ambushed by the slaves, then slaughtered and their horses killed, with the supplies and weapons now on the back of a slave. His force now numbering twenty-five warriors in total! Fifteen warriors with him and ten riders making their way towards him. The road was covered in snow and on both sides of the road stood thick forest. Malak never liked forest, give him rolling hills or rolling waves of the sea any day. As they rounded a bend in the road that took them to the right and closer to their destination of Erath, he noticed a lone figure standing in the middle of the road, a hundred paces ahead of them. He told his men to hold and to continue their slow walk. All of his men loosened their weapons but didn't take them from their belts. As they walked their horses closer, he could make out one strong tallish figure holding two weapons. As he got closer, he recognised the figure and realisation dawned on him. He had found him!

The fifteen warriors walked their horses within twenty-five paces before a voice rung out.

"That's close enough, you rapist mongrels!" yelled Demon-boy.

Malak saw the smile on the face of the Demon-boy! Malak knew this slave and knew him better than any other slave. The legend he had created in the pit spreading around the Outlander nation. This one could fight, indeed could kill with cold precision. But against mounted warriors, the outcome was predictable, and he had no hope in hell of winning.

"It's been a good hunt, slave!" Malak shouted.

The smile on the Demon-boy's face just grew bigger. Malak knew there would be other slaves hiding in the forest on both sides of the road; slaves armed with knives. Sure, there would be a few pit-rats that could handle themselves. As the thought crossed his mind, he heard the galloping noise of horse hoofs striking the hard ground. He looked over his shoulder and saw ten more of his men arrive and join his group. Twenty-five mounted warriors against this one pit rat in front of them and possibly, a few more hidden in the bushes to the side of the road.

Returning his look to the Demon-boy, the Demon-boy was now approaching the group, short sword in his left hand, blade across his chest. In his right hand, a hand axe held out wide. "Get down from your horse, son-of-ugly-pig, and let's see how well you fight!"

Malak laughed. His men laughing along with him.

"I don't think so. You think I am that stupid, Demon-child?"

Demon-boy was about to reply when Malak shouted at his men. "Take him!"

The horses lurched into action; they had run only ten

paces when around the bend behind Demon-boy came forty mounted warriors. Demon-boy took off into the forest to his right. Malak and his men halted at the sight of the mounted warriors bearing down on them. Malak was confused, he waved his hand in the air as the other group approached at a gallop.

"What are they doing?" said one of his men.

Malak started to shout out a greeting when arrows tore into them from the approaching group. Five of his men went down. Malak was shocked and turned his horse around to move off, his men following him. Too slow, as the other mounted group hit them at full charge! It was carnage and Malak's men fell. Malak himself ducked under a heavy swing from a two-handed sword. At the same time, he ducked, another horse hit his, and he and his horse went sideways. He fell from the saddle hitting the ground hard. He looked up and saw his men galloping off in the opposite direction, the mounted warriors that had attacked them in pursuit. He was about to scream out to the warriors that had attacked him when the world went dark and he was struck into unconsciousness.

Malak awoke to see he was tied and gagged. He looked around and saw he was in a dense thicket of shrubs. He could see bodies further to his right, wrapped in blankets sleeping. To his left, he saw Demon-boy with three other pit-rats. He noticed Funny-boy and recognised him, the slave that had made a name for himself in the pits! Many tales had been told about the strength of this dark-skinned slave. They all looked over and saw he was now awake. Demon-boy rose from his sitting position and made his way over to him. Demon-boy sat in front of him.

"We need to talk you and me! I'll take your gag off, if you yell, I'll cut your toes off one by one, then go to work on your fingers. Understand?"

Malak nodded his head. The Demon-boy took off the gag and continued to speak. "Your men are gone. Most of them killed in our little ambush but five of them managing to get away." he said with a small smile on his face.

"Who were those other warriors? They didn't look like slaves!" said Malak.

"They were not slaves. They were warriors from the village to the east."

"Warriors from Erath? How the hell did you get them to attack us?"

"Simple. One of the slaves who looks like you bastards, ran in with no weapons and little clothing. He explained about the escape from your Chief's province. He also explained that the slaves had armed themselves and had stolen horses, now looked like warriors from Hura." Demon-boy's smile grew bigger. "They didn't need much convincing and rode out immediately to catch the slaves that were spotted just west of their village!"

"You will die a horrible death for this once they realise their mistake. They will not want the anger of my Chief coming down on them and will hunt you all harder than we will."

"No. I will not face death yet! The time they realise their mistake, we will be long gone."

There was silence as Demon-boy looked at the warrior. Malak then asking the question that he had at the front of his mind since waking. "Why am I alive?"

"You are being kept alive to pass on a message to your Chief."

"What message? You know that he will hunt you and never rest until he catches you. You killed his son! He wants you to die slowly!"

"I am sure he does. But he will not catch me."

"And the message you want me to give him?"

'He killed the closest thing I had to a father. The closest thing any of the slaves here had to a father. He also killed Trainer, a slave we all had respect for and liked and was like a brother. His son paid some of that debt, as did the fires. But he still has a price to pay."

"My Chief will not see that as a fair deal. You burned half the settlement!"

"Half? Better than I expected."

"Don't gloat! What's the message?"

Demon-boy thought about it before continuing. "There is still a price to be paid. We took his son and half his settlement, but he still owes for all the lives he has taken in the slave camp, for the death of the Trainer and he still needs to pay. Tell him that one day, he will have to pay that price! That one day, we will cross each other's path, and I will exact the price myself"

"You will set me free now, slave?"

Demon-boy chuckled as did his three friends that were listening to the exchange. "No not yet.

"Get some rest! On night fall, we will move off from here."

Demon-boy pointed off to his left "One hundred paces from here at the base of a large tree, we have left a knife and some food. Once we leave, you can make your way to that tree, sliding across the ground like the worms your people resemble. Free yourself there and go where you will. You will not see us again! And if we do cross each other's path, I will not hold back the slaves from doing to you, what you have done to them."

Malak was about to speak when Demon-boy quickly gagged him again. Malak watched him move off into the bushes to his left. The other three slaves watched him for a bit and then continued to eat their food. Malak knew he had to get to his Chief but was not looking forward to telling him he had failed. The thought bringing dark thoughts swirling to his mind as he closed his eyes to rest.

Malak woke as the light started to fade from the sky. He witnessed the slaves organising themselves to move. He was quietly impressed. He prided himself and the warriors under him for being efficient and following orders well. They hadn't a thing on the slaves however, and he watched as they collected themselves and the small amounts of belongings they owned. Very quickly all of the slaves were ready to move. He watched the way Demon-boy moved around the temporary camp, the other slaves reacting to a comment or advice he gave them. Automatically obeying whatever he said. A natural leader with natural authority. It was not long before all the slaves had moved off. Malak had managed to count how many there was. Over forty he thought. Before long, Malak was alone and he started to move across the ground on his belly, heading towards the direction Demon-boy had pointed when talking of the knife and food that had been left for him. With his legs tied together and his arms tied in front of him it was not easy. He was determined to make the most of the chance he had been given. He would warn his Chief and tell them all he knew. Hopefully, he would not be killed but after losing his son, the Chief would not take the news of failure well.

Two days after they had battled with Malak and his men, the pit-rats where resting up in a large valley. It was protected from the wind and the worst of the snow. Silent-boy had set watches and five pit-rats were standing guard whilst the others got rest. Most of the pit-rats were lying wrapped in their blankets under bushes or low trees sleeping. They could not risk a fire so soon after the first run in with the outlander patrol. Silent-boy was standing under a tree wrapped in his blanket quietly talking to Bulldog-boy.

"The stress is starting to show on him, Silent-boy," said Bulldog-boy.

"Yes, it is. But then it is starting to show on all of us," replied Silent-boy.

"True. How are the younger ones? I am too busy with myself and watching out for Demon-boy."

"Mostly good. They are struggling more than the more experienced of us but are handling it better than can be expected," said Silent-boy.

"Good. I am not sure how much more I can take. At least

as a slave we had a warm bed at the end of the day. Even as pit-rats we had a bed and food waiting for us."

"You want to go back?" whispered Silent-boy as he stared out to the mouth of the valley, they were hiding in.

"No. Just tired, and bloody cold," replied Bulldog-boy.

"We all are brother. But it will be worth it once we reach the border!"

Bulldog-Boy stared out at the valley mouth as well. Adjusting his blanket, he turned to walk away. "I'll get my head down then."

Silent-boy nodded.

Bulldog-boy walked away heading towards a low bush he had found earlier, looking forward to lying down and getting some sleep. He had reached the bush when he heard a war cry. He spun around in time to see Silent-boy charging from the tree he was standing under. His blanket falling from his shoulders as he drew his two-handed longsword. Bulldog-boy ran in the direction Silent-boy seemed to be heading, looking for what or who had screamed the war cry. He ran from behind a tree and finally saw what Silent-boy was charging at. He was shocked, they had found them! Galloping with speed up the valley floor was what looked like forty horsemen, screaming as they came. He did not hesitate but charged to catch-up with Silent-boy. They had to delay them enough to give the other pit-rats time to roll form their sleep. He was about to shout a warning when he heard Silent-boy's voice boom out across the valley, loud enough to wake the dead.

"PIT-RATS AWAKE! PIT-RATS AWAKE!" screamed Silent-boy.

His voice echoing loudly across the valley, waking all of the pit-rats form their slumber. Bulldog-boy caught up and was running beside Silent-boy as they ran towards the oncoming horsemen.

"How did they get past the watchers?" shouted Bulldog-boy as they ran.

"Don't know, we need to slow them down!" shouted Silent-boy.

Before Bulldog-boy could reply they had reached the charging horsemen. Silent-boy stepped to the left of the first horsemen and swung his longsword up and over the horse head, crashing into a rider's gut, slicing it open and throwing him for the saddle. Bulldog-boy jumped into the air mid run which put him at the same height of a second rider. As he reached the apex of his jump, he swung his right-hand axe into the throat of the rider. He missed and instead the axe smashed into the warrior's mouth, blowing apart his teeth, mouth and jaw. As bulldog boy landed back on the ground, he had to step to the right to avoid the next horsemen and his spear. He launched and threw his right-hand axe at the back of the warrior's head. It struck the riders back, snapping his spine instantly.

"Stupid son of a goat" Bulldog-boy cursed at himself.

He only had one small hand axe in his left hand, not good.

"BULLDOG!" shouted Silent-boy.

He spun round in time to see a spear flying through the air. He changed his axe to the right hand and caught the spare with left. Another rider was almost on him, he threw his arm back and launched his second axe. It flew straight and hit the rider full on the face, digging in and getting stuck. The rider fell from his still galloping horse.

Silent-boy almost received a sword to the face after throwing the spear to bulldog-boy. He managed to swerve just in time. As the horsemen galloped past, he focused on the next warrior, bringing his longsword up and swinging it at the rider's head. He missed as the rider swayed in the saddle. He did not strop his momentum however and continued swinging the sword around to his left. Unfortunately for the rider that he had just missed, as the rider had slowed and circled his horse to the right. As the rider pulled up, he received Silent-boy's longsword to the chest, the sword not cutting in but snapping ribs with the impact. The rider screamed out and tried to follow up with his own sword, but he was too slow. Silent-boy had already recovered and stabbed his sword into the rider's throat.

Bulldog-boy was battling with a rider that had been unhorsed, using the spear he had to keep out of reach. He had never been trained with the spear and time seemed to slow for him. What was moments seemed like a lifetime and had him wondering if the other pit-rats had even heard the call. He was about to scream out again when the warrior he was facing was struck in the face with an axe, and collapsed. He raced to the body and grabbed the sword the warrior had dropped. As soon as he had it, he let the spear drop to the ground. He spun around to see where the axe had come form and saw Demon-boy running straight at the riders, all of the other pit-rats behind him.

"KILL THE OUTLANDER BASTARDS" screamed Demon-boy.

The running pit-rats let out a huge scream as they came on in against the riders. Bulldog-boy lost sight of Silent-boy but had other things to worry about. There was still thirty-five or so riders galloping in against them. Demon-boy reached him and without stopping ran past and ripped his axe out of the head of the dead rider. Bulldog-boy ran after his brother. He stayed at his shoulder as they battled. Each covering the others side as they took down rider after rider.

"SNOW WEASEL!" he heard Funny-boy yell.

Looking around he saw Funny-boy charge a mounted man and crash into the horse at full speed. The horse was thrown off balance and as the rider tried to correct, Funny-boy grabbed his arm and yanked him out of the saddle. As the rider hit the ground Funny-boy sent his short sword around quickly, opening the throat of the rider.

"I need a bloody bigger weapon than this" said Funny-boy to himself.

Bulldog-boy was then lost in the battle. Kill a rider, dodge more attacks, grab another fallen weapon and repeat. He was covered in blood and his body was tiring quickly. Although the pit-rats were superbly fit, chasing horsemen around was not what they had trained for. He almost got taken again as a warrior came at him. He just managed to dodge to his left as the spear aiming for his chest, ripped a cut through his right arm instead. He stepped into the attacker, grabbing his leather armour. He then pulled him into a sickening headbutt which dazed the attacker. He then butted him again, and again, and again. When he dropped the attacker, his nose was broken and spreading blood all over the place. He grabbed the short sword and dagger the outlander had on his belts, he slashed the attackers throat as he lay on the ground and charged another rider that was bearing down on him.

Demon-boy moved through the riders killing them brutally. There was no time for grace or tactics, no time for skill or strategy. It was dodge and slice, move on and do it again. He was not counting how many had fallen beneath his blade, all he was concentrating on was staying alive. The other pit-rats were doing the same. And although it seemed like a full day, the battle was over quickly. Bodies everywhere as the escaped slaves took count of who was left.

Demon-boy was sitting on the ground, catching his breath. His left hand holding a torn rag to a cut in his right arm. Bulldog-boy and Funny-boy approached.

"Good to see you survive brothers" said Demon-boy as they sat down next to him.

All three of them carried cuts although none of them life threatening. Bulldog-boy laid his hand on Demon-boys shoulder.

"Good to see you charge in brother. That thrown axe saved my life. Thank you" said Bulldog boy

"No thank you brother. If you and Silent-boy had not held them, the rest of us would not have made it in time. Where is Silent-boy?" said Demon-boy

"Checking on the watchers. He wants to know how they got in without any warning," replied Funny-boy.

"I think he will find we have no watchers. The only way they got in was by finding and killing our watchers first" said Bulldog-boy.

Demon-boy stood slowly.

"Well we cannot hang around here waiting to be found by more outlanders. We need to gather ourselves and move. Fast and far" said Demon-boy.

"Agreed. Let's gather the others and get out of here," said Bulldog-boy.

Silent-boy had checked and Bulldog-boy was right. The attacking outlanders had sent in scouts to find the watchers. Once found they were quickly killed. Only then did the outlanders charge in on their horses. It had been a costly battle for the pit-rats. They had lost many in the attack. All carried injuries and a two had serious injuries. Demon-boy would not hear of them being left behind. Somehow, they would bring the two injured with them. In all, fifteen had been lost in the battle in this cold valley. The bodies of the pit-rats had been stripped of anything useful and placed beneath some low bushes. Then they were covered in snow. If the battle site was found, the bodies of the outlanders would be the only thing found until summer. Bulldog-boy had gathered a few of the younger pit-rats he had taught to hunt. Together they took the meat from some of the dead horses. They took the meat from the side of the hind quarters. When they had taken enough, they managed to flip the dead horse on the other side to hide what they had done. Whilst Bulldog-boy gathered meat and food supplies of the dead outlanders, Silent-boy focused on gathering other supplies from the dead warriors. All boots were taken and distributed amongst the escaped slaves. Now most of them had leather boots that would help keep out the damp. They did not all fit perfectly, but better than nothing. Funny-boy did not have boots. His feet too huge to fit any of the boots they had found. Many jokes were thrown at him, he just smiled and wrapped extra cloth around his feet. They did not take the socks form the dead. As Bulldog-boy put it best "I am not wearing smelly socks of those bastards". The others agreed. Of course, all the weapons apart from the spears had been taken. None of the pit-rats had been trained with spears, and apart from a few that were used to stretcher the two badly injured, they were left behind. All pit-rats now carried weapons. In fact, all now carried many weapons. All had a short sword or a hand axe at their waist. Along with many daggers tucked into various places on their bodies.

Silent-boy had also stripped the dead outlanders of any warm clothing, which was not much. A few cloaks and blankets. These were given to the two injured first, then the younger ones that were struggling the most. Once all of the dead had been stripped of anything useful, and Bulldog-boy and his hunters had grabbed as much meat as they could carry, a quick meeting was held.

"We need to get away from this valley. Any suggestions?" asked Demon-boy.

"I'll scout a head with some of the fitter younglings," said Bulldog-boy.

"Good idea. We need another place to hold up for a few days. We need hot food and time to patch ourselves up," said Demon-boy.

"Done," replied Bulldog-boy as he walked off.

"Good plan. After this we do need a few days to rest," said Silent-boy

"Yes, we do. All of us," said Funny-boy.

"Anything else we need to do?" asked Demon-boy.

"Not that I can think of. The bodies have all been stripped of useful things, we have food," said Silent-boy.

"Good. We will get out of this valley and start walking towards the border still. Who were these outlanders?" said Demon-boy.

"I think they are form the settlement of Erath," said Silent-boy.

"Would make sense. They would need to catch us quickly after the trick we played on them. Old chief of the outland bastards will not think it's funny," said Funny-boy.

"True. Best we gather the others and leave then," said Demon-boy.

Bulldog-boy and his scouts had found a small hollow in a hill half a day's walk from the valley. It was well sheltered with dense forest that was hard to get through. There was no way they could be surprised here as the only decent entrance was through a narrow riverbed that wound its way down the small hill, and any watchers could see a great distance down the river bed.

A fire was started and horsemeat set to roasting. Silent-boy set the watchers and joined the others. The two injured had been carried on makeshift stretchers using spears and cloaks. They were in some pain but hid it. They had been laid closest to the cook fire in order to keep warm. Demon-boy looked around. All the faces showed how tired they were. They all looked exhausted and beat up. He should say something but thought hot food and sleep would be best for now. He approached Silent-boy.

"Watchers set?" asked Demon-boy.

"Yes. I choose them myself from the freshest pit-rats we had. I'll keep an eye on them," replied Silent-boy.

"No, you won't," said Demon-boy.

Silent-boy looked confused.

"I'll take the watch. You need rest as well," said Demon-boy.

"I'm fine," said Silent-boy.

"I hope we are not going to argue about this brother. You had the watch when the attack happened, where as I had gotten some good sleep. Get your head down and then I'll wake Funny-boy and he can take a turn on watch," said Demon-boy.

Silent-boy stood and looked at his fellow escaped slave. His brother.

"No, we are not going to argue. I'll get my head down," he finally said with a smile.

"Good. If it was not for you and Bulldog-boy, we would have been caught and killed. You screamed the alarm and held them. Long enough for the rest of us to wake and get there. You two saved us. Thank you," said Demon-boy.

Silent-boy nodded and walked towards the fire. He passed the others and found a spot under some bushes. He wrapped himself up and fell asleep.

Demon-boy walked to the small rise that looked out over

the riverbed. He could see the other watches hidden in bushes. He sat himself down under a tree that had no snow and wrapped a blanket around himself.

Demon-boy changed the watch himself some time past midnight. He wanted some sleep and ended up curling up behind Silent-boy, back to back to stay warm. He slept restfully.

The next day they had some proper hot food. The horse meat had been slowly roasted for most of the night and when the pit-rats woke, the air smelled of roast meat. The pit-rats fell on the roast meat and ate their fill. They were already looking better for a good night's sleep, and with hot food in their belly, the life returned to their faces and smiles started to appear. Silent-boy handed some more meat to four of the younger pit-rats and told them to go take watch duty. They nodded and with tree barks for plates, piled with roast meat, they went to replace the pit-rats that had been up all night.

For three days they stayed here and rested. The two badly injured pit-rats had died at different times. One from blood loss from his injuries, the other Silent-boy said was from his head injury. The bodies where once again stripped of anything useful and placed under bushes.

When the pit-rats left the small hollow, refreshed, feed and as healed as they were going to be, there was only thirty-two of them left.

For a further ten nights, they moved through the cold of night. They had encountered no problems with patrols or Outlanders, but they had encountered worsening weather. Winter was now in full force, every night the snow becoming heavier and heavier. The night moves becoming harder and harder as the snow got deeper. The boots they all now wore made things easier. Their feet stayed dry, although they still ere cold. Demon-boy didn't like to raid the villages they passed but due to the weather, they had no choice.

One settlement they didn't know the name of had offered the most loot as Funny-boy called it. Two nights after leaving behind their resting place in the hills, they had come across it. It looked smaller than the last village but had large buildings that were locked. They had snuck into a warehouse of sorts and found boxes of woollen socks, and other woollen clothing. Silent-boy commented that this part of Pulnuk, was well known for its sheep herds so this warehouse was no doubt the finished products ready for the summer markets. Demon-boy had risked it and snuck all the slaves into this warehouse whilst the settlement was asleep. Once in there, they had sorted themselves out. All of the slaves discarded their cold damp, dirty, badly fitting clothing and threw them in to an empty crate they found. Demon-boy and Silent-boy then rationed out the new clothing. It was enough to stay warm but not enough to weigh them down, which would cost them speed.

Every slave now wore long sleeve shirts that was made from a mixture of goats and sheep's wool. On top of that, they all wore their slaves' shirt and although not clean, was useful at adding another layer. Over that, was the woollen vest that would add warmth to their cold bodies. They all now had full length woollen trousers with warm woollen socks. Once the warm woollen socks were on, it made the leather boots they had stolen so much warmer.

In their supply blanket, they had one extra pair of woollen socks, a spare shirt also made of wool, small amount of food and of course a second blanket. Bulldog-boy had taken some extra blankets and cut them into small squares. The slaves then wrapped these around their heads to keep the head and ears warm. Sometime when the nights were very cold, they would use the second blanket and wrap it around themselves as they moved through the countryside. Demon-boy smiled at the memory of the night that the slaves had all put their new clothing on. Many were smiling and whispered conversations were happening amongst all the slaves. Many quiet jokes were exchanged, you could feel them all relax a little. It was the first time in their gruelling escape that they now had hope and it was a nice feeling to cherish. The best find was finding a pair of old boots that actually fit Funny-boy. Bulldog-boy had been checking a side room of the warehouse and came across them. They were old, stiff and had a couple of cracks in the leather. He came out of the room and threw them to Funny-boy. He put them on and smiled.

"Little tight but they will stretch," he said with a huge smile.

That raid had saved them from the bitter cold and probably death. They were still cold as it was winter and snow was everywhere with the wind ripping the cold through them, but with more layers, the head scarves made from woollen blankets, it was bearable. Over the last ten nights, they still managed to lose one slave to illness and cold. The younger pit-rat had been concealing an injury. The blood loss and the cold combining to end his life. Silent-boy had created a buddy system and assigned the remaining younger slaves with an older one.

The number of pit-rats that were lost was difficult for Demon-boy and although he understood it was not his fault, it was still hard and didn't sit well with him.

They had passed the border of Pulnuk two days after they had raided the warehouse for clothing. A further ten nights had seen them move silently through the next province of Youst. There was less settlements in the province of Youst and they were forced to stop and hunt for food, struggling to find any game as winter pushed most of the wildlife into hibernation. They had stopped for two days when they found a sheltered clearing in a forest, taking time to hunt game, get some hot food into themselves and rest. This was not a choice they had made, rather a snowstorm had hit, and it was impossible to move in the storm as it blew its rage across the province. They had taken shelter under some short trees that had branched close to the ground, creating a dry space underneath were snow couldn't get them. Funny-boy had made the comment, it was like hiding under the cook's skirt. Once they had all got a hot meal into them, they were looking and feeling better. According to Silent-boy, they still had another ten to twelve days of travel before getting to the county of Irik. He had told them of the last province they had to get through and warned them of it.

Varac was a heavily populated province. There were only three main settlements but hundreds of smaller villages. Silent-boy had explained how hard it would be to get through. The Outlanders of Varac were always on the watch for runaway slaves and had constant patrols. Although he could not guess how many would be out during winter. Demon-boy and Silent-boy decided when they reached the border, they would wait for a few days and keep an eye on the settlements next to the border, then come up with a plan after that.

It had been thirty-three nights since they left the capital of Hura, burning half the settlement down in their escape. The escaped slaves now took turns sleeping and keeping watch as Demon-boy and his three friends kept watch on the settlement below them. They had reached the border between Youst and Varac the previous night, setting up a small camp in a clump of trees where they could watch this village. According to Silent-boy, they were in the middle of two of the major settlements. One to the north that was on the border between Youst and the province above. The other settlement on the sea. Silent-boy said it would take them a further five nights of travel to cross Varac if they took their time to be careful and reach the border of his home country.

All of the slaves had eaten the last of their food when they arrived the previous night. There was nowhere to raid apart from the small village they watched below, and no way could they hunt without being seen. The lack of food and the almost non-stop running was really starting to tell on the slaves. Most were irritable and tempers started to flare. Silent-boy, Funny-boy and Bull-dog spread themselves out and calmed tempers where they needed too, and sometimes threatened extreme violence to get their point across. Over the last quarter moon, Funny-boy and Bulldog-boy had started to take more responsibility off the shoulders of Demon-boy. Silent-boy had mentioned to them both quietly that the strain was starting to show, and even great leaders needed a support circle. Funny-boy and Bull-dog boy needed not to be asked twice.

It was almost midday, Demon-boy and Silent-boy talked quietly overlooking the village.

"We need the food, Silent-boy."

"Yes, we do, but raiding a village this close to the border could end badly."

Demon-boy stared at the village that was only three hundred paces below them. "How many do you think live there, brother?"

"Hard to say, but I would estimate fifty to sixty people.

How many of those are warriors, I am not sure," replied Silent-boy.

Demon-boy thought about it before swearing. "If I knew there was only warriors down there, I would not hesitate to try and raid it, killing any Outlander-bastards we find. I won't do it knowing down there could be women and children, they could get caught in the fighting."

"The Outlanders would not hesitate if in our position," said Silent-boy.

Demon-boy turned to his brother staring at him intently. "You advise raiding and possibly killing women and children?" Demon-boy said with a slight tone.

"No, my brother. I was heading towards making a comment on how hard it is sticking to honour when the bastards we fight have no such problems committing atrocities."

"True. Very true. I am sorry."

"It's fine, Demon-boy. You are hungry and tired."

They both continued to watch when they saw from the far left of the valley, twenty mounted warriors galloping their horses over a small rise and headed towards the village. The warriors had left on first light, the reason they left was unclear.

"What do you think of that, Silent-boy?"

Silent-boy watched for a few minutes before answering. "Could be anything. If I had to guess, they are patrolling looking for us, or perhaps they are patrolling their herds, watching for wolves."

"If they have a routine, we may be able to hit the settlement whilst they are away. Women and children would not fight back, and as long as we made them understand that we are just after some food and will cause them no harm, it could work."

"Would still put innocents in the way! If the women decided to fight, we would have to defend ourselves."

Demon-boy nodded, once again accepting the counsel of his friend.

The warriors galloped without slowing down and within minutes entered the settlement. Silent-boy and Demon-boy watched the warriors' dismount. The warriors were surrounded by women and children welcoming them back. The warriors all vanished into their respective homes.

Silent-boy and Demon-boy continued to watch. Both had blankets around them to keep warm and sat shoulder to shoulder. Before long, Bulldog-boy joined them sitting beside them with his own blanket around his shoulders. He said nothing, just watched the village.

After some time, the twenty warriors had come out of their homes and stacked bags of what looked like food stuffs on their horses. They all mounted, waved, and took off at a gallop heading in at the direction they had come from.

"Interesting. They come back for supplies," said Bulldog-boy.

"Yes. We don't need to hit the settlement. We lie in wait and hit the warriors as they return from the village, bringing big bags of supplies," said Silent-boy.

Demon-boy was one step ahead. He had thought of that as soon as he saw them mount up. He was now planning how his pit-slaves, many of them young and inexperienced, could ambush twenty mounted warriors without losing anyone. After the last battle with horseman, Demon-boy was nervous and he was sick of losing his brother slaves. Demon-boy pointed to the small rise the warriors just rode over, heading back to wherever they came from.

"See those low bushes? We should be able to hide our numbers in the scattered bushes and hit them when they come out. Although, if there are more of those bushes on the other side of that rise, I would prefer if we hit them there, out of sight of the village."

Silent-boy and Bulldog-boy nodded.

"We could move tonight under cover of darkness and be in position by the time the sun comes up tomorrow. Although it will be a cold morning hiding in the bushes," said Silent-boy.

"No help for it. We need food or we will not have the energy to make it to the border," said Bulldog-boy.

Demon-boy nodded slowly, staring over the terrain, he committed it all to memory.

"Wake everyone and I'll tell them. We are going to have to risk ambushing the warriors and that means even the young ones will have to fight. Although I have an idea that will strengthen their resolve and motivate them."

All three of them moved off, waking the sleeping slaves. Once all the slaves have gathered into a tight circle, sitting close to keep warm with blankets over shoulders, Demon-boy informed them of what was planned.

"We will all hide in the bushes scattered close to the road. On my word, the first group will move. The first group will be made up of myself and all of the senior pit-rats. We will rush in and surprise them, attacking as savagely as we can. The second group will be made up of the young ones and be led by Funny-boy. They will charge in on his word."

Demon-boy had already informed Funny-boy of his role. The young ones looked up to him and drew strength from his size and personality. Demon-boy knew that if Funny-boy charged in, the young ones would follow.

Demon-boy continued. "We must engage and put them down as quickly as we can. The longer they hold us off, the better chances they have of winning. Numbers are slightly in our favour but once again we are facing horsemen. If one manages to get away to the settlement, it's over. They will bring reinforcements that will over run us. As you know, there is little cover and nowhere for us to hide."

Demon-boy let his sink in before turning and nodding to Silent-boy. Silent-boy took his queue, stood up and addressed the slaves. "We have all made it this far together! We have fought beside each other and learnt to trust one another. Many have died but we are still here. With the food they are carrying, we will have enough food to reach the border."

Demon-boy nodded, then spoke again. "We are all brothers here. Captured by these Outlander-bastards and forced into slavery! You all followed me out of that slavery! You have followed my lead and earnt your place in this brotherhood. There are still a few more fights before we get to the border, but if we do not win this one, we will have no energy to reach our destination."

He looked around the group of slaves that had become his brothers, the only siblings he would ever know. In their faces, he saw determination and strength. Even in the younger faces, he saw this. The one thing he didn't see, was fear. "Get as much rest as you can. We move as soon as it is dark enough."

Demon-boy moved away and went back to his spot overlooking the village, trying to think of ways the ambush could go wrong. As Smith had always said, expect the best but always prepare for the worst.

One by one, his three friends came up to him, put their hand on his shoulder, squeezed his shoulder and said "brother."

They all stood shoulder to shoulder looking over the valley. It would be a long night, but with his brothers beside him, he would survive.

The cold was seeping through him. He was under a bush and the ground was dry enough with no snow. He also had one blanket under himself to keep the chill off but still it was cold. He watched the road for the returning Outlander warriors, moving his toes to keep circulation going. What was worse, he really needed to relieve himself but didn't want to lie in his own urine.

The slaves had moved as soon as it got dark. They quickly scouted the surrounding area and found more than enough bushes to hide in on the opposite side of the rise from the village. The attack would not be seen by anyone in the village. Their blankets with spare clothing had been stashed a small walk to the east under the large roots system of a dead tree. Demon-boy and the other Eighteen pit-rats in his group were in bushes beside the road, further down towards the flat ground. Funny-boy and the younger slaves hiding in bushes closer to the top of the rise, ready to charge in when Funny-boy gave the word. Every slave battled the cold as best they could as they lay under the bushes. Demon-boy was worried as the Outlanders hadn't yet returned and he estimated it was only a short amount of time before the sun was at its highest point. He was thinking whether to go and talk to Silent-boy when he heard the sound of galloping horses. His bush was the furthest towards the north, in order to give Demon-boy a better view and more time. He looked and watched as mounted warriors came around a bend in the path. He counted them, 10, 20, 25, 30, 40, 50, then finally 60. He swore. This was triple the number of warriors that had come in the previous day. Thirty-two slaves against close to sixty mounted warriors; it would be a slaughter. He watched as the warriors sped past his position. He knew the other pit rats would see how many warriors there were. This would sap their morale. He watched them go over the rise and despair welled up in him.

By now, the warriors would be in the settlement, gathering food and supplies. A voice from across the road, no more than a loud whisper could be heard. He poked his head out from under the bush where he lay and saw Silent-boy's face also peering through a bush at him. Silent-boy cupped his hand and spoke. "Numbers mean nothing snow-weasel. We need that food or it's over for us!"

The words washing over Demon-boy, steeling his resolve. A smile spread across his face. He stopped to think of Smith and Trainer, and felt his confidence rise within his rage.

Chapter Sixteen

He heard the galloping horses and the sound grew closer. Any moment, they would ride over the rise and he would give the call to attack. He was once again detached, as if he was back in the pit again. He could feel nervousness down in his belly, but ignored it thinking of his friends and the people he had lost. Before he knew it, the Outlanders had ridden over the rise and galloping towards his position. As the lead horse approached a distant of twenty paces, he called out in the loudest voice he could. "PIT-RATS. ATTACK!"

He rose and threw himself out of the bushes, charging the lead horseman. The horses slowed slightly as the pit-rats rose from bushes around them and charged in. Demon-boy yelled at the top his voice and threw his hands in the air. The lead horse, frightened at the sudden noise, rose on his hind legs, tipping the warrior off. Demon-boy charged in and brained him with the spike on his axe. Turning, he dodged a sword thrust at him from another horseman. As he raised himself to counterattack, he saw the warrior stabbed in the belly by

Silent-boy, his longsword going all the way through and coming out of his back. All of the senior pit-rats were now engaged, slashing, and cutting with quick efficiency. Using all the skill they had learnt in the pit and using all of their endurance and strength they had trained for. Demon-boy jumped in mid-air, bringing his axe down towards the neck of a mounted warrior. It was blocked by the shield and as he landed, he spun in a circle to his left, bring his sword around in a reverse grip to stab the warrior in his lower back. Moving on, he didn't have time to see how the slaves were doing as a warrior came at him on foot with a double handed axe. He took a step back and to avoid the swing, he stepped quickly aiming a sword stab at the warrior's throat. It grazed the warrior's left cheek before he had to take another step back to dodge another swing of that fearsome axe. The warriors had all dismounted and were engaging the slaves on foot, losing their main advantage.

Silent-boy thanked whatever Gods were listening as he ran his sword though the shoulder with his two-handed sword. Pulling it out and spinning on his back foot before delivering a crushing blow with the flat of his huge blade to the head of the warrior he was engaged with, knocking him out. Silent-boy smiled to himself as he linked with Demon-boy, engaging another warrior.

Demon-boy had killed three enemies in quick succession and was standing beside Silent-boy as they advanced. Three of the senior pit-rats in Demon-boy's group were down and four where moving to link with Silent-boy and Demon-boy. Demon-boy was just thinking it would be a perfect time for Funny-boy to engage, when he heard a massive roar coming for the rear of the warriors that made him smile and Silent-boy laugh.

"SNOW WEASEL!" roared Funny-boy as he launched himself at the rear of the warriors. His deep voice carrying over the small battlefield. As he suspected, the young ones were at his side chanting as they ran. "SNOW WEASEL, SNOW WEASEL, SNOW WEASEL!"

The rear group hit the rear of the warriors like a boulder hitting the sea, smashing their way through the rear ranks, killing as they went. Funny-boy's strength and courage flowing into the younger ones around him, who discarded all thoughts of self-defence and fought like the slaves they were, like pit-rats.

Many Outlanders were down as Silent-boy and Demon-boy advanced further into the middle of the battle. Protecting each other's side, moving, cutting, killing, and then moving on to the next warrior. They could both hear Funny-boy shouting insults at the enemy as he fought, they could hear maddening laughter coming from somewhere that sounded suspiciously like Bulldog-boy. Silent-boy caught a blow on his arm that cut deeply, blood squirting from a large cut in the middle of his bicep. He dropped his sword and drew his large knife with his good arm and continued to weave and cut. Demon-boy moved closer, protecting his injured side. Looking around at the damage being caused by both sides, he saw Stonefist-boy go down to a vicious swing on a large sword but almost lost his focus, an axe coming in too close and almost taking out one of his eyes. He stepped to the side to avoid it at the last second. He then jumped forward past the warrior, slicing his sword in his left hand up and into the groin of the warrior before moving forward to engage the next one. Standing in front of him was Bulldog-boy, hands on hips breathing hard. He was covered in blood and had a massive smile on his face.

Fighting stopped and the survivors made their way to

Demon-boy standing around breathing hard. Funny-boy came up and put his hand on Bulldogs-boy's shoulder. "Crazy slave!" he said, smiling.

The others all laughed as they had seen what Bulldog-boy had done. Demon-boy would not learn the details for a while. Demon-boy looked around and surveyed the bodies. The Outlanders dead to a man. He counted only forty-three bodies, so some had stayed in the village. Thankfully, the site of the battle was far away enough from the village that the clash of weapons and shouts couldn't be heard.

He dropped his weapons to the ground and walked around to survey his own losses. Standing was twenty-six pit-rats. They had lost another six pit-rats in the battle! Demon-boy was very surprised they did not lose more. All of his three friends had survived with minor cuts and bruises. Silent-boy was trying his best to stem the large cut to his arm. Demon-boy was quietly shocked as he remembered back to their initial escape, remembering all of the fifty-four faces of slaves that had made it out of the slave camp. He shook himself and gathered his thoughts.

"Capture the horses and raid any food supplies you can," he said before continuing. "The bodies of our brother slaves move over to the bushes. Grab any blankets or weapons you may think you need. Keep yourselves light as we still have five days of hard travel. Get this done, then we make for the dead tree and rest for the remainder of the day."

The pit-rats all moved off getting done what needed to be done. Demon-boy went back to the warrior he had slain with the double handed axe. Reaching the body, he picked up the large double headed axe and looked at it. It was a fine weapon! Not perhaps as good as the one the Smith had made for Angry-man, but a good axe, nonetheless. He walked toward Funny-boy who had preferred a large weapon such as this but fought with two hand axes from lack of options. He shouted out to Funny-boy and hefted the axe in his direction. Funny-boy caught it mid-air and regarded it. He swung it a few times then smiled. "Good balance," he said.

"Will suit you better than the two toothpicks you normally carry!" said Silent-boy.

The four of them laughed before moving onto the task of quickly gathering what they could and getting away. Demon-boy went back over and picked up his weapons. Wiping them off on an Outlander's body, he put them away at his side before going through the packages that the other slaves were bringing in from the horses. On quick inspection, he discovered smoked meats, bread, cheese and some small flasks of Firemer. He sighed in relief. They would now have the food to give them enough energy to reach the border.

That afternoon as they rested, Demon-boy finally got to hear the tale of Bulldog-boy. Funny-boy was whispering it softly as Demon-boy and his three friends sat together and ate.

"He did what?" said Silent-boy.

"He passed his axe to the bastard. He threw it gentle and said, 'Arse face, have this,'" said Funny-boy.

Silent-boy and Demon-boy chuckled. Bulldog-boy just looked embarrassed and said nothing.

"Then what did he do?" asked Demon-boy.

"Then whist the bastard was trying to catch the axe thrown to him, Bulldog-boy ran up and smashed his other axe into the outlander-bastard's face," said Funny-boy.

They laughed, including some of the other pit-rats that were not yet asleep. The tale of Bulldog-boy had been told a few times and had spread.

"Then, he ran up and jumped up on to a horse behind

another bastard. He whispered into his ear then cut his throat," said Funny-boy.

The pit-rats laughed again.

"What is your problem Bulldog-boy? And what did you whisper to him?" said Demon-boy.

"I told him this might hurt," replied Bulldog-boy with a small grin.

All of the pit-rats listening laughed, long and loudly.

"Funny-boy is right. You are going crazy," said Silent-boy.

Bulldog-boy just smiled and then laid down, wrapping his blanket around himself.

"Still. We did well. I am surprised, and happy we did not lose more," said Demon-boy.

"Yes. The younglings fought well. Perhaps in the morning you say something Demon-boy," said Funny-boy.

"I will. If you promise to stop yelling 'Snow Weasel' every time we have a bloody battle," said Demon-boy.

They all chuckled. The talk was easing the tension. They had all been very lucky in the battle that day. Silent-boy had also witnessed the youngling he had taken under his wing get his first kill. He mentioned it to Demon-boy.

"Yes, I saw it. He needs a name that one. He is game and one tough little fighter. Did you teach him that move?" asked Demon-boy.

"I did," replied Silent-boy.

The youngling had run as fast as he could at an opponent on that had been thrown from his horse. As the warrior had levelled his spear, the youngling had executed a tumblers roll. He rolled and came up with his short sword, plunging it into the warrior's chest.

"Dangerous move, but it worked," said Demon-boy.

"Yes. The lad has courage and is not scared of anything,

apart from Bulldog-boys unwelcome advances," said Silent-boy tapping Bulldog-boy on the chest as he was lying down.

Demon-boy laughed before getting up, "I'll take the first watch. Get some rest."

He sat under a tree with his blanket wrapped around himself. He looked over the snow-covered ground, remembering back over everything that had happened. He was lost in thought when Bulldog-boy arrived and sat beside him.

"Thought you would be asleep by now?" said Demon-boy.

"Still too pumped from the battle. Could not sleep," replied Bulldog-boy.

"Sounds like you are starting to enjoy battles."

"Nah. Just getting more and more pissed off every time we come across more outlander-bastards."

"Don't take too many risks brother, do not want to lose you at this stage," said Demon-boy.

Bulldog-boy just smiled and said nothing. They both sat in silence, looking out over the frozen hills, snow gently falling. Demon-boy thought of something.

"Brother. I owe you an apology," he said.

"For what?"

"All those moons ago when we fought in the pit. Everything you said was right. I needed to stop feeling sorry for myself," he said.

Bulldog-boy looked at him with surprise on his face before speaking.

"That was a long time ago brother."

"Still, I am sorry," said Demon-boy.

"To be honest I remember the fight, but not what was said," said Bulldog-boy honestly.

Demon-boy chuckled. "You always remember the fights though eh?"

"Always. It's all I have. All I know."

"It is not all you have. You have me, Funny-boy, Silent-boy and a whole lot of other brothers who rely on you."

"True. But I enjoy the fights, especially against the outlanders. I have dreamed my whole life of hurting them. And now every time we face them, I get to live that dream."

Demon-boy nodded "I understand that. Perhaps one day we can truly bring the fight to them"

"Now that is a dream worth having. Nothing would please me more than to come back with a few thousand warriors, as fit and tough as pit-rats, and wipe them all from this land. A children's dream."

"Well you never know. Hold onto that dream. I also want to return. I made a promise to son-of-angry-man, and that outlander we captured. I want to keep that promise," said Demon-boy.

"Well we need to get out of here alive first. Once we have done that, who knows what will happen."

Demon-boy looked over at his brother slave, "Do you accept the apology brother?"

Bulldog-boy put his hand on his brothers' shoulder. "Nothing to apologise for, but if there was, I would accept it."

They both nodded and went back to looking out over the land.

"Is that the only dream that keeps you going? Revenge I mean," said Demon-boy.

"No. I am really hoping to feel the soft touch of a woman before I die."

They both laughed. Demon-boy had to wipe a laugh tear form his face.

"Well there was not much opportunity for that in the training camp, unless you fancied the cook," said Demon-boy.

"I asked and she said no," replied Bulldog-boy.

They both laughed even harder.

"Do you not think about the touch of a woman?" said Bulldog-boy.

"No. Can't say I do. My life has been one of pain, fighting and death. The thought has never crossed my mind."

'You call me crazy?" replied Bulldog-boy.

They smiled and continued to watch. It was sometime before Bulldog-boy brought up something that had been on his mind for a while.

"What was between you and Trainer? We all respected him but when he was killed it hit you harder than anyone."

The question caught Demon-boy by surprise. He took a deep breath and looked at Bulldog-boy. Once he had steadied his breathe, he launched into the tale. Telling him all, from the first time he had meet trainer to all the secret conversations. When he finished his tale, his friend was nodding.

"No wonder you kept it all secret. The bastards would have not liked the relationship between you. It would have been like losing your eldest brother," said Bulldog-boy.

"Yes. Which is why I do not want to lose you, or Funny-boy, or Silent-boy."

They both smiled. Bulldog-boy stood up and stretched.

"Time to get some sleep. Smith would be proud of you brother, how far you have got us. You truly have led us. Yes, we have helped where we can, the others and I. But it was you everyone followed. The Smith would be very proud, just as proud as I am," said Bulldog-boy smiling.

He said nothing else and turned and walked away.

Demon-boy had not thought of the Smith in many days. But he thought of him now. He remembered all the conversations they had. He found he could think of the Smith now without getting upset. He watched Bulldog-boy walk away.

"He would be proud of us all," he whispered.

For five nights they ran. They still rested by day but took Silent-boy's advice and picked up the pace at night. They would spend the entire night half running and half walking. All of the pit-rats were at the end of their endurance. They were tired, weary and had very little left to give. Silent-boy although nursing his injury kept up. He explained it was important to get through this last province as quickly as possible, as by now Chief Hura would have worked out where they were heading. They had left enough bodies on the trail and it was not hard to work out.

The food and supplies they had won in the last battle, had indeed seen them through. The first day of rest after the battle saw a lot of them falling asleep drunk from the Firemer they had managed to get their hands on. Bulldog-boy, Demon-boy and Funny-boy had kept watched together throughout the whole day. They had sipped a jug of the spirit to keep themselves warm but remained alert. There was no follow up from any outlanders. As they kept watch no words were spoken, just silence. A silence that they felt comfortable with. There was no need for words between the three of them, all comfortable in each other's company.

There had been no pursuit after the battle, just battles against the elements and coldness as every slave moved as best as he could. They had kept to their routine to traveling at night only. They stopped short of the border. The sun was not yet up, and they would prefer to approach in full light. There were no trees to hide in, so they had made do sitting tightly in a hollow and covering their blankets with snow. They could clearly see the border, the large fort, and the settlement they must reach. The settlement walls made of stone and standing the height of three to four grown men standing on each other's shoulders high. If the slaves were shocked at the size of the walls of the settlement, they were speechless when they noticed the border walls. Wooden walls made from large full-grown trees disappeared in both directions of the border. They were also to the height of three fully grown men. The large trees, no doubt, cut down and squared off, then laid on their sides; stacking four trees on top of each other to raise the walls to height. The walls were painted black and Demon-boy wondered how long it took them to paint the walls considering the length of the border. The point, of course, giving protection to the wood from the rain and snow.

The slaves had done their best to keep warm through the early morning. They had run out of food the day before and only had water skins left. They huddled together in the hollow, keeping warm and sharing body heat. The time the sun started to rise, they were still asleep, the energy of the group gone. Demon-boy was awake with his three friends. Silent-boy had done his best to stop the flow of blood from his arm that he received in the last battle. He had used cold snow each day to numb the pain and the bleeding had stopped. It ached him more than he would admit.

Demon-boy sat, staring at the border. As soon as he saw movement on the walls of the settlement, he would wake them all up and make a move. He couldn't make out details of anyone on the wall, the settlement still too far away, but he could see the gate clearly and was waiting for it to open. He didn't have to wait long, as when the sun slowly rose into the sky, the gate could be seen to be opening.

"Everyone up!" he yelled. "We move and we move now!"

Although asleep, the slaves were up instantly on hearing his voice. The sound of Demon-boy's voice cutting through their dreamless, exhausted sleep. They threw off their blankets and left them on the ground. They were all in a group as they moved off and walked at a speed that could only be described as a fast walk. All were quiet as they marched along. Funny-boy was walking beside Silent-boy, carrying his gear for him. His arm in much pain, causing him to grit his teeth together.

As they got close to the settlement, Demon-boy saw warriors on the walls now. He could make out details as they were a short distance walk from their freedom. He saw the warriors gathering on the walls, pointing at his slaves as they marched along. As they moved closer, he saw warriors exit the gate on horses carrying long spears. There was over fifty of them and they blocked the entrance to the settlement.

Demon-boy then realised the warriors were not in fact pointing at his broken ragged group but pointing over them in the direction that they had come from. He stopped and turned around, looking off in the distance. What he saw took the breath from his throat. Riders, hundreds of them. He knew in his gut who it would be; Angry-man! He was not sure how far away they were but knew that they were close enough to make it a race.

"OUTLANDERS BEHIND US, SPRINT!" he yelled.

The slaves automatically obeyed him, without feeling the need to look for themselves, trusting his words and sprinting. Funny-boy was at the back half-dragging Silent-boy as the gap opened up between them and the rest of the slaves. They sprinted for all their worth, never taking their eyes off the gate.

Demon-boy reached the gate and the line of mounted warriors first. He spun around to see the other slaves not far behind him, Funny-boy and Bulldog-boy at the rear a little way back now, each with one of Silent-boy's arms in theirs, carrying him along.

"Who are you and what do you want?" said one of the mounted warriors.

Demon-boy turned back. "We are slaves, escaped many days ago and looking for freedom!" he said, trying to catch his breath.

"So, you say. You don't look like slaves!" said the speaker.

"We don't have time for this. We are slaves, we stole clothing and weapons to get here. Those horsemen you see are after us," he said, in frustration.

Demon-boy looked back over his shoulder and saw the horsemen were not far away and would reach them soon. He felt his anger rise as he turned to face the mounted warrior.

"We were told that Irik offers safety for runaway slaves! That Irik offers freedom! If this is how you treat slaves, then you are no better than the Outlander-bastards that we are trying to escape," he forced out, his patience gone.

"We are NOT Outlanders!" replied the mounted warrior.

Bulldog-boy jumped into the conversation, his anger on his face showed he was also out of patience as Funny-boy held up Silent-boy on his own.

"No, you are not Outlanders! Outlanders have at least half a brain and some honour, you gutless PIECE OF SHIT!" he yelled.

As one, Bulldog-boy and Demon-boy both drew their weapons, turning and walking to the back of the group to face the oncoming horsemen as Funny-boy stood holding Silent-boy in front facing the warriors of the border.

"Draw weapons! It's clear these bastards have no honour. On my command, charge the Outlanders and kill them!"

All of the slaves turned and faced the oncoming warriors.

Demon-boy and Bulldog-boy fired up, didn't hear the conversation going on behind them. All of the pit-rats not caring about the odds they faced. They were tired, pissed off and would follow Demon-boy in the next battle, like they had in the other battles.

Funny-boy and Silent-boy made it to the horsemen.

"We are slaves, we will die if those horsemen reach us," said Funny-boy.

"Who says you are not criminals hiding from justice?" said the mounted warrior.

"I say, we are slaves!" said Silent-boy.

"And who are you, injured one?"

"I name myself as Jorga, son of Weelan. I lived in the fishing settlement of Wiak, just east of the Capital of Iriksec. I was captured ten summers ago when our fishing boat was sunk."

There was silence as he continued. "I say we are slaves, and if you doubt the words of your own countrymen, then my friend has it right. You are worse than scum."

The Outlanders were only two hundred paces from their prey, the slaves they had stalked and tracked throughout the last thirty days. At their head, Chief Hura had a look of rage on his face, holding his sons hand axe in his right hand. To the Chief's left was his warrior, Malak. Malak hadn't been killed by his Chief and once again rode beside him. The warriors started to whoop in anticipation of the kill. Two hundred riders had been hungry for action and were now about to see it. The Chief started to laugh when he realised the men of Irik were not going to let the slaves pass. His heart pumped faster as he saw the Demon-child standing at the front, his weapons in his hands and waiting to fight.

Within moments, the chance to kill this Demon-boy slipped through his fingers. Hundreds of Irik warriors rode around the slaves and assembled in his path. He saw one of the mounted warriors lean down and say something to the Demon-child before he lost sight of him and the other slaves. Hundreds of horsemen now blocked his path, shields raised sitting in a perfect line. He called the halt and his men slowed to a trot, then to a walk before standing still not fifteen paces from the horsemen of Irik

"You know the rules, Outlander. You may not come closer than this to our borders," shouted the mounted warrior that had whispered to Demon-boy a few moments before.

" I am chasing the murderer of my son. Hand them over!" Chief Hura replied.

"Are they slaves?"

"Yes. Slaves that killed my son and burnt down half of my capital."

The horseman of Irik all looked surprised and some of them were quietly impressed. Burning down half a settlement was quite the achievement.

"I grieve with you for the loss of your son, but you know the laws. Slaves are not kept in Irik and if Outlander slaves make it to our borders, then they are free once they cross."

"They only crossed because you let them, donkey brain!"

The mounted horseman blew out a large whistle. Instantly one hundred archers on top of the wall drew back their bow strings with arrows held to their cheeks. At this range, they would not miss.

The leader of the horseman spoke again. "They are free according to our laws. Is our conversation finished?"

Angry-man looked at Malak, a warrior that he had

spared. The anger in his eyes evident. Malak knew his time was up, even before he had time to close his eyes, his Chief raised his son's axe. The axe sliced through his throat and he fell off his horse. The Irik horseman said nothing but just looked on. The Outlanders turned themselves around and trotted off in the direction they came. As the Irik horseman returned inside the walls, the leader kept watching as the Outlander's rode away. Finally, muttering to himself before also turning and riding back into the gate. "Bastard Outlanders!"

Chapter Seventeen

Once through the gates, the pit-rats had been ushered along a straight road, paved with stone. All of the pit-rats were nervous. Silent-boy had told many stories of his people and how different they were compared to the Outlanders. However, the incident at the gate hadn't helped. Along with the fact that everywhere they looked, people looking like the Outlanders went about their business. The large town of Bordik had more of a civilised feel to it as did the residents. Dressing differently to the Outlanders that they were used to, by wearing cleaner clothes with more style and none walking around in armour was a good sign. At least, it should have been, but the pit-rats were still nervous.

The pit rats continued walking until they were ushered into a large building. The building was two storeys and made completely of stone. The stone itself looked like grey river stones that had been squared off into bricks. The corners of the building had a dark grey, almost black stone running up the full height of the building. The same dark stone framed the massive double doors they entered through. The pit-rats felt naturally out of place and all of them constantly looked around for a tree to hide behind. The thought made Silent-boy smile. He looked at Demon-boy and noticed he hadn't calmed down from the confusion at the gate. The look on his face was clear for everyone to see. He was pissed off and would not take much for him to be set off. He would have to be careful here and head off any disaster. He knew Demon-boy's moods, and even though as the man had grown, he had become more in control of his emotions, he could still sometimes be unreasonable.

They were led into a room with a large wooden table, people were stocking it with food and jugs of drink. Word had no doubt been passed along before they arrived. The man leading them said nothing but just pointed to the chairs, indicating they should all sit.

"Help yourselves to the food. You are safe here in Bordik. Eat your fill and our Mayor will be here soon to greet you," the man said, before turning and walking away.

The pit-rats sat down and looked at the food. The man had spoken with a strange accent. They understood the words mostly but struggled with some of the meanings.

Silent-boy spoke up. "Eat. The board is full, and my people would not harm you. We are safe!"

The relief in the room was instant. All of their shoulders sagged, the weight of the escape being lifted slightly. It would be many days before the pit-rats were fully at ease, Silent-boy realised. He looked across at the table at Demon-boy and saw him filling his cup with water. He drank slowly before putting the cup down and watching the other former slaves eat. Former slaves! The thought a pleasing one as Silent-boy reached for some roast chicken. He savoured the flavour as the chicken drumstick soon disappeared. This was the best food most of the pit-rats had ever eaten and the smiles around the table told Silent-boy that they were enjoying it. He looked across at Funny-boy and nodded his head towards Demon-boy. Funny-boy knew exactly what Silent-boy was meaning. Funny-boy looked over at his friend, who was one chair down.

"Would have taken a few bruises taking on all of those horsemen at the gate, snow weasel!"

The table laughed and even Demon-boy smiled finally.

"Yes, more than a few," replied Demon-boy, finally grabbing some food and eating.

Funny-boy looked across at Silent-boy and winked. Silent-boy was once again amazed how Funny-boy could cheer Demon-boy up. Simple words from him could cut through even the darkest mood.

Bulldog-boy joined in. "Yeah, Demon-boy. I am surprised you didn't challenge the bastard that was not letting us in?"

The table laughed again.

"I did!" he replied.

The table laughed harder.

It was some time before the pit-rats had stopped eating. They now just relaxed where they were sitting. Talking to each other and getting used to the feeling that they were no longer on the run. Before long, the Mayor walked in. Silent-boy assumed it was the Mayor, not knowing what the word 'Mayor' meant. He was better dressed in a shiny black leather waistcoat, a bright white woollen shirt with dark grey woollen trousers. His tall black boots, the same shining leather of his waistcoat. He sat down at the head of the table.

"Greetings. My name is Golix. I am the Mayor here. Let me welcome you to my town and your new freedom."

The pit-rats all smiled and sat up straighter. Two other men came along to Silent-boy and ushered him to follow them. Demon-boy, ever protective jumped to his feet before the Mayor spoke again.

"It's okay. We are sending him to a room to get that wound seen too. He will be safe; you have my word. Besides, we would not hurt one of our own, would we? By the way, welcome back to your people, Jorga, son of Wheelan."

Silent-boy smiled and nodded his head as he was led away. The Mayor continued and Demon-boy sat back down.

"Shortly, you will be taken to our local barracks. There you will be given beds to rest in for the next few days. You will then be taken to our baths, where you can get clean. We will give you some fresh clothes whilst your current clothes are cleaned, mended, and then returned to you. We ask that you leave your weapons in your rooms that we provide you with."

Demon-boy stiffened and looked at the Mayor. The Mayor saw the look.

"Do not be concerned. You can keep the weapons you have won; we just do not want people walking around our town fully armed. You may carry a knife if you feel the need, but please leave the weapons in the rooms."

Demon-boy understood and nodded his head. Two other men entered, and the Mayor nodded towards them.

"Now that you have eaten, please follow these men. They will take you to the temporary accommodation and get you cleaned up," said Golix.

As the pit-rats stood, the Mayor looked at Demon-boy.

"May I have a moment of your time, please?"

Funny-boy looked at Demon-boy, who nodded his permission and Funny-boy left with the others. Demon-boy sat back down. Once the room was empty, the Mayor moved to the other side of the table, directly across from Demon-boy.

"They seem to follow your lead!" he said.

"Yes. I have earnt their trust during our escape," replied Demon-boy.

"Now that we are alone, I apologise for the incident at the gate. Please understand that even though we do take in runaway slaves, we have never before had such a large group of escaped slaves arrive at our gate at once. Usually they arrive alone, beaten, bloody and exhausted!"

Demon-boy breathed slowly, understanding where the Mayor was coming from.

"I understand that. We were perhaps dressed and armed a little too well to look like the slaves we are."

"Exactly, and as I said, we usually see them arrive alone or maybe once in a while two will arrive together. Never a group of twenty-six!"

"There was more of us that escaped, but we lost many on our journey here."

"How many started out?"

"There was fifty-four of us that escaped the camp the training camp we lived in"

"You lost that many?" said the Mayor, shocked at how many had perished.

"Yes. Some we lost to the Outlanders when we first left the settlement, then lost more to the cold and more in our last battles to arrive here."

"When you were seen approaching our gates, there was many arguments as to who you were. Some argued that we should send the horseman out to slaughter you. Others like myself advised caution and to go slowly."

"The Mayor is in charge, yes?" said Demon-boy.

"Yes, but we have a council and always discuss different ideas before committing to an action.

'What is a council? And, what is a mayor?" asked Demon-boy.

"A council? A mayor? You do not know the word?"

"No. As a slave, there is still many words that I have not heard before."

The mayor smiled. "No longer a slave, remember."

Demon-boy smiled as well. "It will take some time to get used to being free."

The mayor smiled and chuckled. "That is why I am talking with you. Before any decisions are made by yourselves, take a few days to get used to sleeping in clean beds, safe and warm. A council is a group of men and women that are more senior in age, and hopefully wiser. They lend their advice to the Mayor when needed in order for the Mayor to choose the best way forward. The mayor is like a leader of a town or settlement. He or she is responsible for settlement and makes all the decisions. But getting advice form the council first of course. When the Mayor is away, the council will rule in his absence."

Demon-boy took another drink of water as the mayor continued.

"You and I will catch-up again soon along with any other senior members in your party. Many decisions you will need to make for yourselves. Where to go from here? What to do with yourselves? Many things to be discussed. The first thing would be to honestly say I would not call out Opix, the man that questioned you at the gate. He is a great warrior and even though he respects the rules, he is not someone you would want to challenge."

"How did you know I wanted to challenge him?" Demon-boy said with a half-smile on his face.

"Opix did. He said you had a mad look on your face and thought you would be the type to hold a grudge. He said you may call him out."

"He is correct. The thought crossed my mind."

"I would not, he is a great fighter with or without weapons. He would not go easy on you!"

Demon-boy roared with laughter at the thought. Although he was not an arrogant man, he was confidence in his skills he had learnt in the pits. Fighting for one's life usually sharpened the skills somewhat.

The Mayor looked at Demon-boy waiting for him to stop his mirth.

"You mentioned decisions need to be made. To be honest, they are decisions that I never thought I would have to make. What do runaway slaves usually do when they reach here?"

"When they arrive, we do exactly what we have just done. Feed them, bath them, and give them fresh clothes. After a few days of getting used to your new freedom, we discuss what they want to do with their lives."

"What do these other slaves do?"

"Many have decided to remain in our country, moving to another settlement and building a life for themselves. Learning a new type of work or perhaps fitting in with work that they are familiar with. It all depends what type of work the escapees are trained to do. Some have even sailed across the ocean, searching for their family when we can find them passage. That is only a few, as I said most choose to settle here. If I may ask, what line of work are you and your fellow involved in?"

"Pit-rats," said Demon-boy.

"Pit-rats? I have never heard the term before!"

"We are trained from an early age. Fitness, hand to hand combat and then weapons. Once we reach eighteen summers, we are chucked into a pit in the ground where we fight with other slave to the death," Demon-boy said casually.

The Mayor stared at him in shocked silence. "We had

heard that the Outlanders were indulging in blood sports again," whispered the Mayor.

"Yes. All of the slaves with me came from one training camp in Hura."

"That's on the other side of the nation!"

"Yes, close to forty days of hard running."

"You made it in forty days on foot? No wonder, you are short on patience when you arrived. An enormous feat and no wonder you laughed when I told you not to challenge Opix."

Demon-boy smiled. "I now understand why so many of us is somewhat of a problem. Single slaves are easy to slip into your way of life, but now you have twenty-six escaped slaves that have only been trained to fight and kill. What will you do with us?"

"That is a decision that I have said is yours, but you and I will need many talks I think to come up with a plan in what to do with you all. Go get cleaned up and rest. We will talk again soon.

Demon-boy stood and looked at the mayor. "On behalf of all of the escaped slaves, I thank you."

He turned and left, falling into step behind another man that he didn't know as they made their way through the streets of this town. Demon-boy didn't know what a bath was but was looking forward to sleeping.

Later that evening, the pit-rats or former slaves relaxed in the barrack rooms that they have been provided. Small rooms that held two beds and little else. The windows were large but shuttered against the snowstorm that had hit that afternoon. The remaining eleven that had made it, sat around a raging fire in a common room that was at the end of the corridor that lead to their rooms. The pit-rats had never been this warm, relaxed, or indeed clean. The taking of steam baths was a new experience to them, sitting in a stone constructed room with tiered seating that had been built into the walls. In the centre of the room, are large stone bricked box. In this was rocks that had been heated by fires outside before being brought in by workers. Then cold water from a bucket beside the stoned box was ladled onto the hot rocks, creating steam that filled the room. They had been nervous but soon relaxed in the hot room, feeling the warmth seep into their cold and exhausted bodies. Most had stayed for far too long before leaving. The four friends, however, had stayed in even longer, not speaking but finding calm in each other's company. Later that evening, they all adjourned to Demon-boy's room to discuss what had happened and talk eventually turned to what to do next.

"So, we get to choose where we go or what we do?" asked Bulldog-boy.

"Yes, that is what the Mayor told me. He said that many of the escaped slaves move to different settlements in this land and build a life for themselves. A few take ships and try to return to their old life."

The three others listened as Demon-boy spoke. He told them all of the conversation that he had with the Mayor. After the Demon-boy had finished telling them of the conversation, it was Funny-boy that spoken first. "I have no idea where to find my homeland and would not know where to start!"

The others nodding their heads in agreement! It was Silent-boy who cut to the heart of the problem. "Building a life here will not be as easy for me as I thought it would. I am sure I could find my home village and some family, but I have grown up with you three. You are my family!"

They all smiled before Demon-boy continued to talk.

"Finding work for us should not be too hard but what the hell do we do? We have only been trained for one thing and one thing only, to kill."

Just then, a figure walked through the door of his room, standing in the doorway looking at all of them. It was the warrior Opix that had originally greeted them at the gate. Demon-boy felt his heckles rise. He looked over at Silent-boy, who very slightly shook his head.

"Sorry for intruding, I wanted to speak to you," said Opix, staring at Demon-boy.

Demon-boy rose from his bed and approached. "No need to apologise Opix. In fact, it is me that owes you an apology," said Demon-boy. Opix raised his eyebrows and crossed his arms as Demon-boy went on. "My curt words were a result of exhaustion and tiredness. I apologise for the words and the meaning behind them. You were just doing your job."

The words were not easy for Demon-boy but they were genuine. Silent-boy had spoken to him in the steams regarding his way of letting his emotions control him, and how he needed to stop taking everything as a challenge.

Opix smiled. "Apology accepted, and please accept my apology for my curt words."

Demon-boy approached and held out his arm. Opix looked at it, then stepped forward and grasped it in the warrior fashion. The other three slowly rose and took Opix's arm in the same grasp, thanking him for letting them in. Silent-boy was the last to grasp arms and as he returned to his seat on the bed, he patted Demon-boy on the shoulder.

"Also, I am sorry for overhearing parts of your conversation as I walked in," said Opix.

"It is no secret," said Bulldog-boy, before continuing. "We are discussing what the hell are we going to do with our lives now!"

"Yes, I can't even imagine how you are all feeling right now. From what the Mayor has said, you were pit-rats. In fact, as I walked in one of you said the only thing you have been trained in is to kill!"

"Correct, but apart from returning to the pits, we have no way to make a living from that skill," said Demon-boy.

All of the pit-rats laughed. Opix was smiling but with a look on his face that clearly showed he was thinking. "Maybe there is!" said Opix.

The four pit-rats looked at him as he stood in silence. A large smile crept across his face before he continued. "Do any of you know what a brotherhood is?" They all shook their heads. "It is a company of men that are paid to fight in other countries wars, or battles."

It was Demon-boy that clicked first. "You mean mercenaries?" said Demon-boy.

His three friends also caught up, being a mercenary had been the Smith's occupation before he was enslaved.

"Yes, that's it exactly. That is what the Southerners call them, but here we call them Brotherhoods. We have five such companies here in Irik. They are small private companies that often travel to the southlands, getting paid to fight battles. If you are trained to fight, then perhaps that is where your future lies."

All of the pit-rats were looking at each other, digesting what they had just been told. Already an idea was forming in Demon-boy's head. He was not sure why, but the idea appealed to him. He didn't enjoy slaughter or killing, but he was good at it. If this gave them an opportunity to make a living, and perhaps travel to the south, then they would be fools to discount the idea. Finally, Demon-boy spoke. "It is an idea."

"I have contact with a few of the Captains that run these Brotherhoods. If you want, I could make enquiries?"

Demon-boy looked at his friends one by one. They nodded their consent and he turned back to Opix. "Yes. That would be good, thank you."

"All of you will be interested?" asked Opix.

"Those of us in this room, yes. The others would have to be asked individually," said Silent-boy.

"Of course. Well, I have duty soon, so I best be going. I will get word to my wife's cousin Joren who runs one of these Brotherhoods. As soon as I have a reply, which won't be long, I will let you know." said Opix.

They all nodded their thanks and he left.

Demon-boy looked at Silent-boy. "You would come with us?" he asked Silent-boy.

"I said before, you are my family!"

"We will have to talk to the others. Some of them may join us, but some may not!" said Bulldog-boy.

"I'll do that," said Funny-boy.

Demon-boy nodded. "You speak to the others tonight, so we know how many will come with us," said Demon-boy.

They continued to speak before all moving to their own rooms and sleeping. As Demon-boy lay in his warm bed with many blankets, he relaxed. His mind was still trying to work its way through the adjustment of not being a slave. As he drifted off to sleep, he had a contented look on his face.

Word from Opix's cousin came faster than they were ready for it. He had been in the town of Bordix visiting his sister when Opix had told him of the runaway slaves who were trained to kill over dinner. The next morning, he rushed to the barracks to meet them. Opix and the Mayor had gone with him to make the introductions. As Opix lead his cousin-in-law to the barracks, he smiled at the conversation they had the previous evening. His wife's cousin had been excited at the prospect.

"Twenty-six slaves that were trained in killing! Are they any good?" asked Joren.

"I am not sure as I have not seen them fight, but according to the Mayor who has heard their stories, the oldest four were unbeaten in the arenas of the Outlanders. The one that leads them was quite often put in the arena against two other warriors, but still he won."

"Leader? Will he accept orders, do you think?"

"I am sure he will. They are all very disciplined, but do not forget he led them across the Outlander nation. I have not seen him fight but I can tell you, the others follow without question. If he had ordered them to attack us at the front gate, I have no doubt they would have."

"I will have to test them to see if they are any good. I have a few men with me, do you think they will refuse?"

"They will not refuse, cousin, but make it with wooden weapons!"

Joren laughed. "I will do that. We had three squads wiped out in our last job in the autumn. I am down to sixty soldiers. I need to replenish the ranks if I am to stay in business."

"I understand that."

As the Mayor, Opix and Joren walked into the common room of the barracks, the former slaves were waiting. The room was warm with the fire going but not uncomfortably so.

Demon-boy was the only one standing as the three entered. Quick introductions were made and then Joren stepped forward.

"My name is Joren. I run the Brotherhood called Bloodchildren. I have a small settlement and training camp not far from our capital, Iriksec. I have been told of your journey across the Outlander nation, a truly remarkable story, and have been told of your previous occupation."

The previous evening, Funny-boy had told the other pit-rats what a mercenary company was and what they did, so all of them knew exactly what Joren was speaking of.

Joren continued. "With the training that you have received and experience as slaves, I think you would fit in nicely with my Brotherhood. I need good men, men who obey orders quickly and fight like devils. Not all of our work involves fighting battles. Some jobs may require us to protect wagons of goods and some jobs may have us training new troops how to fight."

Demon-boy spoke finally. "What do we receive for this?"

"You mean payment?"

Demon-boy and the others had never heard this word before, but Demon-boy just nodded as he didn't want to seem unknowledgeable in front of this man.

"Payment can be discussed later, but my company pays the best rates. Also, I provide armour, food and weapons"

"We have to find our own place to sleep?" asked Demon-boy.

"No. We have a barracks where every solider gets his own room."

Demon-boy looked over at Opix, who stepped forward and spoke. "Some of these ideas and words you may not have heard before, but this is a fair deal and in fact, it's exceptionally good. There is more risk working in a Brotherhood, but the rewards are well worth it."

"In that case, it seems fair. Where do we go from here?" asked Demon-boy.

Joren breathed as he looked at Demon-boy, knowing what came next would be a little difficult.

"Before any agreement is made, of course, I would need to test all of those that wanted to join my Brotherhood."

Much to Joren's surprise, he saw all of the former slaves nod their heads.

"We understand that. Tell us how you will test us, and I am sure you will find that we are up to the challenge." said Silent-boy.

All of the former slaves nodded their agreement. 'Interesting,' thought Joren! This Demon-boy was the leader, but he had a solid second that he didn't mind deferring too. Perhaps Opix was right. The two standing in front of him already showing potential leadership qualities and he liked how all of the former slaves referred to them. He spoke on. "There would be a fitness test and, of course, I would like to see some training bouts!"

All of the former slaves were smiling; large smiles spread across their faces. In fact, most of them looked like they were trying not to laugh. Demon-boy turned back to Opix.

"This is fine, just name a place and we will take these tests!"

At this point, the Mayor stepped forward. "Across the settlement, we have an indoor training area that is large enough for these tests. Perhaps after lunch, we can all meet there then?"

"That would be fine. Nine of my men and I will meet you all there after lunch. I have one more question if I may?" asked Joren.

Demon-boy nodded.

"All of you will be wanting to join my Brotherhood?"

Demon-boy looked at Funny-boy, who then stood and made his way forward.

"No. Twenty-two of us are looking at joining you. Four want to find a life away from violence."

"I understand that. In that case, I will see the ones that are interested after lunch."

The mayor, Opix and Joren left the room, the former slaves talking amongst themselves.

"You're worried about their 'tests'? said Bulldog-boy, as he joined the others.

All of them laughed loudly.

Joren and his nine men arrived at the indoor training area. He had with him two sergeants and seven of his better soldiers. All of them had been traveling to see family in the town and had jumped straight up and joined their captain when he had told them of the tests. They walked through the large wooded double doors into the large indoor area. Inside was a floor of hard packed earth over stone. The ceiling was high and vaulted with large, old wooden beams. The building itself was roughly seventy-five paces long by twenty-five paces wide.

Joren was surprised to see the former slaves already running slowly around the outside. All sticking together in a group as they looped easily around the outside of the training area. Joren and his men made their way to the centre of the training area and watched. The mayor was sitting in a long wooden bench along the opposite wall from the main door, deep in conversation. Beside them, a pile of wooden weapons.

The former slaves completed five laps before Demon-boy told them to stop. They all sat on the ground and helped each other go through a serious of stretches. Once this was done, they got to their feet and approached Joren. He smiled as they approached

"You started without us?" he said, with a large smile.

"Just a quick warmup is all, Joren. So, what is the first test?" asked Demon-boy.

Joren nodded to his first sergeant called Dolac, who stepped forward.

"I would like to see you run twenty circuits of this area matching my pace."

Demon-boy nodded and gave the command. The former slaves followed Dolac to the outside. Once they were all lined up, Dolac shouted. "GO!"

They all took off. Dolac setting what he thought was a good pace that he would call half speed. Easy at first but this pace over twenty laps would sap the strength of the former slaves. He was smiling to himself as they completed the fifth circuit. The former slaves still running right behind him and sticking to him. At ten laps, he was not smiling as the slaves still kept pace and said nothing. Not one complaint did he hear. Then at fifteen laps, he was surprised as he heard the two right behind him talking.

"You think he will increase the pace, Demon-boy?"

"Not sure, Bulldog-boy. Do you think we should ask?"

The slaves at the front laughed. Dolac called back to them. "No talking in the ranks!"

Funny-boy yelled back at him. "You are not yet in a position to give us orders, Arse face!"

ALL of the slaves laughed aloud before Silent-boy looked over at Demon-boy and nodded with a smile on his face. Demon-boy smiled back before yelling out to the former slaves. "Increase to training pace, on my word."

They all started whirling their arms as Joren and his men watched. They could hear every word, of course, and Joren was not sure to smile or be annoyed at the lack of respect shown. His other men had blank looks on their faces as well, not knowing how to react to the flippant attitude of the former slaves. As they started their sixteenth lap, they heard Demon-boy yell out. "Training pace now!"

The former slaves all overtook Sergeant Dolac who had a stupid but surprised look on his face. They gathered speed and all stuck together as a group, powering down the track with the sergeant in pursuit. He managed to keep up for one lap before stopping and walk over to his captain. He was trying to catch his breath when his captain looked over.

"They know how to run!"

The men all laughed as Sergeant Dolac watched the former slaves. They powered through the remaining laps but instead of stopping at lap twenty, kept their pace up for another five laps. At lap twenty-five, they slowed back down to the original pace that the Sergeant had set, completing another five laps. At thirty laps, they all came to a halt in front of the captain. Captain Joren could see slight smiles on all of these men. His two sergeants were pissed off and the other four soldiers amused.

Once the former slaves had caught their breaths, Joren motioned for the Mayor, who with the help of Opix brought over the wooden weapons. The pit-rats all took up wooden weapons that they were comfortable with, as did Captain Joren's men.

"Sparing match rules. Fight is concluded when what would be killing blow with steel is landed. This is just a test of your basic fighting skills and not a battle, so go easy."

Demon-boy could see by the look in the Captain's men, they didn't intend on going easy.

One by one, the pit rats took turns and faced off against Joren's men. Bulldog-boy went first and won convincingly. The experienced solider not expecting such furious combat. The solider was defending himself constantly and on the back foot for the short fight. Bulldog-boy then kicked the soldier's feet from beneath him and then held his short wooden sword to the throat of the soldier. Four of the other pit rats went next and held their own against the experienced soldiers. Even the youngling that Silent-boy had taken under his wing, a pit-rat that had never had a death bout, lost his bout but still managed to earn some respect. The other three pit-rats Surly-boy, Food-boy and Horse-boy lost their bouts, but it had taken the experienced soldiers longer than they expected. Funny-boy, of course used his overwhelming strength to good effect. Using a larger two-handed wooden sword, he charged his opponent, dodging a sword thrust to bring his sword out wide and aiming high, his wooden sword tapping his opponent lightly on the head. Silent-boy was still recovering from his injury. He fought with a wooden short sword and not the normal two-handed sword he liked to use. Even though it was his off hand, he still won quickly. Defending every attack easily, flowing through the combat and always being in control. He won with a quick move that was hard to see, his sword tapping the sergeant's throat lightly. Joren was impressed by all of the former slaves and amazed at the skill level of Silent-boy. It was clear Silent-boy had only ended the bout as he was bored.

Next Demon-boy stepped up. Wooden hand axe in his right hand, short wooden sword in his left hand. Sergeant Dolac would be facing him and although the other former slaves had shown great skill, Sergeant Dolac was confident. He was the best fighter in the company and as he stood there loosening his shoulders, he stared at Demon-boy. Demon-boy stood there, still but for his hand axe that occasionally moved.

Joren was looking forward to the bout. He waited until the last two left the circle and called out. "Fight!"

Demon-boy exploded into movement, faster than anyone expected, apart from his three friends, of course. Demon-boy charged in low on Sergeant Dolac's shield arm. He threw his sword in a reverse thrust at the shield, the sergeant blocking it. As the sword hit, Demon-boy had already stepped to the right behind Sergeant Dolac and whacked the blunt side of his axe against the sergeant's arse. As the sergeant spun around leading with his sword, Demon-boy thrust his sword out to block and slipped his axe into the gap between shield and swords, right into the neck of the Sergeant. The axe was slowed at the last second landing lightly.

"Killing blow" yelled Joren

All of the former slaves cheered, as well as the Mayor. Opix knew now why the former slaves were so confident. Their skills with weapons being a good cut above most soldiers.

"Test over. I would be happy to offer you all places in the Bloodchildren," yelled Joren.

More cheering. Demon-boy shook the hand of the sergeant and moved back to his friends, them all slapping him on the shoulder. Demon-boy was not even out of breath, noticed Joren. Demon-boy looked at his three friends and the smiles on their faces. Their future was looking secure. More secure than any other time of their lives. Only five quarter moons ago, they were slaves, being thrown into the ring to fight for their lives. They were worth nothing and only a painful death awaited them. Now, they had a chance at earning a living using the skills they had learnt from the Outlanders. The thought pleased Demon-boy and his only wish was that one day in the future he and his brothers would use these skills against the very people who had once rejoiced in them, the Outlanders.

Epilogue

"A nasty business Hura. And I also morn for the loss of your son," said Chief Pulnuk.

Chief Hura said nothing, he just took a sip of his drink and nodded. It had been two full moons since he had returned to his capital of Hura. His men on the return journey had said nothing, scared he would end their lives for losing the slaves. His temper worse than ever! He had already started rebuilding his drinks hall when two neighbouring chiefs had arrived with supplies and workers to help rebuild. He was thankful, but no number of workers would return his lost son to him.

"So where do we go from here?" said Chief Erak.

"What do you mean? They escaped!" said Hura.

"Does not mean we cannot get to them brother?" said Pulnak.

"You want to invade Irik?" replied Hura.

"May not come to that. We could scout out where they are then hunt them down. Hopefully they do something stupid like sailing south to the southlands," said Erak.

"True. Then we know we can get them," said Pulnak.

Hura thought about it. Whilst the slaves were in Irk, he could not get to them. If they sailed south, then things would get a little easier.

"Yes. If they decide to go south, then we can get them easy enough. We have many contacts in the south and it would not be hard to find them. They would stick out after all and the story of escaped slaves would travel far," said Erak.

Hura smiled for the first time since they had arrived.

"You would both come with me? If I went after them?" said Hura.

"Yes brother, I would," said Erak.

"As would I," replied Pulnak.

Hura nodded.

"I will send word to our contacts to keep their ears open then," said Hura.

"I am sure we could a few of the other chiefs involved as well. Been a while since we have all warred together," said Pulnak.

"Yes brother. It has been a while," replied Hura.

About the Author

Nath always had a huge imagination. As a small child he was known as the story teller. He started writing short stories in his early twenties as a way to get his feelings and ideas onto paper. Life, as it sometimes does, took him down another path away from his creative side and he spent the majority of his life managing bars, hotels and restaurants.

In his late thirties he started Stand-up comedy and found this a good outlet for his stories and imagination. Enjoying his time on stage and entertaining people. However, when New Zealand went into isolation holiday (Lockdown) for Covid-19 and he was meant to be writing his first hour comedy show, he got side tracked and wrote the first draft of Slave boy instead. He found he had missed his story telling and found a new love of world building, which he had been doing his entire life in his head without realising it. He found drive and focus in his life that had been missing for a very long time.

Share the journey with Nath, and get just as lost in reading the story as he got writing it.

If you have purchased a copy of this book, we would love for you to send us a selfie of you and the book on your preferred platform:

facebook.com/RealDawnBates
instagram.com/realdawnbates
twitter.com/realdawnbates
linkedin.com/in/dawnbates

…so we can thank you in person.

With love and gratitude,
From all at Dawn Publishing